Resou
CIT

CROSS

Books of The Wess'har Wars by
Karen Traviss

THE WORLD BEFORE
CROSSING THE LINE
CITY OF PEARL

ATTENTION: ORGANIZATIONS AND CORPORATIONS
Most Eos paperbacks are available at special quantity discounts for bulk purchases for sales promotions, premiums, or fundraising. For information, please call or write:

Special Markets Department, HarperCollins Publishers, Inc.,
10 East 53rd Street, New York, N.Y. 10022–5299.
Telephone: (212) 207–7528. Fax: (212) 207-7222.

KAREN TRAVISS

THE
WORLD
BEFORE

An Imprint of HarperCollinsPublishers

EOS
An Imprint of HarperCollins*Publishers*
10 East 53rd Street
New York, New York 10022-5299

Copyright © 2005 by Karen Traviss
ISBN-13: 978-0-06-054172-9
ISBN-10: 0-06-054172-5
www.eosbooks.com

First Eos paperback printing: November 2005

HarperCollins® and Eos® are trademarks of HarperCollins Publishers Inc.

Printed in the U.S.A.

10 9 8 7 6 5 4 3 2 1

For the Brigade of Gurkhas

Acknowledgments

My grateful thanks go to Charlie Allery, Bryan Boult, Debbie Button, and Dr. Ian Tregillis, for critical reading; to my editor, Diana Gill, and agent, Russ Galen, for keeping me in line; to Andy Tucker, for theological insight; to Benjamin Buchholz, for finding the perfect word; to Malcolm McGreevy and Cliff Allen, who set me on the path that led here; and to Chris "TK" Evans, who made that path a whole lot smoother.

THE
WORLD
BEFORE

Prologue

Ouzhari, once known as Christopher Island, on Bezer'ej: 2376 in the calendar of the *gethes*.

"What am I, then?" asked Sergeant Bennett.

Aras walked ahead of the human, picking a path between the decaying bodies on the shoreline. A conversation among the dead felt unseemly, but Aras knew that Ade Bennett had seen many battlefields and had learned to handle the horror. He wasn't irreverent. He was simply trying to cope.

"If you're asking if your appearance will change as mine has, I can't answer that."

"Am I still human?"

Aras turned and looked hard into the soldier's eyes for a sign of greedy excitement. There was nothing, not even fear, although that would have been reasonable. Ade—he insisted Aras use his nickname—was what Shan Frankland had called "a good bloke," a solid professional soldier known as a Royal Marine. There was no monarchy any more, and he was twenty-five light-years from his own seas, but humans clung to those ancient identities. They even gave their warships names.

Judging by his unwavering gaze, Ade was still waiting for a fuller answer. Aras understood the mix of dread and desperate curiosity all too well.

"Mostly human," said Aras. "But a little isenj, a little bezeri, a little wess'har. A little of whatever host that *c'naatat* passed through."

"And what will kill me, exactly?"

"For all practical purposes, almost nothing. How your

c'naatat achieves that and adapts you will depend on what you experience and what it takes a fancy to. You may simply find the changes . . . a little disconcerting."

Ade nodded as if he understood, and wandered away to check something at the waterline. The sand had once been white. Now it was blackened and vitrified in places by the blast of cobalt-salted nuclear devices.

And every few meters there were more decaying bodies of bezeri beached by the tide.

Without their bioluminescence, the corpses of the bezeri were a colorless translucent gel. There were four or five in a cluster at Aras's feet. It was hard to count because the mantles were decomposing and the outlines merging, but it looked to Aras like a family group—two five-meter males with their great tentacles coiled back, a female distinguishable by her narrower shape, and a smaller, possibly juvenile male.

"Whoa, over here," called Ade. He slung his rifle across his shoulder and crouched down. Aras went to see what he had found.

There was a faint flicker of green light in a small shape on the waterline. It was another juvenile. And it was still alive.

Ade bent closer. "Is there anything we can do?"

Aras took out the signaling lamp that he had always used to communicate with the bezeri in their language of colored lights.

"No," he said.

There was nothing much they could say, either. *Sorry: sorry I failed to protect you. Sorry I didn't wipe out all the carrion eaters, all the* gethes, *when I first had the chance.*

He said what little he could and the lamp translated.

I'm sorry. I let you down.

The response was a small flicker of that same green light, incoherent, barely enough to raise a faint breath of sound from the lamp. It was just a cry. It was fading.

Aras squatted close to the dying juvenile and comforted it as best he could in words of light.

I'm here, little one.

Ade's brow furrowed briefly. The creature's tentacles looked as if they were already rotting. "Have you got Eddie's camera?"

"You can't make education or entertainment out of this."

"People back home need to know what we've done." Ade held out his hand for the small device that the journalist Eddie Michallat had given them. "I think this says it all."

He aimed the camera, still looking detached but emitting a scent of agitation that Aras could detect even through the powerful ammonia stench of rotting flesh around them.

Aras remembered a human scientist called Surendra Parekh who he had executed for killing a bezeri infant, and wished again that he had executed all the *gethes* when he had the chance.

Except Shan Frankland.

The juvenile bezeri flickered again, this time an unusually deep blue.

Can you see me? asked Aras. *Did any of you escape?*

There was no response. Ade glanced at him and they waited long minutes, but the bioluminescence had gone forever.

Ade stood up and panned the camera across the beach, capturing more devastation. There were no lights in the water any more.

"So this is collateral damage," he said.

Aras checked himself again, examining his skin for signs of lesions. He was unmarked. Apart from his all-consuming grief and anger, he was fine. *C'naatat* could handle gamma radiation. But the microscopic symbiont had existed in the soil of Ouzhari, and it couldn't have withstood the temperatures of a nuclear blast.

It was no threat to anyone here. There was no need for the gethes *to destroy it.*

There were two things Aras knew *c'naatat* couldn't do. It couldn't save its host from fragmentation; that was the way all the wess'har troops infected with *c'naatat* had eventually ended their lives.

And it couldn't save a host exposed to the vacuum of space.

Aras looked up at a hazy sky where Wess'ej appeared as a crescent moon. She was out there somewhere, Shan Frankland, not wholly human, and so determined to stop humankind taking her *c'naatat* that she chose death instead. Ade wouldn't discuss it any longer. But Aras knew that spacing yourself was a terrible way to die.

"How long?"

Ade looked away from the camera. "What?"

"How long does it take a human to die in vacuum?"

"Stop it, Aras."

"How long?"

Ade paused. "About twelve seconds. At most."

Aras thought about it, counting. He closed his eyes. Ade had witnessed it and he hadn't. Ade had—

"No, I can't stop seeing it," said Ade. His voice was suddenly hoarse. "And I know bloody well that you blame me for it, so let's just agree that I'm the bastard who let her die."

Aras stifled urges to punish Ade. He also pitied him. His scent said *brother:* he had Shan's genes now, just as Aras did. He couldn't—*wouldn't*—harm him.

He would save his balancing vengeance for Commander Lindsay Neville, who had detonated the bombs here even if she hadn't known the full consequences of her actions. And he would spare some for her accomplice, Mohan Rayat. Rayat was a *spook,* as Ade called it. Neville was a fool. And Ade was a victim of circumstances they had created.

"I suggest we get decontaminated and return to Wess'ej," said Aras. "Eddie will be impatient for his pictures."

Aras was mired in his own bereavement as he walked among the bodies. For all the foreign genes his *c'naatat* had acquired over the years, he was still wess'har, but the human components within him were screaming *me, me, me.* In that brief moment, he would have sacrificed all Bezer'ej and even Wess'ej itself to bring Shan back.

She was his *isan.* He could hardly function without her.

But he would have to learn.

1

The Federal European Union greatly regrets the loss of life on Bezer'ej and the deaths of Superintendent Frankland and her ussissi aide. We condemn the actions of Commander Neville. Let me restate our position: we did not and would not sanction first-use of nuclear devices. As we have no effective military structure left on Umeh, there is no direct disciplinary action we can take against Commander Neville or the troops under her command; but they are now dismissed the service, and in the absence of FEU enforcement, they fall properly within the scope of your own judicial system as the protectors of the bezeri. Our representative Dr. Mohan Rayat will offer every cooperation.

BIRSEN ERTEGUN,
Foreign Minister, Federal European Union,
in a statement to the matriarchs of F'nar

F'nar, on Wess'ej, August 2376

Ade Bennett clung to his schedule twenty-five light-years from home in an alien city that was coated entirely in pearl.

He ran ten kilometers every morning at dawn and there was no reason to stop doing it just because the sun was now a different star and he was a prisoner of war. He pounded along the terraces of F'nar and down its stepped slopes.

Wherever the sun warmed smooth stone, the *tem* flies would congregate and deposit a thin layer of nacre. The iridescence was insect shit: Shan had found that funny, Aras said. She liked irony.

And she's dead. And it's all your fucking fault. You let her die.

Ade wanted to erase the final picture of her standing in

the airlock, seconds from death. But it was the last scrap of
her that he could still grasp, the memory of a woman he had
never expected to love and to whom he had left everything
unsaid. Something in him wouldn't let it go. He had decided
to confront it instead.

The native wess'har paused to stare at him as he made his
way down the terraces. Some acknowledged him with stiff
nods of their sea horse heads. He was a POW in a city where
he was regarded as a hero, but every day he was here served
only to remind him that he was alive and Shan wasn't, and
that he'd failed the basic heroic qualification of saving what
you loved.

Sweat prickled its way down his back. He made his way
through the alleys that honeycombed the lowest level of the
city at the bottom of the encircling caldera. Beyond the city
lay the irregular mosaic of fields and allotments that blended
into the natural landscape, and beyond them were the plains
that were arid in summer and covered with quick-growing
vegetation in the brief, wet winter. F'nar had been built
where it would have least impact rather than the most convenient location. Wess'har didn't seem to have the same prior-
ities as humans.

Ade's route took him south of the caldera and up the rock
face of a volcanic plateau that looked down onto the fields
and the city itself. He liked climbing: it was one of the basic
mountain warfare skills he had learned as a Royal Marine,
and he could lose himself in absolute concentration. Free-
soloing—climbing without a partner or equipment—was
what he did best. That was just as well. There was no other
way to climb on Wess'ej.

The rock face was smooth enough in places to attract the
attention of *tem* flies and it was embossed with the pearly
shit they'd laid down in the summer. If he half-closed his
eyes, the reflected glare made it look like a snow-streaked
peak back on Earth. He felt above his head with his right
hand for a secure hold and locked his fingers into a horizon-
tal crevice.

For a few moments he hung with his full weight on one hand, face against the cool gold rock, looking up at another hold thirty centimeters beyond his normal reach.

Combat boots were lousy for climbing. He jammed a toe-cap into a pocket of rock and transferred his weight, lunging upwards to grab hold of the outcrop above him. He knew every hold on the ascent now. He could climb it blindfolded.

What he really needed now was a good, solid hex to jam into the fissure above him to take a rope. He wondered if the wess'har might be able to make him some kit for the harder climbs. But for now he was reliant on his free-climbing skills alone, and he reached for another hold. The crevice accepted his fingers. It felt secure.

And the moment he hung all his weight on that hand, he knew that it *wasn't*.

The rock came away from the face and suddenly there was no sense of pressure under his fingertips at all.

He flailed, grabbing instinctively. He felt his right humerus snap as his arm clipped an overhang and he landed flat on his back with an involuntary shout as the air was slammed out of his lungs. He couldn't breathe. His head was filled with a single high note like a tuning fork's. For a second he wondered if it was his own scream of pain, but then he realized the noise was somehow inside his head, probably triggered by a shattered spine.

He'd been told that happened. It was funny how you could think rational things when you were dying.

Shit, shit, shit—

It occurred to him that he deserved to die anyway. Shan was dead, so if he died too, then at least he'd never have to wake up to that realization again. The pain filled his mouth. He had no idea how long he lay there paralyzed and wondering when the sky would go dark.

You can't die. Aras said so. But he was dying, he was sure of it: and now he wanted it over with.

Instead of being filled with creeping cold, he felt he was burning. Then the searing pain ebbed and he found himself breathing, first reflex, shallow gasps while he tested his ribs, and then deep breaths.

Eventually he eased himself up on his left arm. His right arm was throbbing, but he could move it. It took him a few more minutes to recover enough to stand up and understand what had happened to him.

So this was *c'naatat* at work. A fall that would have killed or crippled him was now a temporary but painful—and terrifying—inconvenience. It didn't take a genius to work out how valuable *c'naatat* was or how open it would be to abuse. It was just a shock to experience it so spectacularly.

"Shit," he said. "You couldn't give me a way out, could you?" But that wasn't fair. Aras needed him now. Somehow, they had to get each other through the bleak days ahead that were all Ade's fault. There might even come a time when he could go for hours without thinking of Shan and what he had done, but that wasn't now.

He stood staring at the backs of his hands for a few minutes to see if anything else was changing, and when he was satisfied that nothing was happening he looked up at the rock face to work out a new route to ascend.

At the top he stood and scanned the landscape. The secluded cairn he had built looked out over an idyllic vista; without a grave—without even a body—he desperately needed a place where he could commemorate Shan. He needed somewhere to apologize and grieve. Maybe he'd bring Aras up here one day, but not yet. Now was too soon. And he preferred to cry on his own.

It wasn't as if they'd even had a relationship.

If Shan ever belonged to anyone she had belonged to Aras. But she was the Boss, even if she was a police officer and so not part of his chain of command, and for Ade she always would be. He ought to have called her the *Guv'nor* as coppers did. But she had never seemed to mind.

He knelt down and added a few pearl-coated stones to the mound.

"There you go, Boss." The word hurt. He took his medals out of his pocket and folded the brightly colored ribbons around them before easing them into a gap between the chunks of rock and the fine pearl pebbles. "All tidy. Sleep tight."

He paused for a few moments, entirely incapable of prayer because he had seen too many things that no reasonable god would allow, and turned to start his descent. His palm itched and he glanced down at it. *Right to receive, left to pay away;* that was what his mum used to say. Beads of green liquid were welling up from his skin and he wiped his hand on the leg of his battledress, but the fluid emerged again like one of those miracles that was supposed to happen to the statues of saints.

It was no miracle and he felt as far from sainthood as any man ever had. It was the bioscreen being removed a cell at a time. *C'naatat* was purging him of all his implants and the organic battlefield computer grown into his palm. But it hadn't touched his tattoos, and Ade thought they were the sort of thing *c'naatat* would have wanted to tidy up. Aras had warned him that the parasite wasn't predictable.

"Sergeant?"

He thought he was alone. He wasn't. "Oh, Christ," he said. His heart pounded.

Nevyan Tan Mestin was standing right behind him and he should have heard her approach. He was a commando, for Chrissakes; she shouldn't have been able to ambush him. The wess'har matriarch cocked her head and looked past him at the cairn with four-lobed pupils dilating and contracting visibly in bright yellow eyes. *Sea horses.* Eddie's description was unnervingly accurate.

"Why do you not walk up the slope to this summit?" she asked. Wess'har voices were weird, tone and overtone like a chorus, each word made of two simultaneous components. *Will I sound like that one day?* "You choose a hard route."

"I like climbing, ma'am. I need to keep active."

"What are the stones for?"

"To remember. It's a memorial."

"To *Shan Chail*?"

"Yes." Wess'har didn't even bury their dead, let alone erect monuments. They left them for the scavengers. "It helps."

"But you won't forget her."

"No, never. But I come here to think about her."

"And the pieces of metal?"

"They're—they're my medals." Ade was too embarrassed to explain what medals were and how he had won his. "It's an old human habit. We leave valuable things for the dead."

He'd said it aloud now, the word *dead*. It had its own finality. He felt he'd betrayed Shan by letting it slip out. Nevyan stood looking down at the cairn, thin multijointed fingers meshed in front of her like an ornate basket, and her iridescent white matriarch's robe was as bright as the shit-covered pebbles.

"I miss her too," she said at last. "May I come here to think of her?"

No, thought Bennett. *This is private. This is for me. This is just for me to get my head round this, if I ever can. It's for me and the Boss and nobody else, maybe not even Aras.*

"Of course you can, ma'am," he said, fighting reluctance, and felt robbed.

But Nevyan had been Shan's friend, and this was her planet and her city.

"We will recover her body, I promise you, and you shall have your grave." She gestured towards F'nar. "Now walk with me. Let us discuss what will happen to your comrades."

Ade obeyed, which was not unreasonable given that Nevyan was now the leader of F'nar and he was technically her prisoner. But it reminded him how easily he followed orders and how he had done what Commander Neville had ordered. He had said *yes, ma'am* when she asked him to land nuclear weapons on Bezer'ej and he'd said *yes, ma'am* when she asked him to capture Shan Frankland.

He should have said *sod off, ma'am*. Maybe both Shan and the poor bloody bezeri would all be alive now if he had. He had no idea how he was going to live with himself in the very long future ahead of him or what it would take to atone. He walked beside Nevyan, but whatever she was saying to him he couldn't hear it. He could only see Shan through the shuttle hatch, choosing a cold hard death rather than surrender *c'naatat* to anyone. The image intruded more frequently every day.

If it mattered that much to the Boss to safeguard the damn thing, then it would matter to him.

"You know that we don't take prisoners," said Nevyan. "What am I to do with your comrades?"

Yes, he knew that. Wess'har killed, period. They were strict vegans and respected all life, but once you were at war with them it was to the death. "You mean Izzy and Chaz? The two marines still with the colonists?"

"I mean all of them."

"The other three are still on Umeh."

"We shall be asking the isenj to return them, along with Commander Neville and Dr. Rayat."

Ade managed to keep up with her stride. "Sorry?"

"Your government has abandoned you."

"I didn't think they'd be sending a limo to pick us up."

"I mean that they have dismissed you and turned you over to us."

Ade wondered for a moment if Nevyan had misunderstood, but her English was fluent to the point of being peppered with slang that he recognized—painfully—as Shan's. "Ma'am, what exactly did they say?"

She cocked her head, not slowing. *"Dismissed the service."*

The fragile world that Ade had begun to think of rebuilding had collapsed before him again. His gut churned. He knew they'd face an enquiry but he hadn't expected to be kicked out and dumped in the enemy camp. The FEU didn't know why he surrendered or that he was far safer among wess'har than his own kind; as far as they were concerned, they were shitting on him from a great height. Lindsay Neville had asked for it, but not the detachment.

You're the bloody sergeant. You should have stood up to her.

He could hear his own heartbeat pounding in his ears. Nevyan stopped and stared at him, head tilted, pupils opening and closing. Aras said wess'har could actually smell what state of mind you were in by the scents you gave off. She looked like she could smell him clearly enough.

"Sergeant—"

"I'm not a sergeant any more, am I?"

It hurt. Ade had been in the Corps since he was sixteen. It was his refuge. It had given him self-respect and the nearest thing he had to a family, and now it had been torn away from him by some file-shuffler in Brussels who'd never been closer to war than his news screen. He wondered what the hell he still had left, stranded 150 trillion miles from Earth and never, ever going home again.

Sod it. He was whatever the Corps had made him. He'd bloody well find something.

He peeled the sergeant's stripes off the sleeves of his pullover. He'd leave them at the cairn tomorrow.

"It's Ade, ma'am," he said. "Just Ade."

Nevyan slowed her pace and they walked an unmarked path that took them south of F'nar and led into the city like a processional route into an arena. From most positions you couldn't even see F'nar until you were right on top of it, and now Ade was looking straight into its heart. The caldera was almost a complete ring, with homes and terraces cut into the rock. With the icing of pearl laid by the *tem* flies, it looked like a wedding cake turned inside out.

He found himself thinking that it would be a good location to defend but a hard one to escape.

"I won't harm your comrades," said Nevyan. "If they want refuge here, we will accept them. My argument is with Neville and Rayat."

"That's very generous of you, ma'am. Don't you hold us all responsible?"

"Did you or your detachment activate the bombs?"

"No, but—"

"Then the act itself was not your responsibility."

If Ade needed another reminder that wess'har didn't think like humans, this was one. He struggled with the concept. "That's . . . generous."

"I think your government are a *bunch of tossers,* yes?"

It was just what Shan would have said. Delivered in that voice-upon-voice, it sounded utterly surreal.

"Yes, ma'am," said Ade. "Tossers."

Jejeno, Umeh: August 2376 in the calendar of the humans.

The city of Jejeno was not a smoking ruin when Minister Par Paral Ual's vehicle made its way through the packed streets between his office and the human habitat.

Ual had expected it to be. He had expected war. But it had not yet come.

Where Umeh Station stood, there was no pall of smoke or dying fire. It was still there, its translucent faceted dome glittering in the forest of tall buildings east of his office. The wess'har hadn't aimed their missiles at it in retaliation for the humans' nuclear attack on Bezer'ej. Perhaps the destruction of *Actaeon,* the Earth ship, had satisfied their need for balance.

He doubted it. It wasn't like them at all.

Ralassi—his ussissi aide—sat beside him, silent behind his breather mask.

"We shall end up like Mjat," said Ual's driver. He showed no impatience as isenj pedestrians parted ahead of the ground car, moving according to strict unspoken traffic rules in the densely packed city. The whole planet of Umeh was crammed with cities, and all cities were like Jejeno. "They wiped us out on Asht."

"Bezer'ej," said Ual. The wess'har had renamed it. *This is*

not your world, and never will be. This is the world of the
bezeri. "The wess'har call it *Bezer'ej,* and the humans *Ca-*
vanagh's Star Two."

All isenj remembered the fate of Mjat, their colony on
Asht. Mjat was now a synonym for holocaust. The event was
five hundred years ago as humans calculated, and it was not
the only massive loss of life in the wars with the wess'har:
but it had a special place in the isenj consciousness because
it had resulted in the death of millions, mostly civilians.

And the Destroyer of Mjat still lived, centuries after he
should have been dead. The driver was fascinated.

"So he's real, then, sir? Not a myth?"

"He is." It seemed impossible. "And living on Wess'ej."

"The humans caused the death of his female. Do they
know what he did to Mjat?"

"Yes."

"And are they afraid?"

"I'm not sure if they have the sense to be. And I'm not
sure that I fully understand the wess'har logic of culpability." Ual knew what the ussissi told him, and what his genetic memory recalled, and what the archives recorded. But he
had never met a wess'har. "And that ignorance is something
I must remedy very soon."

The ground car pulled up at one of the airlocked en-
trances to Umeh Station. "You mind yourself, sir," said the
driver. Ralassi trotted out in front of Ual. "Humans are said
to be aggressive when crowded."

Inside the dome, Umeh Station was in chaos. Ual wandered unacknowledged into the humans' fragile bubble of a
settlement and decided that they might benefit from a lesson
in how to create order among large numbers.

The dome was strewn with the detritus of a project still
under construction. Nearly three hundred humans were now
crammed into a space built for two hundred, the numbers
swelled by evacuated crew from the unlucky *Actaeon.*

Ual was looking for one of *Actaeon*'s company in particular. He found Commander Lindsay Neville in the site of-

fice, arguing with a civilian over arrangements to feed the dome's population. Humans, it seemed, would not wait patiently for meals like isenj. Neither the commander nor the civilian looked like healthy and well-rested specimens of their kind.

Ual clicked impatiently and waited. He didn't have two highly visible eyes, and humans needed something called *eye contact* to get attention. Ual supposed he looked like any of the many isenj workers to them—multilimbed, spiny-coated and anonymously alien. Ralassi slipped between the humans, all teeth and anger, and interrupted.

"Minister Ual is visiting you *in person*," he snapped. "You will do him the courtesy of postponing your argument."

Both humans fell silent. So this was the one that Eddie called *Lin*.

"I note you did not go down with your ship, Commander Neville," said Ual.

The civilian male picked up a paper from the desk and walked out. Lindsay, standing stiffly as if used to deferring to superiors, was wearing something they called a *uniform*. Ual thought it odd that humans fought so much among themselves that they needed markings to divide allies from enemies. Similarity should have united them.

"*Actaeon* wasn't my ship, sir," she said, seeming to miss the point. "We don't appear to have an ITX comms link to Earth any longer. I really need to talk to Fleet. Might you be able to help with that?"

The entangled photon link was the technology that held the humans in the alliance: it was isenj technology, not theirs, and it was not shared, merely lent. "These are nervous times, Commander," said Ual. "I thought it might be safer for everyone if we restricted communications between this base and your government. It is not *secure,* as you call it, and I fear the wess'har could overhear something that might provoke them further."

Neither of them had said the obvious. *You attacked a wess'har protectorate.* Ual wanted to see how she would broach the topic. She didn't know it yet, but her masters had abandoned her and her soldiers to the mercy of Wess'ej; he'd seen the Federal European Union's message, and it was time to tell her.

"I didn't know the devices were salted with cobalt," she said. "I was duped. I truly regret that."

"A fine distinction that I fear will carry little weight with the wess'har. Have you heard of Mjat, Commander?"

"Your colony on Bezer'ej. Well, your former colony."

"It was erased. Completely, and without trace. And that was for accidentally polluting the bezeri's marine environment. Wess'har are not a forgiving people, and Aras Sar Iussan is even less forgiving than most."

"Okay, and I helped his precious Shan space herself. I get the picture."

Ual doubted it. He doubted that Lindsay understood at all: she would not have risked violating Bezer'ej if she had. It seemed an appropriate time to break bad news.

"Your foreign minister sent a message condemning your actions and used an interesting phrase—you and your troops are *dismissed the service*." Ual searched for his most colloquial English. "She has washed her hands of you and told the wess'har that they may deal with you within their law."

Lindsay said nothing but she was blinking rapidly, something Eddie Michallat did when an interview became strained.

"That's just great. *Great*." Ual wasn't sure if she was upset or angry. "It's not fair on the marines, though. They weren't party to this. The bastard you want is Mohan Rayat."

"Ah, they did mention him. Apparently he is now the FEU's chosen representative here."

Lindsay's mouth opened slightly as if she was gulping in air. "He's their spook. An intelligence agent. A spy. You know what that is?"

"I do now," said Ual.

He had never had to deal with spies before. Neither wess'har nor ussissi had any concept of deliberate state secrecy; it was alien to isenj as well. But they were now all learning fast. It troubled Ual to discover just how much of the human brain was devoted to deception. He wondered if his own mind would be altered by trying to think as they did, and was grateful that he had already fathered offspring and so would not pass on those memories to corrupt them.

"The wess'har will ask us to hand you over."

"And if you don't?"

"I have my own people's welfare to consider."

"I'll answer for my own actions," she said. "But only if Rayat answers for his."

"I know you didn't act alone, but you're in no position to make bargains."

"And I'm not carrying the can for this on my own. What's happened to the rest of my marine detachment? Three are still prisoners. I'd like them released."

"This isn't the time to make such a request of the wess'har."

Lindsay Neville adjusted the gold braid tabs on the shoulders of her uniform shirt. Then she unfastened them and slid them off.

"Seeing as they've bypassed the court martial, I'll dispense with these, then." She seemed more resigned than afraid of the prospect of wess'har retribution. Perhaps she knew that they killed fast and clean. "But if you can arrange a direct conversation between me and FEU Command, I would consider that a great personal favor. If I go, I won't go quietly."

Lindsay Neville walked out into the melee of soft, larva-smooth humans. Ual didn't like hosting this unstable nest of aliens in his city but he had to concentrate on the more immediate threats. Of those, he was not sure which was the greater: the political clamoring of his colleagues of the Northern Assembly, who wanted answers on the human question, or the wrath of the wess'har.

"Ralassi, ask your comrades what they know," he said. Ussissi were conduits of information. They worked for everyone and served no one; they crewed both wess'har and isenj ships but they did as they pleased and cherished their neutrality. "I need facts. Humans aren't very good at supplying those."

Ralassi disappeared into the crowds outside the site office, weaving between humans and isenj workers. Some ussissi had returned after evacuating when retribution seemed imminent. They would know what the wess'har intended. This was not what the humans called *spying,* because the wess'har would neither conceal their intentions nor broadcast them. They simply acted—arrogant, aloof, alien—without notice or consultation.

Ual wandered around the dome, noting that there were vines creeping across the supports that held the roof panels and a fountain was playing in the central plaza. The base held the promise of being pleasant accommodation when it was finished, with a cool, moist atmosphere. He savored the rare treat of walking unrecognized as a minister of state, eavesdropping on conversations among creatures that had no idea he could understand them.

Perhaps that was what being a *spook* was like. It seemed amusing.

He heard words like *stranded* and *never going home* and *we're not getting out of this.* He heard a few words he didn't understand: *fucked, sitting ducks, shanghaied.* They were the sort of words that Eddie Michallat would have explained to him. He wondered if he might tempt Eddie back to Umeh.

And still the humans ignored him. He was just another alien to them, no longer a miracle of creation but an invisible part of the backdrop to their own self-preoccupation. *You remind us of spiders.* Eddie had always been brutally frank. Ual found that if he made quick darting movements like the terrestrial creature he could get humans to flinch instinctively and look at him. That was amusing too.

It was a brief respite. The days and months ahead would be anything but amusing.

Back in his vehicle, he waited for Ralassi. Ussissi were another species the humans classified by similarity to creatures from their own world: *meerkats*. Eddie said it was their sharp faces and small teeth and the way they all sat up at once when something grabbed their attention. So Ralassi was a *meerkat,* and he was a *spider,* and that was how humans coped with those who were different, by classifying them as lower species.

Ralassi scrambled back into the ground car, his beaded belts rattling. "I hear interesting reports," he said. "The wess'har have sought help from the World Before, from Eqbas Vorhi. They're coming to their aid—a most extraordinary thing."

Eqbas Vorhi. He had heard the name, or an ancestor had. They changed worlds. "Should we fear their intervention?" Ual asked.

"Oh yes," said Ralassi. "They are more numerous than the wess'har of Wess'ej and have greater military resources. And they are far less restrained. Wess'ej and Umeh may have shied away from fighting on each other's homeworlds, but the Eqbas have a different history."

"So it's true, then. They shape worlds to their wishes."

"Indeed. We *know* them. We evolved with them."

The original wess'har homeworld—the ussissi's home planet, too—had never intruded in isenj life. The wess'har in the Nir system—what the humans called Cavanagh's Star, totally ignoring true names again—had arrived thousands of years ago. They had cut off contact with the rest of their people even though Eqbas was only five light-years away by human reference, and that was all he knew.

If the wess'har here could keep isenj from Bezer'ej and effectively confine them to Umeh and Tasir Var, what might the Eqbas do? Ual and his fellow ministers thought an alliance with the humans might change the balance of power.

Now they had certainly changed the future for the isenj, but not in the way he had hoped.

"If the wess'har killed millions of my people when the bezeri had asked for their aid, what will the Eqbas do now that the humans have wiped them out?" Ual said, but it was a rhetorical question. He could work out the sequence unaided.

Ralassi was right: Wess'ej had never threatened Umeh, and Umeh had never attempted to attack Wess'ej. But Umeh had never been host to an enemy base before, a complication that the whole city feared.

"We're on our own," said Ual. "The humans are twenty-five years away. They have limited technology and our only allies are the Federal European Union. The rest of their planet doesn't care or actively opposes them. There will be no *cavalry* coming to our aid."

"Cavalry?" Ralassi consulted his belt full of recording devices. Interpreters liked new words. "What does that mean?"

Ual thought of database images of humans forcing other creatures to carry them into battle, creatures dying from wounds and starvation and exhaustion. "Something else the wess'har would not like about humans."

Ual considered his options on the way back to his office and said nothing more to Ralassi. The vehicle slowed and then stopped. Crowds pressed on its sides as they tried to ease past it.

"What's the delay?"

Delay was relative in Jejeno. The driver listened carefully to his comms link. "There is a disturbance ahead."

Ual and Ralassi squeezed out of the ground car and were nearly crushed by the mass of isenj. Shrill panic had gripped them, and panic was something to dread in a crowded city because it meant crush injuries and death. Ual heard the word *ship* repeated over and over.

An attack.

But there had been no alarm. There was no warning system for invasion, but there was certainly one for civil emergencies like street crushes. The fear that Umeh's immunity from attack had evaporated had swept the city, and Ual expected to hear that alarm.

The crowd was now so tightly packed that all movement had stopped. He could hear screams of pain. People were dying in the melee. He shouldn't have stepped out of the car.

Ralassi grabbed one of his arms and tried to push him back inside to relative safety.

"Ship!" someone shouted.

Ual looked up and there was a vessel dropping through the cloud, unfamiliar in shape, smooth and narrow.

The driver leaned out of the cab section, comlink clutched to his chest, and tugged on Ual's arm. "They say it's just ussissi. It's only the old human shuttle they salvaged. There's no danger."

But it was too late for many to be comforted by that. The fear of wess'har retaliation was so great that even an obsolete transport vessel like this could send them into a terrified and deadly scramble for safety.

"Inside, Minister," Ralassi insisted. "Let this pass."

Ual squeezed back into the car and settled on the broad flat seat with relief. He was now pinned down in a street, unable to drive or even walk away. It didn't bode well for the future. If the wess'har ever attacked, the results would be catastrophic without their needing to fire a single weapon. Cities were vulnerable by their very nature. A planet that was simply one vast city was a disaster preparing to unfold.

"Connect me to my communications," he said. "I might as well use this time productively."

Ual had avoided conversations with the FEU foreign minister for several days, although she had transmitted a number of formal messages of apology and reconciliation. Now he knew what the wess'har had in mind, he could have more than a token diplomatic exchange. And he would insist on speaking to her without filtering or interference from what Eddie called *spin doctors*.

Then he would call Eddie.

He had plans to speak to everyone. No, *not* everyone. *Dare I speak to the matriarchs of F'nar?*

"How do I contact the wess'har leaders?" he asked.

Ralassi's little teeth were just visible, and his eyes narrowed into slits. It was a sign of disapproval. "The Assembly has not authorized direct contact."

Perhaps it was a rash move. Ual had no idea what he might say by way of conversation anyway: all conversations had been in the form of warning statements and counter-warnings since the last ancient war. "You're correct."

The crush outside showed no sign of abating. The car shook a little, buffeted by a wave of movement that had started further away. Ual pondered. He was the foreign minister: it was his job to make decisions about the handling of relations with aliens, a previously insignificant post. Now he was the center of political activity and he wasn't sure if he could handle it with the confidence of the senior cabinet, the ministers who managed interstate relations on Umeh itself.

Ual looked on his previous backwater status with sudden nostalgia. Then the car lurched. "We'll soon have you back now, sir," said the driver. "The city safety patrol has opened a passage. You sort those humans out, sir. They're nothing but trouble."

Ual pulled the covers down on the car's windows, suddenly overwhelmed. The sight of pressed bodies outside was like a prophecy.

When he reached his office the cool pale aquamarine stone seemed less like welcome relief from the street crowds and more like frightening isolation. His assistant, Mas Lij, indicated the communications screen.

"There is another message for you from the FEU," said Lij. "Birsen Ertegun is anxious to talk to you."

Ual settled on the slab of smooth-polished black basalt—a costly extravagance—and rested his legs. The message was two hours old and showed the human minister Ertegun—he noted her new status—in a carefully managed pose, hands folded on her desk. Despite that, she showed the signs of human agitation that the ussissi had noted among those in Umeh Station—rapid blinking and licking of their wet fleshy mouths. Ual couldn't blame her. He shared her fear.

The FEU foreign minister began by repeating her apology and the message that she had broadcast for the benefit of the wess'har. She asked if Ual thought they should evacuate all humans on Umeh, and reminded him that the ship *Thetis* was less than a year into its return journey to Earth and could be turned back.

Ual had started to learn the intricacies of the human mind. He considered the offer.

"We should retrieve our people," said Ralassi. He meant ussissi, Ual knew, but he chose to interpret *our* in the widest sense. "We have nothing to gain from this mission."

"Should I tell them about Eqbas Vorhi, do you think?"

"They might as well know the seriousness of their situation."

The isenj party and their ussissi interpreters were still on board *Thetis* even though the humans had already withdrawn their own people from the ship. The invitation to visit Earth seemed fraught with danger now, and not only for humans. For the past year the humans' news had been full of objections to inviting *aliens* to Earth, although they seemed to have no problem with inviting themselves to the planets of others.

"Turning back *Thetis* will solve the FEU's political problems with the rest of Earth's governments," Ralassi offered.

"And effectively end the alliance with us, too."

Ual could ship the humans back. Umeh wouldn't be a potential target any more. But it would take more than one Earth year for *Thetis* to loop back, and Ual had no idea if Umeh had that much time left to appease the wess'har. They *acted*. They tended not to think.

Ual continued to listen to Ertegun's message.

He wondered if the minister realized that he already knew the scientist Mohan Rayat was, as Lindsay Neville put it, a *spook*. Ual considered replying to say as much, but he had learned a lot from Eddie Michallat about harnessing the ebb and flow of information. He began composing his reply carefully and searched for the correct phrase to indicate that Dr. Rayat might care to present himself to the wess'har authorities too.

This was the Game. He would play it.

2

The crisis may be twenty-five light-years away but that makes it no less urgent. We cannot tolerate a situation where the FEU, and the FEU alone, has contact with these alien governments. The FEU has no mandate to plunge the world into a state of war with nations we have never met. We now have diplomacy by newscast, and that is intolerable. We insist that use of the ITX link be made freely available to this chamber immediately or sanctions must follow.

JIM MATSOUKIS,
senior Pacific Rim States delegate
to the United Nations

**Umeh Station, Jejeno,
northern hemisphere of Umeh, August 2376.**

Lindsay Neville just stood back. She should have intervened, but she was no longer Mart Barencoin's commanding officer. She wasn't anyone's commanding officer any more.

The marine was still limping a little from the gunshot wound to his leg but his aggression was obviously fit and well. He blocked Mohan Rayat's progress across the plaza of the crowded biodome. It was hard not to attract a crowd in this place.

"So you're the boss fella now, are you?" Barencoin was tall, solid and intimidating. However thoroughly he shaved, he always looked as if he'd spent the last forty-eight hours lying in a shell-scrape on observation. "Well, seeing as I'm now way outside the Forces Discipline Act, here's a token of my appreciation as a civilian."

He punched Rayat hard in the face. His fist made a wet *crack* when it landed and Rayat went down with an *unh*.

There was an *aaah* of surprise from the remnants of *Actaeon*'s company and the civilian contractors. Marine Jon Becken grabbed Barencoin's arm and pulled him away.

A couple of onlookers broke into spontaneous applause.

Barencoin shook off Becken's grip and turned to a couple of Regulating Branch ratings, *Actaeon*'s internal police. He massaged his hand. "Okay, I'm done. You can stick me on a charge now."

"Never saw a thing," said the shorter of the two men. "It's a bugger, this bad eyesight."

"Mart, for Chrissakes." Becken had a white-knuckled grip on his arm. "Leave it, will you?"

Lindsay wandered over and stood with her arms folded while Rayat got to his feet, a fat trickle of blood issuing from one nostril. He wiped it on his sleeve as if he was used to dusting himself down after a fight.

"I hope that's proved cathartic," he said, staring at Barencoin. Maybe he was considering revisiting the argument later. "Would you like me to spell that for you?"

"Patronizing twat." But Becken held on to Barencoin's arm.

They had an audience, and that was no bad thing. Lindsay wasn't taking the flak alone. She made a mock introductory gesture in Rayat's direction. "Okay, in case any of you didn't see the news, this is the man who decided to use the Beano bombs. He's an intelligence officer. Spy, spook, respected member of the intelligence community—take your pick. Have I missed anything out?"

She had been immersed in the confidential world of need-to-know and secure information from the day she had taken her officer's commission as a student. She could hardly believe she had publicly denounced someone as a spy. For all that Rayat had done, the act still felt wildly dangerous. But she was damned if he was going to run this place. She wanted him frozen out.

"Yeah. Why use any bombs at all?" The question came from a civilian engineer in an orange coverall. The woman didn't look pleased. "What *did* you target?"

Lindsay gathered her thoughts. Shan was dead. Ouzhari was scoured clean. Aras was beyond anyone's reach and nobody knew about Ade Bennett. She decided it was time for the truth.

"A biohazard. A biohazard some of your companies would have killed to get hold of."

"That's smart," said Rayat. He was standing quite still, looking wary of tipping them into a mob with the wrong move. But he still didn't look as scared as she felt. In fact, he didn't look scared at all. "Any other classified information you want to divulge?"

"It's that immortality thing, isn't it?" said a construction driver.

"Yes," said Lindsay. "And I'll leave you to work out just how responsibly we'd make use of that back home."

The ussissi interpreters who worked for the isenj were standing in a pack by the plaza's central fountain. If the dome had been completed and the number of people housed in it had been halved, it would have been a pleasant deployment. But it wasn't. People were angry and crowded and scared. And the ussissi gave every sign of being equally angry animals who might turn on humans at any time.

Only the isenj—patient, unfathomable, quill-covered bulks on spider legs—seemed to be going about their business on site. Lindsay imagined that any species forced to live at such close quarters as the overcrowded isenj had developed a high level of tolerance to adversity. They watched—or Lindsay assumed they watched, as they had no discernible eyes—while the humans wrangled.

"Who's got primacy here, the military or the sponsors?"

"Why have they cut our comms?"

"We're going to be stuck here for twenty-five years whatever happens."

Rad Jaros, the engineer who had taken on the task of managing the logistics of the emergency, scrambled onto the flatbed of a transport and got instant silence when he stood up. That was something Shan could do, too, but Lindsay knew she never could.

"That guy there's right," said Jaros, pointing into the crowd. "If we're lucky, we're stuck here for the next quarter century. If we're not, the wess'har will fry us, and there's sod all anyone can do about that because there's nowhere to run and nobody's coming to rescue us. So we make the best of it and get this place running properly. We had a schedule before all this happened and now we just have to adjust the numbers. Okay?"

"Who do you want running this place?" asked Lindsay.

"Not you or that spy, that's for sure," said a voice from the crowd. "And who's going to enforce the bugger's authority anyway? Our companies paid for most of this project. So we'll bloody well run this ourselves."

Rayat had never struck Lindsay as a fool. He was on his own out here: whatever government muscle he might have called upon back on Earth was now a lifetime away. He didn't even have a hand-weapon. He faced the thickening crowd.

"I think it's important that we maintain some sense of order here," he said carefully. His hands were relaxed, palms down, making placatory gestures of the kind that you learned would defuse trouble. "If you would rather have a civilian administration, then I'm happy to explain that to the Foreign Office when we make contact with them."

"Who's the ranking naval officer here?" Lindsay asked.

There was silence while everyone in a uniform—ratings and junior officers—looked around them. The reality of the loss of life in *Actaeon* was sobering. A stocky freckled woman with a lieutenant's double gold stripe on both shoulder boards raised her hand.

"Cargill, ma'am."

"Well, Cargill, you're admiral of the fleet out here," said Lindsay. "Make the most of it."

Lindsay found it harder to think more than a day ahead

now. She withdrew to a quiet corner behind one of the water purifiers and sat down with her back against the gently vibrating pump housing. Through the transparent panels of the dome she could see the dense, intricate mass that was the city of Jejeno, separated from this little fragment of Earth by a moat of service roads. It was the only scrap of open space in the city.

What now?

When she had arrived on Bezer'ej nearly two years ago, she had focused on completing the mission and going home to a promotion. When she learned she was pregnant in an alien world, she aimed to cope with that, and no more. When David died just a few weeks old, she existed to exact revenge on Shan Frankland for not using *c'naatat* to save him. And then she had seen the reason why Shan could never save David, and she had taken on the task of ensuring *c'naatat* never fell into the hands of either government or commerce.

It was all about having a goal. But now she had no goal at all.

She shut her eyes and tried to visualize herself the following day, functioning normally and looking ahead. But she couldn't see herself beyond the moment. Perhaps basic survival would occupy her. She braced her elbows on her knees and thought about David, buried in alien soil with a glass headstone to mark his small grave, then let her head sink into her hands.

"Welcome to the world of the leper," said Mohan Rayat, and sat down beside her. "You learn to cope with ingratitude in this job."

"Sod off," she said.

"Eddie," trilled Giyadas, gravely serious. "They're coming. What will they be like?"

The wess'har child walked briskly alongside him, a little seahorse princess just a meter tall but who could already break his arm if she wanted. Eddie Michallat was relieved that she liked him. Wess'har females were formidable, and they started young.

"I've got no idea, sweetheart," he said. "I've seen the same images that you have. But they're still wess'har, same as you, whatever they look like. You'll have lots in common. You've been learning their language, haven't you?"

"We all have." She meant her family, the four males and their offspring who had been taken in by Nevyan when their own matriarch died. Wess'har didn't appear to have stepchild issues. "But we still don't know what they're really like. Nevyan says we left Eqbas Vorhi ten thousand years ago. That sounds like a very long time."

"It is. We were just about discovering how to build cities then."

"Are you really a backward species, Eddie?"

Cute. And tactlessly true, and healthy to be reminded of the chilling reality of not being at the top of the food chain any longer. He had to put his hands up to it. "'Fraid so, sweetheart. Unfortunately, our technology is way ahead of us."

F'nar's autumn weather was cool rather than cold but the pearl layer gave the impression of a heavy frost. Eddie was almost as used to its optical illusions as to its overlength days and higher gravity. On this overcast morning, his room in Nevyan's home had been flooded with a cold white light that made him think he had woken up to overnight snowfall.

It could have been a magical experience. But the threat of a war that he couldn't leave behind on the next available flight stripped the gloss from it. He was heading to the Exchange of Surplus Things to hear about the next escalation in the conflict with the humans.

"I still think it's odd that you lot haven't stayed in contact with each other," said Eddie. Eqbas Vorhi had responded to Wess'ej's appeal for military support. If Wess'ej represented the isolationist liberals, the Eqbas were going to make interesting neighbors. "*We* would."

"What would the purpose of that be if we wished to lead separate lives? And your species originated in Earth's tropics. Do you stay in touch with Africa every day?"

Giyadas had him there. Even the kids here had that inexorable in-your-face logic from an early age.

The wess'har around him seemed as agitated by the prospect as Eddie was. He was passing through a phase of being stunned by how alien they were. The novelty of seeing extraterrestrial life in the flesh had palled quickly, but that was when he was buffered by the company of other humans. Now *he* was the minority alien, living in an alien household, and he had become increasingly aware that the only other creature on the planet that looked remotely like him was Ade. Even Aras—reshaped by his *c'naatat* over the years into a theatrical approximation of a man—was two meters tall and built like an armored vehicle. And he had claws.

"Doesn't Nevyan worry when you're out on your own, kid?" Giyadas was probably the equivalent of a human six-year-old. She kept up with him as he walked towards the Exchange, her tufted mane of amber hair like a Spartan soldier's helmet. It was like looking down on a rocking horse. "Did you tell her you were going out?"

"Why should she worry?"

"Well, what if—"

Eddie stopped himself from explaining what could happen to a small child out on its own on Earth. No, there were no what-ifs in F'nar. Anyone could walk down its terraces in complete safety. Wess'har were communal, responsible creatures who regarded the exploitation of any other animal as the worst possible crime. There were no gangs, no speeding traffic, and no muggers.

And then—suitably provoked—wess'har would wage war without pity and wipe out millions. *Chilled or punching*—that was how Shan had described them. They didn't have a middle setting. Humankind was about to find out what wess'har were like when they were *really* punching.

"I want to go to Mar'an'cas," said Giyadas. The *isanket* was taking her future role as a matriarch seriously. Talking to her was like blotting old-fashioned ink, the information instantly absorbed and faithfully reproduced yet somehow reversed. "I want to see the *gethes* from Constantine colony."

"Why?"

"To see why they're different from you. I want to know why they killed the bezeri."

"They didn't, sweetheart. They helped someone else do it. And it was just a couple of them. They believe in God and that makes humans do some pretty strange things."

Giyadas skipped a step. "Sergeant Bennett said it was *bollocks* because if there was a real god he wouldn't let humans behave the way they do."

So Ade Bennett had taken on the mantle of teaching the wess'har inappropriate English. They'd already absorbed way too much from Shan, and Giyadas was picking it up faster than any of them.

Eddie shrugged. "But the why doesn't matter to wess'har, does it? You only care about what's done, not *why* it was done."

"Knowing is not the same as caring. If we don't know why, how can we stop it happening again?"

"You sure you're a kid and not just a bit short for a wess'har?"

"I don't understand."

"Never mind." Eddie slowed as he merged with the crowd of wess'har approaching the Exchange of Surplus Things. His instinct was to grab Giyadas's hand and make sure she wasn't crushed, but the adult wess'har towering above her gave her plenty of space. He took her hand anyway and she looked up at him as if he were mad. "So you've been talking to Ade, have you?"

"He wants his friends back."

"The other Royal Marines?"

"What's royal? What's the sea got to do with it?"

"It's just an old regimental title. They were sea-going soldiers."

"Will he be our soldier now?"

"I don't know. I don't think any of us know what's going to happen next."

But Ade couldn't go home again, not with the *c'naatat* parasite colonizing his body.

The sergeant was sitting on a packing crate in the Exchange of Surplus Things, the nearest that F'nar had to a center of government, a great vaulted hall cut deep into the wall of rock that cradled F'nar. It was a warehouse where wess'har deposited surplus crops and took others that they needed, without tally or inventory, and the bounty was never abused. It was the sort of system that would never work on Earth in a million years.

Ade didn't look at all changed by *c'naatat*. He still appeared on first glance like an anonymous, average bloke somewhere in his thirties, maybe early, maybe late. It took another glance to register that he was exceptionally fit and taking discreet note of everything around him.

But he hadn't turned into a two-meter alien; whatever the parasite was doing to him, it was doing it internally. He nodded acknowledgment but didn't get up. Eddie sat down beside him and Giyadas stood staring into his impassive face, far too close to be anything but annoying.

"Hi," said Ade, cornered. His voice always seemed too soft for a man who was supposed to bark orders. "You're growing fast, aren't you?"

"Are you remembering what Shan remembered?"

"Sometimes, sweetie."

"You must find that a comfort."

Then she disappeared into the crowd to find Nevyan. They were nearly all males and even Nevyan—shorter than the average matriarch—stood almost a head above them.

"I think they're about fifty when they're born," said Eddie. "They don't so much grow up as acquire more knowledge."

"That's very perceptive."

Ade glanced at him sideways and Eddie knew he had seen that warning expression before. It was Shan's. Nobody knew just how many components of a previous host *c'naatat* would whip out like a conjuring trick. This looked like one of them.

"I wasn't being patronizing," said Eddie, responding to the disapproval of a dead woman.

"The kid's wrong. I don't find it comforting."

"You getting flashbacks? Aras does, all the time."

"Yeah, one in particular. A gorilla and the bloody awful feeling of having let someone down when they needed me."

"I can tell you about the gorilla."

"Later, maybe." Ade had a quiet finality about him when he wanted to change the subject. "What are we waiting for? Match of the Day?"

"Live from Eqbas Vorhi."

"They don't play soccer, do they?"

"No. They don't play anything. Apparently Nevyan's going to be talking to a couple of Eqbas matriarchs. What we're looking at is a city called Surang."

The huge image in the wall—part of the stone itself, it seemed—showed a static view of Surang, at once wholly familiar to Eddie yet shocking. It was every live news feed from a foreign city that he had ever seen, and he half-expected a colleague to amble into shot, adjust an audio implant and ask the gallery how long it was to air.

And it was also a window onto an alien city that was exotic even to the wess'har around him.

Surang was astonishing. It was the first shot he'd seen that took in so much of the city skyline, all impossible curves and billowing organic shapes that reached up into the sky like a growth of oyster mushrooms on a tree. There was a lot of vegetation; but there was also plenty of building. If the wess'har in F'nar built to avoid being seen, then their cousins appeared to represent the less discreet pole of architectural philosophy.

Surang was a statement, whether it meant to be or not. It said *look what we can do, monkey boys.*

Eddie wanted to get those pictures down the ITX as fast as he could find a way of linking into the feed. The excitement boiled in his gut.

"Can you imagine seeing our politicians holding talks in public?"

"You'd be out of a job for a start." Ade scratched his chin. "And so would I."

Something brushed against Eddie's leg. A displaced throwback of a thought said *cat* but there were no cats on Wess'ej. He half-turned and found himself looking down into the matte black predator's eyes of Serrimissani.

"Hi, doll," he said. He liked the ussissi interpreter. She was a sullen, savage, stroppy cow, but she had looked after him on Umeh when the shit was flying. He owed her. "Missing Jejeno?"

"Not a city I care for," she said. Her little sibilant girly voice was at odds with her mouthful of needle teeth. He'd felt those in his shoulder once and he never wanted to feel them again. "And Nevyan does not ask me to pour beverages, unlike Ual."

"I know it pisses you girls off to be told to fetch the coffee."

"I am not deceived by your casual attitude. You grieve for your friend, however casually you refer to her."

Eddie shrugged. "That's how we defend our feelings."

"Aras seems not to feel that need."

"We all cope in our own way." He fought an urge to reach down and fondle Serrimissani's head like an animal. *This is not your pet. This is a person.* He settled for squatting at eye level rather than gazing down on her from a lordly height. "So what are you up to?"

"I have advised Nevyan of the isenj way of conducting themselves."

"She's never actually had any contact with one, has she?"

"No living wess'har has met isenj, except for Aras and a few troops."

Met was an odd word to describe warfare. "I really miss Ual."

Serrimissani slitted her eyes at him, lips compressed. Her contempt could be pretty transparent. But he still counted her as a friend even though she made no attempt at small talk while they waited.

Nevyan arrived, with no minders or minions clearing a

path and no visible deference. Nevyan's mother Mestin, once the dominant matriarch of the ruling clique, watched from the sidelines.

Of all the bizarre facets of the wess'har character, this was the one that Eddie was finding the hardest to grasp. Leaders simply *happened* by dint of their hormonal dominance, and once they happened, they got on with the job. Wess'har had unforgivingly high expectations of their informal governors. It was a duty, not a privilege, and nobody clawed their way to the top or maneuvered for position. Nevyan had fallen into the role; her primeval protective instinct had kicked into overdrive when Shan died.

It was both terrifying and reassuring. Wess'har were militantly altruistic. Eddie wondered how that tendency manifested itself in their bigger, brasher cousins.

Giyadas, apparently satisfied that her stepmother had arrived, returned and sat next to Eddie with all the composure of a duchess.

The two wess'har races didn't speak the same language after such a long separation but they were learning as fast as they could with the assistance of ussissi aides. Eddie wondered if humans would turn out to be the only species in the galaxy that took so long to learn languages.

"Do I need to do that voice thing?" asked Eddie. "The double sounds?"

"How will anyone understand you otherwise?" said Giyadas.

"Do overtones make much difference?"

Giyadas did some rapid head-cocking, staring at a point ahead of her. "Are *say* and *stay* different in English?"

"Yes." She had actually asked a rhetorical question. He never thought the hyper-literal adult wess'har did that, let alone a small child. *Smart kid.* "Point taken. Is that it? Just pronunciation?"

"No."

"What, then?"

Giyadas looked as if she was searching his face for something. "If you say *ripe fruit,* then one word follows the other. If we say *ripe fruit,* we say both words at the same time. If we say someone is *eating ripe fruit,* then that is one word too. There is often one word for the basic things. For new things, we add words together to express them."

"I can tell you've never been paid by the word," said Eddie. He shut his eyes for a moment and imagined a three-dimensional tonal language with a huge and specific core vocabulary and then even more torturous compounds. Shan had said wess'u grammar itself was simple. He couldn't imagine how.

"Perhaps I could write wess'u," he said.

Giyadas enjoyed teaching. "Show me your screen."

Eddie pulled out the sheet and set it to graphic mode. Giyadas prodded a long, four-jointed finger into the fabric and scrawled what looked like the contents of a whiteboard from a management brainstorming session, all radiating curves and symbols like a fishbone diagram. He couldn't see a beginning or end, just a single maze of symbols. Even Chinese and Arabic were linear. Written wess'u wasn't made for human brains.

"There," she said. "That is much simpler."

Eddie, a man who lived by his talent for speaking and writing, was now effectively an illiterate, and a mute illiterate at that. "Do you people ever do straight lines?" he asked. "Okay, you be my interpreter. Maybe you can teach me in time."

The wall image changed, tilting down to show a ussissi draped in multicolored fabric belts. She spoke in wess'u and Eddie glanced down at Giyadas, indulging her growing sense of preparation for matriarchy.

"What's she saying?"

"That Sarmatakian Ve will be talking soon. She's the adviser to the matriarch Curas Ti."

Eddie couldn't imagine any human politician taking a sensitive call from another state with the electorate watching. They'd rather screw in public than be seen getting screwed over. But what Nevyan was doing was a logical, extraordinary extension of the cooperative way wess'har had evolved. Lying wasn't an option when you were consciously aware of scent signals, either. Their transparency was more intimidating than charming.

Sarmatakian Ve and the matriarch Curas Ti didn't look like any wess'har Eddie had met. They were stockier, darker, and short-faced; it was as if a designer had been sent in to update the model for a new market. They looked like . . . aliens.

"Boy, you people evolve fast," said Eddie. He made a quick comparison with Giyadas. The wess'har genome was fluid; they exchanged DNA like some bacteria. "No wonder *c'naatat* likes wess'har hosts."

Giyadas gave him that almost canine head-tilt that showed she was concentrating hard on him. "Do you want me to translate?"

"Sorry. Carry on."

"They say that there is another ship being diverted to this sector, a larger one. A mission is being prepared on Eqbas Vorhi. They would like more information in the meantime."

"About what?"

"About *gethes,* about Wess'ej, about Umeh. About everything."

Eddie had a thought.

"Has anyone told them exactly what *c'naatat* is?"

Giyadas tilted her head further. It gave crosslike wess'har pupils a better focus on the object of their curiosity. "I don't know."

"I wonder what they're going to make of it?" said Eddie.

3

We have waited many generations for this. The wess'har want us to hand over the two humans responsible for wiping out the bezeri. I say that we should agree to this only if they hand over the Destroyer of Mjat, Aras Sar Iussan. We have never had justice for the destruction of our colony on Asht, and the loss of millions of isenj lives must surely warrant at least the same penalty as tens of thousands of bezeri.

PAR SHOMEN EIT,
Supplies Minister,
Isenj Northern Assembly

October 2376, Pajat coast, Wess'ej.

Mar'an'cas was a striking landmark but it seemed the most inhospitable place on Wess'ej.

Aras had never seen the island before. It jutted out of the sea off the coast near Pajatis, well to the north of F'nar, almost far enough north to be as cold as his home city of Iussan. The matriarch Bur had sent a guide with Aras and Ade Bennett to make sure they didn't miss it.

Aras doubted anyone could. It looked like something huge and shapelessly gray had punched its way out of the sea and then frozen.

"Looks fucking grim," said Ade.

"Not as grim as remaining on Bezer'ej."

It certainly wasn't Constantine. But then that island on Bezer'ej had been equally incapable of supporting human agriculture until Aras created a shielded environment for the colonists. Mar'an'cas was now secure behind the same type of biobarrier; the colony might yet rebuild itself, physically at least. Its emotional integrity was another matter.

I killed Josh. If they say they forgive me, I shall tell them the bezeri don't forgive him, and neither do I.

The Pajat guide indicated the shallow-draft boat on the shoreline. "I can steer the vessel for you," he said. "If your business is brief, I can wait."

"I'll drive," said Ade. The marine pushed the craft into the shallows and climbed inboard with the ease of someone who had spent a lot of time on amphibious missions. He checked the controls, holding his hands above the touch-pad carefully and moving them to see what response it produced. "I do this for a living. Come on, Aras. Let's get this over with."

Their business would not be brief.

Aras watched Ade carefully as he steered the boat out from shore, making a good first attempt at the hand movements needed to direct the vessel. He had stripped all the marks of rank from his uniform, from the sergeant's chevron stripes to the little wreathed globe emblem on his beret. He smelled strongly of anger.

"You're upset about your dismissal," said Aras.

"Too bloody right I am. Twenty-three years in the Corps and I don't even get the courtesy of a court martial."

"It's what Eddie calls political expedience. He doubts your command was involved in the decision."

"Ain't that always the way."

"You needn't feel ashamed."

"I don't. I'm *disgraced.* That's not the same thing." He opened the throttle with an upward gesture of his hand and the boat picked up speed. "I can live with what I've done, but I don't see why the detachment should be dishonored because of what that stupid cow Neville did."

The spray from the bows threw a hail of icy water in Aras's face and he turned aside. Even if he was infinitely resilient, he still felt the cold. He wondered whether Ade really could live with what he had done because he looked increasingly like a man who couldn't.

This gethes *shot my isan. He helped Lindsay Neville cap-*

*ture her. His actions led to her taking her own life. I should
loathe him. I should punish him.*

Aras had walked away from Ade more than once rather
than let his own grief and rage take over. Human and
wess'har definitions of responsibility clashed within him.

*Shan chose to step out of the airlock, so Lindsay Neville
has to pay for that. No—that's a human view. Neville has to
pay for Ouzhari.*

Shan had liked Ade very much and wouldn't have wanted
him to come to any harm. Aras liked him too. The *c'naatat*
that had entered his body carried with it a comforting scent
that said *house-brother.* Something of Shan was in him and
Aras's primeval wess'har instinct kicked in, making him
bond with males who had his *isan*'s genes. Through the
same instinctive mechanism, he identified qualities in Ade
that his *isan* might transfer to him through copulation.
Wess'har males influenced their *isan*'s mating choices.

But there was no longer an *isan,* and now there never
would be.

"We could have seized Shan from the *Actaeon* if they had
taken her on board," said Aras. "She had no need to space
herself."

"I think she wanted to be absolutely certain the parasite
was unusable. You know how she hated leaving anything to
chance."

It was the first time in two months that they had spoken
this openly about her death, edging nervously around their
respective raw grief. Shan had left a void. Even Eddie
seemed to be feeling it, and Eddie had never looked like a
man who cared about anybody. Aras suspected it was a
façade that members of his trade adopted. For all his pre-
tence of being untouched, the man was still recording stories
about Shan: the *real story,* he called it, not the *pack of lies*
that others might commit to archive.

Irrelevant, all of it.

The forbidding island began filling their horizon. There

was no vegetation to be seen but as they drew closer Aras spotted the sloping outlines of shelters. It was a very un-wess'har thing to mark the landscape with visible, perma-nent structures, but the displaced colonists had no time to excavate shelters in the ground. He wondered if the stony terrain would permit that at all.

Constantine's underground colony had taken years to carve into the rock. He remembered it all. He remembered helping Ben Garrod, Josh's ancestor, excavate deep into the ground. He recalled how he took part in building—no, carving—the church of St. Francis and creating the indulgent but beautiful stained-glass window with its saint surrounded by animals.

Aras hadn't understood what a saint was. Saints often died for their beliefs. He wondered if Josh Garrod's god would make him a saint now because Aras had killed him.

He found he was thinking aloud. "I shouldn't blame you," Aras said. "I killed Josh and he was my friend. His great-great-great grandfather was my friend and each generation after him. But when it came to duty I did what was neces-sary, even if I still cared for him."

Aras juggled two opposing impulses again. Ade had played a role in Shan's death. He was also his brother.

Ade's jaw muscles twitched. "You think I did what was *necessary* to Shan?" He held his gaze. "Sometimes I really think you want to kill me."

"I can no longer see situations with a wess'har's clarity, Adrian. I have become too human. You were *ordered* to act, and no wess'har really understands the imperative that hu-mans experience."

Ade leaned on the control console, making the occasional casual hand gesture to correct course.

"Only my mum called me Adrian," he said quietly. "Just call me Ade, will you?"

"Very well."

"And *only following orders* is a pathetic excuse. I had a choice and I didn't make it." He rubbed his nose and suddenly looked out to sea, hands on hips, although there was nothing out there worth his attention. "You know what I did? I emptied a whole clip into her. I aimed low because I knew she'd wear body armor and I knew nothing would kill her and I knew that hitting her legs could drop her for long enough to get restraints on her. Now, if I'd had the balls I could have just put a couple of rounds in Neville and Rayat and nobody would have been any the wiser. Twenty-five fucking light-years away, no enquiry, no post-mortem. But I didn't. And I fucking hate myself for that."

Ade lapsed back into silence, head bowed for a moment, then turned to the helm with a tell-tale glaze of moisture across his eyes. Eventually he slowed the boat to run up onto the beach. He seemed to find some solace in using his skills. Aras jumped out to help him drag the craft a little further up the shore and their eyes met for one uncomfortable second too long.

"That's all hindsight, Ade."

"Maybe."

"All your indoctrination is to obey your commanding officer. Human society relies on unthinking compliance."

"Well, I'm not completely human any more so they can shove their compliance up their arse."

Aras understood his pain, and it *was* pain, not simple anger. He had been abandoned too. Communal as they were, wess'har didn't expend energy on hostage or prisoner retrieval, and Aras could still recall how utterly abandoned and hopeless he felt five hundred years ago when he sat in an isenj prison awaiting the next visit from his captors. He'd done what was asked of him as a soldier. Then he was simply one effort too many. He felt that even more strongly since he had known Ade.

His isenj captors had never stopped reminding him that they always went back for their own.

The biobarrier gave Aras a stinging jolt as he stepped through it. On Bezer'ej, the invisible fence that maintained Constantine's ecology and separated it from the rest of the planet simply prickled on exposed skin. This barrier was several magnitudes stronger. Nobody was taking chances on contamination, however unlikely it seemed that anything would cross the species barrier.

There were more than a thousand men, women and children now living on Mar'an'cas. It wasn't the entire colony. Aras knew that a few had refused evacuation from Bezer'ej and were prepared to risk the engineered anti-human pathogen that the wess'har had spread across the planet as a barrier to further landings.

It had been created from Shan's own DNA. Aras had been angry that she hadn't told him she had donated tissue, but now he knew he wouldn't have wasted a single second on anger had he known she would be taken from him so soon.

"Let me go on ahead," said Ade. "If you get any crap from them about Josh—"

"I don't require your protection," said Aras. "But I appreciate the offer."

Wess'har had perfect recall. The memories Aras had struggled to ignore now refused to be brushed aside and pursued him, tormenting him. He remembered exactly how it felt when his *tilgir* hit Josh in the left side of the neck and the impact traveled up both his arms as his blade severed his friend's head. He could feel it now. He could hear the absolute silence that lasted seconds and then the rising crescendo of wails and screams from the colonists who had witnessed the execution. He could smell the smoke when the ussissi burned the body.

But you helped Lindsay Neville deploy the bombs that poisoned the bezeri, Josh. You deserved what I gave you.

It was a very human feeling and it wasn't his. Wess'har balancing was much more detached. This was a remnant of Shan Frankland, locked into him forever by the capacity for genetic memory that *c'naatat* had taken a fancy to when it passed through an isenj. Aras wondered how much of his own and Shan's memories would now be surfacing in Ade Bennett's mind. And he wondered how he had drawn a line between Josh's complicity and Ade's.

Two figures in dappled camouflage uniforms came into view, a man and a woman, marines called Bulwant Singh Chahal and Ismat Qureshi. They weren't strangers. Nobody on this island was. Aras knew them all.

"Hello, Sarge. Hello, sir." Qureshi looked at Aras and nodded her head, but her attention was directed towards Ade. "You okay, Ade?"

"I'm fine. You?"

"We were worried when we lost your signal," said Chahal. He held out his hand and the luminous green display that was grown into his palm danced with data. It was battle-field tech, a living computer and communications device that monitored and tracked and reported. Human soldiers were full of implants.

Ade held up his own palm: it was blankly normal human skin, pink and creased and devoid of light.

"Shit," said Chahal. "What happened to your bioscreen?"

"Long story," said Ade. "It went for a walk with my implants."

Qureshi and Chahal glanced at each other. "Okay," she said. "What do we do now?"

"Fuck all," said Ade.

"What's up?"

"The bastards have binned us. We're all dismissed the service."

Aras hadn't known Ade to use profanities as liberally and unthinkingly as Shan or Eddie; his language was an indication of his distress. Belonging and not belonging to a formal group seemed to matter enormously to him. It seemed to matter to Chahal and Qureshi, too. Their skins, usually quite dark compared to Ade's, took on a yellow cast as the blood vessels constricted. They weren't expecting the news. They swallowed hard and fidgeted for a few moments.

"That's what you came to tell us?" said Chahal. "That we've just been marooned here?"

"That's about the size of it."

"Don't we even get a hearing?"

"Seems not. The FEU told the wess'har they can do what they like with us."

Qureshi and Chahal looked at Aras as if expecting even worse news. They knew what he had done to a scientist from *Thetis* for causing the death of a single bezeri infant, and what happened to Josh. He imagined they were scaling up the consequences for being a member of the force that had managed to kill many thousands more, and fearing the worst.

"Nevyan says you're welcome to stay," said Aras carefully. "You won't be punished. Neville and Rayat will, though, when we find them."

Qureshi's gaze darted between Ade and Aras. "What about Mart and Sue and Jon?"

"If they wish to join you, they can."

Chahal looked dubious. It was a very distinct human expression, chin lowered, eyebrows raised. "This isn't how wess'har normally operate, is it? What's the catch?"

"The catch, as you put it, is that *Shan Chail* had great regard for you and that regard is respected. More to the point, you are not personally accountable for your commander's actions."

"Neither was anyone in *Actaeon*."

"*Actaeon* was given time to evacuate the uninvolved. Those who stayed on board chose to do so."

Ade stepped in, suddenly the sergeant again. "Chaz, just shut it. We nuked the fucking place. There's no moral high ground."

Chahal glanced at Qureshi as if seeking a cue. She had always looked too slight to be a soldier, but she looked even thinner now. It was a testament to the ordeal of the last few weeks.

"We're really sorry about Frankland," she said. "I just wanted you to know that."

Aras wasn't sure if the comment was for him or Ade. Either way he had nothing to say.

"Show me the colony," he said.

They walked in a line behind Qureshi, totally silent. Two hundred meters away from the shore, Aras got a better view of the tents. Aras thought immediately of one of little Rachel Garrod's storybooks with their bright illustrations. The tents were made of elegant turquoise and green patterned wess'har fabric but sewn to the colony's design, looking more like one of the humans' carnivals than a refugee camp.

"Jesus Christ," said Ade. "Hell with soft furnishings."

The Pajat clans had done their best to help out in the emergency but there was a limit to what could be done to make more than a hundred farming families comfortable on a rock. Even though the tents were set in neat lines, it still looked like chaos. The first thing Aras noticed was the constant backdrop of children crying and the flapping of fabric in the wind. Then he noticed the smell.

"We're working on the water and waste," said Chahal. "Sue Webster's really the expert on that. If she wants to come here, we could use her."

And these were orderly humans. These were people used to a tough agricultural life and to following rules of survival on a hostile planet. But they were not the generation that had carved Constantine colony out of the rock of Bezer'ej nearly two centuries ago, and they were finding the experience hard.

"At least we've got the hydroponics rigged," said Qureshi. She turned up her collar against the wind. "We've got salad. Just in time for winter. Nice."

"The bezeri won't see another winter," said Aras.

He walked into the camp. Faces he knew—some well, others not—stared back at him and he found himself at the center of a silence that was spreading like a pool of water. The expressions that he met were hard and hostile. What else did he expect? He had killed Josh Garrod, their leader, his friend. They were seeing him as he was for the first time—an alien, a complete stranger whose ethical code was ultimately at odds with theirs.

Aras didn't understand; his actions were even enshrined in their religious texts. *Thou shalt give life for life, eye for eye, tooth for tooth, hand for hand, foot for foot, burning for burning, wound for wound, stripe for stripe.* What did that mean? If it meant a punishment that mirrored the magnitude of the crime, then none of them should have been spared, innocent or not; all the *gethes* for all the bezeri, just as it said in their Bible. But there were many things in that book that they chose to overlook when it suited them.

Ade prodded him in the back. "I don't think this is a good idea, mate. Let's go."

"I have to see Josh's family."

"Just leave it, okay?"

Aras couldn't. He wanted to, but he had spent most of his life among these people and their forebears and he found it hard to cut himself off from them. The human genes in him were mainly theirs, gleaned by *c'naatat* from their bacteria and shed cells. The colonists were almost family. For generations, before Shan came into his life, they *had* been family.

Ade walked in front of him. He held his rifle by the hand guard and grip, but his finger rested outside the trigger guard. He was checking to either side as if on patrol.

"They can't hurt us," said Aras reproachfully.

"I don't want any more accidental contamination."

"They know what I am. They've never shown any interest in *c'naatat.* But they don't know what you are."

Ade held his rifle a little higher. "I wasn't planning on hugging any of them."

"Bastard," said one of the men as they passed.

Aras hadn't experienced abuse for five centuries, not since his isenj captors had told him what a filthy murderer he was and that he deserved the tortures he was enduring. He was surprised how much simple words stung. The two centuries that he had spent ensuring that the Constantine colony survived were obviously forgotten.

Aras stopped and turned round.

"Leave it, Aras," said Ade. He had been trained to ignore that kind of provocation. But Aras hadn't, and he genuinely wanted them to understand why Josh had to die.

The man who had called him a bastard was named David, he recalled, just like Lindsay Neville's dead infant son. David had two daughters and his wife taught at the colony school. He took a step back as Aras faced him.

"Do you know what genocide is, David?"

David smelled of acid fear. "Josh never set out to harm the bezeri."

"And still they're dead. Your god might care about your intentions, but I don't and neither would the bezeri. If Josh had helped destroy beings who looked like you, would you understand better?"

"The parasite had to be destroyed."

"It was a life-form like you or me. Do you know what else lived on Ouzhari?"

"No."

"And now you never will. Did you think what else the bombs might destroy, or did you think a neutron device and the cobalt poison would be selective in their action?"

David stared back into his face. The scent of frying garlic jostled for attention with the smell of the latrines. "But you *know* us. The Garrods were your family."

"My family was Shan Frankland," Aras said quietly. "And she's dead too."

Ade took his elbow and pressed gently. "Come on. Let's find Deborah Garrod and get this over with."

Word traveled ahead. Deborah was waiting for him, standing outside an incongruously patterned tent and holding six-year-old Rachel by the hand. Her teenaged son James, as square and lean as his father, watched Aras suspiciously. He stood a little in front of his mother.

Deborah said nothing. She had a fine-boned oriental face and fatigue had painted dark circles under her eyes. James disappeared inside the tent and came out cradling something in his arms.

"We can't feed them," he said. "You take them."

Aras held out his hands to receive two live rats. Black and White, as he'd named them, were laboratory animals he had confiscated from Mohan Rayat soon after the *Thetis* party landed on Bezer'ej. They had been young animals then, lively and with fine silky coats, and now they were not. They were tubby and their fur was coarser. They were aging fast, as rats did, and they scrabbled to get inside his coat for shelter.

"Where are the others?" asked Aras. He felt the rats burrow into the layers of his tunic and settle, little hearts pounding. They had a clean dry scent very much like a ussissi.

"We had to leave them. We set them free."

"But they have no food. They can't digest native Bezer'ej plants. How could you do such a thing?"

"They're *rats*. You killed my dad, and now you're worried about a few rats?"

Even now they didn't understand. Aras wondered how he could ever have thought *gethes* could learn that their lives were no more special than that of any other species. It was their single defining belief; the colonists even said all *gethes* were modeled on their god. It was staggering conceit. And a god like a *gethes* sounded monstrous.

Aras looked down at Rachel. Once she had rushed to greet him and show him the drawings she had made on hemp paper. Now she pressed into her mother's skirt, hiding her face.

Deborah gestured to James to go back inside the tent. "Aras, I'm praying that I can eventually forgive you," she said. "And I'm truly sorry for your loss."

"Do you understand why I did it?"

"No, Aras, I don't. And I never will."

He thought for a moment that she was going to use the words *punishment* and *sin*. She didn't, but he knew she would be thinking that he had at least paid the same price that he had exacted from her.

"Come on," said Ade. "Enough."

They retraced their steps. Aras wondered if the thin soil on Mar'an'cas could support so many and recalled how long it had taken to get the soil of Constantine to the correct composition to support terrestrial crops. It could be done, though. He'd grown the colony's alien vegetables in F'nar for Shan, to make her feel at home. He could do the same here.

At the perimeter of the camp, a hail of small stones landed in front of them. The marines ducked and turned; some of the colony youths were aiming at Aras.

"Little bleeders," Ade muttered. "So much for our model community."

Another stone fell short. The youngsters closed the gap. Ade stepped in front of Aras as if to block the missiles and a fist-sized chunk hit him in the face. He staggered a few paces and then recovered his balance.

"Fuck you," he said. "Fuck *you*." Blood was running down his cheek. He picked up a large stone and threw it back hard, catching one of the fleeing youths squarely in the back. One of the adults grabbed the boy and cuffed him sharply across the head.

"Sorry," the man called, fist still clutching the boy's collar. "That wasn't meant for you."

"You okay, Ade?" said Qureshi. She rummaged in her belt pouch and unwrapped a dressing. "Let's have a look at that."

Ade took the wad from her and moistened it from his water bottle. He wiped the cut carefully. "No need, Izzy. I'll be fine."

"I heard it go crack," she said. "That's broken bone."

Qureshi took a step forward and he took one back. She stared at him for a few seconds and then her expression changed; Aras knew what she had seen. Ade's wound was already fading.

"Oh shit," she said. "Ade, what happened to you?"

"Don't ask."

"You've caught it, haven't you? That's why you surrendered."

"It was an accident. Shan head-butted me when I was trying to restrain her. It's spread by body fluids."

"Who else knows you've got it?"

"Lindsay Neville."

"Rayat?"

"By now, who knows?"

"Shit." Qureshi went as if to reach out to him and then dropped her arms awkwardly as if afraid of contact. "You poor sod."

Aras wasn't sure whether Qureshi was more worried about the consequences of discovery or Ade's prospect of permanent exile. She seemed genuinely upset, reeking of agitation. Chahal just shook his head.

"Are you going to come back to F'nar?" Ade asked.

"How can we?" Qureshi shrugged. "They need us here to get sanitation and power running. At least we'll be doing something we're trained for."

"And after that?"

"I don't know. I really don't. What about you?"

Ade glanced at Aras. "I'm staying."

The chances of any of them getting back to Earth looked so remote as to make the comment superfluous. Aras felt Black and White shifting position inside his tunic.

"When you want to leave this place, notify me," said Aras.

If there were surplus crops after Eddie and the rats were fed, then he would send them to the marines. He wondered if they might not all be better off on Umeh.

Ade was silent on the boat back to the mainland. At one point he took the bloodstained wad of fabric out of his pocket and stared at it as if the real nature of his condition was starting to dawn on him.

"If your comrades had returned with you, what would you have done?" Aras asked.

"I don't know," said Ade. "The last thing you want in F'nar is a bunch of bored Booties hanging about. Maybe it's just as well they're occupied elsewhere."

"I realize how distressing this is for you."

"I'm not the one they were aiming the stones at."

"I'm not that offended."

"You looked after that colony from day one. That's got to hurt."

"I have greater pain to keep me occupied. And disappointment. What is the one thing none of them asked?"

"Dunno."

"They didn't ask about the gene bank. They brought it to this system for safekeeping. It was important enough for Shan to be sent here to locate it. And now it is forgotten."

"But not by you."

"No. Not by me."

If Ade was seeking a new purpose in life, then so was Aras. This seemed a fine one. When he had settled his scores with Lindsay Neville and Mohan Rayat, then he would be trapped with destructively bitter memories unless he moved forward. Restoring Earth's endangered and extinct species was something Shan would have wanted: she had cared enough to leave her life behind to retrieve the gene bank for her government.

It was a very different *gethes* government now. The wess'har held the gene bank. It was safely out of human hands.

Aras wondered what an Earth without *gethes* might be like.

Ual's forebears lived in his mind. He searched the memory embedded in his genes and looked for wisdom from his fathers and mothers before him, but there was nothing to prepare him for the situation he faced now. He gripped hard on the data cube that Ralassi had found for him, still disturbed by its images, and sought courage.

When he walked into the Northern Assembly debating chamber the roar of angry sound hit him like a shock wave.

The scene before him was more like a street in Jejeno when something had gone badly wrong—when someone had fallen or another unplanned event had disrupted the flow of pedestrian traffic and thrown up chaotic eddies and turbulence. The delegates were milling, arguing, cursing. A choppy sea of glittering black shapes threatened to engulf him; he felt he might drown if he slipped from the podium.

Of course they were in disarray. War had never actually come close to Umeh itself before. They could all remember that and be certain of the accuracy of the memory. Ual wondered at what point he might need to play the data in his belt to his audience. Ralassi had collated archive material on Eqbas Vorhi for him, a little history lesson for the Assembly.

"Minister Par Paral Ual has been summoned to explain the current situation," said the Arbiter wearily. "Let him be heard, will you?"

The chamber grew quieter. Ual could see ministerial colleagues from other departments huddled in a group, shimmering with resentment. Alien Affairs had always been regarded as a junior post, a do-nothing backwater keeping an eye on the wess'har in case they let their defenses down on Asht, a department autonomous through insignificance. But now the rest of the regional administration had noticed him. Ual feared that they might ally to reshape the cabinet.

For a moment he longed for the human solution of a single executive leader. But Eddie had told him that didn't do a thing to stop infighting and alliances; it just created more people to *stab you in the back,* a situation that Eddie assured him seldom involved actual weapons.

"We find ourselves in a difficult position, colleagues," said Ual. And to his utter embarrassment, the words came out in the human's English, shaped by sucked air.

The chamber really was silent now.

He gathered his composure and repeated himself in his own language. "These are challenging times. The wess'har have summoned aid from Eqbas Vorhi to deal with the humans, and if we're not prudent they'll deal with us too. We've never faced anything like this. We need to consider radically different solutions."

"Is it true that the wess'har planted a pathogen on Asht to

stop us returning?" The question came from a location delegate he didn't recognize. Full assembly sessions mixed the representatives of neighborhoods with regional overseers and ministries, and they all had a vote. "What are you going to do about *that*?"

"Absolutely nothing," said Ual. "It's not an immediate problem."

"And why did they do it now? They've had generations to do it."

"Perhaps they couldn't, until now," said another delegate. "Perhaps the humans helped them. And what about *Thetis*? What will happen to our colleagues on board?"

Ual had a sudden nagging thought and dismissed it. Why now, indeed? He pressed on. "The humans are also subject to biological countermeasures on Bezer'ej." He paused and corrected himself. *Preserve me, I actually called it Bezer'ej.* "My apologies. *Asht.* It's fully quarantined."

"It didn't save the bezeri. At least any damage we caused in the past wasn't deliberate."

"Order!" shouted the Arbiter. "If you don't comply with the rules of this chamber I'll close the session. Let the minister speak."

There was a disgruntled scraping of limbs across polished stone but the delegates shut up. Ual pondered the wess'har reputation for bioengineering skills. The ussissi said they came from a world of naturally changing genomes: they knew a great deal about the fabric of life as well as the manipulation of molecules. He would worry about that later.

He made another attempt. "Unfortunately our human allies have placed us in an impossible situation, and I'm led to question what benefit they are to us."

"Hand over the individuals responsible for the attack on Asht."

"The wess'har haven't asked for them yet. Do you want me to deliver them?"

"If need be, yes. That is how their minds work. They decide who's responsible and take only them."

"And how would you define *responsible*? And what constitutes *responsible* to an Eqbas wess'har? Do you understand their framework of ethical logic? They don't invade. They will, however, intervene when asked, and they intervene robustly and then they never *stop* intervening and they create yet another enclave of their own culture."

Eit, the supplies minister, cut in. "We've asked for wess'har troops to face our justice for the destruction of Mjat for generations. Aras Sar Iussan lives in F'nar and as long as he does I say we should not give them the two prisoners they will demand."

"I sympathize," said Ual. "But if we don't comply, we give the wess'har a reason to take action against us, something they will find a great deal easier with the assistance of Eqbas Vorhi." Now he took the biggest risk of his political career. He felt for the data cube and readied himself to place it in the slot to project images for his colleagues' education. "If we surrender to our past then we lose a greater opportunity for the future. Rather than pursue a symbolic feud with the wess'har, I think we might be better off negotiating with them to secure their help—the help we once thought we might get from humans."

"And *we* invited the humans here," said a surly voice to Ual's left. "The rest of Umeh won't forgive us for that. It's made us a potential battlefield. Throw them all out—now."

Eit interrupted. "If you're suggesting a course of action, you're not making it clear." He lobbed a small polished stone in the direction of the voice. There was a loud *ping*. "Expand, Minister Ual."

Ual felt he was sliding into a pit, a deep one dug for him by Eit. But he felt strongly and—as always—that overrode his suspicion that Eit was luring him into making a rash statement. He almost certainly was: but it still had to be said.

"Observe," said Ual.

The images that appeared around the walls for the delegates to watch were old, *very* old. They were navigation aids that the ussissi pilots once used, pictures of approaches to landing areas and locations of ussissi settlements where they could find accommodation. Some showed fine, wide rivers, others mountains, others plains and icy tundra, exotic images for the city-bound isenj. The worlds looked largely wild and unspoiled.

And in each picture, discreet and almost unnoticeable unless you searched for it, was a building or two in a curious sinuous style like a fungal growth, almost blended into the landscape.

"There are nearly twenty separate images here," said Ual. "And each is of a different world that was once heavily populated. All have been visited and subdued by forces from Eqbas Vorhi over the millennia. If you want to study the various reasons why they intervened in each place, I have more history archives. But perhaps all you need to know now is this. They arrive, they remake the world into what they see as its natural ideal, and they stay. They create outposts. They *police,* to use the human word. And they *adapt* to each environment."

The chamber was silent. Ual felt he had made his point. The same silence had descended on him when he viewed the images alone in his offices.

"Are you saying they might do that to Umeh?" asked Eit.

"I am."

"And the humans?"

"I think it inevitable, judging by this, that they won't escape correction either."

Ual let the delegates chew over the implications. The unexpected images were a stroke of theater that Eddie had taught him without realizing. Sometimes you had to make your point any way you could.

"Humans are no longer a beneficial ally," said Ual.

"But they still want the instant communications systems."

"Yes, but they have nothing to give us, except the return

of our diplomatic delegation from *Thetis*. Perhaps we should seek different alliances and re-examine all those things we thought were fundamental to our culture. What matters is that we resolve our population and environmental problems on this planet and Tasir Var. Everything else is negotiable."

It was so quiet he could have heard a bead drop from a quill. He waited for one lobbed in protest to hit him. He waited for someone to demand that they fight the Eqbas if they tried to rehabilitate Umeh to their own taste.

But he knew what they were thinking. He decided to say it for them.

"We have never defeated the wess'har and I'm certain the Eqbas will ensure we have no chance of ever doing so." He paused, seeing Eit's quills beginning to lift. "Perhaps *they* might be the allies we need. Better that we negotiate a lasting settlement than live in fear. You've seen evidence that the wess'har *can* save Umeh."

But at what price? Nobody asked. It was silent.

Then the chamber erupted. Ual never got the chance to say which part of the wess'har civilization he suggested they approach first. The fact that squabbling had broken out—a rare breach of self-control for a race used to tolerating each other in crowded conditions—suggested some of the delegates agreed with him.

He stepped down from the podium and didn't wait for the vote. As he left, a hail of small stone beads, some red, some blue, some green, bounced off him with angry *pings* as some delegates showed their disapproval.

It would mean a very different way of life, a terrifying prospect for a species that knew its past intimately and lived with generations of memories every second. But Umeh needed an environmental solution. And the prospect of expansion off-world now seemed impossible.

Whether the vote went with him or not, he was going to talk with the wess'har. He would surrender himself to chance as an act of good faith. Umeh had been mired too long in fretting over the Destroyer of Mjat and other historical wounds. Ual felt the beads under his footpads, sharp and treacherous.

Beads.

He didn't want to, but he thought of a red corundum bead he had given a curious Eddie Michallat, one still attached to a shed quill. It wasn't the only access the human might have had to isenj tissue. But Eddie was the only human he knew with direct contact with the wess'har.

Exactly what I might have done in his position. But he was still shocked by how deeply betrayed he felt by a creature he thought of as a friend. *Did I misjudge humans that badly?*

Betrayer or not, though, Eddie Michallat had saved him from being forced into a course of action that could end only in another lost war on Bezer'ej.

Ual swallowed his discomfort and thought of Umeh's future.

4

Well, we've still got incoming broadcast—only five channels, but one of them is sports so we can follow the footie. You'd be amazed how sane that keeps you. Our food situation isn't much better than yours, mate, but at least I haven't got people singing hymns next door at six in the morning. Is Ade okay? Next time Eddie comes to Umeh, I hope he brings him. I want to see Lindsay Neville's face when he walks in.

Message from Mne Mart Barencoin to Mne Ismat Qureshi

"You haven't lost your touch for stirring up shit," said Mick, the duty news editor, not looking up from his sandwich. Then he glanced up at the cam, and he simply said, "Oh . . ."

Eddie was making use of one of the comms screens in the Exchange of Surplus Things. Every conversation was effectively a live outside broadcast surrounded by curious wess'har, and he forgot that Mick hadn't seen the wall-sized image of Surang before.

"Where the fuck have *you* been?" said Eddie.

There was a five-second delay on the last leg of the relay, the router that joined the ITX to light-speed links near Earth. Mick's gaze was aimed past him. "What's that behind you?"

"That's a live feed from Eqbas Vorhi. Look, I thought I'd been cut off for good. I haven't had an incoming call from you for *weeks*." Eddie glanced over his shoulder, counting to five again. He hadn't quite worked out the technology yet, but the images moved in the wall itself as if the very stone was changing color and shifting, perfect from any angle. It was one of the many things in wess'har technology that could have earned a fortune if they were a commercially minded people. "So?"

"What's Eqbas Vorhi?"

Mick didn't appear to recognize the name. Either the FEU didn't know about the Eqbas, or they weren't saying. The increasingly heavy ball was back in Eddie's court. "It's another planet." He waited for the ITX line to go dead, but it didn't. Perhaps he wasn't being monitored, or maybe the FEU was curious too. He changed subjects. "What's been happening?"

One, two, three, four five. "The Defense Ministry's getting shitty about relaxing its control of the ITX link, with or without pressure from your isenj chums. Your last piece really caused political meltdown here, naming Rayat."

"Yeah, I can see that having an intelligence officer nuke a neutral planet would cause some raised eyebrows."

"The opposition parties ganged up and invoked the Information Act, so we can at least talk to you, and transmit five channels of quality programming, twenty-four seven, for the ex-pats in your neighborhood." Mick's mock sales-patter tone faded and his gaze flicked slightly to one side, weary and irritated. "And good morning to any of our FEU monitoring chums from Brussels who might be watching. Nice to have you with us. So, hot shot, you got anything for me today or did you just call to whinge?"

Eddie had spent too many years slipping reports past censors in a dozen countries to be fazed by an uninvited audience. It simply made him more combative. "I might have another piece ready later today."

"We could do with something from Umeh Station. I thought you and the minister were drinking buddies."

Jesus, does anyone know? Does anyone know that the Eqbas are coming? If I tell them, will the transmission get pulled? All Eddie's instincts said *don't let them cover this up.* But he wasn't the old Eddie whose blind priority was to get the story first. He'd started thinking of consequences. The transmission delay only made it worse.

"I'll try." He groped for the clumsy but effective code he

had used to tip 'Desk off before that something was amiss. "Are you still mad at me about claiming expenses for that Conqueror stuff?"

He calculated while he waited. The FEU and BBChan received the ITX output at exactly the same time. He could compress a report and send it as a burst, though, and then it was a case of who was faster on the draw. If the BBChan techs were, they could relay the burst to individual subscribers' personal handsets and implants before plugs were pulled and lawyers filed instant e-junctions.

And pulling the plug on a public ITX transmission would be a very visible act, noticed by nervous governments. He had them either way.

Is this your news to break?

Mick leaned back in his seat and winked. Good: he understood Eddie was up to something. "You're not still trying to claim more bogus expenses, are you, mate?"

"I'll send them over when I'm done." When? *When?* "I'm sure you'll go through them with a bloody knife."

"I'll await them with my usual interest."

Eddie closed the relay. Mick would now have techs standing by to watch for that burst, however long it took to send it. He didn't know what was coming, or when. And Eddie couldn't warn him. He couldn't take the risk of being blocked.

Eddie stood with his hand in his pocket, feeling the outline of his bee cam for a few moments, and wondering if he was doing the right thing. It wasn't just a bloody story. He was lobbing a grenade into Earth society.

And if you don't?

The wess'har didn't care what humans knew. And this wasn't live. He still had time to think about it.

He took the cam out of his pocket and tossed it into the air as he moved among the wess'har crowd watching the almost organic skyline of Surang. The bee cam followed him and positioned itself so he could record his piece to camera right in front of the shimmering wall. Humans might have yelled at him to get out of the way so they could watch the screen, but wess'har, being wess'har, simply stared at him as an interesting addition to the spectacle.

"I'll be as quick as I can," he said, and smiled weakly in the hope that some of them understood him and that they wouldn't interrupt. He focused on the cam's tiny red eyeline light and exhaled slowly.

In three . . . two . . . go.

He talked. He explained the image of Surang, and the contact with Eqbas Vorhi, and the implications for the Cavanagh system and for Earth. And—finally—he spoke of *c'naatat,* and the truth behind the bombing of Bezer'ej, and what had happened to a disgraced police superintendent called Shan Frankland. He shut out the peripheral images of curious wess'har and concentrated on revelations that would kick all other news items off the menu for at least a day, maybe more.

Then he signed off and fell silent, holding his position for five seconds.

Eddie knew without looking at the time code that the piece ran at four minutes, a hefty chunk by news standards. When that downloaded into some poor bastard's entertainment implant, it would probably make them shit themselves.

Eddie beckoned the bee cam back to him and slipped it into the breast pocket of his shirt. The wess'har parted to let him pass and carried on sorting vegetables and glancing at the image of Surang.

"Why did you tell them?" said a voice from waist height, and he looked down.

It was Giyadas. She studied him, head tilted.

"I haven't, yet," said Eddie. "But my government either doesn't know the Eqbas are here, or they haven't told anybody else. One or the other."

"*Isan* says they can't do anything about us anyway." So *isan* meant "mother" as well as "wife." *Boss-woman.* "Eqbas Vorhi will go to Earth and deal with the *gethes.* It makes no difference whether they know or not."

Giyadas reached up and took Eddie's hand like a regular

human kid. They walked slowly to a corner of the vaulted hall and sat down on a couple of crates.

"Let me ask you a question, sweetheart," said Eddie. "Is there anything the *gethes* could do that would make you all change your minds about going to Earth and sorting us out?"

Giyadas considered the idea with much dilation and snapping of her cross-shaped pupils. *Oh, God,* thought Eddie. *I'm making the decision of my life by discussing politics with a child. I'll be plunging Earth into panic on the strength of a kid's analysis.*

"No," she said at last. "How could you change enough to be acceptable?"

"Not all humans are bad. Shan wasn't bad. What if acceptable humans ran the planet?"

Giyadas made a little rumble in her throat. "Why don't they run your planet now?"

Sometimes it took a child to remind you what reality actually meant.

I can't sit on this.

If he dithered much longer, the situation might shift. The ITX might not be available. He took a deep breath and pulled out the bee cam.

"Let's see what happens," said Eddie, and put the cam back in his pocket.

Ual sat on the polished stone dais in his office and drew comfort from the silence for a while. There was a skittering sound from the corridor. Ralassi was coming.

The ussissi stood staring at him as if awaiting a reaction.

"You missed the vote in the chamber," he said, all disapproval.

"Well, then?"

"The decision is to demand the return of Aras Sar Iussan in exchange for the two humans."

"So *we* launch the war of demands, do we?"

"You risk your office by even hinting at surrender to the wess'har."

"My office," said Ual, "might well be rubble if we do not. And surrender is somewhat of an overstatement."

"Shall I make contact with Nevyan Tan Mestin?"

Ual shook himself a little and considered the rattle of his blue corundum beads. "I shall do that myself. We both speak the humans' language. Isn't that ironic? The source of our dispute has also enabled us to talk to each other directly for the first time in our history."

If Ralassi was disturbed by the thought of losing his usefulness as an interpreter, he didn't show it. Ussissi didn't care. He would come and go as Serrimissani had once done, a reliable helper but ultimately answerable to nobody but his own kind.

Ual looked at the screen. He needed to choose his words carefully. Eddie Michallat would have found the words: the journalist had a curious gift for speaking in such a way that those who heard him could derive two entirely different meanings from what he said. It was part of the nature of English, but it was also the skill of timing and emphasis. Eddie called it *weasel-speak* and Ual wondered if he might one day learn it from a weasel, whatever that might be.

Ual's console showed him the ITX relay status, but he wasn't sure where the outgoing channel would connect. The image in front of him changed from a diagnostics screen to a large chamber filled with wess'har.

Ual hadn't seen so many at one time. In fact, he had never had contact with one at all. They were extraordinary, long and narrow, and two-legged.

"I am Par Paral Ual," he said in English. "I wish to speak to Nevyan Tan Mestin."

Staring into the clustered wess'har faces, he wondered if any of them understood English. Perhaps he needed to call back Ralassi after all. He waited: they knew what an isenj looked like and that, he hoped, would be enough for them to fetch an appropriate matriarch.

They were still staring at him, huddled together and making musical noises. Then the little knot parted and a much taller wess'har with a plume of soft fur on its head—not unlike a human's—stepped into the foreground.

"Minister Ual," it said. "I am Nevyan Tan Mestin."

A thought that had just been an outrageous idea when he was speaking in the chamber now had seconds to become a sensible plan. Others in Jejeno would be listening and he was not the only minister who had access to English-speaking ussissi—or humans, come to that. This called for very delicate phrasing.

"Matriarch," he said. "My government wants me to ask for the return of someone they regard as a criminal."

"As do we. You will now hand over Lindsay Neville and Mohan Rayat, and we will *not* give you Aras Sar Iussan."

Perhaps he should have asked for Eddie. The subtle distancing of himself from his government's request had not put her in the frame of mind he thought it might. He steeled himself against erecting his quills, not because he feared revealing that he felt defensive but because he suspected it might appear aggressive. "I understand. May I ask if you would be prepared to send Eddie Michallat to discuss this with me?"

Nevyan paused. "Why? What is there to discuss?"

"My English is far from perfect." *No, it's quite excellent. I'm proud of it.* "Eddie will be able to interpret some of the more ambiguous terminology. In fact, I'm anxious that he should. I wouldn't like any misunderstanding of my intent." He leaned a little on the *my*. "I promise you that we *will* be able to reach a solution."

Nevyan said nothing. Wess'har had eyes, like humans did, large wet voids in their skins. It was most unnerving to see them flicker and alter shape.

"One way or another," she said, "the bezeri will have justice. I'll send Eddie Michallat."

"I greatly respect this gesture." The image faded. Ual shivered involuntarily and let his quills spring up for a few moments.

He turned. Ralassi was at the doorway.

"That was not exactly the unequivocal demand that Eit suggested you make," he said.

"I was not present to hear Eit's exact wording," said Ual, luxuriating in his new-found skill of speaking *weasel*.

"How can you believe wess'har will negotiate? It's not in their nature."

"Then why did we ask for the Destroyer of Mjat in the first place? Did we think we could take him by force? We tried, if you recall. The definition of stupidity is doing the same thing again and expecting a different outcome."

Ralassi made a long hiss like escaping steam. "A valid point."

Ual wondered how transparent his plans were. Deception was a human behavior trait; and while he wasn't entirely sure how to go about lying or what use it would be, he had discovered *omission*.

Genetic memory was a source of strength, stability and wisdom. It was also a mechanism for becoming hidebound. Ual would have traded it in an instant for the ability to see the future rather than the past.

It's time to break the pattern. Forget national pride, forget feuds. Think about the future.

He was going to defy the Northern Assembly. And he was going to ask Eddie Michallat to help him do it.

Eddie adjusted the straps that secured him to the bulkhead of the transport and concentrated on the footage playing back on the editing screen spread on his lap. Giyadas's earnest little seahorse face bobbed and tilted in shot, repeating simple wess'u phrases for his benefit. It was sobering to learn a language from a child, but not as humbling as her lessons in politics.

"What are you doing?" asked the ussissi pilot.

"Learning wess'u," said Eddie.

"Fool," said the pilot.

Eddie rolled up the screen and put it back in his pocket.

The pilot's contempt—not unkindly meant, just stating the obvious—made him more determined.

"How civilized that wess'har and isenj can operate vessels between each other's space without starting a war," said Eddie.

"We operate their civilian ships," said the pilot. "And *none* of us take kindly to being shot at."

"Well, that's one way of achieving peace."

"Both races need us in their way. Yes, there is a certain stability in necessity."

"Nothing like a strong trade union, eh, comrade?"

The pilot didn't answer. Eddie practiced the wess'u overtones for hours at a time, hand on one ear as he sang a single note, listening hard for the different harmonics within it like a Siberian khoomei singer. Occasionally it split into two notes and he felt it in his throat and skull, and it was weirdly exciting. He was still making quite a reasonable resonant *aaaaaaahhhhhhhh* when the shuttle landed at Jejeno.

"If you do that on the return run I shall bring you back here and you will wait for the next scheduled transport," said the pilot. "Employ an interpreter like everyone else."

"Have a nice day," said Eddie.

Ual spoke English. He spoke very good English indeed even though he had no true lips or pharynx. He modified the airflow through his throat as if he had been given a crude laryngectomy. He sat on the aquamarine stone dais in his spacious chambers like a black porcupine Buddha, legs folded round him, piranha mouth open in an approximation of a human smile.

"It's very good to see you," said Ual. He had no visible eyes either. "How unfortunate that times are so tense."

"You haven't booted all of us off your planet, then," said Eddie, sitting on the black slab opposite. Outside the window, hundreds of thousands of isenj flowed up and down the streets like a single shoal of fish. "I'd have gift-wrapped

Lindsay and Rayat and left them on Nevyan's doorstep without being asked."

"Where might we *boot* you?" asked Ual. "Wess'ej?"

"We still have a ship inbound. *Hereward.* They could evacuate."

"You still have a ship Earth-bound. *Thetis.* With isenj delegates on board. Both are many years from their destination, if either ever reach it."

Eddie tried to divine the real message. Wess'har were literal: they said what they thought and they meant what they said. Their language was precise—so Serrimissani said—and there were no double meanings or euphemism. Isenj were a little more like humans. They liked playing with words even if they hadn't progressed to outright, blatant dishonesty. And that was why he was here.

An isenj aide skittered into the room with a tray and Eddie found himself flinching. *Oh, God. Spider.* He was hardwired to react to that movement. He tried to see Lij as a person.

"Thank you, Lij," said Ual. "Mr. Michallat, I have acquired tea for you."

"That's very kind." Lij backed out of the room and Eddie's peripheral vision tracked the creature involuntarily. "Minister, I'm happy to see you again, but given the situation I'd like to think I was helping the situation rather than just boosting viewing figures."

"A war twenty-five years away is fiction for your people. It doesn't affect them now and they have no loved ones fighting in it. We, however, are a maximum of five years from the reach of Eqbas Vorhi."

"So you know they're coming. What are you going to do when they show up?"

Ual shimmered and rattled like a chandelier in an earthquake. His many quills were decorated with rough-tumbled sapphire beads. They bothered Eddie, and not just because reporters dreaded rattling things that interfered with a cam's mike. They plagued him because they reminded him of a shed quill he had pocketed for the wess'har so they could have isenj DNA to create the biodeterrent on Bezer'ej.

He wasn't proud of doing it. If that was how Mohan Rayat had to live his life, then Eddie pitied him.

"You don't have your camera, Mr. Michallat."

Eddie shrugged. "It's in my pocket."

"Then we are having an informal discussion."

"Yes. Just a discussion."

"Thanks to your news channel, I am aware that Earth is no more united in its approach than we are."

"Most governments are now demanding direct access to the wess'har. Years ago we all agreed that we'd share first contacts with aliens, but that was when we didn't think it would actually happen."

"Extraordinary how simple communication conduits shape worlds."

"You understand what's happening at the Earth end?"

"That your own government is in what you call a cleft stick." Ual's command of English never ceased to surprise Eddie. "If you prevent access to us, the other nations will turn against you. If you open up the ITX link, then you lose control of the situation—such control as you have at such a vast distance, of course."

"This all hinges on how other Earth governments show their disapproval. It might be trade sanctions, which won't make much of a dent on a territory the size of the FEU. Or it might be armed conflict, and that's a different kettle of fish."

"I shall remember that phrase. And who might be able to take on such a federation?"

"The Sinostates and Africa are strong enough. Africa's been making the most noise."

"I noted that."

"Then there's the Pacific Rim States. They're vocal but they're small. The Americas don't play much these days. But Canada might back the FEU if it decides it wants an excuse for more American territory. They've really developed a taste for warmer weather." Eddie scratched the bridge of his nose. "It all depends how they gang up. We love a good family brawl."

Ual made a gargling noise. It might have been amusement. "But this would have less to do with our dilemma here than the opportunity to change the balance of power at home."

"How well you know us." Eddie decided to try the tea. Without milk—even soy milk—it was mouth-puckeringly tannic. Given the state of supplies in Jejeno it was a generous gesture. "But don't forget there's plenty of people who really oppose what we did here. It's just that they're not high in the global pecking order."

"Do politicians think so many years ahead?"

"They think in *days*." Eddie took another gulp of tea. *Now here's the big one.* "Have you told the FEU that the Eqbas are coming?"

"Yes."

"Ah." Devious bastards: they *were* sitting on it after all. He had to send that report now. The thought almost diverted him. "How did they take it?"

"They thanked me for the intelligence."

Ual sipped something from his cup, wafting a faint aroma of something yeasty and savory. Eddie could hear his own pulse pounding in his ears as he raised the bowl of tea to his lips: the sound of his own swallowing was deafening. He'd fallen off the tightrope at last. He'd wobbled a few times, tilting between observer and player, but he had always felt he could regain his balance.

Now he'd lost it for good. The next question was going to demand an answer that was tantamount to political advice. It wouldn't make much difference to Earth, but it might make a huge difference to Umeh.

"Okay, we've done the dance," said Eddie. "Now what do you want me to say to Nevyan? You must know that they're never going to hand over Aras."

"I know the wess'har mean what they say."

"What, then? What do you want?"

"I want you to talk to the Royal Marines at Umeh Station."

Eddie tried not to jump too far ahead. You couldn't second-guess aliens. It was all too easy to listen to Ual and think he was human, and then misjudge him totally. "About what?"

"I would like them to do a job for me."

"Interesting."

"I wonder if they would be willing to arrest—that's the word, isn't it, arrest?—Commander Neville and Dr. Rayat."

"You're going to put them on trial?"

"No, I intend to take them to F'nar and hand them over to Nevyan Tan Mestin, and I won't be expecting an exchange of prisoners. That's what your marines do well, isn't it? They captured Frankland. They can certainly take these two."

Eddie never knew if he was being observed covertly or not. That usually didn't matter: there was a silly kid at the heart of every journalist who got a buzz out of thinking they were dangerous enough to be spied upon. But it mattered now, because Eddie knew he had slipped well out of the neutral zone and into representing the interests of Wess'ej.

"This isn't what your cabinet colleagues have agreed to, is it?"

"No, Eddie. This is my decision and I don't have the authority to make it, but make it I have. You see my reasoning here."

"You're putting your hands up. A white flag."

"I think I understand that. Yes. It is, I suppose, a surrender."

Holy shit. Ual was doing a Mossad. He was going to kidnap a target and sort things out via the back door. Eddie thought for a second that there might be a trap laid for him here, but he considered the world from an isenj point of view, and it looked terrifying enough to explain rash measures.

"We expected Umeh Station to be destroyed in retaliation," said Ual. "And I still believe that even if Wess'ej doesn't exact some retribution, then Eqbas Vorhi will. Ask the ussissi." He held out a stick-thin arm and offered Eddie a cube of what looked like gray rubber. "Do you have the means to play back this data?"

"I doubt it. What is it?"

"A little summary of Eqbas activity over the last few thousand years." Ual turned on his dais and called out. "Lij? Lij, fetch me a data player, please. Mr. Michallat needs one."

Eddie was distracted by the promise of new information from the data cube. The history of the World Before seemed more urgent now. He still found their cultural attitudes to information totally confusing, because while no race—wess'har, isenj, or ussissi—made any effort to conceal information, neither did they go to any lengths to share it. The ussissi confused him most of all. They traveled between the various worlds but they seemed not to put information at a premium.

Perhaps only humans thought knowledge was power. Maybe he was seeing the universe through a journalist's eyes, where information was more than simple currency: it was life itself.

He finished his tea and got up to stare out of the window onto the streets below. Lij crept in like a spider, clutching a small box.

Eddie couldn't see any pavement in the road beneath. All he saw was isenj, close-packed and moving at a steady rate like flowing liquid. He wanted to walk among them again, but he recalled the last time he had done that and been swept up helplessly in the current of bodies. He could see the dome of Umeh Station from here. It was within walking distance.

"Your government is going to go ballistic when they find you've given away their bargaining chip."

"But you and I know there is no bargain to be struck here." Ual made that chandelier sound and Eddie didn't look round. "This world is a high price to pay for one ancient soldier. It's time we moved on."

"Humans don't, if that's any comfort. And we haven't even got genetic memory to keep our feuds alive. We've really got to work at it."

"Will you help me? If I walk in to Umeh Station and ask

for a Royal Marine, I fear my plans will quickly become public—especially if they refuse."

"I could ask Nevyan," said Eddie. "But we don't know who'll be listening on the ITX, do we? Leave it to me."

"Thank you."

Eddie felt a pang of guilt about the use he had made of Ual's shed quill. But at least he now knew that isenj too could play double games, and he had purged his guilt a little. "If they agree to this, how are they going to make contact with you?"

"I'll visit the base, as I have before. Culturally, we're poor at covert behavior, so the shorter the communications chain, the better."

"You'd fit right in on Earth," said Eddie.

Things had certainly moved on at Umeh Station.

As Eddie stepped through the airlock and took off his breather mask, he was struck by the progress in completing the accommodation sections. He also noticed the tropical temperature.

"Lots more bodies than this place was designed for," said the harassed site foreman. "We're working on it. Who you looking for, then?"

"The marines," said Eddie. "Ex-marines, rather."

"Probably on the building site in the accommodation section. Big strong boys. Even the girl."

Eddie had never thought of Sue Webster quite that way but she was engineer-trained and good at rigging water supplies. That probably required a bit of muscle. He didn't know what Jon Becken's non-combat specialty was, but he suspected Mart Barencoin's wasn't construction.

"I always knew you'd make a good brickie's mate," said Eddie.

Becken looked down from the top of an accommodation cube with a length of conduit in one hand like a spear, an archetypal tribal warrior in an incongruous T-shirt that read *Fly Crab Air.*

"I'd offer you a beer," he said. "But we're on rationing."

"How's things?"

"Piss poor as usual." Becken swung himself down from the roof, getting a foothold on a doorframe. Ladders were clearly for wimps. "I'll find Mart and Sue. Is Ade with you?"

"He's a bit busy on Wess'ej."

It seemed Qureshi and Chahal hadn't shared the news of Ade's awkward condition. Maybe they thought that the fewer people who knew, the better. Eddie looked around.

"Ma'am is in the office," said Becken, shaping *ma'am* into an expression of obvious contempt.

"Yeah, I do have to talk to her some time."

"So you've not had any contact with her since she kicked off War of the Worlds, have you?"

"No." This was too public a place to discuss Ual's proposal. "Can I have a word with you and the others?"

Becken wiped the palms of his hands on his backside. "Interview?"

"No, a conversation. Private. Has anyone mentioned Eqbas Vorhi to you?"

"If that's what the ussissi call the World Before, yes."

"Want to do a bit of peacekeeping?"

Becken adopted a carefully blank expression, the sort Eddie read as a strong desire not to react. "Let's find Mart and Sue, shall we?"

Barencoin and Webster were fiddling with a water pump. Webster's rosy, scrubbed face and buxom frame made her look like a paramilitary milkmaid.

"Eddie's got a dodgy proposal for us," said Becken.

Am I that obvious? "You might be able to do something really useful."

Barencoin exchanged glances with Webster and Becken. "We're pretty useful here."

"Do you know that the isenj are talking about exchanging Lin and Rayat for Aras?"

"I'm glad I wasn't holding anything fragile when you said that."

"Don't take the piss. Are you up for solving a problem and saving a lot of shooting?"

"Depends. We've been kicked out of the Corps, in case you hadn't realized. Sue and Jon weren't even involved. Bastards."

Eddie hoped he had read Barencoin correctly as a man who nursed his grudges like babies. "Elements in the isenj administration want to hand over our two colleagues and forget about Aras, just as a goodwill gesture."

"They're shitting themselves about what's coming over the hill, aren't they?"

"House-bricks, mate."

"Okay, as long as we don't get shafted again, we'll do it for free. Compliments of the Corps."

"Really?"

"You thought we'd refuse?"

"You haven't asked me or Jon," said Webster, a little steel glinting through her bucolic veneer.

"Okay," said Barencoin. "Hands up everyone who wants to defend hysterical bezeri-killer Neville and slimy spook Rayat and watch the wess'har turn this place into charcoal. Nobody? Well, carried unanimously. Let's get to it."

Webster gave him a weary look and stood a little closer to Eddie. "I think you'll find *anyone* in this place would gladly turn them in. Why the secrecy?"

"Because the isenj won't let Lin and Rayat off the planet unless they get Aras. Ual's being a very naughty spider."

"You trust him?"

"More than I trust the FEU. It's his arse that's in the firing line."

"And then what happens to *us*?"

Eddie paused. He was way out of his depth, but Aras had said Ade's comrades were welcome to join him. That was permission enough. "You can stay on Wess'ej."

"At least we'd all be together," said Jon.

Barencoin wasn't giving up. Eddie thought that if he'd been shanghaied by his masters, he'd be wary too. "And are they treating Ade okay? Why's he separated from Izzy and Chaz?"

Barencoin showed no sign of knowing that Ade had *c'naatat,* even though he had been with him when Shan was captured. Eddie, surprised that Lindsay had kept her mouth shut this long, skimmed the surface of a lie. "He's fine. They're just keeping him in F'nar with Aras for a while. I promise you he's okay." *Shit, I'm losing this.* "Look, are you going to do the fucking job or not?"

Barencoin was no more a fool than Ade was. Eddie wondered why the FEU didn't just dispense with officers and let the enlisted troops run the show. They'd have made a better job of it.

"You're not telling me something," he said.

"Ade's in a bit of a state about Shan." Well, that wasn't even a lie. It was simply a fragment of reality from which you couldn't identify the rest of the picture. "Yes or no?"

"Yes."

"I'll let Ual know, then, and he'll contact you when he's ready to roll." He gave them a shrug. He didn't know what else to say. Shit, what *did* you say when you'd just trampled over the democratic will of a nation? This didn't feel at all like the game back home. "I ought to see Lindsay now. I have to do it sooner or later."

Eddie stood outside the site office for a full minute. He'd doorstepped everyone in his time. He'd banged on the doors of gangland bosses and disgraced government ministers; he'd thrust a cam in the faces of parents and asked how it felt to know that their child's body had been found. He believed that after twenty years in the game, there was nothing that could raise his pulse rate or dry his mouth.

He was wrong. His stomach churned.

Lindsay Neville weighed just fifty kilos, a woman emotionally wrecked by the death of her baby, a moderate and mediocre naval officer. She'd been a friend. But he was scared. This wasn't an interview; it was a rebuke. What did you say to an old friend who had personally deployed nuclear weapons when there was no war to fight?

"Hello, Lindsay," said Eddie.

She rested her forehead on one hand while she scribbled on a pad. She wasn't thirty yet but she could have passed for a lot older. Events had taken their toll. "Hi, Eddie. Slumming it?"

Well, that sets the tone. "Working."

"I've seen. Exclusive from the Cavanagh system. It's made your career."

"Oh, didn't it meet with your approval?"

She laid the stylus down with exaggerated care and meshed her hands in front of her.

"Why didn't you say *why* we did it? Why didn't you mention what we had to destroy?"

"Because immortality tends to knock murdered squid off the news agenda, Lin. They had to concentrate their minds on that first. And nobody can hurt Shan any more. Trust me, I'm running the story. Soon."

"What was it you said? It isn't what's true that counts, it's who gets their story in first."

"I know this is going to sound harsh, but if you nuke a neutral planet you've got to expect some criticism."

"I didn't bloody well know that Rayat had salted the warheads with cobalt."

"Silly me. Of course. There's nothing wrong with detonating ordinary high-yield neutron devices. It's adding a side order of cobalt that makes them bad."

Lindsay's pupils were wide and black. Just above her neat collar her throat was flushed. "In the last couple of months I've heard every variation of that line you can imagine. *I can't change what happened.* If I could rerun time I'd still destroy that parasite but I'd do it differently. Do you think your smart-arse armchair analysis can make me feel any worse than I do? I'm at rock bottom now. I've got nothing left to lose. Now sod off."

He had to ask. It was a reflex. "Do you want to talk about it on camera and put the record straight?"

"It's too late for that. Ask Rayat."

Eddie turned to go. It was amazing how little you could know about someone even after you'd lived in their pocket for nearly two years. There were now fewer than ten people alive in his entire world that he knew well enough to count as friends and he'd just lost one more.

"I have to ask you this, Lin. Shan really did die the way Ade said, didn't she?"

The anger that sealed Lindsay's expression crumbled for a brief moment into something that looked like real regret.

"Yeah," she said quietly. "She just stepped out the airlock. A real Titus Oates job." She started writing again, ticking items off a list. He imagined it was some rota or other: she always found comfort in order. "When are they coming for me, Eddie?"

"I don't know." He felt his plans were tattooed on his forehead for all to read. He concentrated on reducing his blink rate but it was very, very hard. "But they're not going to forgive and forget, are they?"

"I know that. Just tell them when they do to make sure they take Rayat as well. I won't carry the can for this alone."

Eddie reminded himself there was no reason for him to feel guilty; he wasn't the fool who'd wiped out a fragile species. But Lindsay really did seem to think that it was the act of salting the devices with cobalt that had catapulted the event from essential asset denial to an act of war. She couldn't see that *any* destruction on Bezer'ej would have provoked the wess'har to retaliate.

And the FEU hadn't told anyone else that it had attracted the attention of a massively powerful military civilization. What did these people use for brains?

His priority now was to get to an ITX relay and send that bloody report, something he should have done there and then. *Sod it.* The transport back to the shuttle was waiting for him at the entrance along with Ralassi.

"You have a message for the minister. Yes or no?"

"Yes," said Eddie.

Ralassi said nothing else. He showed no sign of knowing what Eddie's business had been about, but ussissi didn't get involved. They oiled the wheels, that was all. The ussissi pilot who hurried him into his seat on the shuttle seemed equally devoid of curiosity.

"You have a message," he said.

"I need an ITX link out, first," said Eddie. "Can I use the ship's system?"

The pilot fixed him with a disapproving slitted stare. "Now?"

"*Now.* Please. I need to transmit to my news desk."

The pilot handed Eddie a wess'har *virin*, a soft translucent hand-sized device that could have passed for a bar of glycerin soap had it not fired up with lights and images when the pilot squeezed it into life. Eddie struggled to find the right sequence of finger positions to activate the interface with his cam.

"Like this," said the pilot irritably, and took the cam and the *virin* from him. The ussissi squeezed the device and the news of Eqbas Vorhi and *c'naatat* instantly, silently, reached the relay close to Earth, and—*one, two, three*—it arrived at the BBChan router. Nothing visible had taken place. It was a strange way to make history.

"Well, that's going to get the shit flying," Eddie muttered.

The pilot peered at the *virin* and handed it back to him. "And now will you take your message? You have a message here from Nevyan Tan Mestin."

"Read it for me."

"She says it is urgent and personal."

I've just filed a bombshell. Shut up. "Read it to me anyway."

The pilot settled in his seat and placed the *virin* back in its housing on the console. He made irritated chattering noises.

"I said go ahead."

The pilot hissed.

"She thought you needed to know they have located a body."

5

We strongly suggest that you allow all governments access to the ITX system. It will aid you in defusing the tension between the FEU and other states. Your priority is surely both to be assured of the welfare of your citizens on Wess'ej and Umeh, and to keep open a potential diplomatic channel between yourselves and the wess'har; and we wish to be reassured of the welfare of our colleagues en route to Earth in Thetis. We assume you understand the significance of the entry of Eqbas Vorhi into the situation.

MINISTER PAR PARAL UAL,
Northern Assembly,
to Birsen Ertegun

A halo of shimmering hot air formed around the Eqbas patrol ship as it slowed and eased itself down on the plain north of F'nar. It was the worst possible time it could have chosen to arrive.

Nevyan was anxious to leave. Time would make no difference to Shan any more, but she had no intention of leaving her body drifting in space for a moment longer. And she had no choice. The first of the Eqbas ships had arrived.

"Are you worried, ma'am?" asked Ade Bennett. He stood to one side of her. She knew he hoped to accompany her to recover the body, but she had made her position clear. "Historical moment, isn't it?"

"I'm anxious," she said. "Our ancestors left this way of life behind. I've changed everything by summoning them here."

"Needs must," said Ade, but she didn't understand him.

The ship was a smooth bronze cylinder tapered at both ends. A band of brilliant red and blue illuminated chevrons danced horizontally along each side. Dust rose beneath the hull. It was remarkably quiet but very, very visible.

Nevyan clutched her *dhren* to her throat. Serrimissani, ready to interpret, showed displeasure with half-closed eyes and arms straight at her sides.

Ade frowned. "They don't believe in stealth, do they? You're really going to notice *that* patrolling your airspace."

"I doubt anyone has countermeasures to trouble the World Before."

The hatches opened with a long hiss and several ussissi came out sniffing the air. They stood perfectly synchronized, heads bobbing in unison, and then went back inside. Serrimissani began trotting towards the ship.

Nevyan waited with Ade, hoping she would have nothing to regret later. Serrimissani was now with one of the Eqbas ussissi, talking to her, mirroring her movements while they talked. Serrimissani was fluent enough to interpret without the aid of another ussissi, but Nevyan hoped to use her own hastily acquired command of eqbas'u.

Serrimissani beckoned.

Nevyan was about twenty meters from the ship when she saw the first Eqbas step out. She was wearing an environment suit. She was shorter and thicker-set than Nevyan had expected, even though she had seen their images on screen, and when she took her helmet off she revealed no tufted mane but close-cropped brown wisps.

But it wasn't a matriarch at all. It was a male.

Nevyan could smell that now. She hadn't expected a male to lead the vanguard.

His face was short-muzzled and light brown, and although Nevyan could see the similarities with wess'har features, the visitor reminded her more of a ussissi. This was a wess'har from her origins, a world her forebears had left long ago. The branches of the species had diverged rapidly; wess'har adapted to their environment fast.

Nevyan shook off her suspicion. Being wess'har was about what you did, not how you looked or what you said.

Shan had been wess'har: so was Serrimissani. Ade and Eddie were fitting in as well. Wess'har could take many forms.

More of the crew trailed out, all male, all hesitant. She stared.

She almost forgot Ade was behind her and stopped dead. The Eqbas tilted his head, gaze darting between Nevyan and Ade, pupils snapping open and shut. *We must both look alien to him.* But he had familiar wess'har eyes with four lobed pupils, not the single unnerving void of a human eye. He was kin.

"I am Nevyan Tan Mestin," she said, and waited for some reaction. "Where is your matriarch?"

The male warbled, and although he appeared to have a reasonable command of wess'u she had difficulty understanding him. There was the tantalizing hint of syllables and tone chords she thought she understood, but whole sentences were elusive and she failed to grasp them.

Serrimissani relayed the answer in English. "He says he is Da Shapakti, the commander of this vessel, and he has no matriarchs on board. He asks if Ade is a *gethes* and why he's here."

"Shall I thin out, ma'am?" asked Ade.

"What?"

"Would you like me to leave?"

"No. Stay and observe."

No matriarchs. Why was this Eqbas male without his *isan? Jurej've* needed constant cell renewal from their matriarch, and if this patrol had been in space for some time then they should have been showing signs of ill health.

Perhaps Shapakti was. Nevyan wasn't sure what a healthy Eqbas male looked like.

"Ade is human and has made a great sacrifice for us," she said carefully, avoiding the word *gethes.* "Why don't you have *isan've* on board?"

The ussissi chittered. "His *isan* is on Eqbas, as are those of his colleagues. He says that if you are asking about *oursan,* then they are medicated and do not require it on patrol."

"What's *oursan*?" asked Ade.

Nevyan ignored him. This was unnatural. Matriarchs always accompanied their males on long journeys and families were never separated. She stared at Shapakti, appalled. And without a dominant matriarch, where could she begin to discuss the complex politics of driving back the *gethes*?

"When will your next ship arrive?" she asked. "One with a matriarch in command?"

This time Shapakti's answer was intelligible. "Some days."

She stood staring at him. His gaze still seemed torn between her and Ade.

"Do you want to enter the city? There's accommodation for you if you need it."

"For your sake, we stay here."

Nevyan looked to Serrimissani. "I didn't understand that."

The two ussissi exchanged chatter. "He thinks it would be better for both societies if each became familiar with the other more slowly, and they respect your wish for separateness. They have sufficient supplies."

It seemed reasonable. The Eqbas were here to make environmental and political assessments, not to fraternize. Understanding might come later, if at all. She acknowledged him with a nod and turned to go back.

"You mean to walk?" said Shapakti.

"Of course I do," said Nevyan.

"A vehicle for our equipment?"

"What equipment?"

"Communications, defense assessment, bio-analysis."

He seemed to hesitate and leaned down to the ussissi. Serrimissani listened to the exchange. "He says you have not yet answered his question about the presence of the *gethes*."

Nevyan had to be certain. "Are you sure that's what he said?"

Serrimissani lowered her head and exchanged more high-pitched chatter with the Eqbas ussissi. Her eyes were now disapproving slits. "Yes, *chail*."

Nevyan took three steps forward and cuffed Shapakti casually around the head, just hard enough to make her point. Perhaps he hadn't got the message that he should defer to her. He yelped; she needed no translation. Now he knew his place.

"Tell him," said Nevyan, "that I have already explained that Ade is our *friend*."

Nevyan summoned a ground transport on the *virin*. She reminded herself that Eqbas was industrialized, a world away from the carefully preserved agrarian simplicity of Wess'ej. That was one of the reasons that her people had followed Targassat's teachings and sought a separate life of what Eddie called *minimal ecological and political impact*.

Eqbas were perhaps more like *gethes* in many ways. They expected *transport*.

"Well, that went well," said Ade, raising his eyebrows in that human gesture that said it definitely hadn't. "What was all that about?"

A ground car passed them on its way to the ship. Nevyan found she was clutching the collar of her *dhren* even though the garment was self-shaping, and she made a conscious effort to lower her hands. "I fear our cousins have a very different social order to our own."

"Boys only, eh?"

"I don't understand."

"No *isan* embarked." He had picked up some words fast. "Come on, what's *oursan*?"

Nevyan recalled a dead friend posing the same naive question. She missed her and she wondered how much more she would miss her as time progressed. "Shan called it *shagging*."

Ade wafted agitation as he walked. "I think this is more than I need to know."

"It's not copulation in the sense of reproductive activity, but as Shan said, it's *as near as makes no odds*. We exchange and repair DNA during *oursan*. Without it, the cells of the male deteriorate."

"Ah," said Ade.

His face was much pinker now. Nevyan had seen that before. *Embarrassment.* "I didn't suggest that it was unpleasant. Far from it. But it seems the Eqbas have *medication* instead."

Ade said nothing more until they reached F'nar. Nevyan realized it was the mention of Shan that had silenced him, because he didn't seem the kind of human who was easily embarrassed by bodily functions. They sat on crates with Serrimissani in the Exchange of Surplus Things and watched the Eqbas crew—six males—set up equipment at the back of the hall, supervised by Serrimissani.

"Are you sure you don't want me or Aras to come with you, ma'am?" asked Ade, returning to his main preoccupation.

He didn't use the word *bodies.* Shan and Vijissi were drifting in the void somewhere between Bezer'ej and the isenj homeworld of Umeh, and Nevyan wondered if Ade ever remembered that the ussissi aide had died with Shan rather than abandon her. Mestin had asked him to stay at her side, no matter what.

"You have preparations to make here, Ade. We won't be away more than a few days."

"Understood, ma'am." He paused and looked at her as if expecting her to change her mind if he was persistent enough. His clutched his green fabric headdress in both hands and he was twisting it like a cleaning rag. "You said I was your friend."

"You are."

"Why? I don't understand why you don't blame me for Shan's death. And the bezeri."

"You persist in asking this."

"It's because I don't understand."

"Even wess'har have to draw a line somewhere in the chain of circumstances, or we would execute parents and grandparents for a child's wrongdoings. Your superiors set the bombs. Shan chose to die." Nevyan, broken-hearted again, inhaled sharply to smell Shan in Ade's scent. "And I know that if she were alive now, and I went to punish you, she would stand in my way and defend you."

Ade smoothed out his headdress and put it in his pocket. "Okay, ma'am."

Serrimissani approached as he walked out of earshot. "It's as well that the crew has no matriarchs on board," she said. "Or you might be criticized for leaving at such a critical time."

"Recovering my friends is important."

"For Aras and Ade," said Serrimissani.

"For *me*. Because I said I would."

Nevyan wondered if she should have sent Aras instead, however traumatic it would be for him. *No.* She had promised.

She would make the retrieval quickly, though. These were testing times for F'nar and all Wess'ej.

Da Shapakti was fascinated by the concern shown for Shan's corpse. Aras had begun learning Eqbas'u with Serrimissani's mediation and there was one word that leapt out at him above all others: *suta'ej*.

Shapakti used it a lot. It meant *of use*. The Eqbas commander trailed after Aras and Ade through the center of F'nar, making urgent sounds and smelling of excitement.

"His crew don't say much," said Ade, glancing behind him. He would always be a soldier, sizing up risk, needing to know terrain and locations. Aras thought it was a good habit to retain. "You sure it's safe to let them go through your archives?"

"There is no harm in knowledge."

"That's not how we see it."

"Wess'har don't use knowledge as *gethes* do." Aras had agreed to follow Ade without knowing where he was going. Ade had a digging tool in one hand, a soldier's implement that folded in half. "What do you wish to show me?"

"Somewhere that matters. Something for Shan."

They walked out onto the plain and towards one of the lava-topped bluffs that dotted the landscape. Shapakti followed. Ade stopped and turned back to him.

"This is private," he said.

Shapakti looked at Aras, bewildered. He could tell Ade was annoyed: even if the Eqbas couldn't read his body language, he could smell him, and Ade now had a distinct wess'har alarm scent when he was stressed.

"Ade isn't *happy* that you're following us," said Aras, hoping he had the right eqbas'u word.

"I want to see," said Shapakti. "I want to find out as much as I can about *gethes*."

"This isn't a good time."

"Is Ade *c'naatat* too?"

"Yes. We both are. The only two left alive."

Shapakti thought visibly. Aras could see the process on his face. "When you recover the body, may we examine it? *C'naatat* is fascinating."

It was a very wess'har attitude, utterly pragmatic and moral, examining only dead creatures because interfering with live ones was anathema. It was an approach that humans would have done well to adopt. But Ade wouldn't see it that way. There was a part of Aras—the part shaped by nearly two hundred years of living with humans—that didn't see it that way either.

"What's he want?" asked Ade.

"He wants to learn. He also wants to examine the body to find out more about *c'naatat*."

Ade's face drained of color. "Tell him he'll be examining the butt of my frigging rifle if he so much as looks at her." He glared at Shapakti. "*No*. Understand?"

Aras paraphrased. It was from unfamiliarity with eqbas'u, not diplomacy. "Ade is very upset about Shan. He blames himself for the events that led to her death, so I advise you not to raise the subject again. He's a restrained man but when he angers he's capable of injuring you badly."

"Does that word *no* indicate refusal?"

Ade appeared to latch on to the one English word in the sentence immediately.

"No," Ade snapped. "Absolutely not. And we're not leaving her for the scavengers, either. She's going to have a proper burial."

Shapakti stopped where he stood and let them walk on. Ade glanced back over his shoulder now and again as if checking. Eventually he stopped. When Aras looked, Shapakti was gone.

The top of the lava formation had precious little soil on it, barely enough to plant yellow-leaf. If this was the site for Shan's grave, they would have a hard time digging one. And it would be shallow.

"This is a cairn," said Ade.

A carefully built pyramid of rocks and pebbles stood a couple of meters from the edge of the plateau, about waist-high to a human.

Ade rubbed his nose on the back of his hand. "I couldn't bear her not having a proper grave."

"A gravestone?" Aras suddenly felt excluded, but he'd always known that Ade had desired Shan. The marines had teased him about it. Shan had desired him, too. He wondered if Ade had ever seen him as an interloper. "I made a headstone for Lindsay Neville's baby. It was colored glass."

"You understand, then."

Aras did, but he had never understood why some humans were repelled by the idea of their bodies being devoured by creatures like rockvelvets. What did they think decomposition was? Decay and predation were both consumption, returning the components of life to the great cycle. Even the colonists of Constantine, who believed inexplicably in resurrection, adopted the local custom.

"Shan was raised as a Pagan," said Aras. "I don't think she would mind being left for the *srebil.*"

"She certainly wouldn't like being used for research, I know that much. Jesus, she was EnHaz. You know how she felt about scientists."

It didn't matter. Aras thought it was an unhealthy preoccupation to care about inert, unfeeling remains when the being that made them beloved had gone. But if it helped Ade cope with his grief, then it had purpose.

"I will dig," said Aras. He held out his hand for the folding spade.

"Okay."

"Are you angry that Nevyan wouldn't take us on the recovery mission?"

Ade looked down at the cairn, arms folded, chin tucked in. "She was being thoughtful. I know she wanted to make sure Shan was . . . presentable before we saw her."

"Have my memories made this worse for you?"

"In what way?"

"Genetic memory. Have you no recollections of her that have originated from me? *C'naatat* does that. Shan had them, so you might too."

Ade appeared to realize what Aras meant. "Not of the kind I think you mean."

It was a great pity: they could so easily have been true house-brothers, like wess'har males united by a shared *isan*. Aras hadn't missed having brothers for many years but he needed that comfort now. And Ade's scent said *brother*.

The soil was hard going. Ade eventually held out his hand for the spade to take his turn but Aras shook his head.

"When do we ask for Neville and Rayat to be extradited?" Ade asked. "Formally, that is."

"When I've thought of a penalty which will achieve something beyond revenge," said Aras.

"Long way to go, then, mate." Ade added another pearly stone to the cairn and stood with his head slightly bowed for a few moments. "Long, long way."

Nevyan had never traveled further than the distance between the twin planets of Wess'ej and Bezer'ej. She was now far beyond that space with Serrimissani for support, marveling at a starscape for once not wholly dominated by her two home planets.

She had promised Aras that she would find Shan's body and bring it home, and it had been very hard to find a corpse in space. The ussissi patrol had patiently followed the extrapolated vector from the coordinates that Ade had provided, seeking not only Shan Frankland's remains but also those of Vijissi. They were determined to bring their own people home, too.

"Will you let Aras and Ade see the body?" asked Serrimissani. "They were most insistent."

"That depends on how it appears and how presentable we can make it before we return."

"They are both soldiers. Neither are squeamish."

"I suspect that's irrelevant when the remains are those of a loved one."

The craft rendezvoused with the patrol vessel, matching its speed as it followed the tiny speck of debris at a careful distance. It was Shan's body, still drifting. Nevyan tilted her head to let her pupils get a better focus as it grew larger in the viewing screen set in the bulkhead. The object was rolling slowly; then she could pick out a human shape, exaggerated by the stark brightness and complete shadow created by Ceret's light. Then it resolved into more detail, showing a human in a position that suggested a fall, arms outstretched, legs slightly bent.

There was no sign of Vijissi.

"Bring her in," said Nevyan.

A suited ussissi from the patrol craft steered himself carefully on the end of a long tether, tracking alongside the body until he was close enough to secure it with a line. As the shuttle hauled it in, Shan's limbs appeared to change position, giving the semblance of life; but when Nevyan concentrated her gaze she could see she was still in the same rigid pose. Shan's face had no visible features or hair, just an unbroken pale sheen that Nevyan assumed was some frozen matter.

Transferring the body from the patrol vessel to the shuttle was slow. Two suited ussissi laid the corpse on the long bench running along one bulkhead in the cargo bay and withdrew as the bay hatch closed and the compartment flooded with air again. Shan Frankland was nearly home.

"This is hard," said Nevyan.

"I will stand with you," said Serrimissani.

Nevyan looked down at the body on the bench and struggled to cope.

The clothing was Shan's. It was her informal uniform, the dark blue jacket and trousers, and it was faded and damaged. Ragged holes peppered the legs and hips, and the boots were cracked and peeling. That detail was all that Nevyan could focus on because she could hardly bear to look at the corpse.

It didn't look like Shan at all.

Nevyan had no idea what was typical for a human exposed to vacuum, let alone one who carried *c'naatat*. The body was emaciated as if it had been sucked dry of all fluid and flesh. No, this was not a *body*. It was Shan Frankland. It was her friend.

Shan was a husk swathed in a milky transparent layer that coated as much of her exposed skin as Nevyan could see. She was simply bone wrapped in tight-stretched paper, hands clenched into fists; her uniform gapped at cuffs and collar as if it had been someone else's. It didn't look as if her death had been peaceful.

She was unrecognizable. Aras would be devastated to see her.

Nevyan reached out cautiously and touched her cheek. The coating was waxy to the touch and it flaked away at the point of the cheekbone. The skin beneath was lined and dry like *efte* bark.

"Fetch me some water," she said. "I'll remove it. I can't let Aras see her like this. He's suffered enough." She brushed away a few more flakes. "And these bullet holes in her clothing—I think that might be too much for him if he's to remain friends with Sergeant Bennett."

Nevyan stood and gazed down at Shan and her heart broke again, just as it had when she had first heard of her

death. It had seemed a terrible sacrifice then and it seemed
even more of one now.

Tap . . . tap-tap-tap-tap.

Something metallic hit the deck, then bounced and rolled.
Nevyan froze briefly at the noise and bent down to see that it
was a small, deformed metal tube very much like the bullets
Shan put in her weapon.

Nevyan picked up the casing and examined it, wondering
how much pain it had caused when it smashed through
Shan's muscles and bones. The number of holes in her uniform indicated she had been hit by at least twenty shots.

And Ade had said she was still hard to subdue even after
taking that many hits. Shan had been right: *c'naatat* was exactly the kind of adaptation that should never fall into the
hands of the *gethes'* military forces.

Serrimissani brought a flask of water and some cloth, taking one piece in her hand. "I'll help," she said. "The shuttle
is resuming the search. Vijissi must be in this sector too. He
went with her."

There was another *tap* and bounce as a second bullet
fragment fell to the floor. Nevyan didn't think she had
moved the body that far, but she had dislodged the fragment
somehow. She began wiping gently at Shan's face with a
wad of moistened fabric.

The eyes were closed, sunk in bony sockets. As more of
the coating fell away Nevyan could see that the mouth was
frozen wide open in one final desperate gasp for air. She almost let herself slip into that motionless state of shock, the
primitive wess'har instinct to stop and assess threat, but she
had to carry on. Perhaps, with more water and the warmth of
the cabin, the body might soften enough for her to close the
mouth and restore some semblance of peace and dignity before Aras demanded to see it.

Nevyan dabbed at the exposed skin. The water appeared
to be hydrating it in places, easing the appearance of parch-
ment into something more like human flesh. Shan had never

seemed vain, but she had cared about looking well groomed. She didn't look groomed any longer.

The coating clung to the cloth and Nevyan had to shake it off into a bowl. Then she placed her hands gently on Shan's wasted cheeks, overtaken by grief and regret and anger that she had lost her after such à short friendship.

"You'll be home soon," she said. Talking to the dead was a foolish thing that *gethes* did, but Nevyan couldn't come this close to her and not speak. "You'll be part of the world again. And then I'll balance the *gethes*."

Nevyan had seen *gethes* mothers kiss their children. She had even seen Aras kiss Shan; it seemed a universal human expression of affection. So she bent and kissed Shan's forehead, alien as the act seemed. The *c'naatat* parasite was dead. She could touch Shan now without risk of contamination.

"I'm sorry, *isanket*. I wasn't there to help you."

Shan's eyes jerked open.

Wess'har didn't scream. But Nevyan did.

6

Frankland sparked controversy in her first appointment as divisional inspector of Reading Metro Nine, where she cut crime figures by 75 percent in her first six months of command. "It's old-style policing," she said at the time. "If anyone steps out of line, they'll get a clip round the ear, and if they do it twice, then they can say goodbye to the ear completely." Her uncompromising approach—typified by frequent use of decitizenization and complaints of brutality—angered some politicians but earned her allies in the wider community. "I learned diplomacy after that," she said. Did she take a more softly-softly approach? "No," she said. "I just stopped shooting my mouth off about it."

EDDIE MICHALLAT,
One Copper's Story,
BBChan Publishing

Shan let out a long rattling breath that trailed off into small gasps.

Nevyan knew that corpses sometimes appeared to move or exhale for perfectly explicable reasons, but this wasn't a trick of expanding air or contracting tissue.

Shan was *alive*.

Her eyelids fluttered and then half closed. But she was breathing.

"This might only be a reaction to temperature changes," said Serrimissani. She seemed calm, as if corpses came to life before her every day. "It is unthinkable that she could have survived so long in space."

Nevyan shook herself out of her freeze reflex and put her hand cautiously on Shan's chest. Humans had pumping hearts, strong enough to be detected.

She felt a brief kick. Then there was another, and another, and then the *thump-thump-thump* became steadier. It was slow, but it was regular; there was a heartbeat, a real human heartbeat.

"It's also unthinkable that she survived being shot in the head, or under water, but she did." Nevyan reached for protective gloves. If *c'naatat* had preserved Shan in these circumstances, it too was alive and it was a risk. She regretted the kiss. "She may be able to hear us."

Nevyan drizzled some water into Shan's mouth from the cloth and waited. The continuous wheeze spluttered into convulsive coughing. "Shan," she said. "Shan, can you hear me?"

There was no response, but she was breathing in great sawing gasps. Nevyan knew almost nothing about human physiology, but perhaps that didn't matter; Shan wasn't wholly human. She was an amalgam of whatever *c'naatat* had collected and carried with it from host to host and then selected for her survival. One organism must have had the capacity to survive hard vacuum and irradiation.

The water was now triggering rapid changes. Shan's skin was taking on a pink color, and her limbs and eyelids were twitching. Whatever mechanism had kept her dormant was now kicking her back to normality. Nevyan hoped that it had kept her oblivious, too; the thought of drifting conscious in the void was terrifying.

"She needs more water," Serrimissani said. "Perhaps we need to immerse her. You said she could survive in water."

"Yes, but—"

"Water is probably her immediate need. Then food."

"Shan? Shan, if you can hear us, move your arms."

There was no response. The pilot, summoned from the cockpit by Nevyan's uncharacteristic shriek, pulled a sheet of fabric from a locker. "Support the corners, and we can fill this with water and place her in it," he said. He unbolted a bench and turned it over to lash the corners of the sheet to its legs. Most of their water supply went to fill it to a depth that would cover Shan's body. Nevyan cut her uniform from her, lifted away the ballistic vest, and immersed her in the makeshift bath.

She weighs so little.

More waxy coating crumbled away and floated on the surface. Shan's open mouth filled with water and she began coughing and retching, blowing great streams of bubbles. Her paper-husk frame convulsed and her eyes jerked open again but she didn't seem to be focusing. Her limbs thrashed weakly and then she sank back, lips opening and closing like a suckling child. Her eyes closed.

She was still breathing, though.

"Do we leave her there?" asked the pilot.

Nevyan and Serrimissani leaned over the bath. "The moment she appears to be in difficulties, we take her out."

"I will send a message—"

"No." Nevyan checked her own immediate urge to notify Aras. It would be agonizingly wonderful news. However welcome it was, it would hit him hard after he had come to terms with her death. And if Shan failed to hang on to life this time, Aras would suffer the pain of losing her again.

There was also the matter of discovery. The world thought Shan was dead, and with her the *c'naatat* parasite colony that lived within her. A careless message over the ITX, as Eddie had named it, could be intercepted by anyone. Once they knew she was alive they would hunt her again.

Nevyan decided the news would have to wait.

They watched Shan intently, counting each breath. She had curled up, bony arms tucked into her chest, knees drawn up, a skeleton plated with thin pale skin. Nevyan could see the pulse in her throat and temples, and the bones that ran out from the top of her ribs and ended at her shoulders.

"How are we going to feed her?" asked Serrimissani.

"If she can swallow water, she can take liquid nutrients."

"We have nothing on board."

"We need to get her back to Wess'ej as quickly as we can."

"No, we look for Vijissi. If Shan survived, so might he."

Nevyan reached under the water, soaking her *dhren,* and

lifted Shan's head clear of the water, noting how much heavier she felt now. She coughed and retched. Water splashed the deck. "If Vijissi is alive, then he has *c'naatat* too and he'll survive until we find him. If he doesn't, then extra time will make no difference to the dead."

Serrimissani stared up at Nevyan, an unblinking matte-black gaze. "Dead, alive, we still search for him and bring him home."

Nevyan knew better than to argue with an ussissi. But her priority was to keep Shan alive. *C'naatat* or not—*miracle* or not—she needed to get her back to Wess'ej. "We leave the patrol vessel to resume the search and we return to F'nar," she said firmly.

Serrimissani simply stared back, grim and feral. It was an uncomfortable moment. A human friend mattered more than a ussissi. It must have seemed that way to her.

"Very well," she said at last, but reluctantly. "That seems reasonable."

Nevyan had never trod that fine line between having a ussissi's loyalty and losing it to the pack instinct. It felt precarious. It was.

She propped Shan's head on the edge of the sheeting and wiped her face while Serrimissani hunted for something to serve as a blanket. The shock and relief of finding Shan alive at all had suspended her horror at the state of her body for a while and now she wondered how Aras would react to her physical state.

"There's nothing suitable," said Serrimissani.

Together they lifted Shan from the water and laid her back on the bench. Nevyan took off her *dhren* and wrapped it around her. This was how Asajin had been carried to the plain to be left for the carrion-eating creatures, with her fine matriarch's *dhren* as her shroud.

Serrimissani dripped water into Shan's mouth. She coughed it back up. "Perhaps her swallowing reflex will return. Her appearance is improving."

Improvement was a relative term. She still looked like a

long-dead cadaver. Nevyan tried to imagine what it felt like
to asphyxiate and for your body fluids to boil. and to drift in
absolute, indefinable nothing for months. She would have
been unconscious. She was sure of that.

"It's a terrible thing to die in space," she said.

"Even more terrible to survive in it," said Serrimissani.

Nevyan's home was deserted when Eddie got back. It was
usually a noisy melee of youngsters and *jurej've* at this time
of the morning, but he made his way through the intercon-
necting chambers and found nobody.

Perhaps they'd gone to the fields early because Nevyan
was due back and they wanted to be home to greet her. She'd
be in need of support, he knew that much: it couldn't be easy
see a friend's corpse, even for a matriarch as self-possessed
as Nevyan.

There was a heavy finality to recovering the body. Now
he accepted that Shan was truly dead, and the feeling that
she might walk through the door at any time was fading fast.
At least he hadn't imagined he still saw her or heard her,
slipping elusively into a crowd or evaporating on closer in-
spection. He wasn't sure he could handle that.

He ladled a cup of water from a bowl and sipped it while
he tried his hand against the console in the main room.
Eventually the screen kicked into life. Without Giyadas to
show him, it took him minutes to find the route into the ITX
link to Earth.

*Jesus, Ual's actually going to do it. He's going to defy his
own government.* Eddie rehearsed how he might tell Nevyan,
with no idea of how she would react. She might launch an attack: wess'har fired up in a heartbeat. *Is this what I was really doing on Earth? Did I just spew out information and
leave a trail of chaos for others to deal with?* There were no
anonymous others to clear up now. He was face-to-face with
the real consequences of his precious truth.

Truth my arse.

With a few prompts from his fingers, the image of the Exchange of Surplus Things rearranged itself in the smooth stone of the wall and he was looking at the holding screen for BBChan's router. He wondered if 'Desk was pleased with the story and braced himself for the five-second time lag.

"Jesus Christ, where the hell have you *been*?" Mick was on duty again, and he didn't look pleased at all.

"Umeh," he said. "I thought you wanted me to get access to Umeh Station."

"Forget Umeh Station. You file a fucking story on an alien invasion and eternal life, then piss off for a day?" Counting to five evidently didn't help Mick's temper any more than it did Eddie's. "No follow-up?"

"I got the piece *across*," he said slowly. "No mean feat."

"Yeah, and—"

"Did you run the frigging story?"

"You want to see? *Here.*" Mick switched him through to an output channel. Eddie expected to see his own brief bombshell against a backdrop of Surang's skyline but it wasn't that at all.

The segment started with a long shot of flames licking through the shattered windows of an office building ringed by a high wall, or at least it would have been ringed if the wrought-work gates weren't hanging off their hinges and the wall hadn't been breached in one place by a truck. The crawler caption said FEU DIPLOMATIC CENTER HEADQUARTERS, TSHWANE, AFRICAN ALLIANCE. The stone-throwing, looting crowd provided a better commentary than any voice-over or textlink.

"Europe isn't flavor of the month in some parts of the world now," said Mick.

"Just on the strength of my piece?"

"Just on the strength of our diplomatic correspondent asking the Rim States embassy in Brussels whether the FEU had discussed the Eqbas Vorhi with them. We're in meltdown here. The emergency debate in the UN is still running. If we're lucky, it's sanctions."

"Not much they can do apart from sanctions."

"Oh, there is. The Sinostates are talking about taking over the ITX-router uplink in a *neutral* capacity to *defuse* the situation."

"Jesus." War: it meant nothing else. "They *knew,* Mick. They bloody knew."

"You can confirm that, can you? Because they're denying it pretty vigorously."

Eddie's mouth opened on a reflex to explain that he could, but then he thought of Ual. All his rules of engagement about on and off the record had flown out the window. Did it matter? If Eddie confirmed it, would that make matters worse on Earth, or would it make them worse for Ual, or both? Wess'har didn't have any problem with information. Eddie envied them. Knowledge was the heart of his guilt.

But the denial was a lie, and lies were there to be exposed. It was pure instinct. "Yes, Minister Ual told them. And either way, the buggers are coming. Does it matter?"

"It does if everyone thinks that's not all they're being told. I need something down the line from you fast."

"You're being monitored."

"I don't give a fuck. You think the FEU's going to pull the plug now?"

Eddie was usually so focused on a story that it ate him alive. This time he had another story, closer to home, and one in which he was equally mired. Both had started tumbling like an avalanche. He had to get to Nevyan and tell her what Ual was planning: and he had a responsibility to events he had helped unleash on Earth.

It never used to be this hard.

"Okay, I'll see if Ual will talk to me about Eqbas Vorhi on camera. Meanwhile, get a talking head. Haven't you got a tame biologist to interview?"

"I want it live from the spot, Eddie."

"You want to come 150 trillion fucking miles out here and do it yourself? I've got a war starting up here."

"So have we."

Eddie made the hardest decision of his life, one that stripped him of his identity more surely than Ade's discarded stripes had erased him as a sergeant.

"Later," he said. "I've got something to do that's more urgent than a story."

And Eddie Michallat ceased to be a reporter, not in name, but in the core of his being. He closed the relay and left.

Ade regretted that his best blues and his white Wolseley helmet were seventy-five years in the past on a planet he could never return to, Earth. It would have been nice to turn out really smart for the Boss one last time.

He made another attempt to press a sharp crease into his DPM combat trousers and reassured himself that under these circumstances it was the effort that counted. You couldn't press crease-proof kit properly with the heated blade of a fighting knife.

He pulled on the trousers, made sure they were tucked neatly into his calf-high combat boots, and adjusted his beret. Then he reassembled his ESF670 rifle and slid the magazine into its catch.

Aras wandered up behind him. "You won't need that."

Ade checked the scope and flicked through the settings. If he had to fire, it would be at close quarters. The calibration didn't matter.

"They want a chunk of her? Well, they're going to have to go through me."

"They know how strongly you feel about it."

Ade didn't trust the Eqbas. He knew how wess'har thought; fragments of Aras's memory gave him a definite emotional sense of the wess'har mind. They didn't mess around with life. But he didn't know how different the last ten thousand years had made the Eqbas. The fact that they asked to do a post mortem at all worried him.

Aras showed no sign of emotion at all, and that worried Ade more than the self-destructive rage and grief that had brought the wess'har to the brink of using a grenade on himself. That was how you made sure *c'naatat* didn't try to put you back together again. Eddie had talked Aras out of it. He could really use words, that bloke: Ade envied him.

Aras put his hand gently on the rifle. "Shooting is unnecessary."

"You stick to your job, and I'll stick to mine."

"Ade, I know how hard this is."

"You can't know. You ever caused the death of someone you cared about?"

Aras made a small *huff* that could have been contempt. "I've lost many, many people."

"It isn't the same. I've had my mates die on me more than once, but I handed Shan over *to die*. You think about that. I can't ever put that right, but I can bust my arse trying to make sure she actually does rest in some sort of peace."

Sometimes he didn't feel comfortable talking to Aras. He liked him a lot and counted him as a mate, but Aras always seemed to be thinking things that Ade couldn't even imagine. He made him cautious, afraid of looking stupid. And he had been Shan's choice, and Ade hadn't. It put things in perspective.

"Ade, let me talk to Shapakti."

"You think I'm some knuckle-dragging grunt looking for a fight, don't you?"

"No, I think you're a man who has been through a great deal of stress. It's not unreasonable to be agitated."

"I'm trained to talk to people. When the talking fails, I shoot. But I talk first. You ever done urban peacekeeping? You want to know what you do when you're being stoned by women and children?"

"You threw the stones back, if I recall correctly," said Aras. "But I'm sorry. I'm not handling this well." He indicated the door. "Go on. Do what you feel you have to."

Ade was instantly reduced to shame and embarrassment by the wess'har's soothing tone. Shit, Aras had lost his *wife*. His own grief blinded him to that.

"Sorry. I was well out of order there."

"We've all been *well out of order* in recent weeks. It would be insulting to Shan if we were *not* diminished by her death."

Aras seemed suddenly calmer for finally knowing where Shan was. "I'd better be off, then," said Ade.

F'nar was like one of those housing estates they built to cut down on crime. With its single frontage of curved inward-looking terraces, everyone could see you come and go; and everyone knew where Ade was going.

"It's cold," said Lisik, one of Nevyan's four husbands. He had picked up a little English from Nevyan or maybe even his daughter, Giyadas. He didn't seem intent on learning more than he had to. "Vehicle, not walking. I take you?"

Ade thought it was just a pleasantly crisp day, but wess'har felt the cold. "Thanks."

"No Aras?"

"Aras is preparing the grave."

"What is grave?"

"Never mind."

F'nar didn't have a shuttle port. It wasn't the way wess'har built, not here anyway, although the pictures of Eqbas Vorhi seemed to suggest that they once did. The jungle of pipes, conduits and service buildings needed to handle its few flights was somewhere underground where it didn't spoil the scenery. Lisik stopped the vehicle apparently in the middle of nowhere.

"You sure this is the right place?" said Ade.

"We wait," said Lisik.

Ade picked specks off his lovat pullover. He'd wanted a body to grieve over and so had Aras, but now that it was a reality it was also a reminder—if he needed one—that he'd fired at least twenty rounds into Shan's body. He'd taken enough gunshot wounds to know how much pain they caused.

And she'd head-butted him. She'd sworn at him, called him a *frigging idiot,* despised him in her final moments because he had failed her. He didn't protect her. He hadn't protected his mum from his father either, not once. No wonder his dad had called him a gutless little bastard. He was.

People said they would give everything if they could spend just five minutes again with someone they'd lost, but what Ade had never known was just how powerful and painful that feeling could be until now.

There was no sign of Shapakti or his crew. If they wanted a sample of *c'naatat,* they could take it from him. He didn't care any more.

"Not long," said Lisik.

A muffled *boom* like shelling in a distant war broke the silence. A craft was beginning its descent. The small point of reflected sunlight became a blue disc and then resolved into a blunt-nosed cylinder that spiraled lower and then descended vertically, kicking up a skirt of dust.

How are they going to bring her out?

The hatch remained closed.

Wess'har don't give a shit about bodies. No coffins, no body bags. Oh, God.

The clicking of cooling metal gave way to the *chunk-chunk-chunk* of securing bolts being withdrawn. The three-part hatch door cracked open and the lower section peeled out into a ramp. Serrimissani scuttled down it and Ade stepped forward, rifle shouldered, stomach churning, wanting it all to be over and hating himself for his haste.

"I want you to remain calm," said Serrimissani.

Oh, God, no. It was going to be bad. He made himself look towards the open hatch. It felt like every moment before the first shell landed, before the shooting started, before the ramp went down on the assault craft, except he didn't feel trained and armed against this at all.

"Get inside," she said.

The shuttle smelled of panic. Ade had never consciously noticed scent before, and he realized that his senses were changing just as Aras had said. He wondered if his bowels would let him down. He knew it happened to plenty of people—plenty of seasoned combat troops—but he wished it wouldn't happen to him. There was something about harmed women that triggered it badly. He thought of his father knocking seven shades of shit out of his mother.

You could have saved her.

Ade didn't recognize what was lying wrapped in a piece of iridescent fabric on the bench. Nevyan was leaning over it. He passed through that familiar split second where the rest of his field of vision was gray fog and he could see just one awful detail: and this time it was the back of a skull, two cords of tendon flanking a knob of vertebra.

"Oh God." *Don't turn the body. I can't cope with seeing her face. Don't—*

Nevyan's head jerked round, eyes vividly yellow like an animal's. "She's alive," she said. "We didn't dare send a message. Nobody must know."

Everything was playing back to him delayed by a second. *She's alive.* Ade heard the sound but the meaning didn't sink in. Then there was absolute silence.

The skeletal, hairless head moved slightly.

Ade felt his legs start to buckle under him. He could hear himself saying, "How? How? *How?*" over and over again. But his training kicked in and he seized it gratefully, blind to what he was looking at because it was too awful to dwell on.

"Is she conscious?"

"No," said Nevyan.

He couldn't call for medical support. And whatever Shan's body was doing, it was well beyond the skills of anyone trained to deal with ordinary humans. If *c'naatat* had kept her alive through all that, then there wasn't much else to be done except to give it some energy to draw on. It looked as if it had already eaten her alive.

"Get her back home." Ade couldn't work out why his hands weren't shaking. "Just get her back home. *Now.*"

*   *   *

Aras didn't want to bury the swiss with Shan's body. While he understood the human need behind Ade's request, Shan had no use for it.

But I do. It was a comfort to him.

Shapakti watched while he hacked out the grave, turning occasionally to look out from the cliff across the plain.

"A corpse can't see the view," he said unhelpfully.

"This is an act for the living, not for the dead."

"Burying it will obstruct the scavengers."

Aras laid down his tools and stood up. "*It* was my *isan*," he said. "And if you make any attempt whatsoever to touch her body I will personally kill you, and if I do not, then Ade Bennett will. Confine your curiosity about *c'naatat* to me. Do you understand?"

It was unthinkable for one wess'har to even consider threatening another. They were a species built on consensus, but Aras's humanity had swept that aside in its pain. Shapakti cocked his head, suitably chastened.

"Sir," he said.

"This medication you take. Does it reduce your emotional longing for your *isan*?"

"A little."

Aras had wanted to hear the word *completely*. But it was unlikely the drug would have breached his *c'naatat*'s robust defenses anyway. Perhaps trying to forget his pain was an act of betrayal. He knelt down and sat back on his heels, waiting.

"What is the red object?" asked Shapakti.

"A swiss. A device for communications and data gathering, among other things. It belonged to Shan Frankland and she valued it greatly."

"May I examine it?"

"No."

It wasn't Shapakti's fault. He was simply being wess'har—pragmatic, exact, unsentimental. The position of the grave didn't matter and neither did the swiss; nothing of Shan would be here to enjoy the vista, and Aras had embedded memories of his *isan* more vivid than those in the swiss. But the modest ritual *mattered*. That much of him was human, he realized.

So he waited. Shapakti said nothing and waited with him.

Irregular scrambling footsteps and tumbling pebbles announced an approach. Aras expected Ade to appear with the body, and he braced himself for the moment, ashamed of dreading it, but it was Serrimissani. She was running. The wind was in the wrong direction to smell her state of mind but Aras needed no scent cues to tell she was extremely agitated.

He feared the worst, but under the circumstances he was at a loss to think what *worse* could possibly be.

Maybe they hadn't found Shan after all. The thought was agonizing. He had prepared himself for this and it had not been easy. He stood up.

"What is it?"

Serrimissani stood panting. "This will be hard for you to understand," she said. "You must come with me. Shan is alive."

She wasn't making sense. "Don't. Don't do this to me."

"She is *alive*."

"That's impossible."

Serrimissani turned to go back down the slope but Aras grabbed her by her decorative belts, jerking her back. Shapakti was forgotten for the moment. "She *cannot* be alive. Unless Ade lied."

"He didn't."

Shapakti didn't appear to understand the conversation but he had certainly reacted to the excitement. He was standing absolutely wess'har-still, alarmed: Aras was seeing more similarities than differences in the Eqbas now. He beckoned to him.

"Go back to your crew," Aras said carefully. "We have no body to bury."

"Were the ussissi mistaken?"

"That's not your concern. Go."

Serrimissani was *wrong*. There was a rational explanation
for this, and it would be heartbreaking. Aras prepared himself for the distress and waited until Shapakti was well out of
earshot. He turned on her, angry in anticipation of having his
hopes dashed.

"Not even *c'naatat* can survive in space."

"But she *has*. We can argue about the mechanism later.
Come. But prepare yourself—her appearance will upset you."

Aras struggled. Over the years he had picked up the human habit of suppressing his reactions. "And this is *not* a
shock? That she has survived in space?"

"She's not conscious."

Aras didn't want to hear any more. He wanted to *see*. He
set off at a run and eventually he couldn't hear anyone behind him. He didn't look back.

7

*Shapakti, I don't understand. Why do humans say they were
only following orders? Don't they understand that it is even
worse to obey a bad order than to give one? I suspect that
they delight in being loathsome.*

SARMATAKIAN VE,
adviser to the council of matriarchs of Eqbas Vorhi,
commonly known as the World Before

Eddie sprinted along the terraces. His lungs were screaming for air but he needed to find Nevyan. She wasn't responding to the *virin*.

He headed for Aras's home. He needed *not* to be alone
with what was now in his head. Wess'har going about their
business took no notice of him, probably thinking he was
like Ade, just running for fun.

*Fun. What the fuck's happened to me in the last two
years? How did I get to be a go-between?* His lungs struggled and he envied Ade his fitness. *Maybe that's all I ever
was, a fucking messenger boy.*

One wess'har stepped out and stopped him, catching him
roughly by the shoulder. "Body is home," he said. "Understand? Body is home."

Eddie understood all right. They said things came in
threes. Ual was kicking over the traces, the FEU was under
siege, and now Shan Frankland's body had been brought
back for burial. However urgent his problems, Ade and Aras
would be in far worse shape than he ever would.

"I understand," said Eddie. "Thanks."

He set off again, this time at a prudent fast walk. He
wiped the sweat off his face and pushed cautiously on Aras's

door. There was no sign of Nevyan. He could hear Ade and Aras talking.

"Is she responding at all? Is anyone thinking of how we feed her?"

"Nevyan said she's coughing up water."

"Can she swallow?"

"Not as such."

"What do you mean, *not as such*?"

"Best she could do was drip it down her throat."

It didn't make sense.

Eddie walked into the small side chamber that had been Ade's room. *Why's he taken the body in there?* Aras and Ade were leaning over the bed and they both straightened up and turned to look at Eddie at the same time. And Nevyan was standing watching them in silence.

Body. Oh God, God, God.

"Eddie," said Nevyan. "I should have called you. Shan's back."

"I know."

"No, she's *alive*."

There were days when so much water poured down the pipe that one more bucketful didn't make you drown any faster. He turned the word over in his mind. He looked at it and nothing made sense.

"She can't be alive. That can't be her."

Nevyan simply beckoned him forward. "It's true."

Eddie forced himself to look at the body and he heard a little *uhhh* noise that he thought might be her, or even Ade; and then he realized it was his own voice, his own disbelief and shock escaping from his throat.

Shan looked dead—no, she looked worse than dead. She looked *mummified*. She didn't look like a woman and she didn't look even remotely like Shan. Ade pulled a *dhren* across her body, frowning at him. Eddie hadn't even noticed that she was naked.

"She wasn't drifting?" he asked. He couldn't even form a question.

He'd seen plenty of dead bodies before. He'd seen—and smelled—bodies in ditches at the side of the main road into Ankara, hacked about, misshapen kit people in pieces who only looked real because there were flies swarming on them that billowed up in a black cloud when he leaned a little too close to look. A small white dog had been eating one of the bodies, worrying at the shattered skull of a young woman. It was a poodle with a blue glittery collar; a civilized thing gone feral, like all the humans around it.

The roadside dead were strangers. Shan was a friend, more or less.

"Eddie," said Ade. "It's a shock for all of us. Take it easy."

"What?"

"Don't ask how. All we know is that she's still alive."

Eddie said *alive* to himself several times. He tried not to put his hand to his mouth, but it was hard.

"Oh my God," he said. "Oh my *God*."

Real shock was a strange thing. Eddie found that another part of his brain took over and said *training, training, training*. He reached for his camera. It was only Nevyan's crushing grip on his arm that stopped him.

Ade showed remarkably little emotion. He'd probably seen a lot worse on the battlefield. There wasn't the slightest hint that the marine was looking at a woman he cared for, or even that he had misgivings about having emptied a magazine into her. He knelt down beside the bed and looked for all the world as if he was praying. Aras slid his hand under Shan's head and moved the pillow.

Ade stood up again. "I can intubate. If you've got a tube about so wide, I can get it down her throat." He indicated the width with close-held fingertips. "I can do basic first aid."

"Well, neither of us can, so that makes you the brain surgeon," said the part of Eddie that was coping. The other part was still staring at an unrecognizable skeleton that had once been a woman who physically terrified him. "I left some brewing kit here. Tubes, squeeze-bulbs, that kind of stuff."

"Close enough."

Eddie rummaged through the jumble of *efte* boxes in the storage area he had once used as a bedroom and pulled out the coils of tubing and funnels that he'd filched from the *Thetis* mission's lab. It felt like a lifetime ago. His hands were shaking. Alive. *Alive.* He'd forgotten the news he'd run up the terrace to break.

"It's not sterile," he said.

"I don't think that's going to make any difference now," said Ade. He uncoiled the tubing and measured a length against Shan's chest. "Why don't you find something liquid enough to pass through this?"

"Force-feeding will hurt her," said Aras.

Ade's shoulders stiffened. Eddie had never picked up the slightest hint of aggression from him but he was sensing it now. "Yeah, but I don't know how to do a percutaneous endogastric tube," said Ade irritably. "Besides, cutting a hole in her abdominal wall will hurt her a fucking sight more, so just get the nutrient, will you?"

There was a brief moment of silence. Then Aras simply walked away.

Ade stretched out the tube and took the end in one hand. "Eddie, can you steady her head so I can get the tube in her nose?"

"Okay . . ." *Oh God.* "How do you know when it's in the stomach?"

"Stomach contents siphoning back."

"Has she got any?"

"Look, I've measured the bloody thing. Halfway between the end of the sternum and the navel, okay?"

Eddie had never thought of himself as squeamish but there was something horrific about touching a very frail body. Shan's scalp was unusually hot against his palm and he could feel the ridges of bone. He thought briefly of his bee cam and accepted, just this once, that it was neither the time nor the place. He let Ade work.

"Easy, sweetheart. There . . . yeah, I know . . . I know . . .

take it easy." Ade made a couple of abortive attempts to get the tube past Shan's throat. For a dead woman, she was doing a credible job of struggling and gagging. She crunched down hard on his finger: he yelped and tried to pull free, but she had latched on like a snake and it was a few seconds before her bite tired and he could withdraw. He wiped blood on his pants, seeming unconcerned. "Just as well I'm already infected, eh? Come on . . . let's try again, sweetheart."

Her struggling grew weaker and eventually he managed to ease the tube past her throat. He glanced over his shoulder. "Where's Aras with the bloody mix?"

Aras returned with a glass flask. The contents looked substantial. Ade seemed unconvinced.

"What's in it?"

"Beet jaggery, the last of the barley flour, and some *jay* juice," said Aras.

"You sure you haven't got it in her trachea?" said Eddie. *Oh God.* "The tube, I mean."

"I'm sure," said Ade.

"How do you know how much to feed her?"

Ade paused for one beat before replying and it was as eloquent as a balled fist. "Maximum stomach capacity's three liters, normal capacity half that, but she's wasted away. So we give her half a liter slowly every two hours and keep an eye on her. I might even be able to feel the distension manually, seeing as there's nothing of her. That's what you do with animals, anyway."

Eddie reconsidered his view of Ade as a simple if excellent soldier. "Animals?"

"You feel if the stomach's full. I've bottle-fed orphaned foxes." Ade's face was suddenly different, distracted, recalling something he didn't like remembering. "At least I did until my fucking father smashed their heads in."

The room was silent except for the liquid sounds of the nutrient working through the tube. Occasionally Eddie had glimpses of what had made Ade Bennett into the man he was and the visions were like a sightseeing trip to hell. Maybe that was what Shan had spotted. She had an unerring eye for damaged men who needed her solid reassurance.

And here she was, alive. And she shouldn't have been. There were lucky escapes, and unbelievable escapes, but this was off the scale.

"Looks like she's taken it okay." Ade glanced at Aras, chin lowered. "You want to keep an eye on her while I find something to secure the tube? Then we can leave it in place for a couple of days and not have to put her through that each time we feed her."

Eddie noted the placatory *we*. He didn't feel that included him. Ade busied himself sorting through the contents of his pouch belt and seemed to find something in his emergency medical kit that satisfied him, a small roll of adhesive tape. He handed it to Aras almost submissively. Aras accepted it, and with it Ade's silent indication of where he should place the tape to best anchor the tube.

"Rota," said Ade. "Two hours' watch each. Okay?"

"What if she's brain damaged?" said Eddie.

"I've seen an isenj round blow a hole in her head you could almost put your hand in and she recovered from that just fine," said Ade, wearing his soft voice again. "And if she doesn't pull round from this—well, then we're going to take care of her for as long as she needs it. She's home."

Aras indicated the door with a sharp nod of the head, effectively dismissing Ade. "I will take the first watch."

Eddie, well used to observing the gamut of emotional reactions to shocking news, found himself on the terrace staring at his own shaking hands. The adrenaline was beginning to ebb and the enormity of events was kicking in, making him rerun the last hour over and over again in his mind, each time finding the shock of revelation fresh and breathtaking. Nevyan and Ade joined him.

"I regret not warning you," said Nevyan. "But this was hardly the information to commit to a public channel."

"Jesus, no."

"It is . . . extraordinary."

Eddie struggled. "And there was I thinking I had news for *you.*" He licked dry lips. It was definitely time for a beer. "You need to know this. Ual's . . . um . . . decided to hand over Lindsay and Rayat, no conditions, but his own government doesn't know. He's going to get the marines on Umeh to abduct them."

Nevyan didn't turn a hair. "Bold. And sensible."

Eddie, one duty done, fretted over abandoning a story. "He doesn't want a war."

"How will he achieve this? How am I to contact him if his government isn't privy to this?"

Ade came out onto the terrace with three mugs of beer and handed them out. Eddie took a tight grip on the smooth glass but could hardly feel it. He cupped one hand carefully underneath. "I don't know," he said. "I have no idea. I'll call him—"

"That can wait now," said Nevyan.

They drank in silence. It was a disgustingly yeasty brew but it did the job. Nevyan sipped it gingerly, just once, and then stood nursing the mug.

"You can't get drunk, not with *c'naatat,*" said Eddie, mouth on autopilot now. "Shan told me so."

"I know," said Ade. "But I have a great imagination." He gulped it. "Here's to the Boss."

"How are we going to keep this quiet?"

"Shapakti's going to be all over this. But who would believe us anyway?"

The best stories were always like that. "Who's Shapakti?"

"The Eqbas commander who landed. Yeah, they're here. I should have said."

They're here.

Eddie was making a soft landing now, seeing the world in the familiar context of sound bites and angles again. His brain had wrapped up the fact that Shan Frankland had survived where absolutely no complex organism could, and had hidden it while he calmed down. That shock had made the situation on Earth somehow more manageable.

"I ought to call 'Desk," said Eddie.

He sat down at the small console in the main room, not quite seeing the detail of the screen, and reminded himself that he had seen an awful, *awful* lot of bizarre and terrifying and momentous things in his career. This was just one more.

Jesus, she's really alive. It kept washing back over him. No, this wasn't just one more thing. It changed everything. The BBChan portal opened.

"Mick," he said. "Mick, I'm back."

There was no recrimination over his abrupt exit. "You look bloody awful. What's happened?"

Eddie swallowed a particularly large lump of yeast and hoped the most recent events didn't manifest themselves in a large cartoon think-bubble above his head. "Yeah," he said. "I ran here. I can get you some footage of the first Eqbas forces. Maybe today."

"Now *that's* what I call a story."

It was asking for trouble to promise 'Desk anything, but he did it anyway. "Sorry I had to run," said Eddie.

"Hey, you were going after the Eqbas. But tell me that next time, okay?"

"Okay," said Eddie, and knew there were things he would now never tell a living soul.

Each day, Lindsay made sure that she knew exactly where Mohan Rayat was.

She was dead already. She just needed to make sure Rayat got what was coming to him as well. There was nowhere to run on Umeh, but she was determined that he wouldn't just melt away into the endless heaving mass of isenj.

Rayat was in the communications center today, an optimistic name for a single room that wasn't doing much communicating. He was having an argument, and she had to hand it to the slimeball: he could keep his cool.

"Why can't I send this?" demanded one of the contractors.

"Because it contains more than the basic okay message the isenj will allow past the relay."

"That's no bloody use."

Rayat had that resigned and immovable look of a man Just Doing His Job. He didn't seem like a spook at all. His hands were meshed in front of him on the table like a newscaster.

"You can transmit what you like," he said. "But if it doesn't consist of the exact words 'I am fine' or 'systems operating normally' then the relay is set to bounce it back. So I'm told."

"My company needs this information. It's just operating data from the CO_2 scrubs."

"The isenj don't know that it's not a sophisticated code containing a message that'll provoke the wess'har."

Rayat said it with a commendably straight face. The contractor, hands braced on the table, let his head drop between sagging shoulders in submission to the might of alien bureaucracy. "Okay. It's bloody stupid, but okay."

Lindsay watched the man leave and slid into the space he had left.

"Reckon we'll get to the riot stage?" she asked.

"Not if the food holds out," said Rayat.

He looked inexplicably calm for a man who had unleashed careless massacre. Lindsay now had a very different view of the words *extinction* and *genocide*. Dead bezeri had helped her see that the two were identical if you just deleted the notion that it was different for humans.

"Is that the management *we* or the royal *we*?" she said.

"We all have to pull our weight here."

"And how do you see your future?"

"About as bleak as yours. But at least we both know we don't have to worry about *c'naatat* any more."

"Well, that's about all," she lied, thinking of Ade Bennett raising two contemptuous fingers to her as he left the shuttle, showing her how fast his broken nose had healed. Rayat couldn't possibly have seen that. It had to stay that way.

And Aras didn't count. Nobody could take a wess'har, and a wess'har wouldn't spread *c'naatat*. But Ade Bennett had it, and he was human, and one day he might be home-sick or desperate enough to find a way of getting back to Earth. She'd failed to eradicate the risk—and there was nothing she could do about it now. She'd have to rely on the wess'har to keep Ade confined.

She wondered if she'd have surrendered if it had been her, or how long Shan would have held out in exile. But Shan didn't have any of the appealing human weaknesses that made people care and love and pine.

"So . . . I seem to recall your screaming your head off at Frankland calling her every name under the sun because she wouldn't use *c'naatat* to save your baby," said Rayat.

"Thank you for reminding me."

"What if she had?"

Lindsay didn't want to hear any more. She was coping with bereavement, at least in the sense that she hadn't yet fallen apart. It had been more than a year since David had died, thirty days old, and with occasional medication she'd managed her bewildered grief.

She knew. *What if.* Her son would have been as danger-ous and endangered as Shan, and very probably as dead. And who might have felt obliged to kill him in case he proved a risk? And what sort of life would he have had, iso-lated as a biohazard?

Lindsay walked out.

There was sanctuary in the maze of plant beneath Umeh Station. She'd put her name down on the rota to dose the feeder tank for the hydroponics system, recycling nutrients from the rapidly growing supply of human waste. It was a sudden hard lesson in ecology. There was adequate water and power, but beyond what could be grown in this biodome there was no food, and the mission hadn't planned to accom-modate a hundred extra people on the ground. It was a damn shame that they hadn't had time to unload all of *Actaeon*'s supplies before the ship was hit.

She went back to the sewage processing plant and climbed down the ladder to the service ducts and machinery spaces. So this was what they were planning to build on Bezer'ej when *Actaeon* set out from Earth twenty-six years ago. It was just as well the isenj had chosen to make space for it on Umeh; the wess'har would have blown it into orbit for daring to intrude on the landscape.

Among the pipe runs and filter housings there was no smell apart from new plastic, but the thought of circulating feces was a psychological deterrent for most. A musical rhythm thrummed in the quiet motors and intermittent rush of fluid from pipe to pipe, as soothing as a Zen garden in its way. Lindsay leaned on one of the separation tanks and rested her forehead on the cool surface.

Poor bloody bezeri. She couldn't imagine a species so fragile and so localized that fallout would devastate it, but she had to accept that was the price she'd paid without thinking. Why did they pick that chain of islands to spawn in? Why didn't they spread around the planet?

Bloody stupid squid.

She wasn't a monster. She *knew* she wasn't. But now she was wondering what monsters really were. She was so preoccupied with the fear that she might no longer know what was right and decent that the insistent gurgling of her stomach caught her unawares.

It was time to eat. Her stomach was gnawing its way out again, objecting to a meager diet of ten-day lettuce and beans when it wanted plenty of fat and sugar.

"Boss?" said a woman's voice behind her.

"Sue?"

Webster stood with one hand on her belt and an apologetic smile on her face. Lindsay thought she looked like the sort of girl who teachers described as "helpful." But she had her ESF670 rifle slung on her webbing and she hadn't earned a green beret for being helpful.

"It's time," she said. "You knew this was coming, didn't you?"

"I did." But she was still suddenly scared. And she wanted to *run*. "Oh God."

"Let's walk out of here with a bit of dignity, shall we?"

"And Rayat?"

"Leave him to Mart."

"He's not going to slime his way out of this, is he?"

"I don't think so."

Lindsay walked out and Webster followed behind. If the marine could take this with equanimity, then so could she. She wondered how the wess'har might settle the score and knew that whatever they did, it would be fast and efficient, which suddenly turned out to be little comfort.

She really didn't want to die.

Webster kept right behind her as she climbed the access ladder to ground level and walked through the dome to the entrance. She looked around to see who had come for them. Ussissi or isenj? Nobody going about their business in the dome was behaving as if anyone unexpected had entered.

"Where are they?" asked Lindsay.

And then she saw Rayat. There was something wrong— more wrong than being taken away by alien troops for some unspecified death. Barencoin and Becken were frog-marching Rayat towards the door. Small knots of crew and contractors stood aside to let the men pass, staring and doing double takes.

Rayat's shocked white face said *pain*. As he came within a few meters of Lindsay, she could see he wasn't just being forced to the door: from the angle of his arms, his wrists were cuffed behind his back.

"Ready?" said Barencoin. "We haven't got much of a window. She didn't put up a fight, then?"

"I just asked nicely," said Webster.

Lindsay turned just as she realized that Webster wasn't accompanying her. She was *arresting* her. Nice, capable, helpful Webster held her rifle in both hands now.

"Come on, Boss," she said. "I've got to hand you over in one piece. Don't do anything daft."

"And what about you? What do you think they're going to do to *you*? You think being at the bottom of the command pile will stop the wess'har coming for you too?"

"Yeah," said Barencoin. "So far, it has."

Rayat stumbled. Barencoin had hold of his collar. Lindsay was right behind them, Webster's rifle in her back. All she could think of right then was that she was hungry and that she hadn't had time to go to the toilet. When it came to it, she was as reluctant to face death as she had been on Bezer'ej, when she was so convinced that she was prepared to blow her grenades and take Shan Frankland with her.

You don't have the guts.

She would never erase Shan's rebuke. The woman's contempt for anyone with less reckless courage than herself was an ever-present toxin weakening Lindsay at every turn. Shan Frankland certainly knew how to haunt you.

"I think I'll hand you over to Ade," Barencoin told Rayat. "He could do with a laugh."

"Discipline doesn't take long to fall apart, does it?" said Rayat. "I'm an officer of your government. I was acting legally."

"Technically, so were we, but we still got ours and now you're going to get *yours*."

"Think of it as peacekeeping," said Becken. He slipped on his breather mask as they stepped through the airlock. An isenj ground transport swept up to the entrance and Lindsay found herself pushed flat onto its floor, Rayat landing with a thud beside her.

"It's worth it if I see you go first, you bastard," she said.

"Where are we going?"

"Shut it," said Barencoin, and put his boot flat on Rayat's cheek. "And keep your bloody heads down."

"Why?" Lindsay just thought *riot*. The isenj blamed them. They'd riot if they saw them. There was a ussissi driving and it didn't turn to look at them.

"I said *shut it*."

She inhaled a scent of damp forest. She knew that smell, too: there was an isenj in the vehicle.

"I regret the drama," said Minister Ual's voice. "But this is more to protect me from my own people's reaction than to prevent your escape."

"Where are you taking us?" asked Rayat.

"F'nar."

"You don't have jurisdiction over us."

"I'm simply carrying out your government's wishes." Ual suddenly leaned over them like a collapsing Christmas tree, glittering with royal blue beads. "My problem is simply that I am not carrying out the wishes of my *own*."

Nevyan found it hard to keep the news of Shan's survival to herself. Secrecy was a very unwess'har thing. Her husbands had known why she had left in a hurry, and now they wanted to know what had been done with the remains. Humans had strange rituals. There was a certain curiosity about a species that preferred to hide its dead. But they were *gethes,* carrion-eaters: so they did such things.

Secrecy was unimportant now that Shan was safe on Wess'ej. The news reached most of F'nar before midday.

Giyadas insisted on seeing the human who had come back from the dead. The *isanket* led her stepmother by the hand along the terraces, tugging with uncharacteristic impatience. Nevyan remembered to knock on the door. Human territorial privacy was a difficult concept to grasp.

"Is she recovering?" she asked.

"We think so." Aras was mixing something in a bowl that smelled full of *evem.* "Her temperature is very high, which is a good sign that *c'naatat* is modifying her. She's still not conscious."

"May we see her?"

"She owes her life to your persistence. She would be glad to know you were here."

Ade was sitting beside the bed with a piece of what the *gethes* called smartpaper, a data storage medium that was a thin white sheet of fabric. He was reading aloud from it but he stopped when he realized Nevyan was standing in the doorway.

"Just in case she can hear," said Ade, clearly embarrassed. *"Barrack Room Ballads."*

Shan didn't look peaceful. She looked agonized and ill, and there was a transparent tube taped to her cheek and extending into her nose. But she didn't look as horrific as when Nevyan had first seen her. The bones in her face seemed less prominent and her skin was flushed pink.

Giyadas stared at the tube, hands tightly clasped. "What's that for?"

"For putting food directly into her stomach," said Ade. "She can't swallow properly."

"She must have been very frightened. Will her hair grow again?"

He ran a fingertip over Shan's scalp. "It's already growing. I can feel it."

It was hard to think of her as she had once been. Even though Shan was shorter than most matriarchs, Eddie had referred to her as a *strapping girl,* a tall and athletic female by human standards. It was also hard to imagine that she had survived in the vacuum of space and returned with any scrap of life in her at all.

Eddie wandered in and joined the solemn contemplation. He leaned closer and looked into her face. "Come on, you old bag," he said. "I bet you can hear me. Come on. Get up and take a swing at me. Stop slacking."

"Why do you say things you don't mean?" asked Giyadas.

"Because it's easier than getting upset because she looks so awful."

Ade exuded a strong scent of agitation. He fidgeted with the smartpaper, clearly annoyed at the interruption. "I don't think she'd enjoy being a spectator sport."

"That's my cue," said Eddie, and walked out.

C'naatat had turned out to be even more extraordinary

than Nevyan had imagined. She understood why it provoked such extreme reactions in humans; they were solitary creatures, competitive rather than cooperative, and *c'naatat* had all the makings of a very desirable military advantage. What it meant to individuals also set on avoiding the natural progression of life she could only imagine. Their ability to close their eyes to what would happen to the world outside their heads constantly amazed her.

And yet there were humans like Shan and—she dared think it—Lindsay Neville who went to extreme lengths to stop it becoming available to their own kind.

"Where are her lights?" asked Giyadas.

Nevyan looked carefully at Shan's hands for signs of the bioluminescence she had once displayed, a legacy of the bezeri. Shan hadn't been sure quite how *c'naatat* had managed to collect that genetic material, and it had distressed her at first. Giyadas had found it fascinating.

Ade took one of Shan's hands and turned it over carefully. He could touch her with impunity; he was already contaminated. "Nothing yet," he said. "They might come back when she's better."

"There are others who wish to visit," said Nevyan carefully. "My mother."

"I'm sure Shan would love to see Mestin. When she's awake."

"Very well. I understand."

"Please don't think I'm being ungrateful, ma'am. You found her and we owe you everything. But Shan wouldn't like too many people to see her in this state."

Humans were obsessed with appearance. Nevyan noted his use of the word *we.* "A considerate thought, Ade Bennett."

He gave her an awkward smile without any display of teeth and went on reading. Nevyan wondered how this odd narrative about soldiers in ancient Earth wars might be of comfort to Shan, but there was a great deal she didn't know about her yet, nor about Ade Bennett. Eventually Aras came in with the bowl of liquid food and more tubing. Ade put down the smartpaper and stood up.

"Let's leave Aras to it, shall we?" He ushered Nevyan and Giyadas to the doorway.

Nevyan knew she could do nothing further for Shan but she waited anyway, watching Giyadas interrogate Eddie on the nature of human secrecy. Ade, incongruously alien in his landscape-patterned battle clothing, polished his boots with rhythmic strokes. Eddie said he didn't need to polish them at all, but he did it anyway. His weapon was propped by his seat.

"So does everyone know she's back?" asked Eddie.

"I imagine so." Nevyan waited for disapproval, knowing Eddie's attitude to information, but none came. "Have you told the other soldiers?"

Ade shrugged. "Haven't seen them to tell them. I bet Izzy and Chaz have told the others about me, though. Haven't had a message from them in days."

It didn't matter who knew now. There was nothing the *gethes* could do to take *c'naatat,* and nobody else wanted it.

"Does *c'naatat* think?" asked Ade.

Nevyan considered the idea and wasn't sure if it disturbed her. "I don't know. It seems to make decisions, but I don't know if it's aware of its host's feelings any more than we're aware of this planet. It merely treats it kindly, as do we."

"See, we'd want to find that out." Ade considered the degree of shine on his boots and seemed to find it wanting. The polishing gathered speed. "Back home, they'd want to take it apart and find out all about it."

"We don't feel the need to."

Ade seemed satisfied with the answers for a while and sank back into the rhythm of polishing. "How did it keep her going? What was she like when you found her?"

Nevyan cocked her head. "She was covered in a transparent substance. I assume it offered some protection while *c'naatat* kept her in suspension."

Eddie was checking something on his little fabric screen. He made *uh-uh* sounds as if understanding something he had not understood before. "Some organisms can go dormant and survive in space. *Haloarcula* can. So can *Synechococcus*. Look." He offered Nevyan the screen. "They can form a coating. Neat."

"And valuable," said Ade. "The top brass would be *very* interested in that. The more shit you throw at *c'naatat*, the tougher its host gets."

"Nietzsche," said Eddie. "He said that which does not kill me—"

"Yeah, I know who Nietzsche was, thanks."

"I wasn't inferring that you didn't."

Ade's jaw muscles clenched and he went on polishing, eyes cast down. Giyadas was transfixed by the spectacle.

"You're a species that likes to keep busy," she said. Eddie laughed, showing every sign of doting on the *isanket*. The tension subsided again.

After a while Ade paused and cocked his head, then slipped his boots back on and reached for his rifle very casually, as if he was going to subject it to the same cleaning ritual as the rest of his equipment.

Eddie paused. "What's up, Ade?"

Ade shook his head. But he stood to one side of the door, and as it opened he lunged forward and knocked the visitor off his feet. His rifle was hard against Shapakti's head in one movement.

"Fucking well *knock*," said Ade, face flushed. "You can get your head blown off that way." He eased his weapon away from Shapakti's head and hauled him up by his clothing. "Like this." Ade opened the door and rapped his fist against it. "Knock knock. Hello? Come in. Understand?"

"Wow," said Eddie. "Is that an Eqbas?"

Aras appeared in the doorway of Shan's room. "I'll explain to him. Shapakti hasn't learned enough English yet."

"I'll teach him," said Giyadas. "I can do it."

Shapakti warbled in the odd mix of eqbas'u and wess'u

he seemed to be developing with Aras. Nevyan could follow it more easily now. "This *gethes* is dangerous. Why does he hate me?"

"He thinks you're ambushing him," said Aras. "Humans have private spaces. And they don't like being observed excreting or reproducing. This is why we have doors inside this house as well."

"Are the females aggressive? What about the female *c'naatat*? We had no idea the organism was so persistent. Can we—"

"You will leave my *isan* alone."

"Esganikan is very curious about her condition."

"Esganikan can wait."

Nevyan intervened. But she shared Aras's anxiety: the Eqbas had suddenly become intensely curious about *c'naatat*'s characteristics rather than its control. Shapakti smelled excited.

"*Shan Chail* will *tear you up for arse paper* if you irritate her," said Nevyan, hoping she'd recalled the phrase correctly. "Why have you come here?"

Shapakti appeared to grasp the broad meaning. "To inform you that there is a vessel on a direct approach from Umeh."

"The ussissi fly shuttles between worlds all the time."

"This one carries an isenj minister with two *gethes* prisoners. He wishes to talk to Nevyan."

Nevyan looked at Eddie, whose gaze was darting between Aras and Shapakti as if trying to follow the conversation. "What's up?" he asked. "Look, can I talk to this guy? Can someone interpret for me?"

Nevyan ignored the request. Eddie could do as he wished; she didn't understand why he always asked permission. "Ual seems to be delivering Neville and Rayat personally," she said. "Your diplomatic mission was successful."

"I knew he'd keep his side of the bargain," said Eddie, gaze still locked on Shapakti.

"There is no bargain," said Nevyan.

*   *   *

The ussissi pilot made a conspicuous point of bringing his vessel to a halt a thousand kilometers outside wess'har space. He eased himself out of his seat and peered over the back of it at his passengers.

"This is as far as I go without explicit landing clearance from F'nar."

Ual hadn't enjoyed his first experience of space flight at all. Zero gravity was terrifying. Fragments of quills broken by his free-fall collisions crisscrossed the grille across the air vent, and he wondered how ussissi tolerated so much time between planets. Ralassi was actually eating something, drifting a little against his restraints, utterly unconcerned.

"Call F'nar again," said Ual. "Invite them to board to carry out security checks."

The three human soldiers were actually dozing. Ual found that degree of serenity extraordinary, but they behaved as if this was as commonplace for them as it was for the ussissi. It probably was. Mohan Rayat was reading from a small square object. Considering his predicament, he didn't appear appropriately distressed either.

But Lindsay Neville was agitated. She fidgeted, rearranging her collar. She had hardly spoken throughout the journey and odd sounds were coming from her body, liquid gurgling sounds. Ual turned and looked at her, alarmed that she might be about to spawn young.

"That's my stomach," she said. "I haven't eaten in twenty-four hours. Do wess'har feed prisoners?"

The ussissi didn't look up from the console. "They don't take prisoners at all."

"I regret the discomfort," said Ual. "It makes little difference in the end, though."

"You're a callous bastard, sir."

"You seem to forget that I might disapprove of your action on Bezer'ej for reasons other than the diplomatic embarrassment it causes us. Isenj don't engage in wanton destruction."

Ralassi held out his hand, offering whatever snack he was devouring, but it seemed not to appeal to Lindsay despite her claim of great hunger. She looked away and there was no sound except the various hums and rattles of the hull and the ussissi pilot's high-pitched conversation with F'nar.

His chatter stopped. He seemed surprised.

"This is not encouraging," said the pilot.

"Told you so," said Lindsay. "This is where they shoot first and worry about hand-over negotiations later."

"F'nar isn't replying to my message," said the pilot. "This is the commander of an Eqbas vessel standing off our stern. She asks us to cut our drive and allow her vessel to take us inboard."

Ual had to think about that request for a few seconds to make sense of it.

"What Eqbas vessel?"

"The one that has just made itself known to us."

Ual had known they were coming, but the reality of arrival—and the speed—was a shock. "I had expected the wess'har to board us."

"Unless I have misunderstood the ussissi on board, the commander means to take this entire *vessel* inboard."

Ual had planned to admit a boarding party as an act of good faith. "Are you correct?"

"She said *vessel*." The ussissi beckoned him forward. "Minister, look at this display. This is a hazard system." He passed a hand across a smooth white surface and shapes welled up from it, three-dimensional and subtly colored. "It detects objects and hazards. The small object *here* is us."

There was a bead-sized lump on the surface. Close to it was a curved raised area that ran off the edge of the screen. Lindsay edged up behind Ual to look.

"*That* is the Eqbas vessel," said the ussissi.

"Oh *shit*," said Lindsay.

Ual began to wonder if he had made a very grave error of judgment. But perhaps it didn't matter which wess'har na-

tion he met first; one thing he did know about wess'har—
from both his ancient memory and his own experience—was
that they meant what they said.

Humans didn't.

"Follow the Eqbas commander's instructions," said Ual.

8

She could see lights. She could see red and green and gold and violet and something she didn't have a name for.

She didn't even have a name for herself or a sense of her shape or substance. But she could *see.*

She could taste something familiar yet alien, earthy, alive, and then it was gone again. She was moving fast through water. Then she was on dry land, tight-packed with others she knew, enveloped in familiar smells and dryness. And then she was looking down on black grass.

It was all familiar and yet completely strange. She wasn't afraid any more. She simply had a sense of urgency.

She had to do *something.*

The things she could see and feel and taste were *inside,* but she couldn't define how: they just were. There was nothing *outside.* She was vaguely aware of the form of herself, but she couldn't feel anything that told her where she ended and the rest of the universe began.

Then she could see, and she was aware that what she saw was something *outside*; a brilliantly clear night sky without horizon. Its clarity was impossible. For a few moments—

and she had no idea how long those were—she couldn't make sense of it.

When she did, she wished she hadn't.

It was indeed a sky; but it was an infinite field of stars, and she was *in* it. She tried to turn to look over her shoulder but she couldn't move. Animal panic began to rise from the pit of her stomach and something said *get a grip* and she tried to control her breathing.

Then she realized something.

She wasn't breathing.

When Shan opened her eyes again, the star field was gone.

She was clear who she was, and for some reason she was very pleased about that. Warm, soft fabric touched her palms. Something appetizingly spicy wafted on the air.

I'm Detective Superintendent Shan Frankland, Environmental Hazard Division. For a moment she wondered if she'd overslept and she tried to remember what shifts she was working that week, and then she recalled that she hadn't worked shifts since . . . since . . .

She tried to reach out for her swiss.

"She's not breathing. Fuck it, she's *not breathing.*"

Oh shit.

I'm not on Earth. I'm twenty-five light-years away. I've got a parasite. I'm not—

There was something in her nose; no, it was in her throat, and she tried to swallow. Whatever it was, it hurt like hell. A tube? *Sod that.* She grabbed it instinctively and pulled, feeling something rip from her face and scrape the back of her throat. She gagged. Her stomach rebelled. She rolled to the edge of the bed and vomited.

Someone took her shoulders. She tried to push them away out of embarrassment but she couldn't. A voice was calling, "Get Aras! Now!" and she still struggled to get that damn thing out of her mouth.

"Whoa, whoa, whoa, *steady.*" A man held her down— yes, she could smell it was a male, it was all flooding back—

and the tube pulled clear of her throat with a painful jerk. "There. All gone now. Take it easy."

She was staring down at her stomach contents. "I don't remember eating that," she said, but her voice cracked. The face looking down at her was one she knew. She just couldn't place it. "Sorry . . . sorry . . ."

"Don't you worry about that, Boss. Do you know where you are? Do you know me?"

She had to think about it. It took a while. He wiped her face with a cold wet cloth.

"Ade?"

"Well done, Boss. Yes, It's Ade. How do you feel?"

I had a row with you. Her skin burned. "Too hot."

"Let's clean you up."

It was more than a row. She'd hit him, shot him, something like that. "Sorry . . . what's wrong with me?" She couldn't understand why tears were streaming down his face. Maybe she was coming round from a major anaesthetic, although she couldn't imagine why. She knew she said stupid, embarrassing things when she was regaining consciousness even though they sounded sensible at the time. *Shut up.* "Can I have a cup of tea? Sorry I threw up."

"You throw up just as much as you want. Hold still." She felt the sudden chill as he took the cover off her and a lovely iridescent white one went in its place. *Dhren.* She recognized that. "Yeah, you bet you can have a cup of tea."

Then she managed to concentrate on her hands and forearms. They didn't look like hers. They were just bone. "Oh God, what's happened? What's—"

"It's okay . . . *sshh* . . . *sshh* . . ." He put his hand on her shoulder and she wanted to shake it off, but she couldn't. "You're home now."

"Jesus, look at the state of me." She struggled to put her hand to her head. *Where's my hair?* She could see her own outline under the *dhren* but she was just peaks of bone, nothing at all. "How long have I been out?"

"Don't you worry about that. You just rest."

A wonderful scent like sandalwood hit her, rich and oily, and she knew instantly who had entered the room and what he meant to her. The memory was vivid, clear, and shocking.

"Aras. *Aras.*"

"*Isan.*" There was that hint of an alien double-tone resonance in his voice. She looked up into the face of a creature that was almost human but still reminded her of a heraldic beast. "Do you recognize me?"

"Course I do, you silly sod," she said. "Isn't some bastard going to tell me what happened?"

"She's back all right," said a third male voice.

Eddie.

The gaps began filling in, first a couple of flash frames and then a torrent of disjointed images: a shuttle cabin, farms, a church window. She'd have to write them down. She'd have to get some order restored. That was her *job.*

But few images kept returning. At first they were hazy. But then she was absolutely certain about them, and she didn't like them at all.

One was a painfully vivid memory of being slammed to the cool gold ground of Constantine, meters underground yet bathed in light, and being handcuffed. The other was of hearing a hatch close behind her and seeing open, raw blackness speckled with impossibly sharp stars filling her field of vision as the shuttle bay opened to space and the escaping air tore past her.

I stepped out—

The pain of cold and vacuum was worse than she could ever have imagined but she recalled it anyway, accurately enough to make her gasp.

I'm dead oh God it hurts I can still see oh God let me die let me die let me—

Aras Sar Iussan, the final thought in her mind as she was dying, folded her in his arms and the comforting vibration rumbling from his chest almost made the images fade.

"You're right," said Aras. "She's not breathing."

F'nar Plain, November 1, 2376.

The Eqbas ship was huge. Eddie didn't know much about wess'har traffic control, but he could tell from the size and color of the symbols on the projected screen that the target was a whopper. The reactions of the wess'har around him confirmed it: they locked into position and didn't even twitch, that freeze-and-wait reaction that was typical when they were assessing a potential threat.

"When will we be able to see it?" said Eddie.

"Very soon," said Nevyan.

Nevyan's mother, Mestin, and the other senior matriarchs of F'nar had gathered in the Exchange of Surplus Things to watch the progress of the inbound vessel on the screens. Eddie had always thought of them as unassailable military muscle but seeing them transfixed by the arrival of the Eqbas worried him. He remembered cowering beneath the shadow of huge wess'har ships as they swept over Bezer'ej, feeling like a baffled caveman. And this vessel was a magnitude greater than that.

The giant ship waited for clearance. Eddie had spent a sobering hour looking through the images that Ual had given him, pictures of the worlds where Eqbas Vorhi had intervened before; worlds that were now orderly, and peaceful, and *invaded.* The Eqbas could walk in whenever and wherever they wanted.

"Are you glad you're not running the show any more?" he said.

Mestin blinked. "If you're asking if I have confidence that Nevyan will handle this more effectively than I could, then yes. She's far more dominant in a crisis. She has much more *jask.*"

"Is it a crisis?"

"Wess'har are a cooperative species," she said. "But we prefer this agrarian way of life, and it's evident they do *not.* The adjustment may be disconcerting for both."

Eddie wasn't sure if she was saying that the Eqbas would have to get used to walking everywhere or that it was the end of civilization as they knew it. He took out his bee cam and checked its status. Giyadas watched his hands with the intensity of someone trying to work out how a conjuring trick was done. It was one shot he couldn't miss. He'd been denied two headlines of a lifetime—DISGRACED HALF-ALIEN COP CHEATS CERTAIN DEATH, ALIEN MINISTER KIDNAPS HUMAN WAR CRIMINALS—but he was buggered if he was going to let this one pass by doing the decent thing.

Besides, Earth needed to know what was coming. It would focus a few minds. He was clear about that now: he had done the right thing—probably. Those riot scenes from Southern Africa wouldn't leave his mind even when he tried to make them.

My fault. It's all my fault again.

Nobody needed to walk far out onto the plain to see the craft. Eddie heard it long before he saw it, a steady low-frequency throbbing right on the threshold of his hearing that made the back of his tongue itch. Then it dropped slowly through the cloud a good five kilometers away, and it was *colossal.*

F'nar fell uncharacteristically silent.

"Holy shit," said Eddie. "And don't you dare repeat that, Giyadas, you hear?"

Some shots didn't need commentary, and this was one of them. The bronze ship hung in the sky and waited while the small party of matriarchs approached. Then its airframe began to alter.

Eddie thought his eyesight was playing up; but the outline wavered and the cylinder thinned at two points like a bubble of hot blown glass being twisted by a craftsman, creating another bubble on either flank. The belt of red and blue chevrons faded and then reformed perfectly on each separate vessel.

Eddie was mesmerized. He'd seen ships and aircraft on Earth that could separate into independent sections but the

technology was one of hydraulics and bulkheads: this sleight
of engineering hand appeared to be utterly fluid, even organic.

The bee cam recorded it faithfully. The Eqbas cruiser—it
helped Eddie to think of it in those terms—was now a large
ship with two escorts, two destroyers. The smaller sections
drifted away from the main section and rose out of sight
through the clouds in a tooth-shaking rumble. Where were
they going? He'd ask.

"Well, this gets the top slot for the next bulletin," he said,
as much for self-comfort as anything.

"Most impressive," said Nevyan. Giyadas clung to her legs.

It was just a ship, a visiting ship. But it felt like an invasion. If this was one routine vessel diverted simply because
it was closest to Wess'ej, he didn't want to think about what
was waiting on Eqbas.

The ship settled on the plain and the sound of its drive
dropped an octave as it powered down. The bee cam hovered, motionless. Then a huge Eqbas stepped out of the airlock onto the ramp and stood looking around before walking
with an easy rolling gait towards Nevyan.

It could only be a dominant matriarch. Her long multijointed hands were clasped in a prayer-like grip as she
walked and a spectacular mane of tufted copper red hair extended in a line down her forehead. Eddie was immediately
put in mind of a muscular and angry cockatoo. He didn't
fancy asking her if she wanted a cracker.

"Esganikan Gai," said Nevyan.

"Big girl," said Eddie, awed. "Wow. *Big* girl."

Esganikan, like all wess'har, didn't appear to know much
about personal space. She came close enough for him to
smell her slightly spicy breath and stared into his face, then
looked to Nevyan and trilled in a double-voice contralto. He
could smell a pleasant scent of fruit. Her ussissi aide,
Aitassi, settled beside her.

"She greets you and says she has several more of *these* on
board," said Aitassi, indicating Eddie.

Nevyan trilled back and Esganikan cocked her head both ways sharply. Eddie had never seen that before. He assumed Nevyan had spoken eqbas'u and that her fluency had come as a surprise. Or maybe she'd told Esganikan to watch her lip because *she* was the boss woman round here; it was hard to tell with wess'har. But at least neither of them had started throwing punches.

Esganikan turned towards the ship and more females emerged, equally formidable, wearing ornately quilted knee-length tunics in various shades of green and gray. There were males in the crew, too. Eddie was struck by the fact that the gender split seemed more equal. If there was one thing he had come to think of as normal on Wess'ej, it was that there were many more males than females.

"Extraordinary," said Nevyan.

"I thought so too," said Eddie, and assumed they were noticing the same thing.

"I thought you understood no eqbas'u."

"I don't."

"She said the detached craft had been sent to Bezer'ej and Umeh."

"Blimey, they're not starting a war already, are they?"

"They'll carry out a reconnaissance of Umeh from orbit and an environmental damage assessment on Bezer'ej. What did *you* find extraordinary, then?"

"Lots of females," he said. "Didn't you?"

Nevyan made a head-rocking gesture like an Indian dancer and didn't reply; Esganikan walked back to the ramp and waited, warbling to someone inside the hatch.

Then Ual appeared on the brow and there was a collective *ssssss* from the assembled matriarchs of F'nar.

They froze. Then they tilted their heads, riveted. Ual was the first isenj ever to set foot on Wess'ej, and Eddie let the bee cam loose for posterity.

And right behind Ual was Lindsay Neville.

She trooped down the ramp with Rayat, herded by the

three marines, but Nevyan didn't react. Her eyes were on
Ual. Out of the context of his crowded but intensely orderly
city, he looked shockingly sinister.

But he's almost a friend. I like him.

Eddie tried to steer Nevyan back to the subject of the
prisoners. "Beelzebub and his lovely assistant," he said help-
fully, nodding in their direction. Nevyan knew what a Royal
Marine uniform looked like so it should have been a simple
process of elimination. "What are you going to do with them
for the time being?"

"Kill them," she said calmly. "What is Beelzebub?"

Oh boy. But this wasn't Earth, and there were plenty of
places back home where they would have opted for summary execution with equal ease. It was none of his business.
"Just a name. Can I interview them first?"

"If you feel it might be useful."

Ual moved towards them with all the grace of a drinks trol-
ley with one broken wheel. Nevyan held out both arms and for
one awkward moment Eddie thought she might actually give
this old enemy a hug, but she was simply indicating that she
was the one he had to talk to. There was no reason for him to
pick her out from a group of apparently identical aliens.

"Thank you for not opening fire," he said, in perfect but
gasping English. "So this is where you choose to live, Mr.
Michallat. Matriarch Nevyan, you now have custody of the
two humans."

Nevyan paused, perhaps baffled by the use of the hon-
orific *matriarch.* Wess'har weren't much on protocol. "I
hadn't expected you to bring the prisoners personally. But if
you think you will return with Aras Sar Iussan, we will never
hand him over."

"I realize that. The risk I've taken is not what will happen
to me here but what happens when I go home after defying
my own government."

"And empty-handed."

"That depends on what I came for."

"We don't bargain. You have nothing that we want."

"Ah, but you have something *we* want."

Nevyan could do the silent routine as well as any interviewer. She waited, gaze fixed. Eddie wondered at what point he should do the diplomatic thing and break the impasse.

But Ual spoke at last. "I want a sustainable peace. I want wess'har to come to Umeh to help us resolve our environmental crisis."

Nevyan showed no shock or any emotion at all. Eddie, as he always did at times of crisis, just let the bee cam keep rolling.

There was a loud thump of a body hitting flagstones. It was hers. Shan was still having moments of not knowing where she was in relation to her body.

"Sod it," she said. "Sod it, sod it, *sod it.*"

She'd been so sure she could make it across the room to the toilet. She tried to kneel and was surprised how suddenly easy it was until she realized Aras had walked in and lifted her.

He scooped her up in his arms, laid her back on the bed and wrapped her tightly in a blanket, hissing with annoyance.

"You're to call me when you want to get up," he said, and put his hand on her chest. "You appear not to be breathing again."

No, she wasn't. *C'naatat* had found some other mechanism in its box of tricks for oxygenating her blood. She made a conscious effort to inhale and exhale, seeking the primitive unthinking rhythm again. "I got out of the habit. No jokes about breathing through my ears, okay? And I want to pee."

"I'll help you." He didn't seem to understand the joke. "You smell extremely dominant, so you must be feeling better."

She sniffed the back of her hand. There was a scent of mango with undertones of sawn wood. It was the wess'har pheromone that signaled matriarchal aggression, *jask,* powerful enough on occasions to make other females cede their authority to her. She'd changed F'nar politics once before without realizing it. This wasn't the time to be doing it again.

"I used to be able to control that," she said. "I promise I won't depose any more *isan've* by accident."

"You seem remarkably ebullient."

"I feel . . . okay."

Each time she shut her eyes and opened them again the miracle of being alive and *home* was fading. Aras's wonderful, mouth-filling sandalwood scent was the last thing to pall. *Hey, you're my old man.* She savored the elation of seeing again the one person who was in her thoughts as she died, but the police officer within, the one she knew had been there all her life, was telling her to calm down and get on with the job.

Don't be such a fucking girl. You didn't die. You're back. You're fine.

She wanted to surrender to tears and didn't know how. "I still need the toilet."

"I'll help you."

"I can manage, thanks. I don't suppose lavatory functions bother you, but they bother me." She paused at an embarrassing thought. "*Do* they bother you?"

"If you're asking if we dealt with your bodily wastes during your coma, we did not. You didn't excrete at all."

"It's your bedside manner I fell for," she said. "And who's *we*?"

"Ade and myself."

Ade. Oh yes indeed, she remembered Ade in detail now. She remembered, and she was waiting for him to come back into the room. "Christ, were you selling bloody tickets for the show?"

"Ade wanted to help. He's very distressed."

It was too late for that and it wasn't her condition that was troubling her. It was the big gaps in her knowledge; she didn't like gaps and she made a point of never having them. The absence of knowledge was more than the irritating whisper of a Suppressed Briefing. That, at least, let her know there really was some memory drug-programmed into her subconscious even if she didn't know what it was until some event triggered it. This was genuine oblivion.

The last thing she had done was to step out of the shuttle's cargo bay, apparently months ago. *Jesus Christ, I really did it, didn't I?* Now she was back on Wess'ej. Apart from the brief moments of awful consciousness while she drifted in the void, she didn't know what else had happened between the two events.

But she remembered about Lindsay Neville detonating nuclear devices on Ouzhari all right. Her recall of that was perfect.

"Where's Ade?"

"You said you wanted a cup of tea. He's gone to Nevyan's home to get some from Eddie."

Ade was a good soldier and good soldiers followed orders, including orders that said *get these bombs to Bezer'ej.* She couldn't blame him for that. *Lying on the ground deep in Constantine, mind-numbing pain in her legs and her guts, tape over her mouth, Ade threatening Lindsay that he'd slot her if she didn't put the grenades down. Fuck you, you shot Vijissi.* Oh yes, she remembered it all right.

He'd stopped Lindsay killing her—*really* killing her— with a grenade, so she owed him her life. It just didn't feel that way. She remembered the impact of rounds sputtering into her legs, her pelvis, knocking her down, punching through bone.

Later, girl. Take it easy. "Where's Vijissi? Did they find him too?"

Aras shook his head.

"He wouldn't leave me. Mestin told him to stick with me and he did, the poor little bastard."

Another friend gone, then, and she didn't have many. In fact there was just Aras, because she hadn't yet come to terms with Ade. *Aras.* She realized how precious he was to her, and how the full sweet realization of that in her final dying moment was being entombed forever behind her workaday indifference. She didn't want to lose the feeling. She reached for it desperately; it started to slip away. She panicked, clutching at it like a key falling into deep water.

"I know I should say something really significant."

"*Isan,* I wish you would rest."

"You were my final thought." *It was your last few seconds and you'd have given anything to tell him you loved him. Now you can't even say the fucking word out loud.* "I didn't tell you how I felt."

It just never came out the way it should. Perhaps she really didn't have any normal human feelings, just like Lindsay had said. She wanted Aras's unerring gift for saying what he felt, and being able to feel in the first place.

Aras did that canine head-tilt, and she knew exactly which part of her was the hard-arsed copper who found his openness and courage utterly disarming, and which was wess'har, altered by *c'naatat* and bonded to him biologically through *oursan.*

"I was never offended," he said. "I know you're not a demonstrative person."

"Do you want me to say it?"

"When you feel ready." He ran his palm over her scalp. Her hand followed his: the stubble felt like someone had given her a buzz cut. "Your *c'naatat* needs feeding. See how fast it restores you."

"I'm starving. I could eat a scabby cat with piles."

"I recall that was your requested menu last time you were injured," he said. He could approximate a human smile, but he never showed his teeth. "I have more appetizing solid food."

"Bathroom," she said. She wanted to ask him why he wasn't more excited to see her alive but perhaps it was the shock. You couldn't just snap out of bereavement. She had to give him time. "*C'naatat*'s definitely working overtime."

She let him carry her to the toilet door and she shut herself in, still draped in the blanket because she couldn't bear
to look at her own body. The toilet bowl was handsome
aquamarine glass shot with deliberate bubbles and flaws, a
work of art that deserved better appreciation than the steady
assault of waste. Wess'har were master glassmakers and a
generous but anonymous individual had made the bowl and
cistern to a design provided by Constantine colony. Shan
pulled the flush. The water swirled.

Constantine was gone too.

She remembered preparing the colony for evacuation.
Three paces outside the toilet, her legs buckled again. Aras
rushed to pick her up but she waved him away, panting. She
crawled on all fours, frustrated to be helpless, but she felt . . .
better, hungry and optimistic, strength and energy building
in her. Sweat stung her eyes: *c'naatat* was burning her up,
stoking her metabolism and making up for lost time.

It didn't quite get her as far as the bed, though. She got to
her knees but it was one effort too many and Aras had to lift
her onto the mattress.

"I'm glad we don't have any mirrors," she said. She could
see the pity on his face and his un-wess'har reluctance to
meet her eyes. "I look like hell, don't I? Okay, don't answer
that. Tell me what I've missed."

"What do you remember?"

"Everything." *C'naatat* didn't believe in the blissful era-
sure that normally went with serious trauma. It spared her
nothing. "Right up to the time I stepped out—" She stopped.
"I *had* Lindsay Neville. I swear I put a round through the
bitch but she was wearing a vest. She *did* detonate the bombs,
didn't she?"

"She did."

"And Bezer'ej? The colony? Why Eddie and Ade are
here?"

"Perhaps you should wait until you're feeling stronger,
isan."

"Well, that's guaranteed to pique my curiosity. My brain's strong enough, thanks. Tell me."

Aras made that long, slow hiss of annoyance. "The devices were salted with cobalt."

Shan wasn't a scientist but she'd worked in EnHaz long enough to have a good grasp of the league table of biohazards. "Shit."

"The area is heavily contaminated. We've yet to find any bezeri who aren't dead or dying." Aras shut his eyes. "Nevyan ordered the destruction of *Actaeon*. And the World Before has now sent two vessels to our aid, with others to follow."

Oh God. There was only so much you could take in at one sitting. "Where's Lin now?"

Aras didn't answer. It wasn't a good sign. He still had that blisteringly frank wess'har habit of saying the first thing that came into his head so anything that interrupted the unedited flow had to be serious. It meant he didn't want to upset her: it also meant he knew she might do something extreme if she knew where Lindsay was, and *that* told her either the bitch was accessible or she had escaped.

But where the hell could anyone escape out here?

"I'll make your meal," he said, and left.

She fumed. A few minutes later Ade appeared with the promised mug of tea. He spent an inordinate amount of time turning it in his hands, looking like a man trying to find the right words.

"Come here," she said, trying very hard to choke down anger that for once had no specific target. Ade edged towards her. Something inside her was burning to be out, to get at him, to . . .

"Boss," he said. He was standing over her, turning the mug in his hand. "Boss, I . . ."

Shan gathered what strength she had and brought her right fist up hard, smashing the mug from his hands and sending it shattering on the floor. He stepped back, mouth open in the formation of some excuse that she didn't want to hear. She'd rarely lost control, *ever.* Now she abandoned herself to rage.

"You bastard," she hissed. "You *bastard,* you fucking well let her get me, you fucking well—" She slumped half out of the bed, spent by the effort. Adrenaline consumed her. Then it ebbed and faded, and she was left panting, hanging off the edge of the mattress. Ade went to lift her. "Fuck off—fuck off out of my sight, you bastard—"

Aras slammed open the door and was between them in three strides.

"Enough! Go, Ade. Leave her. And you, *isan,* you will calm down, do you hear?"

Ade's face was stricken, devastated. He froze for a moment and then strode out, crunching over broken glass.

Aras lifted her back onto the pillows and she accepted his hand on her forehead. He slipped into a characteristic infrasonic rumbling, the kind wess'har fathers emitted to comfort a fretting child, and shame washed over her along with the profound and irresistible feeling of warm heaviness.

You lost it. Where's your discipline? You never lost it out there. Get a grip.

In an instant, she wanted both to beg Ade's forgiveness and to kick the shit out of him for helping useless, make-believe officer Lindsay fucking Neville transport bombs to Bezer'ej and force her to space herself.

"I don't think I handled that well," she said at last.

Aras's comforting rumble trailed off into silence. "Did you fire first, or did Ade?"

Perfect wess'har recall dredged up the exact sequence of events on Constantine with an unflinching accuracy that her human memory once struggled to achieve. She was looking down at Lindsay, rifle to her forehead.

"Maybe Ade, maybe Mart." It was almost instantaneous: she could feel the trigger yielding under her finger, the first round hitting her in the pelvis, her rifle discharging into Lindsay's ballistic vest. "But I was putting one through Lindsay."

Aras ahrugged. "What would you have done if you were Ade, or Mart Barencoin?"

Shan felt a flutter of regret in her stomach. If either of them were as hard-trained as she was, then she knew: *she would have fired.* It was an unthinking reflex.

"And I fired back." She reached out for Aras's hand. "I just went on autopilot."

"Well, then," said Aras. He never implied rebukes—he would chide her respectfully—but his reasonable tone was as good as one. "And there's more you need to know."

"Is this going to piss me off even more?"

"Perhaps." He slid his arm round her shoulders and leaned his forehead against hers. "I hardly know how to tell you."

"Try me. You know you can tell me anything."

He took his time. She waited.

"I killed Josh."

She almost asked him how it felt to kill a former friend. Then she realized she knew already, even if Lindsay had survived the attempt.

It was all too bloody easy.

"Well, serves the bastard right." Josh had taken Lindsay and Rayat to Christopher Island—Ouzhari—*knowing* they planned to deploy ERDs. He had his own pious logic. She hoped he had his excuses ready for his god. "But I'm bloody sorry for you, sweetheart."

Aras straightened up. "There are other matters, too."

"Are we getting near the end of the list or what?"

"Perhaps I should let Ade explain. He insisted that he should. Will you promise to hear him out this time?"

"Okay."

Shan had been pretty sure she knew Ade. Reliable, decent, sensible: a solid sergeant, the sort that every army—and police force—was built upon. He did his duty, even when politicians wanted him to do stupid, dangerous things, and even when it meant shooting her. She had come perilously close to sleeping with him but—as always—discipline and the prospect of his bioscreen broadcasting the event to the rest of the marines stopped her.

Bioscreen.

She hadn't noticed the green light in his palm this time. Maybe he'd deactivated it. "So he knew about the bombs."

"None of them knew about the cobalt except Rayat. No, Ade now finds himself in a very difficult position."

"He deserted?" *No insignia.* She could still take in every detail without thinking. *Hey, I'm back.* "Is that why he removed his stripes?"

"He *surrendered*," said Aras. "He had no choice. You . . . you infected him, *isan.* You injured him. Do you remember?"

Crack. Her head smashed into the bridge of Ade's nose as he tried to pin her down. She remembered that. But Lindsay had checked her out. She hadn't found a break in her skin. *Useless cow.*

"Don't be hard on him," said Aras. "He fed you when Nevyan brought you back. He read to you. He is utterly devoted to your welfare, whatever has happened."

Shan shut her eyes.

"Shit," she said. "Oh *shit.*"

9

"That," said Rayat, "is exquisite."

Lindsay saw the wall of shimmering white pearl as they
passed the edge of the inland cliff. She wasn't sure what she
was looking at and then her perspective kicked in and resolved it into the concave bowl of a vast amphitheater.

F'nar looked even more shockingly unreal than it did in
Eddie's reports. It seemed more bizarre, more organic, as if
aliens had found a book on Antonio Gaudi's architecture
and had a stab at making it their own vernacular style. It
was almost captivating enough to divert her from the realization that she had an unspecified but very short time left
to live.

"Yeah, lovely," she muttered, and followed Mart Barencoin's broad back. He still had that habit of looking around
and then walking backwards for a few paces as if he was still
on patrol. "Where are we going? I didn't think they had pris-
ons or police stations here."

"We do not, Lindsay Neville," said a ussissi voice. "You
will go to the Exchange of Surplus Things, unless a clan is
willing to accommodate you. But that depends when they
execute you. An overnight stay might not be necessary."

She glanced down. She had difficulty telling ussissi apart,

distinguishing them only by their taste in bandoleer-type belts of bright fabric or beaded embroidery.

"Are you Ralassi?" she asked.

"Idiot," said the ussissi. "I'm Serrimissani. I'm a female. Ralassi is male. No wonder your species is doomed."

"It's a pleasure to meet you, too."

"I once worked with Ual. I now work with Nevyan."

Lindsay noted she used the word *with*, not *for*. "I thought we'd be dead as soon as we stepped off the ship."

"That would be normal procedure. But there is information required first."

"About what?"

"Culpability. Technology. Whatever the Eqbas require."

Serrimissani certainly spoke excellent English. That didn't comfort Lindsay one bit. She kept her head up as she walked, but this didn't feel like being a prisoner of war. She now had no sense of being on the right side and just unfortunate to be captured: she felt like a criminal. She had always wondered why captives didn't try to escape, why those herded into prison camps never rose and overthrew their guards, and now she knew. Docility in the face of threatening authority was an automatic response. There were very few Shan Franklands in the human species.

But Lindsay knew she was responsible for something terrible, and the wess'har were right. She had to take the blame.

The wess'har she passed simply glanced at her. There were no stones thrown or abuse hurled.

"They're very restrained," said Rayat.

"Shan always said *chilled or punching*. This is chilled." Barencoin glanced over his shoulder at her as if to shut her up. "I think we all know what punching is going to be like."

"And yet you're not on their wanted list, Mr. Barencoin," said Rayat.

Barencoin walked on, oblivious. Jon Becken, right behind them, responded for him. "Yeah, it's our boyish good looks and smart uniforms. Everyone loves a Royal Marine."

"We had friends in high places," said Webster.

At the Exchange of Surplus Things—a big hall with door-less side rooms and absolutely no trappings of grandeur—Ual and Eddie stood talking like old chums while Nevyan and Esganikan watched them with that odd display of head tilting. Wess'har wandered in and out with crates and mesh bags of unrecognizable produce, pausing to stare at the activity in the main hall, but it seemed more curiosity than anger. The place smelled of soil and sandalwood and indefinable vegetable scents. Lindsay felt that she was standing trial in a supermarket.

Serrimissani broke from the discussion and scuttled towards Lindsay, but she slid in between her and Rayat, cutting out the scientist like a sheepdog. "Do you have *virin've*? Communications devices? If so, we require them."

"Yes." Rayat hesitated but Lindsay held out hers. There was no harm they could do with them. "There you go."

"What do you want it for?" said Rayat.

"To determine culpability," said Serrimissani.

Rayat stared down at Serrimissani and she drew back her lips ever so slightly, just enough to reveal a mouthful of close-packed little teeth. He fumbled in his jacket and pulled out his handheld. She took it and he flinched when her paw brushed his hand.

Rayat looked at Lindsay and shrugged. "A show trial, perhaps?"

"Not their style. And they're not taking them because they think we're going to call in air support."

Serrimissani and Aitassi were conferring, brandishing the two handhelds while Eddie watched the exchange with a slight frown of concentration. He didn't look her way, perhaps deliberately. Esganikan Gai drew herself up and covered the ten meters to where Lindsay and Rayat were sitting in a few strides. There was something about her manner that reminded Lindsay of Shan, and that wasn't reassuring.

She stared into Lindsay's face and then into Rayat's, head tilting, pupils flaring and closing, and trilled. Serrimissani trotted up beside her.

"She says she needs to understand who is to blame for the events on Bezer'ej so that appropriate action may be taken—no more, no less."

Lindsay really didn't like wess'har eyes. It was the way the four pupils constricted to a hairline cross: it made them look like the blind voids of a statue's eyes, soulless and unfathomable. Her interrogation resistance training enabled her to simply look through the Eqbas, but it wasn't easy.

"That's simple enough," said Lindsay. There was nothing else left to say. "It was me and him."

Esganikan warbled. Serrimissani appeared to be struggling with the translation and summoned Aitassi. Eventually an English version was extracted.

"She says that fact is not at issue," said Serrimissani. "You did not bring weapons of this kind with you in *Thetis*. So another generation was complicit. The Eqbas need to know who authorized or ordered you to take these actions, and then who took steps to right these wrongs, or did not, because they must be held accountable when we reach Earth."

Reach Earth.

"But half the people you want to punish could be dead and gone in twenty-five years' time," said Lindsay, hearing the words *reach Earth* and desperate to shut out their true meaning.

"Thirty years," said Serrimissani. "And what your people do between now and then will be added to the reckoning."

Ade stood at the door, a new mug in his hand.

Shan swallowed her embarrassment and steeled herself for an apology. Being wrong was easy, and so was admitting error. But real regret—regret at lashing out at someone prepared to give their life for you—was hard. She was sorry for very few things in her life, but every one of them ate away at her.

Something in the back of her mind said she had done something particularly unforgivable to Ade.

"So, you got me killed, and I gave you a dose," she said, saving him the trouble of finding the first words. "I think we're even." No, that wasn't good enough. "Okay. I started the shooting. Sorry."

He looked up without raising his chin. After twenty-five years of nicking guilty bastards she was utterly immune to appealing contrition, even in a man she fancied, but he wasn't putting it on.

"No, *I'm* sorry, Boss. If you think you can hate me any more than I hate myself, you're wrong."

"If I hadn't been about to blow Lin's brains out, would you have fired?"

Ade chewed his lip. "I don't know."

"Well, you stopped her turning me into hamburger. Even *c'naatat* couldn't have put me back together again after that." He was a good meter from her and clearly still too scared to hand her the mug. Her voice sounded like an old woman's, hoarse and cracking. "Shit, Ade, I'm sorry. I should never have said those things to you."

"It's okay, Boss. I know you've been through hell." *Hell.*

She thought again about the moment the shuttle's bay opened to space and she pushed herself off the edge of the coaming into the most profound emptiness a human could conceive. The first minute of dying *had* been hell, yes. They said you could last maybe twelve seconds in space. But that was for regular humans.

The brief episodes of consciousness that followed, with no sense of duration or frequency, were far worse. She couldn't feel a thing: she was isolated in her own head, a place she had never much liked being. The blind, all-consuming panic when she opened her eyes and realized where she was had been worse than the pain. She fought it.

Do your worst. You think you can break me? I can handle this. I can do anything. *Fuck you, I'm going to stay sane because there's nothing more you can do to me.*

She remembered thinking that like a mantra; *fuck you, fuck you, fuck you.* She realized she'd been railing against

God just in case she'd been wrong, and there really was a deity out there somewhere to hear her contempt and defiance. But there wasn't. There was just her, a scrap of dried meat fueled by anger, and she'd still held on to her sense of self. And she had *come back*. Nothing, absolutely *nothing* could ever touch her inner core now.

"Want to talk?" asked Ade. "I mean, it—"

"Maybe later," she said. The detail could wait. "Not yet."

"Okay."

"Is it true you looked after me? Read to me?"

Ade nodded. "Too little too late, eh?"

"I've had my tantrum. The slate's clear."

"Stop trying to spare my feelings."

"I can't be arsed to spare anyone's feelings, Ade." *Spare mine. Stop being kind. Get angry, for Chrissakes.* "Do I get that tea or what?"

"I was so sure I knew what I was going to say to you."

Ade's face fell a little more. He didn't look any different: no claws, bioluminescence or any of the visible retro-fit improvements that her own *c'naatat* colony had added. She'd been devastated when she found out that Aras had deliberately infected her. The fact that he'd done it to save her life was lost in the brief, raging, utterly desolate realization that she would never be able to leave.

"Ade, do you realize what I've given you? Look at me, Ade. You can't go home. *Ever.* You can't have kids. You can't even sleep with a woman again. Do you understand what all that means?"

His lips moved and she wasn't sure if he was forming a reply or trembling. "I know. But I'm alive, and the bezeri aren't." There was a long pause. "So, serves me right, eh?"

"Did you object to your orders?"

"Not enough."

"Well, you probably did all you could." Shan looked longingly at the mug of tea beyond her reach. She would have told Lin to stuff her orders, but then she had never been a soldier. Police had their own way of ignoring instructions

they didn't fancy obeying. She had never been in Ade's position so she had no right to judge. *And I can't expect everyone
to be me.* "If an officer and a spook order you, I don't think
you have a lot of choice."

"No, *everyone* has a choice."

"And having a choice, you must make it."

"Sorry?"

"Targassat. Those who can act, must." She held out her
hand to him. She knew what it was to be a leper. "You did
choose, actually. You stopped her fragging me." Perhaps the
next question was one too many. "What did you feel when
you shot me?"

Ade took her hand reluctantly. It must have felt repellent,
skeletal, but he closed one hand around it and then the other.
"Nothing. The second the firing stared I went on auto. Just
reflex. I'm sorry."

"It's what we all do. Or we end up dead."

"I don't even know how to say this. I'm not Eddie."

"What?"

"When you—when you just stepped out." His eyes filled
with tears: she was shocked by his emotion. Adoration
shone out of him. "You're the . . . you're . . . sod it, Boss,
you're a fucking hero. A real fucking hero."

"Bollocks." She couldn't meet his eyes any longer. "Can I
have that bloody tea now?"

She couldn't quite manage the weight of the mug, not
even with both hands. He held it while she drank. She was so
desperate for the comforting taste that she didn't mind the
humiliation of being fed like a child. It was bliss.

"They're here, you know," said Ade.

"Who? The World Before?"

"Yeah. Eqbas Vorhi." He wiped her chin. She didn't protest.
"Their second ship's just shown up. They don't look like the
local wess'har and they don't speak wess'u. And they—well,
Nevyan can tell you. She's with them now." Ade shut down.
His gaze dropped and he lowered both his chin and his voice.

"And what? Come on, Ade, *what*?"

Aras strode back in to the room, emitting the acidic scent of agitation. He loomed over Ade. "You eat first, *isan,*" he said, and put a bowl down a little too hard on the nearby table. It steamed alluringly, wafting that spicy scent she'd noticed earlier. "And when you're able to walk unaided, you can involve yourself in public life again. Until then, you stay put and *eat.*"

Nobody gave Shan orders. Her normal reaction would have been to walk out and investigate for herself. But she peered under the covers and she could see her ribs, and not just the lower ones like any fit individual might. It was the whole rib cage, top to bottom, with no visible sign of abdominal muscle or pectorals or breasts. It looked as if some zealous medical student had removed every scrap of fat and muscle from a cadaver and then replaced the skin as an afterthought, just to keep everything tidy. She couldn't begin to imagine what her face looked like. At least she hadn't had any looks to lose.

"Okay," she said, swallowing hard. For all the feeling of renewed confidence, a voice inside her reminded her she wasn't that far the other side of dead. *Get a grip, girl. You've come through a lot worse than looking like shit.* "Here's the deal. I eat, and you find me someone to teach me eqbas'u."

"I'll do it," said Ade. "No problem, Boss."

Poor sod. Her anger had burned out. They were three freaks of nature; they had to stick together.

A vague memory of needing to run and hide—not hers—intruded and dissolved again. She settled back on the pillow and decided to pursue it after Aras had finished feeding her.

She didn't enjoy being helpless. Not at all.

Language was frustrating Nevyan. Esganikan was learning wess'u rapidly but Ual was happier with English; ironically, it was the one tongue that appeared to unite them. Mart Barencoin was a welcome oasis of familiar language even if it was an alien one.

He took a few cautious steps towards her in the Exchange of Surplus Things, his two comrades watching him carefully.

"What are you planning to do with us, ma'am?" He was a little taller than she was, and fascinatingly dark: she remained intrigued by the exotic variety of color in human hair and eyes. "We can make ourselves useful."

Nevyan wasn't sure if she should mention Shan to him. "Do you really want to go to Mar'an'cas? It's not very hospitable."

Barencoin shrugged. "Chaz and Izzy could do with some help."

"You have no need to punish yourselves just because I won't do it for you."

"I do feel responsible, actually. In human law, I would be."

"It was Neville, Rayat and the two colonists who took them to Ouzhari who set and detonated the devices. They had the choice not to use them; you transported the devices, which was foolish, but no more foolish than carrying a *tilgir* and then *not* using it to kill someone." She paused to see if there was any comprehension on his face. "Aras has already executed Joshua Garrod. We will locate his companion in due course."

Barencoin reacted visibly to the mention of Garrod with a small jerk of the head; he smelled agitated. Nevyan was never sure whether to check what humans didn't know, another problem in dealing with a species that had such a bizarre and proprietorial attitude to information. They told each other some things and not others. She knew now why they needed people like Eddie Michallat.

"What did Josh do that I didn't?"

"He helped Neville set the bombs and activate them."

"I transported them. Ade and—"

"Can you not see the line?"

Barencoin's bewilderment made him look much more like a human child. "I don't think I'm going to get the hang of this culpability thing, ma'am." He kept glancing at that light grown into his palm, his bioscreen. All the marines had one: so did Lindsay Neville. Nevyan understood why Shan found the device repellent. "Can we visit Mar'an'cas and assess the situation? And can we see Sergeant Bennett?"

So they still clung to their old identities even after their government had discharged them. Nevyan found that sad. They had no other community, not even in the displaced Constantine colony. "Later."

"Just tell me if he's okay. I know there's something wrong."

"He's well." Secrecy was very hard work. She didn't like it at all. "He's had unexpected news, as have we all. When he's ready, you can see him."

Barencoin made that shoulder-hunching gesture and raised his eyebrows, indicating he didn't understand, and she fought a natural urge to explain to him as she would to Giyadas. "We'll wait," he said, as if he had another option.

The Exchange of Surplus Things was becoming what Eddie called a *circus*. He'd explained what that was and she couldn't see the comparison at all. Shapakti and his crew were moving equipment and Esganikan was taking great interest in Ual while Eddie hovered at his side. Fersanye had volunteered to keep Rayat and Lindsay under control in her home because her clan was accustomed to aliens, having provided brief lodging for Shan Frankland. And many wess'har were simply turning up to deposit and collect produce, stare at the extraordinary tableau, and wander off about their business.

Nevyan wanted quiet order again. This was all her doing. *You invited them.* It was an uncomfortable time, but something had changed: Shan was back. She felt her confidence growing. She wasn't alone out in front any longer.

"Hey, Ade!" said Barencoin suddenly. "Where you been, you daft bugger?"

Ade Bennett had come into the hall as if looking for someone. The other marines moved towards him and he came to a halt, smiling, but folded his arms awkwardly and tightly across his chest in that characteristic keep-your-distance gesture she'd seen Shan use so often. Wess'har parted conspicuously to let him pass and Barencoin glanced at them.

"Waiting for you tossers to show up," said Ade, clearly with affection.

"You look bloody well. They treating you okay?"

"Like royalty."

"We brought some guests."

"Yeah. I know."

"What's wrong? I thought you wanted to kick seven shades of shit out of them."

"I'm a bit busy."

"Why didn't you go to Mar'an'cas?"

"I did."

"And?"

"I came back, all right?" There was that slight edge to his tone that said he was the dominant male. Nevyan watched, waiting for the fight. "Look, I have to sort something right now. See Eddie. He'll get you something to eat." Ade turned to Nevyan. "Is that okay, ma'am? Can they go to your place?"

Nevyan felt she was collecting stray humans. It would amuse Giyadas, though. Her adopted sons didn't share the *isan'ket*'s fascination with the *gethes* language, but they would watch them for amusement anyway. "I'm sure Eddie is happy to share his food."

But Barencoin didn't appear interested in a meal. He exhibited rare tenacity. He had spotted something. "Ade, there's something *well* weird going on. What's up?"

"Later," said Ade. "And I fucking mean it, okay? *Later.*"

Then Barencoin reached out towards Ade's shoulder. Nevyan expected it to be an aggressive gesture and prepared to intervene, but Ade took a step back.

"I thought as much," said Barencoin, suddenly red-faced. "Oh shit, Ade. You've got it, haven't you?"

"It's not a dose of clap. And for Chrissakes keep your voice down."

"Shit." Barencoin backed off and turned to his two comrades, evidently appalled. He was still glancing back at Ade and muttering *shit* while he herded them towards Eddie.

"They can keep their mouths shut," Ade reassured Nevyan. "God knows how he'll react when he finds Shan's alive."

"It makes no difference now. *C'naatat* is beyond human reach again."

Ade jerked his thumb in the direction of Shapakti. "Now his boss-woman's here, can she spare him to do Shan a favor?"

"Is that wise?"

"Shan wants to learn the language. She speaks wess'u and so does he. He can teach her."

"I'll ask Esganikan."

"How much does she know about Shan?"

"She knows as much as I do. We don't conceal matters from each other. It's a most corrosive habit and I would like to get out of it soon."

Ade shrugged. "Okay. Shan doesn't know Lin and Rayat are here, by the way. Aras thought she'd go off on one if we told her."

"Is she well enough to talk to me?" Shan would understand that Nevyan had duties to carry out before she could visit a friend. Aras needed time with her first. It occurred to Nevyan that Ade might need that too, but that was a matter for the three of them to resolve. "I should be with her, at least for a little while."

"She's eating everything that doesn't move and swearing like a trooper, so apart from the fact she looks like a corpse, she's getting back to normal."

"A harsh assessment."

"What did you expect me to do, cry my eyes out at the state of her?" Ade fumbled with his beret and shoved it into his pocket. "Done that. She doesn't need reminding what a state she's in."

"Do you want to talk to Commander Neville?"

"I've got nothing to say to her."

"Will you help us to examine the material on her communication device and Rayat's?"

Ade glanced down at his boots. They were exceptionally shiny. "What are we looking for?"

"We want to know who authorized the use of nuclear devices."

"The FEU."

"Personally. Organizations aren't responsible. People are." Nevyan beckoned Aitassi: the aide would trust him to extract information. "And even if they're no longer alive when we reach Earth, those who later contribute to their guilt will be."

Nevyan saw that same reversion to a child's face: Ade Bennett understood responsibility no better than Barencoin did, although both of them clearly wanted to. She wondered how any *gethes* would ever learn.

If they didn't learn, the Eqbas would teach them the hard way.

Ade skipped his daily run for the first time in more than twenty years, barring days when he'd actually been in combat. He'd do an extra few kilometers tomorrow. Once you let things slip, you lost all discipline.

But Shan's alive.

The thought kept rolling over him anew as if he'd forgotten—as if he could. He had a second chance. You didn't get those often and you didn't waste them. He jogged back home along the terraces, occasionally feeling for the two handhelds in his top pocket, and realized that he didn't actually have a clue what he was going to do with that unimaginable opportunity.

He leaned on the pearl-encrusted door and it swung open. The smell of hot oil and caramelizing sugars filled the living room and the table was covered in plates and bowls. Aras, holding a sizzling pan in one hand, gave Ade an exasperated look and motioned him to the table.

"Hey, I just saw Mart and Sue and—" Ade paused. Shan

was up. She was *really* up, in every sense. She was standing in front of the screen that occupied a large section of one wall, a walking corpse in her formal black uniform pants and a white sports vest. Neither fitted her any longer. She looked freshly horrific.

"Shit," she said. "What the fuck's happening back there?" Something on the BBChan news feed was annoying her. Then she stopped and glanced over her shoulder. "Hi, Ade. Find me anyone?"

"Nevyan's going to ask Esganikan."

"And she is?" Shan set an unsteady but determined course for the table and half fell onto the bench beside it. She reached for a pile of *netun jay* and munched contentedly.

"She's the commander of the second Eqbas mission."

"Yeah, I'm going to want to talk to her."

How long had he been away? A matter of *hours.* Shan's arms had some suggestion of sinews and he could no longer see bone across the full width of her chest. Her black hair was almost a respectable crew cut, slightly fluffy and thick enough to make her look more like a woman again. And she was, as far as she was concerned, back in charge of the operation. It was written all over her, from the set of her shoulders to that way she had of clenching her jaw.

"I'm waiting," she said. She was eating like a horse; *netun,* those nice little chewy flat-breads Aras called *gurut,* a bowl of an bright orange *evem* soup, and a large jug of tea. "I can't just sit here on my arse all day."

"You can." Ade decided to distract her from expeditions and laid the handhelds on the table. She was a copper. She'd done more investigations than he'd had hot dinners. She knew her way around records and files. "Take a look at this."

She picked up the handhelds and turned them over. "That reminds me," she said. "Can I have my sidearm and my swiss back, please?"

Aras smelled annoyed, a scent almost like grapefruit oil. Ade was finding that kind of cue easier to pick up now.

"Yes, *isan*. But you have no need to go out and use them, have you?"

"I'll sit and eat until I'm fit to go out. That was the deal."

She examined Rayat's device with one hand, taking a bite out of a *netun* and wiping a stray bead of bright gold filling off her chin with a careful finger. The handheld clicked into life and she studied the image. Ade liked to watch her think. It was exciting to imagine what process was going on in that agile, ferocious mind, as long as he wasn't on the receiving end of it.

"Nevyan needs information from that," he said.

"I really ought to do a verified copy of the data before I go crashing around. You know me, stick to rules of evidence." Her eyes were fixed on the device, appraising and unemotional. Then she almost smiled. "What do you want to find?"

Aras slammed the pan down on the range and leaned across the table, hands flat on it. "Enough," he hissed. "She isn't well enough for this."

"Sweetheart, I'm a big girl and I'll decide what I need to know." She put her hand on his. "This is what I do. I'm a copper." She paused as if something funny had occurred to her. "Do you know, I never put my papers in? I never actually resigned. Is Wessex Regional Constabulary still there any more? Did anyone tell them I was dead so they could release my pension?"

"I can find out for you," said Ade. He never worried about his pension. "Here, have some tea."

"This means you've had contact with Rayat."

"Leave him to Nevyan," said Aras.

"He's alive and here, then?"

"I—"

"Aras, I've managed to keep my head for two months in space without a fucking suit." Her tone was calm and she squeezed his hand, but it was tinted with warning. Ade could see her knuckles whiten. "I'm capable of hearing a sitrep from Ade without going ballistic. Go on, Ade. Brief me."

Ade felt he was pushing Aras's self-control to the limit. Wess'har didn't seem to have much, not as far as anger was concerned. He glanced at Aras's grim expression, and then at Shan: and Shan was the Boss. He deferred.

"Ual brought Rayat and Lindsay here. Mart, Sue and Jon arrested them."

"Result." She gave him an approving thumbs-up, apparently unconcerned. "Nice job."

"Actually, they turned up in the second Eqbas ship. The commander is a big scary bird called Esganikan Gai."

"But you're not afraid of big scary birds, are you?"

"Nah." He grinned, feeling a little precious warmth from her. "Not usually."

She winked. "Good."

"And they've sent teams to recce Umeh and Bezer'ej from orbit."

Shan thumbed the controls of the handheld. "What am I looking for in here?"

"Culpability. That's what Serrimissani called it."

"Explicit orders to deploy ERDs."

"Yeah."

"Personal, not collective, right?"

"Names."

Shan reached for another *gurut* and chewed carefully while she browsed through files. If she hadn't looked so skeletal and swamped by her uniform, she could easily have passed for her old self, in control, analytical, and not about to take any shit: a senior detective going about her business. He wondered if she was going to collapse when his back was turned.

"Get me my swiss, will you, sweetheart?" she said, eyes not moving from the handheld. Ade went to the cupboard and reached for it at the same time Aras did. They stared at each other for a second too long and Ade felt his face redden.

Silly sod. She didn't mean you.

Aras took the swiss and handed it to Ade with an expression and scent that he simply couldn't read at all. If Shan had seen the reaction, she showed no sign of it. But she never missed a trick and Ade felt inexplicably humiliated.

Ade surrendered the swiss. "Thanks," she said. No, she was completely deadpan. He couldn't even smell a reaction, and he was sure he could do that by now. "Now, this is what you do. You shove this in *here*. A little upgrade I borrowed when I was in Special Branch."

Both the swiss and Rayat's handheld made a satisfying simultaneous *chunk* sound and Shan smiled, not at him or Aras but to herself.

"I'd have thought a spook's kit would have been harder to crack," said Ade.

"Yeah, they often think that too," said Shan. "It pays to play Mr. Plod. Anyway, Rayat wouldn't want to draw attention to himself if anyone from the *Thetis* payload picked this up. But all I've done is get in. Rayat's too professional to have obviously encrypted stuff. Anyway, what are we looking for? Some dialogue that shows he was given explicit instructions to use Beano bombs? Okay, tell me what you know about the sequence of events that led up to deployment."

Ade wasn't sure where to start. "When we started planning to use the Once-Only suits?"

"When Rayat got involved."

Ade shut his eyes and imagined himself back on board *Actaeon* again. *Think. In* Actaeon's *armory, Neville and me and Rayat looking at the racks.* "He was using his handheld as if he was messaging someone, and then he wanted to know if we could get ERDs down to the surface in the Once-Only suits. I said yes because they were about thirty kilos each, and I said it was a bad idea. Then Commander Neville said he couldn't deploy ERDs and they had an argument about Beano bombs too. She was adamant they weren't going to use any, and Rayat wasn't going to discuss it in front of me so I asked her if she wanted me to leave and she said yes."

"Well, she's as good as dead anyway so her motive doesn't matter now." Shan scrolled and tapped, eyes moving between her swiss and the handheld. "He couldn't encrypt on the ITX so if he was phoning home, it was either plain language or code. Let's have a look at his message log."

"He won't have one. He'll have done a fast shred."

Shan turned the handheld so that Ade could see it. It was just a screen of numbers and symbols. "Outgoing message paths. He hasn't bothered to erase them. And he's not that careless." She chewed her lip thoughtfully. Aras hovered again, taking her left hand and folding her fingers around a mug as a silent order to drink its contents. "He hasn't sent that many in the past six months, which isn't surprising really. Let's have a look at the address book."

"Not even Lindsay would be thick enough to file a number labeled SPOOK HQ."

"They're going to show up on Earth with a warrant, aren't they?"

"Who?"

"Esganikan and company. They'd better hope the suspects are going to be around in twenty-five years' time. Or maybe they're just looking for an excuse for a punch-up."

"That's not very wess'har."

"No. But they must have thought about the time differential."

"Surely."

"Yeah, surely." The idea was bothering her, he could see that, a puzzle she couldn't crack. "But if the alternative is to say the guilty parties might be dead when you turn up, then you might as well write off the whole crime. And wess'har don't seem to believe in a statute of limitations or spent convictions."

"They said something about *those who later contribute to their guilt.*"

Shan appeared to consider that and then flicked through files. Ade moved to look over her shoulder. She shifted a little, evidently uncomfortable, and then tugged at his pants leg.

"Sit down."

"Sorry."

"Is there any slang term for Beano bombs?"

"That *is* the slang. Biological neutralization ordnance."

"Any *other* names?"

"Oh . . . bleach. Floor cleaners."

Aras sat down at the table opposite Shan and tucked into the pile of *gurut,* making a faint riffling sound like someone flicking through a wad of paper. Ade had never heard it before.

"What are you so pleased about?" asked Shan.

The *urrrring* sound stopped. "You're home, *isan.*"

"Yeah, I'm glad to be back, too," she said. "I really am."

It was a brief moment and one that didn't include Ade. He'd have to get used to that. Shan laid aside the handheld for a moment and wolfed down more *netun.*

"Is it me, or is it hot in here?"

"It's you," said Aras.

"Okay, cool-down time," she said, and made an unsteady path for the back terrace, the rear one that overlooked the plain. Aras had excavated his home at the furthest edge of the caldera. He must have had a hard time coming to terms with being *c'naatat* in a city where everyone was part of a family.

There was an uneasy silence. Aras opened the large container he had built for Black and White and placed food in their green glass bowl. Ade wandered across and stood watching, trying to find the right moment to talk.

Two noses poked out of the nest ball of shredded fabric, then the rats waddled out and snatched chunks of capsicum and soybeans. They rushed into separate corners to devour them.

"You're going to thump me, aren't you?" said Ade.

Aras began *urrrring* again. He could still talk while he was doing it. Ade was fascinated and realized how dully human he must have seemed to Shan by comparison.

"No. I would prefer that she rests and eats, but she's Shan, so she'll do as she pleases."

"I think Lin and Rayat will occupy her."

"She seemed quite calm about their presence. Please help me keep her that way."

"Anything else you want to say to me?" *Back off, get out, leave my missus alone.* "If so, now's the time."

Aras picked up a *gurut* and chewed thoughtfully. "Yes. It's your turn to clean the floors."

If he had wanted to tell him to sod off he'd have done it, Ade reasoned. He went to look at Rayat's handheld, coupled to Shan's machine by a fiber, and realized she had taken her swiss out to the terrace with her.

He stood at the door. Shan was leaning on the stone balustrade, head bent, swiss in one hand. Then she raised her arm and there was a flash of reflected light. He realized she had the swiss's bubble-thin screen on its mirror setting.

She turned, suddenly aware of him, thinly disguised shock on her face.

"You okay, Boss?"

She pinched the bridge of her nose. "Why didn't you tell me how bad I really looked?"

"You're looking a lot better than when they found you."

She ran her hand over her head as if testing how thick her hair was. It was the first time it had occurred to him that she cared how she looked and that her current condition might distress her. She'd always taken care of her appearance, but in an officer sort of way that was more about polished boots and smart uniform than the usual do-I-look-okay fussing of a woman. She'd had lovely long jet-black hair and now she didn't. She had also had a nice arse, and that was gone too, but she wouldn't know that.

"Sod it, I'm over a hundred and twenty." She forced a smile but it was unconvincing. "And I've been a bit dead lately, so all in all I'm looking okay for my age."

"We'll get you some decent fatigues made up."

"And boots. My boots didn't make it."

"I bet I can find a ussissi who can blag a pair from Umeh Station."

"You're a good bloke, Ade."

"Salt of the earth, me."

"Come on, let's get on with rummaging Rayat's bloody data."

She seemed crushed. But he didn't care what she looked like right then and he knew Aras didn't either. It was enough to have her back. He put a cautious hand under her elbow and gave her just enough support to walk back into the living room with some dignity.

"It's all right," he said, giving Aras a help-me-out-here look. "A couple more days and you'll look good as new. It's not worth getting upset about."

"Do I look upset?"

"Yeah. Frankly, yeah, you do. Your hair's growing back at a hell of a rate, though. You'll be back to normal before you know it."

"Don't kid yourself it's about how I look." She placed her swiss on the table and linked it up to Rayat's device again. Aras sat down next to her and put his hand on her arm. "It's what's in Rayat's handheld. It's a bit of a shock when you find that he was briefed by Eugenie Perault. Remember her?"

"The minister who did your Suppressed Briefing for the mission," said Ade.

"Go on, you might as well say it."

"The one who shanghaied you."

Shan stopped short of shaking Aras's hand off her arm, but Ade could see she had braced her frail muscles. If she could do that it was at least a sign that she was regenerating more tissue.

"Maybe," she said. "But I want to know why she briefed *both* of us for the same mission. And I need to know if the bitch knew what was really out here."

10

We demand the following. We require the return of Minister Par Paral Ual, who acts without authority: we demand that you hand over Aras Sar Iussan for trial: and we demand that you withdraw your vessel from our space.

Official request from Minister Par Nir Bedoi, Home Affairs,
to the matriarchs of F'nar

F'nar Plain, November 3, 2376.

Esganikan's ship had become a city in its own right.

Out on the plain, the vessel had changed shape and had rearranged itself into a number of smooth shapes like a series of bronze and blue bubbles. It solved the logistics problem of where F'nar might put two thousand extra wess'har.

"Wow," said Eddie. He thought of the two shiplets that had formed out of the main vessel and gone their own way. "How do they do that?"

Nevyan, walking beside him, tugged at the neckline of her *dhren,* the opalescent white wrap that many of the matriarchs in F'nar wore. It formed itself immediately into a cowl. "You call it nanotechnology." She pulled the *dhren* apart as if ripping it and it opened along an invisible seam like a zipper. "This fabric uses that principle. The ship's materials are created the same way."

"For a bunch of nature lovers, you do employ some dodgy hi-tech."

Nevyan zipped herself up again. "If it were *dodgy,*" she said, "we would not be using it."

Eddie resigned himself to being a caveman again. Wess'har had been a space-faring species when humans thought bows

and arrows were this year's must-have and were starting to realize wild dogs could be their best friends. It put you in your
place.

"I should have asked this a long time ago, Nevyan, but
how far back does the wess'har civilization go?"

"Define civilization."

"Building cities."

"Using your frame of reference, a million years."

"I'm not sure we'd got to grips with fire by then." Eddie's
brain gave up trying to examine the context and settled for
being awed. The wall-to-wall hard-science PhDs of the
Thetis payload had been gently patronizing towards his hum-
ble anthropology degree, but he felt he was now the best
placed of all of them to see how astonishingly nothing *Homo
sapiens* was. "And you haven't started living on pills or given
up sex or uploaded your consciousness into machines."

"Why would we want to do that? It sounds extremely
foolish."

"Well, we always tend to think that's what we'll be doing
in years to come."

"You're a very sad species," she said, without a hint of
sarcasm. "You want to eradicate all the things that make you
a living creature."

"Where were you when I was making documentaries?"
Eddie asked wistfully.

The camp of scattered ship-bits was busy with Eqbas personnel, many of them females. One group was standing in a
circle, gazing down at something on the ground and occasionally crouching to press their hands on the soil. Eddie let
his bee cam loose. It made a slow pass round them and one
watched it in that same carefully hostile way that Serrimissani did. He hoped it would take evasive action fast enough
if the Eqbas swatted it.

"What are they doing?" he asked.

"Finding a water course to tap into," said Nevyan. "They
plan an extended stay."

"And how do you feel about that?"

"Confused."

Nevyan walked past the hydrology team to where Esganikan Gai stood watching the activity in her camp. It had the feel of the *Thetis* mission, setting up a base and trying not to look or feel permanent, two years and a whole messy history ago.

Esganikan made a gesture with one straight arm, beckoning Nevyan towards her like an aircraft director on a carrier's deck. It struck Eddie as a little imperious. If she tried that on Shan she'd get a rude awakening.

Shan. He hadn't been back to see her yet and she'd been conscious for a couple of days according to Serrimissani; the ussissi was a natural journalist if ever he saw one. *Poor old Shazza.* She'd be in a terrible state. He wondered if she'd recognize him. There was always something embarrassingly painful about seeing a once-powerful person reduced to frail dependence, a nasty tap on the shoulder from your own mortality.

He started musing. *What happens to people when they realize they're never going to die? Wow. The whole human existence is predicated on inevitable death.* Maybe Shan would recover enough to talk to him about that. He hoped so. He hoped she would talk to him anyway, even if she never gave him another story, and he accepted that he had finally gone soft and begun caring about things other than his job. He wondered if he'd have felt that way if he'd still been on Earth, in the daily fight to get a story before any other bastard did.

"Greet you," said Esganikan, providing her own fluting chorus. She made that aircraft controller's marshaling movement again. "Learn English for Ual."

"Don't mind me," said Eddie. He stepped over the threshold of a shiplet, now somehow relaxed into a bubble-shaped hut. He found himself in a vestibule that put him in mind of the city of Surang, organic curves and projections even more eccentric than F'nar's. His bee cam followed him inside.

Nevyan knelt down opposite Esganikan and warbled at

her. Eddie decided to stay standing. There was an exchange that he couldn't begin to follow but it appeared friendly enough. Then Nevyan knelt very still, something Eddie had learned to interpret as a negative reaction. She'd heard something that had surprised her.

"Clue me in," said Eddie.

"I'm asking her why she has so many *isan've* with her," said Nevyan. "She says that some *isan've* choose to leave their families behind, in safety, or to delay bonding. It's the nature of many missions."

"But you travel with your whole clan. Mestin took you all on her tour of duty on Bezer'ej. Can't they?"

"We never travel outside this system," said Nevyan. "And it's a relatively safe place." She listened intently to Esganikan again. "She says that we have the luxury of a more backward life."

Backward. Eddie flinched. "Are you going to smack her in the mouth for that?"

"Why?"

"Never mind. Can I take a look around the camp?"

Esganikan considered the request, trilling. "The teaching?"

"What's she asking?"

"She asks if you have any text to accelerate her learning of English."

"A book?" Eddie fumbled in his pockets and took out his handheld. He hated the idea of being parted from it, but this was going to make his life a lot easier. "There's a stack of dictionaries in here, but no language course as such, and it wouldn't be wess'u to English anyway. Not much help."

"A list of words and rules."

"Yes."

Trill, trill, warble. "That's what she requires."

Eddie handed Esganikan the device with the BBChan logo color-coded right through the casing and every component. "Don't break it," he said. "It belongs to the company." He showed her the controls with exaggerated gestures. "I've opened it at the right page. Can you make a copy somehow?"

"Will learn," said Esganikan grimly.

"Yeah, I bet you will," said Eddie, and excused himself while the girls did business.

He walked among the bubbles, nodding politely at any Eqbas who looked his way. One of them watched the bee cam and walked slowly after it, giving him a wonderful but sinister shot. Eventually he recognized Shapakti. A sense of relief flooded him in the way it always did when he was in completely unknown territory and spotted a scrap of familiarity.

"Clever," said Eddie, pointing to the shiplet bubbles and giving him a thumbs-up gesture. Gestures were always dangerous but Eddie doubted there was enough cultural similarity between them for it to mean something offensive. If he got a punch in the face he'd know he'd guessed wrong.

Shapakti stared at Eddie's thumb and made an exaggerated pointing gesture with both arms.

"Safety exits? You'll be coming round with drinks and tax-free purchases later?"

Shapakti burbled and took him by the arm—gently, thank God—to turn him to face the direction in which he'd pointed. *"Gethes,"* he said. Well, that was clear enough. "Who that *gethes?"*

Eddie shielded his eyes with one hand against the glare from F'nar's terraces and focused. The frame was emaciated, and the stride unsteady, but it was Shan. Ade walked behind her.

"Holy shit," said Eddie. *You saw her brought in. You saw how bad she was.* "That's unbelievable."

"Who?" Shapkti constructed his English phrases like a wall. "Who is that?"

Eddie wouldn't get emotional. She wouldn't like that, not one bit. "Shapakti, old son, that's *Shan Chail.* Frankland. Understand?"

"C'naatat?"

"That's it." Eddie, flushed with that perilous enthusiasm

that came with suddenly being understood in a strange language, threw caution aside. "*Shan Chail—isan. Aras—jurej. Oursan.* Yes?"

It was certainly an economic language. Shapakti made a curious roll of his head and let out a long low trill that might have been surprise. It could also have been complete incomprehension. They waited, watching. Shan advanced, stumbling occasionally and being steadied by Ade.

She looked terribly, terribly ill. That was a huge improvement. She paused in front of him, a little shaky, hands on hips.

"Hi Eddie," she said. "Don't I even get a good morning?"

"Bad hair day, doll?"

"Remind me to introduce you to Mr. Truncheon."

"I really missed you, you old tart."

"It's good to see you too, you tosser. It really is."

He stopped short of hugging her. He wanted to. But *c'naatat* made you cautious, even if you had no breaks in your skin and the chance of infection was remote. He hoped she realized that he cared.

Ade stared at Shapakti in a way that would have started a fist fight on Earth. The Eqbas didn't react at all. He was focused on Shan.

"Shan, this is Shapakti," said Eddie. "You've got his attention."

Shapakti inhaled audibly. "Frankland."

"I might even let you call me Guv'nor," she said. "*Teh, g'ne'hek eqbas'u sve?*"

"Hey, clever," said Eddie. She could do the two voices. It was fascinating. "What did you say?"

"I've asked him if he'll teach me eqbas'u."

"Esganikan wants to learn English."

"Our gift to the world. We'll throw in cricket, syphilis and bureaucracy for free." Shan raked one hand through her hair, a little self-conscious. Eddie had never realized she cared how she looked. "Is that a deal, Shapakti? *Teh, mek?*"

"*Mek, chail,*" said Shapakti.

"Good lad. Now let's go and see Esganikan."

"Why?" asked Eddie.

"Nosey bastard," said Shan, playing the police officer again. "Because I'm an *isan* of F'nar and she's on my manor, son. That's why."

Eddie pointed to the appropriate bubble. "In there. Should you be up and about this soon?"

Shan ignored him with the practiced air of someone who was used to asking all the questions and strode ahead, a credible approximation of her old pace. Ade matched her stride. "I hear Esganikan Gai is keen to know more about *c'naatat*. Ade and I are going to show her."

"Be nice to her, won't you, Shan?"

"Any reason I shouldn't be?"

Shapakti fell in behind her, warbling and trilling. It was simply melodic noise to Eddie, but Shan half-turned to deliver a blast of wess'u at him. Shapakti dropped his head a little and lapsed back into silence.

"What did he say?" asked Eddie.

"Cheeky bastard wanted to know if I give *oursan* to the *c'naatat* who hates him."

Shapakti meant Ade. Ade dropped his gaze and found his boots of sudden and overwhelming interest.

"And what did you say?" said Eddie.

"Nosey bastard," said Shan.

Ual found F'nar an extraordinarily awkward city. It was chaotic, disorderly and full of stairways. Isenj weren't built for steep stairs.

The treads were too narrow for him to place his whole bulk on them and he found himself tottering, trying to find purchase with his rear and side legs and failing. Bipeds never had to worry about such things.

"I suggest we stay at ground level," said Ralassi.

"If I'd known our stay would be extended, I would have brought more supplies with us."

"The next shuttle will drop off some food, Minister. Do you want to eat now?"

"Later."

"And do you intend to return to Umeh?"

"You think I can remain here?" Ual hadn't expected this. He had anticipated the rage of his opponents—in government and among the electorate—but he had not foreseen Eqbas dispatching a vessel to Umeh. "I've probably made a disastrous mistake, but I must try to salvage something."

The Eqbas ship hadn't landed. It was just orbiting and gathering data. It was the worst possible situation. How could he now expect isenj to accept the assistance of the wess'har with one of their ships looking like a potential aggressor? Now he had neither his bargaining chip, as Eddie called it, nor a receptive audience for his plan.

The first isenj ever to visit the enemy on a peaceful mission had got it badly wrong. Ual knew he would go down in history and memory as a fool rather than a visionary.

But he had come this far. The cycle of resentment and decline and sporadic fruitless war *had* to be broken. He made his way back down the passage to the Exchange of Surplus Things and tried to find a corner in which to be inconspicuous.

Wess'har came to look at him, or so he thought; but they appeared to be spending as much time sorting through containers of food as studying him. They were all tall and irregularly shaped—vertically symmetrical, yes, but all gangly limbs and long faces.

Eddie, with his talent for comparing all beings to species on his own world, called them sea horses. There were no longer other animal species on Bezer'ej and there hadn't been for many, many generations. Ual had nothing in his environment that he could compare to the wess'har. It was the first time he had thought about the sadness inherent in that.

But some wess'har were shorter than him. A small one with a plume of stiff gold hair across the top of its head, just like the big females, approached him and stood far too close to him. He was a government minister. He'd earned the right to a little more personal space.

"You're in trouble," said the wess'har in perfect English. "I'm Giyadas. Nevyan took me as her daughter."

Ual decided she was an infant. As with isenj, it was hard to tell a wess'har's age by their size: but wess'har had no genetic memory to make them wise from birth, and none of the social restraint that adult isenj learned. Adult wess'har seemed as outspoken as young ones, often to the point of offense.

It was his first impression of them—big, gold, shiny, and rude. They would never show the self-control needed to cope with living at close quarters like his own people.

"Yes, I'm in a great deal of trouble," said Ual.

"Have the *gethes* shafted you?"

"What does that mean?"

"Put you into a difficult position and then abandoned you." The child looked up at him, tilting her head this way and that. "Eddie taught me the word."

Ah. Eddie's accent was discernible. "If you mean that the humans can do nothing more to aid us in exchange for the things we have given them, yes."

"You're hard to understand."

He was a minister of state yet he was reduced to chatting to a small alien child. This wasn't how Eddie's *shuttle diplomacy* was supposed to work.

"My people won't like it at first, but I think we will fare better by cooperating with your people than by fighting them. There is an . . . inevitability about wess'har."

"You mean that we can take you any time we want."

Ual repeated the phrase to himself, appalled. Yes, it was true. And now the Eqbas were involved it *would* happen, sooner or later. Sooner and peacefully struck him as better than a long noble fight to the last isenj. They had made that boast before and lost. And there had been no last isenj, just millions more. "More words that Eddie taught you?"

"Shan Frankland said it."

He had heard small snatches of information about Shan Frankland and was trying to piece them together. Even dead, she seemed still to be pivotal for the wess'har. "The dead officer."

"No, she lives."

Ual decided to let the comment go unquestioned. Humans had some eccentric beliefs about noncorporeal existence and it seemed that Giyadas had been exposed to them. "And what do you think of your cousins from Eqbas Vorhi?"

"They're different."

Ual was being sociable. There was no harm in indulging the child of a potential ally. Giyadas took his arm and tugged a little more forcefully than he imagined such a small creature could.

"I want you to meet someone," she said.

Ual followed her patiently, maneuvering his bulk around crates and containers while wess'har stood back to let him pass. They didn't attack him or even hurl abuse. He was the enemy, the ancient enemy, and he knew what would have happened if a wess'har had arrived on Umeh. Isenj felt the old injustices as vividly now as their forebears did in the days of Mjat.

But there was no hostility. If anything, they seemed no more than mildly curious. He almost tripped over a strange cylindrical fruit on the floor but a wess'har reached down and removed it from his path.

I don't understand them at all. Rude and considerate; peaceful and extravagantly violent; technologically sophisticated and yet living a primitive rural life. *And they have never threatened Umeh.*

Ual had come to negotiate, not to learn, but learning was overwhelming him. No isenj could have any idea what they were dealing with.

He shuffled out into the sunlight of a gloriously clear day quite unlike any on polluted Umeh. The alleys and small courtyards that made up the tangled ground level of terraced

F'nar were fiercely illuminated by the reflection from the pearl surfaces, the polar opposite of Jejeno in every way he could imagine. Giyadas trotted ahead, stopping every so often to check he was keeping up.

"Here," said Giyadas. She tilted her head and clasped her hands, a miniature of the adult matriarchs. "He wanted to see you. He says he's never met an isenj who wasn't trying to kill him or who he wasn't trying to kill."

A huge alien that looked more human than anything stepped out in front of him. He had a face that was all harsh angles, and liquid dark eyes like the soldier Barencoin except that there was far less white visible in them. He wasn't wess'har, and he wasn't human. Ual couldn't identify his species.

The creature flicked a long dark braid of hair over his collar and sniffed the air.

"I'm the Destroyer of Mjat," he said in immaculate English. "I'm Aras Sar Iussan."

Eddie Michallat said there were monsters in human history, and that humans often speculated on how they would exact their social revenge if they met these long-dead criminals. But this monster was not long dead; and now he was simply an extraordinary creature for whom Ual could suddenly feel nothing but . . . astonishment.

This wess'har, or whatever he had become, was more than fifty generations old. And he had survived being an isenj prisoner of war, a very bitter war indeed.

Ual was glad his political rivals weren't there to hear him. The first thing that came into his head was hardly what they would have wanted. But he said it anyway.

"I'm truly sorry for what we did to you in captivity," said Ual.

Aras was completely still. Ual wondered if it was a preparation to spring forward and attack like a ussissi, but the Destroyer of Mjat simply stood there and didn't even blink.

"And I regret that I had to kill so many of you," he said. "I remember, you see. I caught my *c'naatat* parasite from your people when they cut me and tore me. So now I have your genetic memory, and I know what it is to stand outside myself and see me as I am."

"A rare gift," said Ual. "And perhaps one we should all seek. Knowing what you do, then, would you destroy us again?"

"Under the same circumstances?" Aras tilted his head sharply and Ual could clearly see the wess'har in him now. "Yes, of course I would."

Ual took care not to touch him, but he approached close enough to make it clear that he would follow him to talk further.

"Let us look for different circumstances," he said.

Shan hadn't seen Nevyan since she had last left F'nar for Bezer'ej, a long cold lifetime ago. Esganikan could wait her turn.

There was a distinct scent of mango in the air as Shan entered the ship's detached section and it made her indefinably uneasy. It was an indication of the presence of a dominant female under challenge or threat, a pheromone powerful enough to make a ruling matriarch cede her position and become deferential.

She could emit the pheromone herself, but now that she had it back under conscious control again she wanted to keep it that way. Wess'har couldn't override their scent reactions; she could. *C'naatat* had somehow provided her with the capacity for tact that she'd never had as a regular human being and now it was time she used it.

And there was Nevyan, bobbing her chess-piece head and craning her neck to see who was entering the compartment.

You saved me, kid. You saved me. Shan stepped forward.

She'd never been comfortable with displays of emotion. Any sane person would have flung their arms around their rescuer, grateful and tearful. Shan wanted to, but the old control born of years of barricading herself against the world took the impulse and crushed it before she could follow it.

But this was still her friend, the woman who hadn't abandoned her to space.

"I'm not sure where to start." Shan reverted to English for a moment. "Thank you doesn't quite cover it."

Nevyan's scent-burst of contentment—sweet powdery musk—almost overwhelmed the mango aromas. "My friend," she said. "Oh, my friend, it's good to see you." She made an awkward move forward and the two of them stood on that precarious brink of actually touching. Neither stepped over it. Mestin would touch her, always with a reassuring layer of fabric between her and Shan's skin, but most were still cautious. "Look how *well* you are."

Well was relative. "I'm in your debt."

"It's enough for me to see you alive. You owe me nothing."

Esganikan, a head taller than Shan even without the magnificent plume of copper hair, watched them intently. "You're the *c'naatat*."

"Actually, I'm Superintendent Shan Frankland." *Don't start a ruck. Don't start effing and blinding at her.* "And this is my . . . colleague, Ade Bennett. He caught the parasite too. Neither of us planned to, believe me."

"I want to know all about this organism. Is it true you survived in space?"

"I'm here, aren't I?"

"I don't understand."

Rhetorical. She doesn't get it. "Yes. It's true."

At first Shan was distracted by the growing intensity of the dominance pheromone—discernible, but not provocative—and then she was struck by the fact that the interior of the ship was utterly alien: not just wess'har alien, but *alien* alien. There were the trademark organic curves and loops, but the bulkheads were a mass of shifting light and lines, all intense detail and movement.

Shan put her hand on the bulkhead and familiar violet and ruby points of light rippled under the skin of her fingers. Her bioluminescent signaling was back. It tried to match the colors she touched, attempting to respond.

Esganikan studied Shan carefully with much head-tilting, then stared at Ade for a few moments. He stood with his feet slightly apart, smartly upright, hands clasped behind his back. "You carry more than the life-form itself, then."

"I do indeed." Shan flexed her hands, fist to fingers to fist, and the full spectrum of colors illuminated them. "A few genes from the bezeri. Aras is the expert in *c'naatat* activity, if anybody is, and you can see how much it's changed him. It scavenges genetic material."

"You and your kind are exceptionally dangerous."

"Yes, I realize what *gethes* can do."

"I meant *c'naatat.*"

Shan felt something like solidity—and she had no better word for it—settling and spreading in her chest. It wasn't the cold constriction of adrenaline when she was sizing up for a fight: she knew that only too well, primal aggression poisoned a little by fear. No, this was *her*. This was the *her* she had discovered when helpless in the void with only her mind for refuge. A voice inside said *try it, go on, see what I'm really made of.* She silenced it. This wasn't the time to create divisions.

"I know," Shan said carefully. "That's why I ditched myself in space. That's why Aras spent centuries in exile, that's why Ade gave himself up, and I'm afraid that's why Rayat and Neville detonated bombs on Ouzhari. We're not about to hand it over."

Esganikan smelled *dominant*. Shan was fully aware of it but now it was touching her in some way, making her ... cautious. Suddenly she realized what was happening to her.

She's backing you down. She's outscenting you. It started the minute you walked through that hatch.

Shan let go of her control. Her fragile abdominal muscles tightened and she let her skin release the scent that said *I'm the Guv'nor, so don't fuck with me.*

Esganikan's shoulders relaxed a little. Shan felt the moment pass. It was fleeting, insubstantial: she didn't like this silent game at all, but she had emitted enough scent to pro-

duce the reaction. She glanced at Nevyan, who was absolutely still with her muscles locked.

"Will you let us assess the symbiont?" said Esganikan.

"I'll think about it," said Shan. *Yeah, don't try it on with
me again, sunshine.* "I want to see the prisoners."

"Why?"

"I'm a police officer, even if the police force I served is
long gone. You know what police are, do you?"

"I do now."

"I need to find out things from one of these prisoners."

"Will you try to free them?"

"Of course not."

"Then speak to them, but don't execute them." It was a
casual remark, symptomatic of that odd wess'har ambiguity
about respect for life. "We do not yet know if they will be of
use to us in dealing with your governments."

Your governments. So she was still almost a *gethes,* but at
least Esganikan now knew who the Guv'nor was. She was
going to have to talk to Nevyan about this.

Nevyan followed Shan and Ade back outside. At a discreet distance from the fragmented Eqbas vessel, Shan
caught Nevyan by her elbow. She flinched.

"Are you okay dealing with Esganikan?"

Nevyan's hands were clasped carefully in front of her,
multijointed fingers meshed in a way that a human would
have found painfully impossible. "It's confusing."

"Why?"

"I find myself disagreeing with her, but she's very dominant."

"So? *You're* dominant."

"I find I want to disagree about our relations with Umeh."

"It's none of my business, but—"

Ade cut in. "You're right, it's not, Boss. Stay out of it for
a while. Please. Get some rest."

"Yes, I need your counsel," said Nevyan, ignoring him.
Ade's male opinion didn't register on the scale. "She's set

on a course of action and I have doubts. Why do I feel like this? Where is our natural consensus?"

"Maybe she's just bloody *wrong*," said Shan, still rattled by the encounter herself. "What's bothering you?"

"Umeh," she said. "At first, its only relevance was the human enclave. Then Ual asked for our assistance with his world's environmental pressures."

"That's a brave move." Shan looked first for the political flanker that Ual might be pulling but couldn't think of one right then. There *had* to be one. "Are you going to help them?"

"Help is a relative term," said Nevyan. "Esganikan is very keen to assist, so keen that she plans to land a contingent on Umeh, with or without the consent of the various regional governments."

Shan thought about it for a while, chewing her lip. Her legs were feeling the strain of a long walk and Ade put a proprietorial hand on her back, steering her. He said absolutely nothing. He was just comfortingly *there*.

"We have a word for that," Shan said. Ade was right; it *was* none of her business, but she'd played a role in bringing disaster to Cavanagh's Star and she never left a mess for someone else to clear up. "We call it invasion."

The bowl of fried peppers was the first solid food that Lindsay had eaten in nearly forty-eight hours. The sound of Rayat's chewing irritated her and she couldn't work out why it seemed so loud given the constant clamor of wess'har voices and clattering glass in the warrenlike home that was now their prison.

She tried to shut it out.

"No locks," said Rayat. "In fact, no doors."

"So try walking out of here."

"Why do you think they haven't killed us?"

There was a sudden peal of trills somewhere in the house, almost a shriek. Lindsay dropped the bowl and last few strips of peppers spilled across the flagstone floor. Then the musical voices resumed their normal pattern. A scent like fruit—peach, mango, apricot?—wafted through the doorway. Wess'har always seemed to be cooking something. Lindsay's stomach was still growling in response to every aroma.

"Maybe the Eqbas branch of the family does things differently." She picked up the bowl and scooped the peppers back into it, unsure when the next meal was coming, if ever. Wess'har seemed to be conscientious about clean floors so she ate what she retrieved. Rayat, perched on one of the rock-hard recesses, looked down his nose at her and carried on chomping.

"Got a problem?" asked Lindsay. She wiped her finger around the bowl and sucked off the last scrap of oily sauce.

Rayat shrugged. "We were never much of a team, you and I, were we?"

"No. Not *any* sort of team."

"What do you want to happen?"

"What?"

"Rescue? Return?"

"Die, and get it over with. I've lost my baby, I've got nothing to go back to and I'd have to live with being a war criminal." She checked the bowl. It was hard to see if she'd missed any liquid because the vessel was brown and amber swirled glass—hard glass, the sort that could stand being dropped, the sort that the colonists had used to make the bells of St. Francis Church in Constantine. What was happening to the colonists now? "And that's before I think about what the wess'har and the isenj will do to Earth. No, dead's good for me. How about you? I think dead would be good for you, too."

"I didn't plan to kill any bezeri."

"You didn't plan to completely eradicate *c'naatat* either, did you?" She recalled his anger when he found she'd let Shan step out of the airlock. "Asset denial has a lot of meanings."

Rayat remained irritatingly calm. "In the right hands, it

could have been immeasurably valuable. But it's gone now. And we can forget about Aras."

Gone. Right. But Ade Bennett was here. What if he really did get homesick and want to leave? No, Ade had an unshakeable sense of duty, just like bloody Shan Frankland. And even if Rayat found out what he'd become, there was nothing he could do about it, not here.

But she liked the idea of seeing the look on Rayat's face if he ever found out. It was a little comforting scrap of childish vengeance before she died, nothing more. And someone else could pull the trigger, no grenade and no self-inflicted pain. She could just about handle that. *Shut your eyes, think something profound, and try to go with some dignity.* Yes, it was almost a relief.

Rayat swung his legs off the ledge and ambled towards the door.

"Where are you off to?" she demanded.

"Perhaps I can have a chat with someone," he said. "If they haven't done their usual summary execution, perhaps there's some room for negotiation after all."

Lindsay watched him walk through the opening and heard his steps fade in the corridor. She hoped they shot him. What did their weapons do, anyway? She'd never seen them fire one. They looked more like brass musical instruments than weapons.

And there was no more sauce. She put the bowl down on the ledge and sat down with her back against the wall and her eyes closed.

A few minutes later there were footsteps outside again, not the scrabbling dog-steps of ussissi or the thud of a wess'har's gait, but the steps of more than one human.

"Is that you, Eddie?" she called. She didn't need him to mediate for her. She wanted it all to end. "Ade?"

But it was Rayat who walked back through the door, and for once his face was a perfect picture of shock.

Lindsay wondered what might be enough to shock a spy. God, maybe he'd run into Ade. He *knew.* Well—

But it wasn't Ade, and it wasn't Eddie. Rayat, stunned silent, was staring at Lindsay. It was one of those moments when what she saw didn't make sense, but she saw it anyway.

There was a gun to Rayat's head and holding it was a nightmarishly emaciated figure with very short, scrubby dark hair in a loose black uniform. The gun clicked, a good old-fashioned 9mm pistol.

"Okay, sunshine," said a dead woman's voice. "I haven't said this for years. *You're fucking nicked.*"

It was Shan Frankland. Dead, dead, *dead* Shan Frankland.

11

Creatures without feet have my love,
And likewise do those with two feet,
And those with four feet I love,
And those too with many feet.

THE BUDDHA,
566–486 BCE

Shan began slipping the 9mm pistol in the back of her belt out of habit, and then found her trousers weren't tight enough even with the belt on its last notch to hold it securely.

She slid the gun discreetly into her pocket. She didn't want to ruin a grand entrance by letting it clatter to the floor down the leg of her pants.

Lindsay probably wouldn't have noticed anyway. She was still sitting against the wall, hands pressed flat on the floor and mouth slackly open in classic theatrical shock. An actor might have made a better job of it.

Cobalt.

Lindsay was everything Shan despised, the apparently compassionate woman with short-sighted, pig-eyed self-interest buried not far beneath her normal, reasonable girly veneer. Shan wanted to hurt her, and badly. But she had information to extract.

She stood staring at Rayat, a man as unkempt and as far from the image of a spy as it was possible to get. She'd never noticed he had so much gray in his dark hair before. What was the rate of violent exchange for genocide? A good kicking? Knee-capping? Holding his head under water a few times—a lot of times? She'd done it all, and worse, and not one of those recalled acts gave her that light-headed, throat-stopping sensation of savage animal release that made her feel some score had been settled in the universe.

"Sit down," she said.

Rayat was looking her up and down without moving his head, eyes darting, and he had never seemed to be a man who shocked easily. She was glad she'd found his threshold. It was a childish thing, but she'd learned a long time ago that a copper needed to know how to make the right entrance. It often saved a lot of work.

"I said *sit the fuck down.*"

Rayat paused for three beats before sitting slowly. Shan meshed her hands, pushing her gloves hard back on her fingers until the webs of skin hurt. His gaze settled on them for a telling second. *Oh, he's afraid I'm going to belt him. No— he's wondering if he can pick up a dose if I thump him, the sly bastard. He never gives up.*

Shan swallowed her temper. "I've not been well lately, you know."

"You stepped out the hatch," said Rayat.

"Nothing wrong with your memory, then."

"You stepped out the hatch."

"I think you already said that."

Rayat was doing better than Lindsay. She was still sitting on the floor, staring, silent. "Just tell me how."

Shan spread her arms and shrugged. "Beats me. I expect you already realized I'm not like other girls." She wandered across the room. Unbidden, Lindsay placed her hands back against the wall and edged up it. It was a clumsy way to stand when she could have knelt first, but maybe she was expecting a boot in the face. Shan met her horrified eyes. Looking cadaverous had its advantages. "You stupid, selfish little cow."

"Oh God," said Lindsay. "How did you . . . ?"

"Survive without a suit? It's the first minute that's the worst. Want to try it?"

"Oh God."

"Too fucking quick for you. I ought to let the ussissi shred you."

"Get it over with."

"Esganikan would rather I didn't. Not yet."

Neither of them had finished *helping with inquiries,* as her old sergeant used to say. There were helpful people, and there were people who needed some help to be helpful. Either way was fine by her.

Rayat was made of sterner stuff than Lindsay, or at least he seemed to think he was. Shan kept an open mind. He was certainly managing to be more coherent.

"Okay, Superintendent, I know your record with prisoners. You enjoyed your work."

"Don't flatter yourself," said Shan. "What was in your Suppressed Briefing from Perault? Everyone knows what was in mine."

"Why does that matter to you now?"

"Good old-fashioned copper's need to know. What was your primary task?"

Rayat looked through her. There was a definite shift in his expression, as if it was part of a mechanism he'd adopted to resist interrogation. Shan thought that if she were an agent who had no further mission and no chance of escape or survival, then the last thing left to preserve sanity was the satisfaction of thwarting the enemy in some small way.

She could have beaten the answer out of him, given time. He wasn't all that different from her, hanging on to his sense of self in a lonely and frightening place.

But understanding him didn't excuse his crime.

Bastard.

She felt something primeval flare up from her gut and the kick she aimed at him came straight from her subconscious. It caught him under the arm, right in the ribs. He didn't even scream. They usually did.

"Come on, you shit-house." He curled up instinctively,

hands shielding his head. The shock from the next kick traveled back up her leg, and it hurt. "You can take me, can't you? You're *trained*. You're *hard*. What do you want? Want me to draw enough blood that you catch this fucking thing?" She stamped down hard on his ankle because she couldn't get at his balls. She was light-headed and it wasn't from exhaustion. She'd tipped over this brink of rage before. "Get up, you bastard. Come on, you murdering heap of shit—"

He rolled over on his back, gasping. "You're a—" he began, but that was as far as he got because she didn't want to hear, and she didn't want to argue, and she didn't want him to get up again. She kicked him in the back and the kidneys and anywhere else she could reach. She kicked him until she staggered to a halt with exhaustion and all she could hear were his grunts of pain and—at last—her own gasping breath.

If she'd been fitter, heavier, she knew she would have killed him. She'd come as close to killing someone before but she knew when to stop in those days. Whatever Rayat knew didn't matter right then. She wanted destruction. She loathed herself for that and wasn't sure why.

She managed to haul him into a sitting position by his collar so that his face was inches from her. "Do you know what you've done? Do you fucking *know*?"

Lindsay was completely silent, watching them warily.

Rayat uncoiled and spat blood on the floor, white-faced and trembling. But she couldn't make him scream. God, she wanted to.

"You're an animal," he said hoarsely. "And if you think you're hard enough to beat anything out of me, you've got a long job ahead of you, bitch."

"Then maybe I'll settle for just making you fucking *bleed*."

Lindsay was pressed flat against the wall, silent, trying not to be noticed. Shan forced herself upright and walked out.

She got to Fersanye's door and Ade—made to wait outside—caught her before she collapsed.

"What the hell happened?" Ade had a tight grip on her arms. "Did he hurt you?"

"The fuck he did," she said. "I kicked the shit out of him."

"Good for you, but—"

"But it wasn't for the bezeri." The realization crashed in on her. "It was for *me*."

It was accumulated rage; rage at being set up, being shanghaied, being used, being turned into a freak, being expected to clear up everyone else's shit, freeze-boiling to the point of death and beyond . . . and being caught between black and white.

So Rayat killed thousands. Aras killed millions.

But she could still see the difference, just as she could still feel that Perault's motive for consigning her here *mattered* even though her wess'har side didn't give a toss.

If Rayat thought that calling her an animal was an insult, he hadn't understood her at all.

Human would have been much, much worse.

Aras found the smell that Shan called *forest floor* more than distracting. It came close to unbearable.

It took him back to the time long before the first humans came to Bezer'ej, five hundred years ago, when he huddled in an isenj cell on an island called Ouzhari. The smell told him his jailers were coming to inflict more tortures on him. He had looked much like any other wess'har in those days. Minister Ual reeked of that scent.

"I never thought we would have this conversation," said Ual. He lapped from a bowl of yeast broth. Wess'har busy drying sliced *lurisj* in one of the courtyards paused to look at him and then went back to their task. "Without our human friends, we would never have had a common language to do so anyway."

Aras felt the skin rip from his back again. *Murderer, monster, child-killer. You don't deserve any better.* He ignored the insistent smell of wet leaves. "They have their positive elements."

"Perhaps that's their purpose. A catalyst."

Aras had heard enough of purpose and pattern from Ben

Garrod and his descendants. "We had reached a satisfactory equilibrium before they arrived. Did their purpose include destroying the bezeri?"

It wasn't Ual's fault. He hadn't settled on Bezer'ej, and he hadn't tortured him. Aras couldn't understand why he was experiencing this flashback so intensely now when he had lived with the accurate, unchanging memory for so long. Shan had inherited the memories. She'd reacted badly to them as well. He tried to shake off the intrusive images because they were producing an anger in him that wasn't his.

"Are you unwell, Aras?"

It was odd to hear an isenj call him by name. "No, I'm remembering what your people did to me."

"You can also remember what you did to them."

"I can."

A white ball of fire rolled down the street and the screams were deafening. He hid, calling for his family when the silence fell.

But it was the memory of an isenj. And he could recall his own astonishing survival when the prison was attacked and smashed to rubble, and how his comrades couldn't understand how he had survived such an ordeal. It had seemed a blessing, a vital advantage to share with other troops when the small wess'har army faced millions of isenj.

Nobody had known what it really was in the early days. They found out soon enough.

"Can you do for Umeh what you did for Asht? I apologize—what you did for *Bezer'ej*." Ual corrected himself, perhaps making a deliberate point that he could accept massive cultural change. "And by that I mean reversing environmental damage, not . . . reduction in population."

"Of course we could," said Aras. "But you must be aware that you can't sustain the population you have and still restore your environment. Do you recall any natural environment on your world?"

"We do," said Ual. "Our memories span generations."

"And where will you find the species with which you

once shared Umeh? Do you have a gene bank like the one the *gethes* brought with them to Bezer'ej?"

"No."

"Then what can be restored?"

There was no answer to that: a Umeh rich in biodiversity was a memory, no more than that. Ual lapped his drink again. He was decorated with hundreds of small blue rattling gems that caught the light. Isenj had always liked shiny objects.

Aras recalled the musty, sulphurous flavor of the yeast broth. He had never tasted it but he had the memory, just as he could relive the moment when a petrol bomb exploded against Shan's riot shield or when she had beaten a criminal until she broke his bones.

"We need to find a way of reducing the pressure on Umeh," said Ual.

"You must accept that there must be fewer of you."

"I have invited wess'har intervention. I had hoped for a solution I might be able to . . . what's the human expression? . . . *sell* to my people."

"I think you need to discuss this with Esganikan Gai." Aras was remembering far too much now. His distant past churned up again. His first *isan,* long dead by her own hand, unable to tolerate endless life: Cimesiat and all his comrades contaminated by *c'naatat*: and the years in Constantine with the alien newcomers whose strange belief in invisible forces had always managed not to conflict with the principles of Targassat until now. "I find it interesting that we all spend so much time letting the past influence the present, when it no longer exists. We all let our personal World Before rule the world that is."

But there *was* a previous time he wanted to find again rather than forget. He wanted to walk away and return to some semblance of a peaceful life with Shan, and he had a second chance to do that now. Eqbas Vorhi was more than capable of taking on the task of restoring Umeh and even Bezer'ej. He'd done his duty and now it was over.

But even now Shan was struggling around F'nar, pretend-ing she was fit and able to be the Guv'nor again. No, she had done her duty too, and even duty was finite. Aras thought of the Baral Plain, his birthplace, quiet and remote and truly cold in winter. They could live there, Ade as well. Ade liked snow.

"Forgetting the past is a monumental task for a species with genetic memory," said Ual. "But it's exactly what we have to do. Most isenj will resist Eqbas Vorhi's help—will your people help me convince them?"

Aras stood up. He couldn't stand the smell of decaying leaves any longer. "Will you excuse me? I must find my *isan*." He beckoned to Giyadas, watching them from a dis-creet distance with unblinking yellow eyes. "The future ma-triarch of F'nar will keep you company for the time being."

He walked home up the terraces, willing Shan to be there when he returned. He needed comfort. His need made him feel guilty because she was the one in need of care, but for the first time in centuries he felt that he had lost control. When he opened the door, Shan was sitting at the table while Ade stirred a pot on the range.

Aras could smell her distress. She wasn't bothering to suppress it. Ade raised his eyebrows in mute warning.

"What's wrong, *isan*?"

"Nothing. I gave that shit Rayat a good hiding. And what happened to *you*? I can smell you from here."

"I spoke to Ual." He knew that would silence her. "I haven't had a conversation with an isenj since I was their captive."

Neither Shan nor Ade needed an explanation. *C'naatat,* for all its disadvantages, was also a conduit for understand-ing. Ade had never mentioned inheriting those memories but his reaction told Aras that he had. The marine ruffled Aras's hair in that roughly affectionate manner of human males anxious not to appear oversentimental.

"I'm sorry, mate," said Ade. He patted Aras's back a few times and withdrew to the range to resume his cooking, a house-brother in every sense but one. It had been a very long time since Aras had felt that. He missed the intimacy.

"Did it help you?" asked Shan.

"It disturbed me. But it's done. I mustn't live in the past when there's so much time ahead to deal with."

"They're going to invade Umeh, aren't they?"

"Eqbas? Ual has invited them, as we did, whether his people want them or not. Let's see what happens."

Shan reached out and put her hand on his and they sat that way in silence for a few minutes, not looking at each other. "You're right," she said. "There's a lot to be said for clean slates."

Aras meshed his fingers in Shan's and tightened his grip. Ade poured the contents of the pan into a bowl and set it on the table with some mugs. It was very good soup.

"You're not a bad cook at all, Ade," said Shan. And for a moment she looked at Ade in a way that told Aras he *did not exist.* It was a fraction of a second, no more.

Wess'har males can't be jealous. And I want a house-brother.

It was just a random flash of silly human jealousy, another facet of the *gethes'* greed for more than they needed. *C'naatat* normally dispensed with inherited traits that it found troublesome. Aras hoped it would purge him of this one before it became intrusive.

"That's Mar'an'cas," said Nevyan. "The human colony appears to be surviving."

"Why didn't you kill them all when they first tried to land on Bezer'ej?" asked Esganikan.

The spray whipped up from the sea. Jon Becken seemed comfortable steering the boat so Nevyan let him and knelt down on the curved deck. Her *dhren* shaped itself high around her neck against the cold northern weather.

"They were harmless in those days," she said. "And they brought other species with them."

"This is the gene bank I hear about."

"They thought they could preserve Earth's life-forms and then return them when the planet was fit to be restored."

Esganikan made an approving *urrrr.* "A task we can perform. They aren't all despoilers, then."

Becken turned to Webster and Barencoin while he held his hand above the controls to correct the course. The marines chatted, either oblivious or uncaring of the fact that Nevyan could understand them. Their conversation consisted of speculation about Shan's survival, which they deemed *fucking amazing,* and the *weird shit Ade had got himself into.*

Nevyan turned to them. "Yes, it is indeed fucking amazing," she said, and her comment seemed to silence them. She hadn't intended it to.

"Tell me more about the gene bank," said Esganikan, glancing Barencoin's way. "In English."

"The colony brought it with them and Shan was sent to retrieve the strains of edible plants for free distribution on Earth. Human organizations make living things like food plants into commodities that only they can sell to other humans."

"I am not sure I fully understand *sell.*"

"A barter system. They *license* seeds and even other beings, altered genetically so they can track and control them."

"What do they exchange for food, then, if they have no free access to food plants?"

"Labor."

Esganikan pondered the concept. "So they are cooperative?"

"No, their entire society revolves around individuals acquiring more than is necessary."

"The more you tell me about *gethes,* the more I feel they are overdue for our intervention. And what about the other life-forms in this bank?"

"Shan was sent to retrieve unlicensed food plants to *break the cartels.* She had no orders regarding other species."

Esganikan looked at the marines and then faced the bow of the boat again. "There is no consensus among humans."

"No, they all believe and act differently."

"Then we should differentiate between them. We should separate the *gethes* from those who can be wess'har."

Barencoin appeared to take notice of that. Perhaps it had some significance for him, because he looked annoyed. Nevyan glanced at him and he turned away.

When they landed on the island the two marines Qureshi and Chahal were waiting for them. They jogged down to the waterline and exchanged slaps on the back and embraces with the three other soldiers. Whatever privations they faced, they seemed content in each other's company. Nevyan thought that their communal spirit was an encouraging sign.

Nevyan had seen the colonists of Constantine when she was stationed at the Temporary City on Bezer'ej with her mother Mestin. The colony had never been a problem, quiet and absorbed in its pursuit of strange invisible beliefs of noncorporeal life, and it was properly invisible itself, buried in the excavated settlement modeled on Aras's memories of his home city of Iussan. And then the harmless humans had become *gethes* after all, true to their nature, helping Rayat and Neville. Perhaps it was not possible to find many wess'har among them.

Some gathered at the route into their camp of fabric shelters. There were males and females, some clutching small children. And they stank of misery. Nevyan knew an unhappy human when she smelled one.

"I want the person called Jonathan who helped Joshua Garrod enable the *gethes* to bomb Ouzhari," said Esganikan.

Nevyan wondered if they had understood her, because her rapid acquisition of English had not included perfecting the accent of a single-voiced creature. There was a collective murmur that seemed like one moan of despair. It seemed that they had.

"If you don't fetch him, then you condone what he did, and you will be balanced too," she said.

"Like every godless fascist regime that's ever been," said a man at the front. "Burn the churches, punish the innocent, show others what happens to the disobedient. But God will judge you."

Esganikan met the reaction with an explanation, as was proper. "How can you be innocent if you prevent what's right? This is to balance the genocide of the bezeri. If you prevent that, you become part of it. I have no wish to show anyone anything. I care only what you do, not what you think."

They looked back at her, unmoving.

"Okay, I'll do it," said Barencoin.

"No, mate, that's where I draw the fucking line," said Becken. "I'm not hunting civvies for someone to kill them. That's not what we do." Becken glanced at Nevyan. He was a young pale man with a badly scarred nose. "No offense, ma'am."

Barencoin slipped his rifle off his shoulder. "He knew they were nuclear bombs, and if he hadn't helped Neville and Rayat, we wouldn't be in this shit now."

"Yeah, Mart, and we helped the bitch too, didn't we? Or you fucking well did. You landed the devices on the planet."

"Okay, I should have shot her and Rayat and had done with it. But I didn't. So now I do things right. Okay?"

He stepped forward. The little rank of colonists looked about to part and then closed up again. Esganikan watched, apparently fascinated.

"Come on, hand him over," Barencoin said quietly. "They mean it. Wess'har don't piss about, and you know that better than anyone." He paused. "Anyway, Shan Frankland's back, and if you don't fetch him now she'll come and drag him out by his balls."

The colonists stared at him. "She's dead."

"Well, she's not dead now," said Barencoin.

"She's alive? *Alive?*"

"Yeah, but don't read anything freaky into it, will you? God wasn't involved. He's not taking calls, in case you hadn't noticed."

Barencoin motioned with his rifle for them to let him pass

but they didn't move. He sighed and simply walked forward, and *then* they parted.

Nevyan and Esganikan followed him. Nevyan found it interesting that humans could be so compliant even when they outnumbered their captors. There were around a thousand here and many emerged from their tents to watch.

Barencoin cleared a path without even trying. He might have been behaving in that way humans called *bluffing,* but nobody seemed to want to test him. Nevyan thought she recognized one or two of the colonists but it was hard to tell.

"Now that Joshua Garrod is dead, who speaks for you?" she asked.

"Try his wife, Deborah," said a woman. "Or Martin Tyndale."

She didn't recognize Deborah Garrod at all. The woman seemed neither hostile nor afraid, and she had youngsters with her, a small female and an almost fully grown male. She indicated the interior of the tent. "It's cold out here," she said. "Can we talk inside?"

Esganikan ducked beneath the bar above the opening. The tent was a chaos of fabric and boxes and stank of stale food. Nevyan was aware of the young male's fixed stare.

"What's your name?" she asked.

"James," he said.

"You intend to restore Earth," said Esganikan.

"Our forefathers came to Bezer'ej for refuge, to wait it out until the world was ready," said Deborah. "However long it took."

"And what do you want to do now?"

Deborah shrugged. "If prayers could be answered? To turn back time. If not—I was going to say that we would like to go home, but Bezer'ej is the only home we've ever known."

"Would you prefer to return to your homeworld?"

"If the time was right. If the purpose could be fulfilled."

"We can make it the right time," said Esganikan.

Perhaps she was overconfident of her new language

skills. Nevyan watched her, baffled, a little hesitant because the matriarch's dominance pheromone was so convincingly powerful, as strong as her own and sometimes close to overwhelming her.

"How?" Deborah asked.

"You wish to restore your environment. That is what we do, what we have always done. We can do it for you, and with your cooperation."

There was something about Esganikan's effortlessly clear focus that reminded Nevyan of Shan. This was a female used to getting things done. But this was not her friend, not someone she knew well and who had her interests and those of her city at heart: wess'har or not, Esganikan was a stranger.

"Are you offering to take us back?" said Deborah.

"Yes, and the rest of the life from your world."

"And what about Jonathan Burgh?"

"He must be balanced."

"So if we hand him over the rest of us can go . . . home."

"The two are not connected. If none of you hand him over, then none of you will go home, because I will have to balance all of you for complicity in his action. It is not a condition, nor is it bargaining, because we do not make bargains. It is merely a consequence."

"It's a fascinating distinction." Deborah thought for a while, her head in her hands.

James glared at Nevyan and lowered his voice. "Are we just going to let them do what they did to Dad?"

"The bezeri *died,* James."

"It was an accident. He didn't mean it to happen like that. He was destroying the Devil's temptation."

"James, we became involved with weapons that we should have shunned, and we're paying the price of tolerating violence. Don't you think I miss him? Don't you think it breaks my heart too?" She turned James around by his shoulders. "Go and find Jonathan. Tell him he can choose whether or not to surrender. It's up to him. It's not our place to make him."

Nevyan watched, fascinated by the ethical knots the woman had tied and untied. Their logic was wholly alien to her. If Jonathan acted for himself, then Deborah would be innocent of his death. But he would still be dead. In the end, motives counted for nothing but humans never saw it that way. They lived in their heads, not in the world. Perhaps that was why they could never respect life that wasn't like them.

She waited with Esganikan in complete silence; Barencoin stuck his head through the tent flap a few times to see what was happening and then withdrew. Nevyan walked outside and found him standing in a tight group with the other marines, talking in a low voice, rifle cradled in his arms.

"Who's going to do it, ma'am?" he asked.

"I think we've been here before," said Qureshi. "With Parekh."

"It's not your responsibility to execute our prisoners. We'll do it."

Esganikan wandered out to wait with them, effectively stifling all conversation. From time to time she reached into her quilted tunic and took out a hand weapon, a smooth dull blue cylinder notched with small finger-shaped indentations to create a grip. Nevyan watched the marines, wondering if they realized what the instrument was. And they watched Esganikan discreetly. They weren't fools.

"There," said Qureshi.

James Garrod appeared out of the mass of colonists with a man—a man with a gray and stricken face—trailing behind him. So this was Jonathan Burgh. There was nothing about him that would have helped Nevyan single him out as foolishly obedient or violent or even memorable. James kept his gaze on the ground and indicated Jonathan with a gesture over his shoulder.

He looked as if he felt he had betrayed him. It was a curious kind of morality. It seemed hard for humans to feel that same shame for their treatment of beings who didn't look like them.

"I don't want to die," said Jonathan Burgh.

"Very few creatures do," said Esganikan.

She took him down to the shore. Nevyan stayed back to make sure the marines didn't intervene, but they were discussing whether they should stay on Mar'an'cas. Webster wanted to work on the water and power supplies. Nevyan was impressed by their pragmatism.

There was a loud *snap* from the direction of the shore, and then another. The camp fell silent. The marines paused in their conversation too, and then went on talking in slightly different tones.

"I could get this place running a lot better," Webster said. She stopped a man walking past. "Look, do you want us to stay? Can we get some of the solar plant sorted for you?"

"Get out," said the man. "We don't want you here."

"I love civvies," said Barencoin. "Ungrateful fuckers."

"Well, then," said Qureshi. "Our own government doesn't want us and neither does this lot. Anyone for F'nar?"

Esganikan appeared again, tidy and unmoved. Except for Barencoin, none of the marines would look at her. She cocked her head and Nevyan followed her back to the boat. The vessel sat lower in the water on the return journey, weighed down by two extra passengers, and Becken took it a little more slowly.

"I like your friend Shan," said Esganikan. "I understand her. She has clear purpose. She acts wess'har."

"And you seem to like the colonists, and I must say that was not expected."

Esganikan flicked her plume of hair and faced into the wind. She seemed to enjoy being in the open air: it might have been a relief after a long enclosed patrol.

"They want an Earth that lives in balance, and so do we," she said. "And that is why we will take them with us when we send a mission to Earth. They have asked for our help. So we will give it."

12

We have released the command codes for EFS Thetis *so that you can take control of the vessel and retrieve your personnel. The ship is equipped to take up to 400 individuals in chill-sleep and we will order evacuation of all FEU personnel from Umeh Station. We hope cooperation can be resumed when the difficulties over Bezer'ej have been resolved. In the meantime, we ask you to maintain an open communications relay between our systems. We genuinely seek peaceful relations with Umeh.*

BIRSEN ERTEGUN,
Foreign Secretary, FEU

Someone hit her. She couldn't tell who it was but she threw a punch back anyway. And someone was screaming: a woman's voice, shrill and sobbing, "Don't! Don't! Leave him alone, you pig—"

Shan woke with a start and expected—oh no oh no *oh no*—to see black, star-speckled space once again.

Instead she was looking up at gathering clouds in a fading blue sky. She rolled over onto her side and realized she had dozed off on the terrace at the back of the house.

Shapakti stood at a careful distance. "I knocked," he said apologetically. He rapped on the parapet wall, not making much of a sound at all. "It was hard to find something to knock on."

"Nobody else in?"

"No Aras, no Ade."

Well, at least the two of them weren't worrying about her any longer. She didn't like people fussing. It was six days since Nevyan had brought her back and she was mobile and conscious and she could take care of herself. As long as she didn't look at her body in the shower, she was fine. A week, maybe two, and then she'd look a little more like a survivor than a victim.

And then Aras might remember she was his wife, and all that went with that. He was treating her like his child.

Shapakti waited patiently. "I came to ask if you wanted to visit Bezer'ej."

"Yes, it's time I took a look."

"I know these things concern you. You were an environment officer."

"I was a *police* officer. I joined EnHaz late and I didn't do the science bit. I used to nick people for pollution, breaching research guidelines, illegal biomaterials, that sort of thing. Do you understand *nick*? Arrest. Prosecute. Punish." Punishment hadn't been part of her job since she was a uniformed officer on the street, but she did it anyway. Sometimes the informal approach worked best. Sometimes she was so informal that she'd let eco-terrorists do the job for her. "And I'm still a police officer. I don't know how to be anything else."

Shapakti made a cautious circle around her to get to the doorway. "We have started to cleanse Ouzhari. A crew has landed to carry out a survey."

Shan picked up the blankets and folded them, finding herself suddenly in the mood for a large plate of something. She didn't care what. She was ravenous.

"What do you actually do, Shapakti?" she asked.

"I am a scientist," he said. "I study how organisms work."

"Ah, a biologist. Is that why you hang around me? Study the old freak?"

"Do you find my interest offensive?"

"I'd rather you just asked me questions."

"I want to know about *c'naatat*. We all do."

"You're looking at it."

"How does it make its decisions?"

"I think it treats a host like a planet. An ecosystem." She had to use the English word: she had no wess'u for it. "Except it takes a lot better care of it than *gethes* would."

"Can you feel it?"

"No. I can feel what it does, but I'm not conscious of it as an entity. Or a community." She had a sudden irrelevant thought. There was no God, but if there had been one, maybe that was how he operated too. He let humans fuck up because he was too big and too busy to see the piddling small detail. "I try not to think of being colonized."

She looked at her hands and there was more tissue between the skin and the bone than there was yesterday. *C'naatat* had preserved her brain, even if it had to devour all her muscles and her fat to do so. Then it put back enough tissue to make her mobile, to get her away from any threat. And then it began bringing her back to normal levels of organ tissue and lean muscle mass. If it wasn't smart and sentient, then it was doing a good impersonation of it.

She flexed her hand in front of Shapakti, sending a ripple of colored lights up through her fingers. He made a small incoherent sound. It was a great party trick.

"I picked it up from the bezeri somehow," she said. "This might be the last living trace of them. Ironic. You know they made maps? Colored sand pressed between sheets of transparent shell. Beautiful."

"We look for survivors anyway."

Shapakti moved back for every inch Shan moved forward, and that wasn't like wess'har, who didn't know what *too close* meant. "You think I'm dangerous, like Esganikan does?"

"*C'naatat* needs to be controlled."

"No, those who might misuse it need to be controlled. Understand the difference?"

"Yes."

"Tell me, are *gethes* the only species that behaves this badly towards others?"

Shapakti tipped his head slowly to the right. "No. But you sound as if you would want them to be."

It was a sharp observation. Yes, she hated her own kind. She knew that. She was the polar opposite of most humans, who thought that *Homo sapiens* alone was special: and she thought they were the only ones who were *not*. She was going to ask Shapakti how he had spotted that so soon, but she decided to leave it.

"You were going to teach me eqbas'u," she said.

"Humans learn language slowly."

"Tell you what, give me a shot of Eqbas blood or something and see what happens."

Shapakti's pupils snapped open and shut in utterly transparent curiosity. Shan was reminded what poor poker players wess'har would make.

"I just meant blood," she said. "That wasn't a euphemism."

"What's *euphemism*?"

"An indirect and less offensive way of saying something. Don't think I'm offering you anything extra, okay?"

Shapakti thought about it. She could see it on his face. There was a definite wess'har expression when they were realizing something, a slow lowering of the head like a small animal gradually nodding off to sleep.

"I have an *isan* at home," he said stiffly.

"Good for you, son. So you take a few drugs and you don't need *oursan,* right?"

"Correct."

"That explains Esganikan's surly manner." One wess'har word for surly was *ussi'har,* ussissi behavior. "She didn't bring her *jurej've* with her."

"She has none. She is a soldier. It would not be fair to have family." He edged to the door. "I will come for you tomorrow."

Shapakti left, wafting sandalwood, and Shan stood looking into the cupboard-sized bedroom she'd shared with Aras. It was high time she moved back into it. Besides, Ade was confined to the sofa as long as she was using his bed.

She had no idea why she was put there. She wondered if it was Aras's choice.

"Sod it," she said. "That's *my* bed too."

She dragged the *dhren* off Ade's bed. Beneath the piles of *sek* fabric it was just a few broad planks of *efte* wood laid on blocks. *Efte* grew on Bezer'ej, fast-maturing tree-sized plants that shot to full height in a few months and then deliquesced and drained back into the soil, leaving behind sheets of fibrous bark that could be cut, felted, laminated, and made into a hundred different materials. For the first time she wondered if the wess'har had introduced it to Wess'ej. There was still a great deal about their approach to ecology that she didn't know. But it could wait.

What mattered at the moment was getting fit again and trying to recover that state of relative contentment she'd reached with Aras. For a make-do-and-mend relationship, it had been pretty good; there was a lot to be said for necessity. She made up their bed again, holding the sheets of fabric under the cold torrent of the shower spout to wash them, and shook them dry.

Ade, ever the ultra-tidy soldier, had folded his bedding neatly and stowed it in the single cupboard. It was just a couple of camouflage sheets of thin DPM fabric, the sort you could fold down in your pack and even use to make a bivouac shelter in the field. Shan re-created his bed as best she could by wrapping the *sek* blankets around the planks and finally stretching the sheet drum-tight with proper military envelope corners.

She didn't have a coin to perform the old army test for bed-making perfection, so she took a cube of brick-solid dried *evem* from the larder and bounced it down hard on the covers. It sprang back into her hand. She hoped Ade appreciated the attention to detail.

Aras and Ade returned an hour later, muddy from working the allotment and carrying sacks of vegetables. They seemed easy in each other's company for the moment.

I never thought I'd see either of them again.

Shan wondered why relief was so short-lived. When you were in a terrible situation, you imagined that you would live in a state of permanent gratitude if you ever escaped. You would never ask for anything again, *anything,* ever, as long as you could extract yourself from the shit you were in. You would cherish all those things snatched from you and never let them out of your sight again. But it wasn't like that. A sense of gratitude was more fleeting than resentment.

Ade glanced at the open door of his room and went to check.

"You've been a naughty girl, Boss," he said. "You should leave the housework to us."

"I was bored," she lied. "Anyway, you can bounce a coin off that bed."

"I noticed. Tidy job. Thanks."

She studied Ade's expression—cautious, anxious for approval—and recalled the dreamed memory that she had been grappling with when Shapakti disturbed her. It hadn't come from Aras. The vivid tableau of violence had been conducted in English, a woman yelling at someone to stop. She could guess a lot from that: it was Ade's memory.

For a moment she recalled something warm and wet on her face like a spray of saliva, and she put her hand up instinctively to swat it away. Then she felt her stomach roll with nausea.

Whatever that memory was, it wasn't good. And it wasn't saliva, because she'd been spat at too often to mistake it for anything else.

"I'm going to Bezer'ej for a recce," she said.

"We'll—" Aras began, but Shan interrupted him.

"On my *own*. I'll be fine."

"You won't like what you see."

"Funny, that's happened quite a few times in my career."

Ade rinsed his hands and made a grab for his jacket. "I've got to sort out some billets for the lads," he said. His glance darted between them. "Please, don't have a row about this, will you?"

Shan shrugged. "Of course not."

The soul of tact, Ade Bennett. He gave both of them an uncomfortable smile and left. Silence flooded in after him.

"Want to say something?" she asked.

Aras was now accomplished at displacement activity. He

rummaged through the larder. "No, but you do, *isan.*"

"I moved my stuff back into our bedroom. Are you okay with that?"

"Yes."

"No problems sharing a bed with me again?"

"You're offended that I haven't attempted to copulate."

Sometimes the no-nonsense wess'har style wasn't what she needed to hear. "Okay, I know I don't look too good right now."

"You're still frail. It's not appropriate for your condition. I must care for you."

"I thought that we'd be relieved to be together again." *No, I don't need anyone. I really don't, remember?* "I just didn't think it would be this uncomfortable."

"These are early days. I thought you were dead. It's hard for me to adjust too."

"You blame Ade."

"But you're back."

"And you're okay with him?"

"You spaced yourself."

"Exactly. It was my own bloody fault. I didn't have to go after Lin and I was so cock-sure of myself that I didn't think anyone could take me." The memory she had picked up from Ade's blood was one of being violently abused. She wondered what she had triggered in him when she lashed out at him, and she now knew why she felt ashamed. "As long as you don't take it out on him."

Aras tilted his head slightly. "He's my brother. In most senses."

Shan wrapped her arms round his waist and rested her forehead against his chin. Theirs was an accidental relationship, a blend of duty and sympathy, the sort that was based on pragmatism rather than impulse; it was the sort she could trust. "I know this is hard for you too."

"I wanted to use the grenade. Eddie and Ade stopped me."

"Oh, Christ, I'm sorry."

"It's in the past."

"Well, we're both going to find out what we went through, aren't we? Swap-a-nightmare time." *Oursan* was fun but *c'naatat* transferred memories across the receptor cells too, the vivid ones that you couldn't erase. "I think I've picked up some bad ones from Ade just from blood contact."

"I imagine a soldier with a violent father has some very unpleasant memories."

Shan had never known Ade's background, but nobody who fitted into normal family life would have signed up for a deployment like this. She felt the punch again. She wondered what the splash of warm moisture on her face might be and dreaded the revelation.

"You always got on before," Shan said.

"Will you prefer him to me?"

She jerked her head back. "Whoa, where did that come from?"

"You felt pity and comradeship for me and you feel the same for him."

"Hey, I'm not a bloody charity shop."

"If that's what you want, I'd be very happy to have him as a house-brother. But perhaps human monogamy will make you choose between us."

"Don't talk crap," she said. "We had a deal. I don't walk out on a deal. And I'm not Lindsay Neville. I don't fuck someone by accident or because I got tanked up out of my skull either, okay? Don't you know me by now?"

"You said it yourself. You ruined Ade's life. I know how your framework of responsibility operates, and I will respect your decisions, whatever they are."

"You know what? If I had the energy, I'd storm out, but frankly I can't be arsed." She stepped back from him, hands held up in angry submission. "When I'm feeling fit, maybe I'll handle this better."

It was time for a walk. Her anger had been an asset in her career, a savage dog let off the leash when she chose to free it and send people running for safety. It had kept her sane in space. But now her anger wouldn't come to heel. She didn't like being in thrall to any emotion and that included passion.

She walked through the city feeling like a copper on the beat again, a memory from a long and uncomplicated time ago, acknowledging wess'har she recognized and those she didn't. This wasn't Reading Metro. They didn't wrap themselves in defensive anonymity here. And, like a copper, she knew that Ade had been lying—benignly—and that he wasn't sorting out billets for his detachment.

She'd find him. F'nar was compact enough to cover in a few hours and it wasn't a place to hide, so she'd start with known associates and affiliations—Nevyan's place—and work out from there. Like Eddie, she could always find out what she needed to know.

In a world where there were few secrets to uncover, she wondered what skills she might have to learn to occupy herself in the very long future.

Eddie took a deep breath. He was afraid what he would see.

"Okay, kid." He brushed his palm across the top of Giyadas's rocking-horse mane. She had a skill he needed: she could press the correct sequences into the ITX console simultaneously, while he had to tap through them in laborious sequence to activate the image in Nevyan's wall. "Let's see what's on the news, eh?"

"It will be depressing," said Giyadas.

Eddie heard his own phrases in her mouth. She was six as far as he was concerned. Six-year-olds—even matriarchs in waiting—deserved a carefree childhood, protected from concepts like depressing news. But it didn't appear to dent her mood.

There were only two news feeds he could access via the ITX now, and both were running similar images. They hadn't changed much in three days. Apart from the sports and entertainment segments, they spewed wall-to-wall unedited footage of troop movements along the FEU borders with Africa and the Sinostates.

Eddie could hear the voice-over but he didn't want to.

*Unless the FEU agrees to stand down and hand over control
of the ITX link to the UN so that global negotiation can take
place, the African Alliance is threatening to seize the FEU
downlink array at Amman. Sinostates president Yi says she
will deploy troops to ensure that the relay station is handed
over to the UN undamaged.*

The Amman relay was sandwiched on a finger of land between the two superpowers. The Middle East had never been
very good at staying out of the crucible. Eddie exhaled and
thought better of sending 'Desk the images of Eqbas-held
worlds that Ual had given him.

He'd abandoned all the rules of the game. Self-censorship
didn't matter any more.

"Why are they doing this?" asked Giyadas.

"So the other nations can talk to your mother and Esganikan and . . . well, agree some kind of peace." Eddie
rolled the words around in his brain and they left him reel-
ing. "If this has UN backing then the FEU has to give in."

Giyadas appeared to be mesmerized by the sudden
switch to the studio. She tilted her head about as far as it
would go, studying the faces and prodding the console to
switch between story icons.

"There can be no negotiation," she said. "Why do they
think talking will change what must be done?"

There was no point panicking over the political commentary of a child. But Eddie did, because this child thought as the
adult wess'har did, and the adult wess'har of two worlds had
clearly made up their minds that Earth was due for a visit.

"Can you get me my news desk now, sweetheart?"

Giyadas looked over her shoulder at him. "Is this just pictures, Eddie?"

He didn't understand her question at first. He heard a
journalist's question; were there any interviews to follow?
But then he realized she was asking him something more
profound. "For me, you mean?"

"Yes. What is real to you? Do you see your home at war?

Or do you see a clever film, something that makes you feel accomplished?"

Shan had once asked him a similar question about Earth; did the people back home see his reports on the war in the Cavanagh system as a movie, massively distant and unreal?

It wasn't unreal now. And it was still at least twenty-five years before they would see the unimaginable reality of an Eqbas task force.

"I think I see a product," he said. "And that tells me I need to stop doing this job."

He sat on the thin hard bench and stared at the shimmering wall with its armored vehicles full of bots and an earnest young major in a Sinostates uniform explaining that every effort would be made to minimize collateral damage. Troops with a universal expression that Eddie had seen on Ade's face and a hundred others—wide-eyed, unblinking, brows slightly raised—stared from the back of trucks.

"Okay, I've seen enough," he said. "Let's talk to 'Desk."

Giyadas played the console like a concert pianist. The wall defaulted to smooth stone for a moment and then back to the news.

"I can't find your 'Desk."

He could see the transmission: the ITX was still live. "Let me have a go."

Giyadas had a way of lowering her voice as if she was talking to an idiot. "It's not there," she said. "The link has gone."

Eddie didn't disbelieve her, but he stood behind her anyway and laid his hand on hers—cool, suede-like, utterly alien—to move it to the controls he felt might yield a connection.

"See?" said Giyadas. "I am no fool."

The wall was flooded with an inappropriately peaceful powder-blue holding screen. It simply said UN PORTAL in the global and two subglobal languages—English flanked by Mandarin and Arabic.

The FEU had caved in, with or without armed conflict. Eddie wondered what live footage he had *not* seen.

Either way, he was now cut off again from BBChan, the last remnant of what he called home.

"We will return you to Jejeno," said Esganikan, in passable English. "You may need protection from your fellows. Our troops will accompany you."

Ual hadn't quite planned it this way. Ralassi seemed not to be taking any notice and trotted around the ship's compartment, examining the bulkhead displays with an Eqbas ussissi. Ual's fate didn't affect them. Ussissi were beyond sectarian disputes.

"But it's unthinkable for *any* wess'har troops to land on Umeh," he said.

"Then think it."

It was hard to tell if she was massively arrogant or just finding her way through a complex and inexact alien language. She was a big creature and she intimidated him. She knelt on a thick pad of fabric, leaning forward slightly from the waist like a ussissi about to spring.

"There will be a bad reaction," said Ual.

"If we don't land we can't help you. So we land and help or we take you back and leave you. Either way, there will be no further colonization of other planets by your people."

Know the enemy. There were unspoken assumptions about other species that shaped the isenj view of the world. Wess'har believed in balance and would not take life. Humans wanted something in exchange for anything they gave, and they wanted it fast, and they usually wanted more than was fair. Ussissi cooperated with everyone but drew the line at choosing sides. And nobody wanted to die.

Ual had not fully understood the Eqbas capacity for taking you at your word and then refusing to deviate from their plans. *I asked them to help.* Eddie had once told him a human myth about having three wishes, and how careful you had to be about the way you worded your wish.

"What form might your help take?" Ual asked.

Esganikan had that wess'har trait of suddenly becoming absolutely still, not just immobile but *frozen*. "You have problems feeding an increasing population and dealing with the pollution caused by that. The first step is to reverse your population growth." She dipped her head suddenly, the great plume of red fur catching the light. "Normally we would begin reestablishing a sustainable balance between species in the ecosystem, but as you appear to have eradicated everything beyond food plants and marine life then that presents us with problems. There is little to restore. Do you maintain any genetic archive, like the *gethes* do?"

"No."

"A pity."

"But Tasir Var is not entirely . . . urbanized."

"Your moon."

"Have you observed it?"

"We still assess Umeh from orbit. We will break a vessel out to there soon."

Ual pondered *break*. Eddie said the Eqbas ships split into sections. "You could take the remaining native species from Tasir Var."

"Not an ideal solution, but at the moment I can think of no other. Da Shapakti is the expert. His priority must be Bezer'ej."

If Esganikan knew it was called Asht then she was refusing to use the isenj name. Ual accepted that Asht was now beyond isenj reach; and he always had, even though his colleagues and the electorate thought otherwise. Sometimes you needed to trade pride and dreams for a safer reality.

Two Eqbas males entered the compartment and called up wonderfully detailed images of Umeh's topography in the bulkhead. It seemed as if the hull of the ship was a liquid sheet full of light.

"Do you have any means to limit your birthrate?" asked Esganikan.

"Yes, but regions are reluctant to use it in case their neighbors don't and they are overrun. We have never fully developed such . . . unpopular medicine."

"Then we will create a solution that acts on all isenj equally at the same time."

Ual hesitated. "What?"

"A medication. An intervention."

"But how will you ensure that all use it?"

Esganikan stood up and passed her hands across the surface of the bulkhead, creating a closer view of Ebj, the Northern Assembly territory. She put a long multijointed finger on a fine tracery of lines.

"Is this part of the water grid?"

"Yes."

"Does every Umeh region have such a network?"

Ual began to see the Eqbas mind at work. "I would say that twenty such grids serve ninety percent of the population."

"And the remainder?"

"They exist on more remote islands and have their own extraction and pumping systems." Umeh was a world in precarious and shifting equilibrium: discomfort was spread fairly, a necessary thing in a crowded world that needed to defuse tension to maintain order. "You plan to . . . intervene in the water supply, then?"

"It is the least drastic solution and the most universal. You must all consume water."

"So you want me to show you how to access the regional systems."

"All of them."

"Even Ebj?"

"As I said, we will treat all equally. We wish to be fair, and your internal politics are not our concern." She cocked her head. She seemed to be searching his face. "We have your DNA. Are all isenj similar? If not, we shall need more tissue specimens."

Ual heard his beads rattle in an involuntary reflex of quill fluffing. *My tissue. My DNA.* But he concentrated on his duty. "I have not agreed to this."

"We will do it anyway." Esganikan dismissed the images in the bulkhead with an imperial wave reminiscent of a human's. "The alternative is culling, and that is an extreme measure, but we can do that too, and easily, as there are few other life-forms to consider." She glanced at Ual as if expecting a reply: she had odd shiny eyes like a human, too, and the same flat featureless skin. "You don't want us to cull."

Ual had to remind himself she was absolutely literal. This wasn't one of Eddie's verbal games.

"No, but I believe your claim that you will do it if we don't comply."

It was Eddie.

If Eddie had actively handed over that quill to create the bioweapon or had done so from accident or innocence, the result was the same. Asht—Bezer'ej was now out of isenj reach, and he was secretly glad of the removal of one more temptation to overstretch their capacity. But he wasn't wess'har. He *did* care about motive.

I rarely trust anyone. But he was inexplicably hurt that Eddie might have done something *behind his back,* to use the human phrase.

Esganikan did that rapid head-tilting gesture, side to side, pupils dilating and closing into thin crossed lines.

"You misunderstand us," she said. "As long as you remain on your own world and harm no other species in it, your problems are yours to resolve. When you step beyond that line, they are ours." Her English was getting better by the minute. "But your colonizing missions are over. And they are over for the *gethes,* too. You will both learn to live in balance within your own boundaries."

Ual reached down and snapped off a quill from among the older ones by his legs, the ones set to shed soon. He took off the corundum bead and handed the quill to Esganikan. This had to be a conscious act, not a betrayal.

"If you need more," said Ual, "you may simply ask."

In his mesh of fingers, the bead glinted with blue light. He would give it to Eddie. He left the Eqbas ship and prepared to send a message to his mate.

13

The community of Constantine colony wishes to return to Earth. We will remove them from Wess'ej by your year of 2381 and transport them to a location of their choosing on your homeworld during your year 2406. We will also grant their request of aid to re-establish the species contained in the Constantine gene bank in their proper habitat.

This will mean some rearrangement on your part. The transition will be easier if your planet's administrations use the interim period to prepare for a radical restoration of your ecosphere. Do not attempt to hinder this operation. It is for the good of all species with a stake in your planet. It will be carried out.

MATRIARCH CURAS TI
to the UN Secretary General,
on behalf of the joint administrations of Eqbas Vorhi

"Holy shit," said Eddie. He inhaled a chunk of dehydrated wheat sprouts and coughed until his eyes watered. "Coming, ready or not."

He read the transcript of the Eqbas ultimatum several times over breakfast in Nevyan's main room. The ITX link to 'Desk had been down for ten hours. But he could still see the outgoing news feed, and it reminded him that over the years he had slipped story by story, interview by interview, into the position he was occupying now. He had always been a tool for politicians, mostly knowingly, sometimes not.

The Eqbas statement wasn't an ultimatum. That implied the *unless* factor. And there wasn't any *unless* about it. Coming, ready or not . . .

Lisik was trilling tunelessly while he boiled a pan of something red and slimy. Its fumes made Eddie's nose prickle. Giyadas occupied herself in playing with Eddie's

handheld, now retrieved from Esganikan and with an ITX
link to Earth built into it, courtesy of Livaor. Nevyan seemed
to have inherited a stable of impressively capable males.

Serrimissani watched them all, turning her head sharply
from one to the other, as much the embodiment of a meerkat
on guard duty as he had ever seen. And this was a regular
day. *Invasion. Breakfast with aliens. The end of my career.*

Eddie had the recurring experience of standing outside
his own body and observing his extraordinary position;
faced with overwhelming novelty, his brain sought a familiar
pattern and settled on breakfast to buffer the experience. It
was the split second when the cinematic image of war in
your viewfinder suddenly became personal and aimed at you
and you *ran* for it.

"What did you expect?" asked Serrimissani.

"More saber-rattling," said Eddie. "You'd have thought
I'd have learned the wess'har style by now, wouldn't you?"

"Two years is ample time to do so."

She came and went as she pleased in Nevyan's household, disappearing most nights to return to the ussissi warren
with its little half-buried mud-plaster eggshell domes. Eddie
could now see that the Constantine colony on Bezer'ej had
been built to a mix of two architectural styles, the discreetly
buried galleries of northern Wess'ej and the domes of ussissi nests. He was fascinated by the symbiotic evolution of
two burrowing species, but his fascination had to take a
backseat.

Earth was going to get a personal visit from Eqbas Vorhi.

It would happen in thirty years' time, but it was going
to happen and nothing was going to prevent it. The Eqbas
had the same literal finality as their clean-living Wess'ej
cousins.

"I can't complain that I haven't had the best exclusives in
history," he said. He heard his own feeble reassurance. "I
mean, who else could run alien invasion stories live from the
front?"

Serrimissani did her fox yawn, the little whining noise

followed by a snap of jaws. "I understand many of your colleagues have tried over the years."

"I mean serious journalists with genuine stories."

"And you haven't transmitted any material about Frankland's return."

"Okay." He hadn't a clue what to say about Shan, even if he intended to run the story, which he didn't. He'd done enough damage as it was. "I've succumbed to self-censorship again. Let's say I've grown up."

Giyadas sat beside him and peered into the bowl. Then she placed his handheld and screen in front of him.

"I spoke to a *gethes* at the United Nations. She was alarmed."

Eddie's stomach somersaulted. He had no idea the link was being answered. The kid hadn't said a word about it. Jesus, she'd spoken to someone on Earth. "Sweetheart, did you say anything to scare her?"

"I told her who I was and I asked which *gethes* nations would live like wess'har and which would not."

It was a reasonable question for the miniature adult that Giyadas was. But if that call had gone straight through to the UN shortly after the warning from Esganikan had been received, then it might have sounded like a very different enquiry. It might have sounded like *who's going to be on our side and who isn't.*

"What did she say?" asked Eddie.

"She said she would get someone *senior* to speak to me."

He prodded the handheld with a cautious finger and reopened the link. The image that appeared was an office with ornate translucent furniture as if someone had decided to do the rococo look in ice sculpture. Cherry blossoms were suspended within the back of the glass-clear empty chair that occupied the shot. In the way of all small incongruous detail, the pink petals seized his attention.

Then the chair was suddenly occupied, and a middle-aged woman in a high-necked taupe suit gave a visible breath of relief.

"I'm Eddie Michallat, BBChan," said Eddie. "I was hoping to speak to my news desk. What happened to the FEU Defense Ministry portal?"

"Transmissions are being routed through the United Nations now," said the woman. An ID icon sat at the bottom of the frame: YULYA CORT, CRISIS LIAISON. With a job title like that, Eddie thought, she was probably a light sleeper. "May I ask who was using your link?"

"Giyadas . . ." He struggled for the wess'har naming convention. "Giyadas Lisik Nevyan. I'm sorry about that. She's a little girl. So you have control of outgoing ITX now?"

"Access is being allocated at the moment."

"A queue to use the phone, eh?"

"Sorry?"

"Old phrase. Doesn't matter." He gave her a pause to talk but she didn't take it. He wasn't even asking her a question so he made a mental note that she might prove difficult. "Would you mind patching me through to BBChan Europe, please?"

"This is a relay for international community use. If we open it up to the entertainment industry, it would become unmanageable."

No, doll. That's not the way it's done, believe me.

Eddie rarely demanded what he could ask for as a favor, but he felt it was time she understood his connections. "I'm not the entertainment industry, as you call it. I'm a BBChan journalist. Now, I could always ask this kid's *mother* to ask you. Would that be easier? I'm her guest, along with the Eqbas Vorhi advance fleet."

Cort appeared to think about it for a while; then her right arm moved out of frame.

"I'll see what I can do," she said. The screen faded out to the baby blue UN holding portal.

"What is it?" said Giyadas.

"Nothing," said Eddie. He was annoyed that he hadn't been connected, but he had Ual, Nevyan and now Esganikan to exercise a little influence for him. He'd wait. "Bloody jobsworth."

"She doesn't know how important you are." From anyone else it would have been taking the piss. From Giyadas, it was a sincere assessment. "You are one of us."

Serrimissani made a small *ssss* that probably translated exactly the way it sounded.

Reporters weren't supposed to be important or one of *anybody*. It was the final proof, if he needed it, that he'd gone too far. He went back to his bowl of wheat sprouts, reassuring himself that the meager supply of grain was far more nutritious in this state, and suddenly realized the only person who cared about him was an alien kid.

It had never hit him that hard before. Next week, next month, next year, something would change and he would stop crashing through bad and half-hearted relationships. But he never had: that was why he was here, like the rest of them. He was someone with so few emotional anchors on Earth that he could wrench himself out of time to travel twenty-five light-years from home.

Even Shan Frankland—aloof and hard as a whore's heart—had stumbled into communal domesticity. That told him just how alone he truly was. Even Shan could get her leg over here.

He crunched thoughtfully.

"Will you return with the colony?" asked Serrimissani.

He hadn't even considered it. The news was happening *here*. If he did, he would want to return to the Cavanagh system because this was the most fascinating place he had ever been and—the kid had hit the nail on the head—he was *important* here. He couldn't bear the idea of all this going on without being involved in it.

And by the time he got out of the freezer, everyone he left behind here would be at least fifty years older. He didn't fit in anywhere any more. He probably never would.

"I might stick around."

"Ual is returning to Umeh."

"He's a braver man than I am, Gunga Din."

Serrimissani didn't ask the obvious question and continued undistracted. "He will have Eqbas to protect him."

"How? They've got a few thousand personnel, tops."

"Attack an Eqbas and see what retribution follows."

"How come everyone knows so much about them except the wess'har here?"

"They don't want to know."

"But how can they *avoid* knowing what they get up to?" Eddie had no concept of not wanting to know something, nor any idea of how a technically advanced species got to be that way without indiscriminate curiosity. He fumbled in his pocket and pulled out the drab gray isenj data-player with the cube still in it. "Have you *seen* this shit? Do you know what the Eqbas have done to planets who've got out of line over the years?"

"Broadly speaking, yes. We too come from Eqbas Vorhi."

"*And?* Is this okay?"

"Is it any different to what your powerful nations did to those they could subdue and press into their mold, except that Eqbas Vorhi is interplanetary in its reach?"

"No, but wess'har are supposed to be morally superior."

"So if a large human attacks a small human and causes it suffering, then it is *morally superior* to ignore their plight? And what if the attack was unprovoked?"

Eddie hated arguing ethics with her. He usually lost. He was being sucked into an indefensible position: damn, that was *his* job. "Define provocation."

"Do you tolerate cultural differences on Earth?"

"Yes."

"Even ones like stoning females to death for being raped."

Serrimissani had done her homework. Eddie was more convinced than ever that she was a natural journalist.

"That's an extreme example, doll. There are clearly things that are unacceptable, and things that—"

"Clarity for *you*, perhaps," she said, and her tone was

very neutral, not at all her usual hissing contempt. "Understand that *we* have clear lines of acceptability too. At what point do you intervene? Where is the line between cultural difference and unacceptable behavior? I imagine your more barbaric communities feel their actions are acceptable, just as you feel yours are."

Eddie unpacked the sentence and decided that was exactly what it was: a sentence, but in the legal sense.

"Okay, you win. We're a species of verminous fucktards. I still don't understand why the wess'har here can be so uncurious and still have science and technology."

"Eddie, humans seem to have difficulty accepting that others do not think as they do. Nor do they seem to want to try. That shows a singular lack of curiosity in itself."

No, wess'har didn't think like humans. Eddie conceded defeat and returned to his wheat sprouts.

"That was enjoyable," said Giyadas. "What may we debate now?"

On the surface, wess'har behaved very much like humans. Eddie watched Lisik drain the red slime and pack it into exquisite scarlet glass jars that looked almost liquid in themselves, just like anyone pickling produce for the winter. Cidemnet, another of the four males that Nevyan had taken in when their own *isan* died, walked in and checked flat trays of a white sponge sheet that appeared to be drying on the planklike range. It was a peaceful scene of domesticity.

Cidemnet prodded the sponge sheets with a stick of brilliant amber glass and seemed satisfied. He broke some off into a bowl and held it out to Eddie. "You try?" he said. Livaor, rinsing fabric in a bowl of water, paused to watch the show.

Eddie dabbed the sponge with a cautious finger and tasted it. It wasn't just pepper-hot: it was sour and musty and it actually *hurt*.

"Cidemnet makes very good *rov'la*," said Giyadas, and took half the portion.

"I can tell," said Eddie hoarsely.

Cidemnet was also pretty useful with a fighter craft. He

had flown only one mission in his life and that had ended
with CSV *Actaeon* breaking up in orbit around Umeh and its
shattered hull giving Jejeno a spectacular meteor display.
Eddie smiled with all the will he could muster and chewed a
small chunk of searing, choking, foul *rov'la*.

No, they weren't like humans at all.

Ade was sitting on an outcrop at the top of the bluff, collar
turned up against the wind, rifle and Bergen on his back,
swinging his legs idly like a heavily armed schoolboy. Rain
had started to fall, making the day feel colder than it was.

"Who told you where I was?" he said.

"I can still follow a suspect." Shan's legs screamed for a
rest. She sat down beside him. "Nevyan said you had a little
bolt-hole up here."

"You shouldn't be out in this weather."

"Don't be so bloody daft." She held her hand out to him,
more of a hand-it-over gesture than a tender one. He hesitated and didn't take it. "Get your arse back home and let's
not have any more of this crap." She wanted to tell him that
he was a kind, brave and very appealing bloke, and that she
was pathetically grateful for his devotion, but it didn't come
out quite like that. "Come on, move it."

"I'm in the way, aren't I?"

"You come home right now. We'll work it out."

"I bet you said things like that when you were talking
someone down from a window ledge."

"No, I used to say, 'Jump, you pathetic fucker, and stop
holding up the traffic.'"

Ade laughed. It was true but maybe he didn't realize that;
he seemed to think that she was wonderful, noble, heroic.
She wasn't. She didn't care about the rest of the human race.
She cared about him, and maybe she cared about Eddie at a
pinch, but not in quite the same way.

"So that's it, is it?" Shan looked down at the cairn. The
stones were all neatly graduated, big ones at the bottom, de-
creasing in size as they went up. He'd put a lot of effort into

it. "Did many people turn up? Did they say nice things about me and talk about my tireless work for charity?"

Ade sat with arms folded, chin down and eyes lowered, and didn't answer.

"Sorry," she said. "I tend to forget that it's more traumatic for the mourners than it is for the corpse."

Shan got up and gave him a few moments while she busied herself studying the cairn's construction. There was something lodged deep in the stones, a piece of fabric and metal. She worked her fingers carefully into the gap to pull it out, realizing too late that it was a singularly tactless act.

"Jesus, Ade." She spread the medals in her palm and let the ribbons drape over the edge of her hand. Turkey, Macedonia, North Africa; and the ACG and the Military Star. She had no idea that he'd been decorated twice for bravery, but it didn't surprise her. It also didn't surprise her that he'd never mentioned it. "I bet you didn't get these free with your breakfast cereal."

Predictably, he blushed. It was one of those odd contrasts with his roughy-toughy marine image that she found deeply endearing. "Yeah, well . . ."

"If you brought them all this way then they must mean a lot to you. It was a lovely gesture."

Just sometimes—and with less frequency over the years—someone could get past her defenses. Ade did it all too frequently for her peace of mind. He didn't look up but there was a distinct citrus-tinged whiff of a wess'har male under stress. She folded the ribbons round the medals, unfastened his battledress and slipped them into the top pocket of his shirt.

"Sod 'em, Ade. Sod them all. They can't take it away from you." She slid her warrant card out of the swiss. She still had a real card: she always refused implanted technology. "And we have to be more than badges."

She shoved the card between the stones. Superintendent Frankland was gone, and she had to get used to being Shan, the person she'd been cooped up with in open space when she couldn't move or breathe or die.

Ade raised his eyebrows. "Like that's going to change you one bit."

And that was another thing they had in common. It was more than her healthy interest in his fit body and his charming awkwardness. They had both found something of a genuine family in their respective uniforms, and then politicians had taken that from them. There was a sense of shared betrayal.

They took the easy way down from the bluff. It was a tense walk back home and she struggled to make conversation.

"What was Ouzhari like when you were last there?"

Ade shrugged. "Bloody horrific."

"Oh."

"Yeah."

"Right . . ."

Ade walked on a few more strides and then sighed. "I really thought that when you came back I'd stop feeling so bad about things, but I haven't."

"For chrissakes, Ade, let it go."

"I'm trying."

"I fucked up your life with *c'naatat*. We're even."

"My life was fucked long before you nutted me."

"Your dad?"

"Yeah, the shit-house."

"I think I've picked up your memory of him."

"Handy with his fists. He'd have a go at me and my brother and my mum too, except she normally fought back and took a good hiding for us when he was really tanked up. And I did sod all to save her." Ade gave her an awkward nudge, the sort he usually reserved for Barencoin or Becken. "You're a lot like her."

Ah well. Now she knew the psychology of his devotion. "I'm sorry I lashed out at you. You don't need any more violence."

"It's why I find it hard when women need help. I think that's why I crapped myself when I had to rescue Mesevy."

She'd almost forgotten the incident. Sabine Mesevy,

drowning in the bottomless bog outside Constantine, sinking into slime populated by transparent *sheven* that would engulf you and digest you. Ade had gone in without hesitation. He'd thrown up and also lost control of his bowels afterwards, but only afterwards.

"I'd have let her go under," said Shan. "Like it or not, it was heroic."

"I should have done more for my mum. I was the bloke."

"You were a child and your mother was an adult. She chose to stay with a violent man." *The silly cow, being that emotionally dependent on a man.* "Just drop the guilt. You've got enough on your plate now without beating yourself up about the past."

Shan had once thought of Ade as a medium type of man; mid-build, mid-brown hair, mid-brown eyes, the sort of bloke you wouldn't notice unless your business was noticing people. But she had learned he was simply good at avoiding attention, a useful survival trait in both a brutalized child and a professional soldier. There was nothing mediocre about him at all. She thought of the time she had very nearly weakened and succumbed to a quick and unromantic fuck on Bezer'ej, and she realized she had spotted what he truly was from their first encounter on board *Thetis*. He was courageous, a real man by her exacting definition, and not because he was fearless but because he knew exactly what fear was.

She tried again. "Are you getting on okay with Aras?"

"He's a pro." It was almost his highest accolade, one degree short of *fucking hero*. There was definitely a precise hierarchy of personal worth, climbing up from the pits of *shit-house* through *tourist*, *sound* and *pro* to heroic status. "A good mate."

"You've got a lot in common. I know that you and Eddie kept him together. I owe you for that."

"Least I could do."

"You know what the isenj did to him, don't you?"

"He never said exactly." Ade had that look—a compression of the lips as if stifling profanity and a fixed gaze into middle distance—that said he didn't need to be told. "*C'naatat* filled in the gaps for me."

Shan thought of something warm and gel-like hitting her cheek. Maybe it wasn't the time to ask. "I keep recalling your being hit in the face by something wet."

Ade looked blank, gazing ahead of him as he walked, and then he screwed his eyes shut for a second. "Yeah," he said. He didn't expand and she didn't press him, so she waited a few moments and changed the subject.

"We need to talk about the domestic arrangements." She couldn't bring herself to say it. She had to. "Aras is afraid I'll prefer you to him."

"Oh." Pebbles crunched under Ade's boots. The *S* word had still not intruded in the conversation. "I didn't think wess'har were jealous."

"Polyandry's natural for them. He's just worried about being alone again."

Ade nodded, eyes fixed straight ahead. "That's all a bit exotic for me."

He knew what she meant, then. "Okay, I read you wrong."

Ade swallowed audibly. "No. You didn't."

"Changed your mind?"

"No."

"Okay. When you're up for it, just ask."

Ade slowed to an ambling pace. He was blushing again. "You ever fallen in love?"

"No. Loved eventually, but never fallen."

"I didn't think so." He walked on.

This was why Shan felt comfortable with wess'har. There was nothing you could say that sounded gauche or clinical to them. Just the facts, ma'am: either something was so, or it wasn't, and nobody got embarrassed. But Ade did.

And so did she. "Sorry. This comes from never having to beat men off with a shitty stick. I never learned to do this right."

"It's okay. You're just like a bloke, really." He bit his lip, his face a caricature of instant regret. "I didn't mean it like that. I meant that I don't have to guess your mood or explain what my job's like . . . shit, I'm really fucking this up, aren't I?"

"Yes. You can stop digging that hole now."

He put his hands over his eyes in mock exhaustion. "Jesus, I wish I was good with words. Please don't laugh at me. I know I'm not clever."

She dug her nails into her palm to stop a smile crossing her face because he wouldn't have understood that she found him touchingly innocent rather than ignorant. "I'm not laughing. And you're not stupid."

"It was Dave Pharoah."

It was an almost wess'har non sequitur, a sudden leap from one subject to another just as Aras did. "What was?"

"The splash on your face. Corporal Dave Pharoah. My oppo. He was a daft sod, Dave. I got my tattoos on a tat run with him when we were completely hand-carted on rough cider. He bet me I wouldn't have a tattoo done in a really painful place." Ade managed a rueful smile. Then it faded. "He got shot standing right next to me at Ankara and his brains went all over my face. I didn't realize what it was at first. I thought it was bird shit."

Shan wanted to say she understood but she knew she didn't. For all the violence in her job, she had gone home at the end of a shift, selected a menu from the catering service, and cleaned her 9mm. She had never been under fire for days or weeks and she had never wiped a comrade's brain tissue off her face. When you thought you were *well hard,* to use Eddie's phrase, it was always sobering to realize there was someone who had experienced far worse things than you had.

She patted his back slowly. "Sorry I brought it up."

"It goes with the job. You know what you're in for when you sign up."

No, you don't. You couldn't possibly. "I'm still sorry."

"Anyway, I had the tattoo done and it hurt all right." Ade kicked a pebble into the air and caught it in one hand, apparently unaware of how impressive that seemed to her. "If I miss people now, what's it going to be like when I outlive everyone?"

"I think we'll both find out around the same time," said Shan, happy to be counted as one of the boys again.

14

You've dragged the rest of the world into this and we're going to have aliens landing here in thirty years. Plenty of time to come up with a solution? No. The population is going to panic now, and they're going to blame us. I'm going to make the Eqbas an offer, because I'm not entirely convinced that they're the enemy. I think the enemy is standing right in front of me.

CANH PHO
Prime Minister of the Australasian Republic
in a private conversation with Birsen Ertegun

The island of Ouzhari, Bezer'ej.

Shan walked along the shoreline of Ouzhari, suitless and bewildered.

She had never seen the island in its unspoiled state and maybe that was just as well. Many crime scenes during her career had made her punching mad, and a few had even reduced her to private tears, but the scene of desolation notched up a new category: she was numbed.

Esganikan and Shapakti walked at a discreet distance to her right, in environment suits that were soft and flowing like translucent shrouds. She could see them in her peripheral vision. Maybe it had been a bad idea to forgo the suit, but she didn't need one. It crossed her mind that it emphasized to the Eqbas that she was a freak to be controlled at all costs.

She squatted on the sand, elbows braced on her knees and hands clasped. What did you say? What could you even think? She tapped her thumbnails against her front teeth, pondering the enormity of the blast.

"Are you praying?" asked Shapakti.

She could hear him well enough, suit or not. "No. And if I thought there was a deity listening I wouldn't exactly be praying, either."

She stood up and walked further along the shore, stepping carefully over unidentifiable patches of decayed matter that might once have been bodies. She hadn't even expected bacteria here. But something had already returned to profit from the carnage.

They're bezeri. They're people.

She was ashamed that she had to remind herself of that, only feeling the revulsion on an intellectual level rather than an instinctive one. There were nonhuman animals she reacted to instantly at a gut level and those that she had to think about. *It doesn't matter. It's what you do, not what you feel that counts.*

Esganikan said little. She kept an eye on the survey teams, one of them busy carrying out test bores into the soil and the other on a bizarre floating platform that looked for all the world like a glass raft. Shan had no idea why it wasn't swamped by the waves. It had no gunwales that she could see, and large shallow containers didn't remain stable once they took on a little water and it started slopping around. But the Eqbas team of four stood calmly on the transparent platform as if it was solid ground, with their hands clasped against their chests and looking down at something. As bizarre as it looked, it was simply the wess'har equivalent of standing with hands on hips, a comfortably relaxed pose.

Then they all stepped back in one synchronized movement. A column of dull glass rose from the deck of the raft. For a moment Shan thought it was part of the steerage or even the head of a drilling mechanism, but it wasn't. It really *was* water, seawater, somehow lifted intact from the ocean beneath.

One of the Eqbas—a male, by the smaller build—inserted a thin rod like a stylus into the column at waist height and studied it. His head tilted sharply. Then he withdrew the rod and reinserted it near the base of the column. There was more vigorous head-tilting and the column rose higher, an impossible tower of water with no visible support rearing above a raft that shouldn't have been floating. Shan was transfixed.

The column was at least five meters high now, and the whole team was indulging in that head-tilting that said something had completely engrossed them, something they weren't expecting.

"What are they doing?" she asked.

Esganikan stood beside her. When Shan turned, the Eqbas matriarch was staring at her and not at the bizarre spectacle on the glass raft.

"They're testing the sea at different depths to assess contamination and biological activity."

Esganikan was standing so close that Shan felt an urge to shove her in the chest and nick her for *looking at her funny* as Rob McEvoy called it. Rob, her bagman, had been a young inspector who she was grooming as a successor. *Rob. Is he still alive?* She'd never returned his message. She'd forgotten him. It appalled her. She'd make that a priority.

Esganikan stepped back one pace. Shan could taste her own scent of dominance, enough to keep the Eqbas commander in her place. Esganikan could obviously smell it too, even in her suit.

"Did you acquire your *jask* with your wess'har genes or have you always been this way?" she asked.

"I'll show you my file," said Shan, and didn't budge an inch.

"I know who you are and what your task was."

"*Is.*" Shan was distracted by the raft again. It was moving away. "I haven't finished it yet."

The raft was moving fast, and not like a vessel trailing spray or dipping and rising through the waves. It was simply moving, level and utterly unnatural. There was no sign of wind whipping the crew's loose suits and for a moment

Shan's brain told her she was watching a camera shot, a zoom out from a static scene.

"They're in a hurry."

"They have detected something." Esganikan paused as if listening. "It may be another false reading. They found something that looks like the waste products of bezeri in minute dilution."

"Survivors?"

"Or more recently dead."

Shan looked round and watched the land team for a while. They were simply taking core samples with a tube that looked much like the one used by Olivier Champciaux, the geologist who'd been part of the *Thetis* team. He was another person she hadn't thought of in a while: all the remaining payload, as the marines had called the mission's scientists, were at Umeh Station. *All except the dead ones, anyway. And Rayat.* "What were you doing when they diverted you here?"

"We were returning from a patrol at Harsa. I believe Shapakti's crew was assessing environmental imbalance on Nem Ijot. Neither of us are ideal for this situation, but we could reach you far more quickly than those with more specific experience."

"You sound experienced enough to me. Did you want to go home?"

"I did. But this was a vital mission."

"Ironic. That's how I ended up here, too."

Esganikan might have understood or she might not, but now she kept a respectful distance from Shan—still too close for a human's comfort, but distant by wess'har standards—and walked with her to where Shapakti stood with one of the core sampling teams.

"Can you decontaminate the area?" Shan asked.

Shapakti had a handful of soil cupped in his palms. "Yes. A season, perhaps two."

"That's impressive."

"It is routine work. But we had hoped there might be biological material we could use as a template for reconstruction."

"The grass." Shan used the English word. She didn't have the wess'u for it. "Black grass."

"What?"

"There was black grass here. A plant that covers the ground. Aras talked about it. He restored the island after the isenj were driven off it."

Shapakti rubbed the soil between the palms of his gloves. "He had material to work from."

"At least it's just Ouzhari." *Yeah, that's clever, you stupid cow. It's just Antarctica. It's just the Galapagos. It's just the bezeri.* "I meant that the damage is localized. It could have been worse."

"Not for the bezeri."

The bore team stood around their drill, waiting, and then Shan realized their rig was nothing like Champciaux's after all. What she had thought was a solid shaft was a column of soil easing out of the ground in the same way as the inexplicable column of seawater. One of the group took a flat sheet of transparent material about the size of a drinks tray and passed it through the column, which somehow remained intact.

"Does he whip off a tablecloth and leave the plates in place for an encore?" Shan asked, but she had slipped back into vernacular English that defeated Shapakti. "What's he doing?"

"They are examining the soil under great magnification."

"With that thing?"

Shan had a nodding acquaintance with laboratory equipment and no more. She nicked the polluters, the dealers in banned biomaterials, the companies who crunched one gene sequence too many: it was up to the boffins to sort out the detail. The Eqbas held the sheet in his hands and studied it as if panning for gold. When she walked up behind him to look, it was suddenly obvious what the sheet was.

She was looking at an image that could have come straight off an electron microscope, and it might have been grains of soil or bacteria. The magnified image covered the entire surface of the sheet. "Now *that's* serious kit," she said. "Whatever it is."

The scientist holding the sheet touched his glove against the surface and isolated a single shape that made her think of a radial hairbrush. The transparent sheet was busy overlaying it with different images at a breakneck speed, blurring its outline.

"Pollen?" she said. She didn't even know if grass here produced pollen. It was too easy to see familiar shapes and assume that meant familiar biology.

"I don't know," said Shapakti. "We have never seen this before. It bears no resemblance to anything from our databases. May I take a sample from you?"

Shan rolled back her sleeve and held out her arm, which was now showing muscle, although nowhere near at her normal levels. *He wants to rule out contamination by my cells,* she thought. It was basic forensic procedure, and she felt a sudden nostalgic kinship with another investigator.

Shapakti pressed a gloved finger against the skin of her forearm and studied the tip, then dabbed it on the glass tray. Shan had no idea how he could separate a specific sample from the general contamination he picked up on his gloves, but it seemed that he could, because images began moving again on the surface of the tray. It was dauntingly advanced technology. Shan thought she might sit quietly in a corner with a flint and a few bits of straw and try to discover fire.

Shapakti shuffled his boots and pointed at the tray. "See. What you have within you is the same as this."

The hairbrush images shuffled, distorted and lined up. Then symbols that she didn't understand arranged themselves in a cluster at the top left of the sheet.

So this was *c'naatat*. Shan studied it, not really knowing what she was looking at but transfixed by it nonetheless, and suddenly alarmed that he could obtain a sample from unbroken skin. "Can you enlarge it?"

Each bristle of the brush resolved into more brushes,

complex and never-ending as a fractal. This was the organism that had remade her—once, twice, three times at least. It had decided she needed claws, and changed its mind: then bioluminescence, but that satisfied it. And it had taken a fancy to the ability to see shades of blue that only wess'har could see, and the dubious gift of isenj genetic memory, and scent communication, and things she couldn't even begin to guess at because they hadn't made themselves known to her yet.

And it had kept her alive in space.

"Poor little sod," she said to herself, even though she didn't like to think of it as being conscious of its actions. Maybe it was. For now, it was a virus, or a bacterium, or an ultra-benign disease; anything but a decision-making creature. "You don't look like any trouble at all."

"We will still exercise caution," said Shapakti.

"I don't think it can do much harm now."

Shapakti held his arms slightly away from his sides as if he had touched something especially messy. The bore team was suddenly very still and so was he.

"It is not dead," he said.

15

The Pacific Rim States and the African Assembly today issued an ultimatum to the Federal European Union to end its deep space exploration program "immediately and indefinitely" or face armed intervention.

The demand, thought to have the tacit support of the Sinostates, follows yesterday's shock revelation that Eqbas Vorhi intends to land on Earth in thirty years' time. "I might be dead by the time that happens but my kids won't be," said UN delegate Jim Matsoukis. "If we stop this insane colonial adventuring right now we might avert an unprecedented disaster."

It's not yet known if the FEU will give in to pressure to recall its warship Hereward, still heading for the Cavanagh's Star system. "We still have people stranded out there and we won't abandon them," said an FEU spokesman.

BBChantext 1667. See UN debate live at 1800 EUST.

"He should have known," said Shan.

Esganikan walked with her, a rare study in matriarchal patience. They had trailed up and down the Ouzhari shoreline for a couple of hours, stopping to look out to sea as the afternoon wore on and the rest of the survey team trailed back to the ship to eat. Shan could see it from the beach: a luminous copper cylinder, its shape now more like an igloo with an entrance tunnel, with waves of faint light shimmering across its hull as the automated decontamination system swept it clean of radiation. Shan could walk here with impunity but it was still a dangerous, poisoned place for all other life.

Except *c'naatat.*

"I don't understand why this makes you angry," said Esganikan. "An organism has survived. The situation is not completely desperate."

Shan jerked her thumb over her shoulder at the lifeless beach behind her. She fell back on English. "It's a fucking barbecue here. *What's* not desperate?" Esganikan stood impassive and silent. Shan concentrated on wess'u again. "Sorry. Not only is this as bad as I could imagine, but the bezeri died for nothing. And Rayat is a scientist. He knows that even some terrestrial bacteria can survive radiation. This was a big, sloppy, stupid gamble. Look." She held out her arms, flipping her hands over and back again to demonstrate them. "I'm probably here now because some bacteria have a talent for surviving *anything*."

Esganikan brushed something from her soft environment suit. It reminded Shan of a burqa.

"I learned your language in days, but I will never learn how you think. This is all irrelevant."

"Maybe I'm not wess'har enough to feel that way."

"You desire balance. That is what police require, isn't it?"

"Yeah, and we don't often get it."

"And what if the survey team find bezeri still alive? Will that anger you too?"

"Have you got Aras's signal lamp?"

"Yes."

"Then if you find any, tell them Shan Frankland is sorry—again. I bet that's the one English word they don't need translated by now."

Esganikan went back to the ship. Shan sat down cross-legged on the sand to wait for the glass raft to return, suddenly aware she was probably sitting on organisms that had changed her life beyond human recognition. She picked up a handful of soil and sifted it between her fingers.

Shapakti approached her, giving her a wide berth like a nervous beekeeper in his loose pale suit and veil. Everything that wess'har made, even the sinister stuff like weapons and biohaz suits, had a certain functional elegance.

"You haven't eaten." Shapakti's agitation made it clear he didn't want her to get the wrong idea about his offer of food. It wasn't a sexual invitation. "Aras insisted that I make you eat regularly. Come back to the ship."

"I have to decontaminate first or I'll make you all light up. Can't be arsed at the moment"

"Is that a refusal?"

"Yes, it is."

"I will bring food to you, then."

"Don't worry. You're perfectly safe, mate. You're not my type." She saw his pupils snap from four-petaled flower to cross wires even behind the suit's draped visor: he might have been working out what *mate* meant and fearing for his honor again. "Would you do me a favor? Before we leave, can I visit Constantine?"

"Of course. You can go now if you wish, while we wait for the others to return."

"How? I could walk, but it's a hell of a long way."

"What?"

"I can't drown. I've done it. I walked into the water and visited the bezeri. Can't say I enjoyed the sensation, though."

"It is indeed a long way to walk, especially in your condition. I will find a vessel."

He beckoned to her and she followed him back to the craft. Two years alongside utterly alien technology had raised her amazement threshold and she was expecting some part of the small craft to detach itself and form a boat or some other form of transport. But Shapakti simply opened a hatch in the igloo-ship's tunnel of an entrance lobby and removed a milky smooth cube thirty centimeters square.

"What's that?"

"You called it a raft. A *niluy-ghur.*"

"Oh, this is going to be one of those conjuring tricks, isn't it?" She had once watched a wess'har take a simple jointed stick and snap it into a frame that made a stool. Working surfaces emerged like protoplasm from hard flat walls: metal waste biodegraded in hours. Wess'har were good at manipulating two things—solid materials and cells. "White man's magic. Go on. Surprise me."

Shapakti placed the cube at the water's edge and it unfurled itself like an emergency life raft, first folding out into a flat transparent blanket of gel and then becoming rigid. The sea lapped at it. It slid obediently into the water to form a solid platform with one edge still on the beach, and Shapakti walked onto it and stood waiting.

Shan put one foot on the raft. She would have felt safer if she'd had her old boots. It didn't feel quite the same world in the matte gray ones that an anonymous benefactor in F'nar had fashioned for her, even though they were superior boots, silent and thermally perfect and self-cleaning, and they shaped themselves to whatever height and fit she wanted them to be. But they didn't go with the remains of her uniform and they didn't announce her arrival. She missed her old boots.

The raft was rock-solid and didn't move when she put her full weight on it like a boat would have done. As soon as she was inboard—if standing on a glass sheet could ever be considered inboard—it moved away into the shallows and out to sea. A column rose out of the surface in front of Shapakti, a plinth of glass-clear material, and images danced in its top layer almost like the *virin* communicator Nevyan had given her.

Shapakti touched the column and the raft began making speed. If Shan hadn't already seen the vessel in action, she would have abandoned ship there and then. There was no undulation or feeling of the wind in her hair, and she could easily have been standing on an immobile solid floor while the ocean and the landscape moved around and past her and *under* her like a disturbingly good simulation. No water slopped over the bows, such as they were. And she was looking down through the water between her feet. Weed and other unidentifiable debris churned up by the raft's motion roiled in a space trapped between the ocean and the bottom of the hull.

"Tell me this thing doesn't fly," she said.

"Why?"

"I meant that humans don't cope well with seeing the ground a long way beneath them, even if they're on a solid glass floor. They always think they're going to fall."

"You survived in space. You coped well enough."

"Yeah, but I don't want to do it again."

"And it *could* fly if we were to modify it."

Landing on Bezer'ej for the first time: Ade Bennett closed the hatch behind her and she was looking through the transparent section of the shuttle's hull as the AI took over and tipped her out into space. It felt like a long and terrible fall. Her stomach rolled. Shan shook herself out of the memory and put out her hand to steady herself even though there was no movement. A glass column flowed up from the deck to meet it.

It was faintly warm and yielding, like a layer of insulation over steel. "You do like your glass," she said. "Glass utensils, glass drains, glass bells. Glass people."

"You like to be able to see through things, Shan Frankland. So do we."

Shapakti brought his heel down hard on the deck and it extruded a glass booth around him. He slipped off his biohaz suit and the raft swallowed it, sealing it into the deck in a bubble. "Now you," he said. He kicked a booth into place around her. It felt like being shrink-wrapped for market. "Or you will take contamination to Constantine."

The seascape streaked past them, spray and wind held at bay by barriers that she couldn't see. She checked the time on her swiss. Constantine, a hundred miles north of Ouzhari at the top of the chain of islands, was now in sight. The raft must have been making at least ninety knots and yet there was still no sensation of movement.

She stepped off the raft onto a familiar beach and it was suddenly and unexpectedly heartbreaking.

A perfectly spherical stone inlaid with intricate patterns of color stood at the high-water line. It was the Place of

Memory of the First, the memorial to the first bezeri pilot who beached himself to gather information about the Dry Above.

"You know what this says?" she said. Shapakti studied the patterns, just as she had studied them when Aras first showed her the stone. "It says that *the nineteenth of the shoal of Ehek launched himself out of the water and told the waiting ones all he could see of the Dry Above before he died an honorable death.* A suicide mission. After that they developed pod ships with water jets that propelled them back into the water. It was like the early days of space flight to them."

Shapakti followed her down the beach to another large stone memorial, this time a conical one with lines of color spiraling down its sides. Shan patted it. "The Place of Memory of the Returned. The first bezeri who came ashore and made it back. And now they're all gone."

"Perhaps not all." Shapakti stroked his long multijointed fingers over the inlaid stone. "There were several hundred thousand."

"And what if you find a few? A hundred? A dozen? It took them centuries for their population to recover last time and they started out with a lot more. And how can they rebuild?"

"Humans were reduced to hundreds at one time in their evolution."

"And that's a role model?"

"I merely offer a positive future."

"You know what?" Shan began walking up the beach, shaking off memories of when she thought she'd be off Bezer'ej and heading home inside a year, back to a quiet retirement with a garden full of unregistered tomato hybrids. "If you find any bezeri, we should let them have Lindsay Neville. And Rayat. Their call."

Constantine, the Mountain to the Dry Above, was returning to its wild origins. The blue and amber grasses had crept back over the site where the *Thetis* mission had made its camp. Even the recently abandoned fields of the colony

were already being overrun by island species. Without the
invisible biobarrier that contained the colony and allowed a
terrestrial ecology to exist, the crops were dying.

It was a glimpse of the fate that would have befallen the
Constantine mission nearly two centuries before had an ex-
iled alien soldier called Aras Sar Iussan not intervened to
help them survive.

Shan had worked in those fields for a few months. She
walked back through them towards the underground colony,
looking for the discreet skylight bubbles that blistered the
landscape, but she couldn't pick them out. She was right on
top of the colony before she saw it.

At the top of the ramp that led down into the excavated
galleries, she wondered if the tunnels were still accessible.
Nanites had been scattered to reclaim the building materials
and erase all traces of the *gethes*. When Ade and Barencoin
had dragged her bound and gagged from the place, the walls
were already crumbling.

"I'm going to see how far I can get," she said. "I'll call if
I need help."

"I will accompany you," said Shapakti. "A cave-in is less
alarming than the anger of your males."

The subterranean colony, once as striking a feat of exca-
vation as the Nabataeans' Petra, had been robbed of its light
and was now pitch-black. Shan's adapted vision kicked in
and she picked her way through piles of soil and fallen
stone. Her boot crunched on something, and when she
looked down it was the remains of an ESF670 rifle, the one
she had taken from Chahal and tried to fire into Lindsay
Neville's head. The nanites had dismantled most of it; the
buffer pin and return springs seemed to be the last items on
the menu for them.

"They used to have sunlight down here," she said. "Aras
never did tell me how they managed that. Are you okay,
Shapakti?"

"I can see well enough to walk."

Wess'har had evolved from burrow dwellers: low light didn't hamper them, but Shan switched on the flashlight in her swiss anyway. Shapakti didn't have the infrared vision that *c'naatat* had given her.

The map of Constantine was etched in her mind. She sniffed, tasting decay on the stale air. No, not decay: *putrefaction*. She'd smelled that so often in her life that there was no mistaking it for anything else. It was a corpse.

The colonists left their dead for the native rockvelvets. There were no flies here, nor any of the usual terrestrial insects that lived on the dead. The colony had only been interested in resurrecting pollinators from the gene bank.

Shan thought that a good old-fashioned bluebottle would have been just the job right then. "Can you smell it?"

"I smell . . . sulfur compounds."

The wess'har sense of smell was acute. After a couple months in a warm environment bodies had usually peaked in stench, but the microecology here was shot to hell. And rockvelvets only fed in the open. Decay was slow.

Shan reached in the back of her belt for her gun, purely out of habit in a dark and now unfamiliar place, and Shapakti made a little noise of surprise. Maybe he thought she knew something he didn't. His sudden whiff of alarm managed to cut through the smell of rotting meat. The tunnels were silent except for their footsteps and the sporadic sifting noise of falling soil.

"You're not breathing," said Shapakti.

No, she wasn't. It was funny how you could forget to do some things. She made a conscious effort to start again. She headed for the abandoned church of St. Francis, reasoning that if she were a religious colonist in trouble then she'd go there when things got really bad.

GOVERNMENT WORK IS GOD'S WORK

The inscription—archaic, arrogant, delusional—was still legible in the block of hard stone that had come from Ouzhari, the original landing site. Shan just walked in, aware that neither the dead nor the living could harm her but cautious nonetheless. And this wasn't a crime scene with evidence to protect and secure.

The *efte* door was gone and she walked along the aisle as she had first done two years ago, a Pagan disturbing someone else's hallowed ground. But there was no magnificent stained-glass window of the saint who respected all life. The stone frame was empty, the glass pieces safe on Mar'an'cas. And the carved *efte* pews with their dancing angels had been devoured and recycled by the nanites.

She could now both see and smell her target. It was a group of bodies, not one, and when she looked down at them with her hand over her nose and mouth she could see that the group was a man, a woman and two children.

Even if she had known them there was no way she could recognize them now. The woman had long brown hair and there were two hardened slices of bread nearby. One had neat bite marks taken out of it. The cause of death didn't matter any more. But it didn't look as if they starved.

"Stupid bastards," she said. "Some of them wouldn't leave."

Shapakti peered at the bodies, cocking his head in fascination. Of course: if he was going to learn anything about human biology, he would learn it from a dead body, not a live one. Wess'har had no concept of the vivisection of other species.

"Where is the part that still lives?" he asked. "The invisible component?"

"The soul? Oh, that's just crap. A story."

"Like *c'naatat*."

"Shapakti, my old mate, they're *dead*. Trust me. I've seen a few stiffs in my time." *Here I go, copper's lairy mouth again, shutting myself off from it all by being flippant.* "They're not decomposing normally because there isn't the range of insects here to do the job the Earth way. If you want some samples, go ahead."

"The anti-human pathogen worked."

"I'd say. It was based on my original DNA. I always did have an antisocial streak in me." She watched him squat down and place a thin rod at various points in the tangle of misshapen, discolored limbs. The bodies were huddled together, embracing: a family, probably. "Did I look that bad when they brought me in?"

"I believe that your shape was more coherent."

"Flatterer." She thought of a hundred other corpses whose last moments she had reconstructed. "There's a part of me that says put them outside for the rockvelvets, but I'm buggered if I'm going to move them in that state." *Deconsecrated or not, the church is where they wanted to die. Leave them in peace.* "When you've got what you want, let's go."

A little over two months ago Shan had stood here, her back to the altar, and addressed the thousand or so colonists. The man, woman and children lying here had heard her tell them to leave, to abandon all they'd worked for. She looked at the faces and couldn't see who had once looked back at her.

Movement caught her eye.

She aimed her gun two-handed and strained to see. Whatever it was, it was small. She walked into the corner behind the pile of sawdust that had once been the altar and noticed a pattern of tiny footprints and a faint smell. She knew that scent. It was almost like lavender leaves. She put her gun back in her belt and squatted down, looking for rats.

"Come on out, fellas," she said. She made the clicking noise she'd heard Aras use with Black and White to get them to come to him. "Come on. I won't hurt you."

Shapakti edged up behind her. "What is it?"

"Rats. The colony abandoned them. Poor little buggers must be living on the bodies." She didn't dare risk a bite. An immortal rat was a prospect she wasn't ready to contemplate, and she didn't have thick enough gloves to withstand those teeth. Sticking her hand into a hole was a recipe for disaster. She drummed her fingers on the floor until a whiskered nose emerged from a crack in the stone.

"What are they?"

"Earth animals. The *Thetis* mission brought them for experiments."

"Oh."

"Yeah. *Oh.* Aras confiscated them from Rayat and let the kids look after them. He really likes them." She found herself smiling. There was nothing wrong with a man who cared about animals, nothing at all, even if he wiped out cities. She drummed her fingers again and a large beige rat bounded towards her and sniffed her gloves. She withdrew her hand cautiously. "They're tame ones."

She fumbled in her pockets. She always kept something on hand to eat, and this time she found a very old packet of dry rations. It did the trick. In a minute she had assembled fourteen rats of varying sizes and colors, all jostling for food.

"I can't just leave them here," she said. "They'll starve to death. Got a bag or something?"

Shapakti offered her a tube the size of a cigar.

"What's that?"

"A container." He bent it between his fingers and it unfurled into a large open box with curved sides. "Here."

"I bet you were a Boy Scout."

"You are incomprehensible."

"It's just a compliment."

Shapakti picked up the rats, each steadfastly refusing to be parted from its fragment of compressed soya and fruit, and placed them in the box. Shan took off her jacket and laid it across the open top; she didn't know much about rats, but she knew they preferred the comfort and safety of the dark.

"You're undernourished," said Shapakti.

"Give me a few weeks, son," she said, anticipating Aras's delight at the rescue. "Then come and feel my biceps."

They walked a different route through the fields on the way back to the raft. The tayberry bushes were still there, brown and twisted, and it was hard to tell if they were dead or just dormant. Someone should have cut back the old canes to ground level. On a stone facing the sun, two rich black velvet place-mats patterned with concentric lighter rings lay sunning themselves. They shivered at Shan's approach and began sliding off the rock to inch away to safety.

"Rockvelvets," she said. "Human eyes can't see the rings. Did you know that?"

"I would like to know what else *c'naatat* has changed in you."

"I'll tell you all about it one day."

Ceret was setting fast. Skimming south across the sea towards Ouzhari on a sheet of glass in failing light and then in the dark was unnerving, but if you'd drifted in space for a couple of months it was suddenly a long way down the sphincter constriction scale.

Shan was beginning to enjoy sailing. She wondered how Ade might like it. The *niluy-ghur* would have made a great amphibious landing craft if the camouflage could have been sorted out.

By the time they beached, Shapakti was back in his bee-keeper's suit and the box of rats was wrapped in a protective gel film. The Eqbas craft was a gleaming bronze beacon swept sporadically by rippling blue light, looking for all the world like a sleazy nightclub situated on the edge of town because the neighbors objected to the noise.

At the entrance, Shan submitted to decontamination in what she now thought of as a plastic bag and wondered if this was what it felt like to be trapped by a *sheven* just before it began digesting you. It might have been worse than spacing yourself.

"We've brought some guests," she said.

Esganikan was kneeling on the deck with the crew, eating from plates as if they were on a picnic. Shan picked up a dark brown slab and chewed on it, not caring that it tasted like solid yeast extract.

"I hope you didn't mind my bringing back the rats," said Shan. "They couldn't survive here."

"I don't object."

"So? Any news?"

"The marine survey team has located a number of bez-eri," said Esganikan.

"Dead?"

"Alive."

Shan's stomach flipped but she couldn't distinguish between her own relief and dread. So you found someone alive in a pile of bodies, and that was good for five seconds; and then it dawned on you what they would be going through.

"How many?"

"Fifty-four."

"And what shape are they in? Did you manage to use the signaling lamp?"

Esganikan looked for a moment the way Shan had so often felt, shoulders sagging in weary disillusion.

"We may have to work without them to repair the ecosphere. But we *will* repair it."

It was an oddly evasive answer for a wess'har. But their logic was utterly unsentimental. The bezeri were the obvious victims to a human, but they weren't the only species to suffer: others were woven into the ecology.

Shan tried again. "What did they *say,* exactly?"

"They will talk only to Aras Sar Iussan."

In their hour of need, the bezeri had turned to the one outsider in whom they had any degree of trust. Aras would be reassured by that, Shan thought.

She also wondered what they wanted to say to him that they couldn't say to anyone else.

16

This is our final request. We demand that you return both the traitor Par Paral Ual and the Destroyer of Mjat so that they may face proper justice.

MINISTER PAR NIR BEDOI,
Northern Assembly

The vessel that had separated itself to visit Bezer'ej appeared over F'nar, dropping beneath the cloud cover and settling in the Eqbas camp. Aras straightened up and put his hoe aside for a few moments to watch it. The marines stopped too.

Shan was back. He had pined every moment she was away. It had only been two days, but he never wanted to let her out of his sight again, and neither had Ade, but she insisted on going alone.

"She'll be wanting her dinner on the table," said Ade, and dusted his hands on his pants. "Let's get this finished and head home."

"I hope Shapakti took care of her."

"You can bet on it," Ade said. "We had a little chat."

Ade's *little chats* seemed to have a salutary effect. Aras suspected it was the unsettling effect of a polite and modest manner backed up by physical strength and the slightest suggestion that—if pushed—he might kill you. Yes, Ade had the makings of a fine house-brother: Aras would welcome his genes. And the soldier knew what it was to grapple with unpleasant memories and tolerate exile.

"Aras, how do you feel about the Eqbas?" asked Qureshi.

"They're different," he said carefully. So many of them were unmated adults. It was unnatural. "But so am I, so I cannot criticize."

He went to the irrigation node and rinsed his hands and

face under the rushing water. The marines went on hoeing, preparing the ground within the biobarrier for beans, potatoes and something called chickpeas. The area devoted to terrestrial crops had expanded five-fold; there were eight people to feed now who couldn't digest wess'har food and the supplies were running low. For the first time, the Constantine colony had no carefully preserved surpluses to give away. But the marines seemed to be enjoying their rapid instruction in horticulture and had reduced the soil to a textbook fine tilth with precise lines of drills. They were happy to be busy. They didn't seem to care how their time was occupied as long as it was filled with activity.

Aras reflected that it was a perfect image of the *gethes* concept of irony. An alien was teaching urbanized humans how to grow their own crops.

"Painting coal white," said Ade. He squatted down at the end of one of Becken's drills and peered along the line in the soil as if to check for perfection.

Aras considered the concept. "A new phrase for me."

"A pointless activity to keep soldiers busy." Ade took a handful of red beans and began pressing them into the furrow at precise intervals with his thumb. "Is this the right depth?"

"I thought you came from a rural part of Earth."

"Me? Nah. City boy."

"You fed baby foxes. Foxes are wild animals, yes?"

"Yeah, but they're all over the cities. Lots of animals live in urban areas."

Aras felt that he should have realized that. The information—and plenty of it—had been in Constantine's archives. The urban coexistence made the gulf of respect between *gethes* and other species even more incomprehensible to him.

"Yes," said Aras. "That's the correct depth."

"Join the Marines, see the galaxy, and do a bit of gardening," said Barencoin, who had started to look satisfied with his agricultural duties. "Beats getting your arse shot off, anyway."

"You'd fit right in with the colonists," said Webster.

"I don't think Jesus wants me for a sunbeam somehow."

They laughed raucously and while they worked Becken told a joke about a *gethes* with a tapeworm. Aras listened intently. When he had first discovered the parasitic creature while reading the colony archives, he had briefly thought of his *c'naatat* as a benevolent tapeworm. Becken's story alleged that tapeworms enjoyed certain human foods.

Becken had one arm raised with an imaginary hammer in his hand. "So the tapeworm puts his head up and says, 'Where's me bar of nutty, then?' and the doctor goes—*wallop.*"

The marines roared with laughter. Aras, who felt he had some measure of the *gethes'* humor, pitied the tapeworm, who had no choice about the arrangement. His distaste must have shown; or at least he must have smelled agitated, because Ade straightened up from the furrow of beans and gave him a discreet jerk of the head that indicated he wanted Aras to follow him.

"Let's leave this lot to it," he said. "Come on. Can't keep the missus waiting."

There was a perfectly matched chorus of "Oooo-oooo-ooo!" from the marines and Aras suspected he knew what that meant. Ade's face reddened. Aras handed his hoe to Chahal.

They walked away briskly. "I meant *your* missus," said Ade.

"I know."

"I can move out."

"Shan made you return last time. Your leaving will not take away her sense of obligation or attraction."

"And what do *you* want?"

It was easy for a normal wess'har to say what was on their mind. But Aras had been tinted by human hesitation.

He thought for a few seconds, filtering the words. "I miss having house-brothers. I would like us to be a family. But I worry that Shan would feel obliged to choose between us because humans are monogamous."

Ade walked on a little way ahead. He didn't say anything else until they passed through the two outcrops of pearl-coated granite that marked the broken edge of the caldera, as near to a pair of gates as a carefully unplanned city like F'nar would ever allow.

"She'd never leave you. She's not like that."

Aras knew that. But it didn't mean that she would *want* to stay with him. Shan was a creature of duty; the thought of her enduring him if she wanted to be with Ade alone was unbearable. She might grow to resent him in time. He couldn't face that.

"I lost my first *isan* and I very nearly lost Shan. The thought of losing her again terrifies me."

"And you must know what I feel for her. But I've done enough damage. I don't want to do any more."

"The decision will be hers."

They reached the door and there was a moment of hesitation as Aras stood back to let Ade enter first and Ade did the same. There was no natural hierarchy between them yet. Aras stepped across the threshold, flustered.

"I'll get the kettle on," said Ade. "I make a good cup of tea, she says."

Aras had been so certain that having Shan back would make life perfect. But it wasn't working out that way at all. She had a second chance at life, and a very long one at that. He wanted it to be happier than what had gone before.

He would do whatever it took to ensure that.

"And then they will do what, exactly?" demanded Esganikan Gai. She slammed her *virin* down on the table so Ual could see the vague ultimatum from his respected colleague Bedoi. "The isenj will use force if we don't comply? Or is this just talk?"

Her English was becoming excellent, and very rapidly. Ual tried hard to stop his beads shivering on his quills: he had been in F'nar a week now and was becoming agitated. In the Exchange of Surplus Things he had a permanent audience because, as Eddie told him, wess'har *washed their dirty linen in public.*

"There is a great deal of rhetoric in public life that wess'har are unfamiliar with," said Ual. "Sometimes politicians don't think before they speak. Their concern is saying what will satisfy the electorate."

Eddie Michallat, who had been sitting quietly on a crate a little to Ual's right, uncrossed his legs. "Well, that's something our species have in common."

"I will tell you what's going to happen," said Esganikan. A small knot of wess'har was watching her: a few more were more interested in the image occupying most of one of the walls, an image of an orderly city of towering fungus-like buildings and much vegetation. "We have assessed your planet from orbit for restoration purposes. We have so few species to work from that we will introduce those from Tasir Var that appear appropriate. The alternative is that your situation deteriorates until you reach a terminal population crisis and natural disaster overtakes you. Either way, you will be confined to your two planets. Containment measures are being put in place."

We weren't going anywhere anyway. Ual didn't want war. There was nowhere on Umeh to fight one. "When will you take me back to Umeh?"

"When we land, you will be with us."

"And when will that be?"

"Would tomorrow be soon enough? I have some business to attend to with the *gethes* and I would like that completed before we visit your people."

Eddie exhaled very slowly and quietly. Ual took it as suppressed surprise.

"While you're on the blower to Earth," said Eddie, "could you see if they'll connect me to my News Desk, please?"

Esganikan stood up and it was clear the conversation was over. She strode out with her ussissi aide scuttling behind her. Eddie watched her go and then turned to Ual.

"If Shan and that one ever ganged up, I'd leave town," said Eddie.

"A formidable creature. I have not yet met Shan Frankland." Ual felt the need to confide in Eddie. "I have made a great mistake."

Eddie shook his head. "What's the alternative? The Eqbas were coming the minute the bombs went off on Bezer'ej. After that, all you can do is get the best deal for your people that you can. Damage limitation."

"We should have chosen our allies more carefully."

"I don't think anyone planned this. We never do."

"Will you come with me, Eddie?"

He raised his eyebrows. "I've never filmed a lynching."

"We do not *lynch*."

"So what's the worst that can happen to you?"

"Imprisonment. Disgrace."

"Am I going to make that much difference? I don't think having Earth media present is going to deter your people one bit."

"I would feel comforted to have a friend with me."

"Oh."

Ual had not seen his family for some weeks. Long separations were normal: his offspring were too young to live independently, and they were being educated on Tasir Var, a world he had never visited. His mate had gone to look after them. She hadn't yet replied to his message that told her what he'd done and how afraid he was. She might have already abandoned him to find another male. He had no way of knowing.

And now he had grown tired of the pretense with Eddie. He reached into his belt for the blue bead, with every intention of telling Eddie that he knew what he had done with the quill, and that it no longer mattered because he had voluntarily given his own sample: but he couldn't. Eddie had saved him from a decision that might have been catastrophic. *Plausible deniability.* He'd even taught him the concept.

Ual let his arm fall back. "I will attempt to talk my way out of it when we land. I believe that's something you're good at, yes?"

"They do say."

"I might even tell an untruth. Will you help me?"

"Eddie Michallat, the man who introduced lying to the isenj nation. What an epitaph."

"The truth can be very much overrated."

"You're not wrong there."

Ual got up and made his way towards the entrance. It was a bright, clear day. Eddie followed him outside and they picked their way through the alleys and out onto the ill-defined path that led out through the fields to the wild unspoiled plain. Wess'har—Targassati wess'har, anyway—didn't like to leave permanent marks on the landscape if they could help it. It was one of the most interesting facts he had learned.

"Where are we going?" asked Eddie.

"For a walk."

Eddie probably understood. He followed at a distance.

It was the most extraordinary sensation to move without rules on pace and direction, without being required to keep to one side of the road or the other, to stop and start and turn as you pleased. The space he had felt . . . anarchic.

There was nobody he could collide with. There were no open spaces like this on Umeh. The only areas that had not been completely built over were the ice deserts, and even now the huge expense of urbanizing them seemed inevitable if the population was to be housed.

A shape overhead made Ual start. But it wasn't a vessel. It was a flying creature of some kind, in fact a whole group of them moving slowly across the sky with steadily flapping wings. They had no purpose for the wess'har. They simply existed here with them. He had never seen wild creatures on Umeh. Nobody had, not in living memory.

Umeh could have this one day. It wouldn't be authentic, but it would be a new reality. He inhaled the air. Isenj could tolerate a wider range of atmospheres than humans, but good clean air free of the by-products of crowded living tasted sweet whatever its composition.

"Why did they build F'nar here? There are pleasant grass-lands and forests right across the planet."

Eddie shrugged. "They chose the barren places where few native species lived."

"They take that much care?"

"I know. It's hard for humans to understand too. We'd have hogged the best seats right away." The breeze whipped his hair. "I've tried to understand why they're like this. On Earth, the species and individuals that grabbed most sur-vived. Where the wess'har came from, the species that coop-erated best were the ones who made it. I want to go to Eqbas Vorhi. I have to see it for myself."

Isenj were competitive too. Competition had limits.

Ual opened his mouth and took in as much of the clean air as he could gulp down. He spent the rest of the afternoon weaving an irregular path back and forth across the plain of F'nar, stunned by the space and the endless vista of tiny, fast-growing winter plants and bright pearl cliff faces.

He was right. He knew now that he was, and that what-ever price he paid would be worth it.

17

*The detail of Earth geopolitics probably means little to you,
but I want to assure you that the FEU does not speak or act on
behalf of the whole planet. We too are appalled at the events
in your system. We have now forced the FEU to turn back its
warship* Hereward *and we hope you will take that as a token
of our genuine wish to stay out of your affairs. The United
Nations, an international peacekeeping organization that rep-
resents all Earth states, has imposed a permanent and global
ban on travel and exploration beyond our own solar system.
We hope this measure will convince you that there is no need
for you to intervene here to guarantee your own security.*

UN Secretary General MARIE-CLAUDE GARCES,
in a message to Curas Ti

The scent of *jask* hit Nevyan before she entered the Exchange of Surplus Things. Esganikan and Shan were locked
in disagreement. She didn't need to see either of them to
know that.

"They are *below*," said Serrimissani.

Nevyan hurried down the passage that stretched under the
Exchange to the subterranean hangars where F'nar's fighter
craft were housed. The terrestrial gene bank had been placed
there for safekeeping. She followed the scent that Shan had
tagged *mango* and found her and Esganikan standing by the
row of dull gray composite cabinets that held as comprehen-
sive a selection of the Earth's plant and animal species as
anyone could assemble. Many no longer existed on their own
planet. And Shan's posture as she stood in front of the cabinets said clearly that she would not surrender their contents.

Shapakti, two of his crew, four F'nar citizens on mainte-
nance duties and Aitassi stood at a sensible distance from the

matriarchs. A definite space had cleared around the two even though their pheromonally charged debate would have no impact on the hierarchy of F'nar.

To a human, it might have looked like a discussion. Shan was leaning against one cabinet, arms folded, and Esganikan was speaking quietly to her in wess'u, the linguistically neutral territory they had settled upon. But their scent said very clearly that they were jostling for dominance.

"I think it's a very risky move," said Shan.

"Nobody can own this resource."

"I don't claim to own it, but its safety is my personal responsibility."

"It should return to Earth. The species should all be restored."

"And what if we *fuck up* again? The whole gene bank is gone."

"We will ensure that no *gethes* . . ." Esganikan got to grips with the new phrase: her red plume bobbed. ". . . *fucks up* again."

Nevyan stepped across the moat of space around the two females.

"We're discussing what should happen to the gene bank," said Shan, but she didn't take her eyes off Esganikan. "I'm concerned about committing all of it to Earth."

A powerful defensive scent made Nevyan glance towards Esganikan for an opinion and Shan simply turned to look at her. Shan was her friend. And Shan should have been standing where Nevyan was now: the human had outscented Chayyas when she first came to the city, and so the senior matriarchy of F'nar was hers by right. She had chosen to hand that to Mestin. Mestin had ceded to Nevyan.

And Nevyan never thought she might have to test her *jask* against Shan Frankland.

She met Shan's eyes and the message was clear: *are you on my side or what?* She could almost hear her saying it. It was the *or what* that always had such finality about it.

"I agree with *Shan Chail,*" said Nevyan. She did: but

even if she didn't, she trusted Shan's judgment over a
stranger's. She smelled her own determination well up and
add to the pheromonal mix. "Before any of this material re-
turns to Earth there must be a duplicate bank, maintained out
of the reach of *gethes.*"

"I'd go along with that," said Shan.

"Can you do this?" asked Nevyan.

Esganikan's scent was diminishing. She took a step back
from Shan, who unfolded her arms. "Yes. It can be done. We
need access to examine the specimens."

"I'll show Shapakti around later," said Shan, and made no
attempt to step away from the cabinet. She smiled, but there
was no movement in the muscles around her eyes. Esganikan and her party stood blinking for a few moments and
then left.

Nevyan waited.

"Thanks," said Shan. "I think we out-mangoed her."

"I have never known two *isan've* need to confront another
together to achieve consensus." Nevyan had to ask. "You're
quite capable of asserting your dominance over her on your
own, so why did you not do so?"

"I didn't want your job then, and I don't want hers now.
There's a time and a place for throwing your weight around
and this isn't it."

"How do you control your scent?"

"I just can. I suggest we see her together when there's
critical business to be done, or she'll just walk all over you.
And me, if I'm not as hard as I think I am."

It wasn't an insult. It was a statement of fact and a prudent precaution. "I know I can rely on you to support me,
Shan."

Shan stepped away from the cabinet and stood looking at
it, arms folded again and her lips pressed together as if she resented it for dragging her so far from home. She opened it
with a touch on a recessed panel. Cold air rolled out from the
cabinet in a breath of fog, and inside it layer upon layer of thin
shelves held a snapshot of a planet Nevyan had never seen.

"Will you travel back with the gene bank?" asked Nevyan.

"I can't. This is home now." Shan betrayed neither regret nor satisfaction. "My mission was to retrieve the unpatented strains of food crops. Perault never said anything about my returning with them, and I don't reckon she gave a monkey's toss if I came back or not. Once the samples ship out, my obligation ceases."

Shan took a small object out of her jacket, not her own communications device but one like those that had been confiscated from Rayat and Neville. She tossed it a little way in the air and caught it again in one hand. "Guess what?"

"I cannot follow this conversation."

"Okay, I've been going through Rayat's handheld to get names. But I came across correspondence with Eugenie Perault, the minister who gave me my Suppressed Briefing."

Shan began walking towards the exit and beckoned Nevyan to follow.

"And?"

"It's routine. It's just the combination of people that sets my bells ringing. There's no reason for her to talk to a pharmacologist, so she was talking to him as a spy. Now, ministers normally have whole departments of minions who do that for them, so if she was having personal conversations with him, I'm pretty sure they were along the same lines of the one she had with me, because she usually didn't talk to lowly EnHaz coppers either."

"He was not a factor in your Suppressed Briefing?"

"No. But I'm bloody sure now that he knew what he was looking for out here. I just want to know why he was tasked to find *c'naatat* and if Perault was the one who sent him."

"I would think that was obvious."

"Not if you know Perault. She was a devout Christian, and her sister was an eco-terrorist. One of those I helped when I really shouldn't have. I didn't know who she was at the time. Call me naive."

"You sound as if you regret what you did."

"Not at all. I'd do it all over again. I'd just go in harder next time, that's all." Shan stared at the handheld as she walked, apparently willing information to extract itself from the device. "And it doesn't even matter if she sent him with a different set of orders to me, but I need to know anyway. I hate loose ends. It's one of those obsessions that makes me a copper."

"Will he tell you?"

"I get the feeling he wants me to try to thrash it out of him to show he can get the better of me."

"And are you determined to show him he can't?"

"When you put it like that, it does sound puerile."

They came out into the main hall of the Exchange and some wess'har paused to sniff the air, reacting to the wild cocktail of scents that still clung to them.

"You let them live because you want to know these things? Is that all?"

"I let them live because Esganikan told me not to shoot them. But yes, I want to know." If Shan was annoyed by her criticism she didn't let it show. There was no trace of any scent or expression. "I don't like relying on gut instinct, but sometimes it's the best there is and it's saved me on more than one occasion. And something's telling me that I can't close this unless I know what Perault was up to. It might be irrelevant, but I know there's a missing piece and it just might be significant."

"What now?"

"I'm going to get Lindsay and Rayat moved to Mar'an'cas."

"Why?"

"They're sitting on their arses in Fersanye's house doing nothing and eating, and they ought to be earning their keep. They can get their hands dirty with the colonists." Shan tapped at the handheld, distracted. "And perhaps being stuck with a bunch of god-botherers on a cold wet rock for a while will shake Rayat down. Or get him to drop his guard to someone."

"But Lindsay Neville was never part of his operation, was she?"

Shan shook her head.

"Do you wish to kill her?"

"Sometimes."

"Perhaps you have learned to dispense with pointless revenge."

"I doubt it," said Shan.

Ual wondered if the defense forces of the Northern Assembly might try to shoot down the ship before he had the chance to make his case. And if they didn't, then the Maritime Fringe might save them the trouble. It all depended on how keen they were to call down the wrath of Eqbas Vorhi.

Esganikan Gai, who stood at the helm of a warship that had somehow detached itself from the larger vessel, seemed unperturbed. "Your forces have nothing that can penetrate this hull."

"Said an Eqbas spokesman," Eddie muttered, but very quietly. He held a short sleeveless garment up against his chest. "Is charcoal my color?"

"What is that?"

"A ballistic vest to stop projectiles putting a hole through me. I know it works because it's Shan's and she said it stopped an isenj round before." He fastened the vest down each side and flapped his arms as if testing it for comfort. "It's too tight. Funny, she always seemed to be built like an Amazon."

"I have yet to meet her," said Ual. He wondered if he would ever get the chance now: he could imagine the reception he might get in Jejeno. "I didn't believe Giyadas when she said she had survived."

The distance between Wess'ej and Umeh was hours rather than days, a *bus ride* as Eddie called it. Esganikan's liquid fragment of warship began decelerating on its approach to Umeh space. The interior of the ship was all fluid light and shifting displays that took up all the bulkhead space, and the Eqbas personnel were kneeling or sitting in small niches, looking more as if they were meditating than standing by for possible attack.

Esganikan glanced at an unintelligible formation of gold lights set in an amber cloud and passed her hand over it. "When we encounter your defense systems, we will exercise caution."

"I thought you said they didn't have anything big enough to take you out," said Eddie.

"I meant that we will avoid putting the Umeh armed forces in a position where we have to retaliate and destroy them."

"Ah. I can see why that wouldn't get things off to a good start."

It was a wise precaution. The long-range surveillance net on both Umeh and Tasir Var would react to an alien vessel. They were very old systems, created before isenj realized that wess'har would make no attempt to attack them on their own territory—except Asht, of course. Ual had given up thinking of the planet as Asht. He accepted that it was now and always would be Bezer'ej. If others could take that view, the isenj would be on their way to breaking their dependence on a past that couldn't be recreated, and they might look forward to a very different but easier future.

The image of Umeh was an ochre disk on the bulkhead. Ual had now seen his homeworld from space twice, but he compared it with the swirled blue and white surfaces of Wess'ej and Bezer'ej, and even Earth. They all looked so much more inviting.

"Your ground command is warning us," said Esganikan. "Is there an appropriate response?"

"Let me speak to them," said Ual.

It was not a Northern Assembly station but a Maritime Fringe one that had detected the Eqbas ship. Surface Defense at Buyg wanted the ship to turn back.

"I am Minister Par Paral Ual and I wish to land with a delegation from Eqbas Vorhi," he said. *Delegation* was an Eddie word, very *weasel,* and nowhere near as alarming as *warship.* "We require entry to Umeh airspace."

"You're a traitor on board an alien ship."

"The reality is a little more complicated than that. Are

you aware what might happen if Umeh was to carry out an unprovoked hostile act against an Eqbas vessel? Or if the Maritime Fringe did, and was the cause of hostilities that affected its neighbors?"

There was a pause. Ralassi, close at Ual's side, was making little *snap-snap-snap* noises with his teeth. "They won't fire on a vessel with ussissi on board. We would stop crewing vessels for isenj if that happened."

"Power of the union, lads," said Eddie. His voice vibrated uncharacteristically. "That's the spirit."

The Eqbas helmsman didn't look up. He said something in eqbas'u that Ual couldn't follow and Esganikan turned her head to give what seemed to be an order. The bridge crew moved instantly to different positions.

"Let's not start firing," said Ual. "This can be worked out peacefully—"

"We are landing," said Esganikan. "We know now what your target acquisition technology is like and this ship has not been targeted. Aitassi and Ralassi will talk to your ground stations and identify a landing site for us."

"If I have any authority to land at all, it will be in Northern Assembly territory, in Ebj." *If I have any authority . . .* "If anything happens to me, the person you should concentrate your persuasive skills upon is Minister Par Shomen Eit. His responsibility is supplies, which is infrastructure and environment."

"I intend to speak to your whole Assembly."

She alarmed him. "I wish you would discuss these ideas with me a little more in advance of executing them."

Esganikan stared back. "It makes no difference."

Eddie moved slowly forward to stare at the bulkhead display, arms pressed in to his sides as if afraid the ballistic vest would abandon him. Then he took his bee cam out of a pocket and let it hover by his head. He said nothing.

"Is this a dangerous situation for you, Eddie?"

The journalist shrugged. "I've been in worse. And I wasn't sitting behind an Eqbas cannon at the time." He glanced at Esganikan. "Do you have cannon, by the way?"

She seemed almost indulgent. She actually patted Eddie's arm, and he flinched. "If you mean heavy long-range weapons, yes. If you feel vulnerable, you may stay in the ship when we land."

"You must be joking," said Eddie. "This is my bloody story. I'm having it."

Esganikan might not have understood his colloquial language but she appeared to detect something else, and patted his arm again. Ual realized Eddie was afraid. His face was paler than usual and he was breathing more rapidly, licking his lips. Ual wondered if he enjoyed the tension or if he simply lived with it as soldiers did.

Either way, the human was right. There was plenty to fear.

And Ual was completely alone. All isenj prized a little solitude, a luxury in a crowded world, but this wasn't quite the solitude Ual had in mind.

"I'll be right behind you," said Eddie.

Shan woke with a start and realized she was not drifting somewhere between Bezer'ej and Umeh. She was in her own bed, alive, well fed, and warm. The relief was wonderful.

"You stop breathing frequently," Aras whispered.

"Sorry. Does it bother you?"

"Not as long as I can still feel your heartbeat."

"Yeah, that's how I look at it." She buried her head in the hollow of his shoulder and tried to doze again. "You still here?" Wess'har slept in irregular short bursts: Aras would get up and wander off several times during the night, something she had grown used to. "Keeping an eye on me?"

"I thought you might be upset if you woke and I wasn't here."

"Aww. Sweet."

"It's started."

"What has?"

"Recall of your memories."

"Oh."

She felt him swallow. "Most unpleasant."

"Try fucking awful."

"You're very resilient."

"Didn't have a lot of choice."

She started to drift off again, soothed by the delicious scent of sandalwood and the suede-like feel of his skin. This was bliss. She didn't need to be on her guard. She knew her gun was on the table by the bed and it didn't matter that it was a little out of reach. F'nar felt safe in a way that Earth never had.

He nudged her. "And am I forgiven for my reluctance to mount you?"

"Aras, can we work on a bit of euphemism, please? *Mounting* just doesn't do it for me."

"But *you* don't use euphemism. You say—"

"I know what word I use. But mounting is a bit too . . . *agricultural.*"

"Very well. But am I? Forgiven, that is?"

"I reckon."

"Promise me that you won't get involved in Esganikan's missions. I would welcome some uneventful time with you."

It wasn't an unreasonable request. "Provided she doesn't piss me about over the gene bank, I'll leave her to her own devices. I'm not the cavalry any more. I know when I'm done."

Aras made a noncommittal rumble in his throat that might have been either approval or disbelief. She shut her eyes again and rearranged his arm into a more comfortable position for her head; the rumble turned into that purr with its undertone of infrasonics, ebbing and flowing, soothing her just as it would calm a wess'har infant. The outside world receded. She sank into a blanket of endless, blurred gold.

"What if it had been Rayat?" The purr trailed off.

Oh, please. The gold haze evaporated. "What if *what* had been Rayat?"

"If you had infected him. Would you have felt the same pity and . . . obligation?"

"Oh, come *on*." She rolled over on her back. She was wide awake again. "No. Not even with a bag over his head. I'd have given him a grenade and told him to do the decent thing." She got up and checked her swiss: it was still four hours to sunrise and 2318 Western FEU time, as if that mattered to her body clock any longer. "I know what this is about. You want a house-brother, don't you?"

"Yes."

Poor sod. He'd coped with his condition on Bezer'ej, but being surrounded by ordinary wess'har again seemed to have made him more desperate for normality. She wondered how long it would be before he became broody. But a remedy for that longing would always be completely out of the question in so many ways, and she wasn't even going to mention it.

"Look, if you and Ade want to sort out some arrangement, go ahead." *Yes, go on. Save me having to make the decision for once.* "If that's the way you both want it, I'll be perfectly happy."

"That's very wess'har of you."

"There's a lot of me that is."

Liar. That was one part of her that wasn't. Her brain said *one at a time, girl.* She was appalled at herself for even looking at Ade, and she did, oh yes she did. She'd looked at him that way for a long time. It might have been normal and even commendable for wess'har, but a voice inside kept yelling *slut, slut, slut.* Of course polyandry was okay for wess'har: they were . . . *animals.*

And that was another thought she didn't like, and it was equally unbidden. If there was anyone who should have had the most open of minds about nonhuman species, it was her, and here she was relegating wess'har into the category of *not like us.*

She really didn't have an *us* any longer. The *us* consisted of Aras Sar Iussan and Ade Bennett and her. She now had more in common with the yodeling sea horses in the city below and even with the microscopic organisms she had sifted between her fingers on Ouzhari than she had with the monkeys whose worst attitudes still rose up in her when she least expected it.

"When are you going to see the bezeri?" Aras had taken the news of their request in silence. She wondered if he didn't want to leave her on her own with Ade after all. "I could come with you."

"No need," said Aras. "I shall talk to them. I'll leave tomorrow."

He didn't sound happy about it. But that wasn't surprising. There was no comfort he could give them, and apologies were worse than useless.

Outcomes were all that mattered, and Shan couldn't think of any happy endings for the bezeri.

18

We approve of your decision to limit human endeavor to your own system. But your poor relations with other species on Earth make us believe that the common interest still needs our intervention. You appear to be familiar with the concept of third party arbitration and peacekeeping. Our current timetable and intentions stand.

CURAS TI
senior matriarch of Surang and speaker for Eqbas Vorhi in
off-world matters,
in a message to the United Nations

Ade crouched down to look Serrimissani in her hostile black eyes and handed her the sheet of smartpaper. "This is the best I can do, mate," he said. "Rigger's would be best, high combats if not. I'll be really grateful."

Serrimissani studied the traced outline of the sole of a boot and gave Ade the sort of look that he'd seen her give Eddie. He felt stupid. But he'd promised Shan he'd get her some replacement boots, good solid ones, and he was going to do it. Barencoin and Qureshi watched him suspiciously. The Exchange of Surplus Things had become the nearest thing they had to a mess and when they weren't on crop duties they hung around here, and he wished they wouldn't.

"I will do my best," said Serrimissani. Ussissi seemed not to find it demeaning to run errands. "If I have to barter for this, what do I offer?"

Ussissi were new to haggling. Ade couldn't help thinking they would end up being bloody good at it. They always had their walk-away point and you couldn't manipulate them. He fumbled in all the pockets on his shirt and in his pants, and then in his belt pouch, but there wasn't much. The sum total of his negotiable wealth was his fighting knife, his mother's wedding ring, and his medals. That wouldn't be worth much to anyone in Umeh Station. A few kilos of prime steak would have done the deal a lot better.

No, not the ring. He turned the medals in his palm. Barencoin grunted and stepped between him and Serrimissani. "Aw, for fuck's sake, Sarge, not your *medals.*"

"They're not worth anything out here."

"She doesn't need the boots that badly. She's *got* boots. Jesus, all this on the off chance she'll give you a leg-over? You sad bastard."

"Piss off, Mart."

Qureshi pitched in, always the sensible older sister breaking up a fight between the boys. "Come on, they're his and he can do what he likes with them. Lay off him."

"I can't for the life of me think what you see in that bird, I really can't." Barencoin did one of his theatrical eye-rolls of exasperation. "I mean, I know you're not going to get it anywhere else, but you're not much use to her now she's had a bit of wess'har, are you? Not with one dick."

Ade tried very hard not to be his father, always solving his problems with his fists. He was still the bloody sergeant here whether they'd dismissed him or not. He lowered his voice. "I *said* I'd get her the boots, so I *will.* And you can wind your neck in, okay?"

"Suit yourself," said Barencoin, and walked off.

Serrimissani studied the medals and handed them back. When her paw brushed Ade's hand it felt like corduroy, all soft little ridges, but she couldn't have been less like a toy if she'd tried. Her teeth looked like serious business.

"I will find a way to acquire the boots without barter," she said. "And Marine Barencoin is wrong. From what I have seen of Shan Frankland, she will take pity on you and grant you sexual favors whether you offer her boots or not. She has a strong sense of *jask.*"

There were some things a bloke didn't need to hear, and

pity was one of them. Qureshi steered him into a quiet corner and sat down on an empty crate.

"You okay?"

"Yeah."

"You sure you know what you're doing? We don't want to see you get hurt. Emotionally, I mean, because it's not like getting a good hiding from Aras is going to make much difference to you."

"I'm not doing anything. I'm just looking out for her."

"Right."

"She reminds me of my mum."

"Christ, Ade, you never actually told her that, did you?"

"Yes."

"You should never tell a woman she reminds you of your mum. Not even if your mum was Helen of Troy."

"I meant that she's not afraid of anything and she makes me feel safe."

"Well, if you didn't make that clear to her, the boots aren't going to get you very far."

"I'm not getting her boots for *that*." He really shouldn't have mentioned his mother. He could see that now. "So what would work, then?"

Qureshi's expression was that of someone trying to break bad news. "You could always just ask her."

"Izzy, you're not going to take the piss out of me, are you?"

"No, Sarge. She's not *that* much older than you. And she doesn't look it."

"Thanks a lot."

"I've said the wrong thing, haven't I?"

"Think what you like." He occupied himself with his belt, sheathing his fighting knife with exaggerated care. "I can trust her."

Qureshi didn't ask him to explain. They all knew he'd had unrelenting bad luck in his love life. They thought he was bloody soft with women, a pushover, a mug. Maybe he was, but he didn't know how to be anything else.

"What's the Boss planning to do with Neville and Rayat?" said Qureshi.

So she thought of Shan as the top of the command chain, too. *We all need structure.* "She still wants information out of Rayat, but I haven't a clue what she wants to do with Neville."

"I thought she would have jobbed her by now." Qureshi mimicked Shan's two-handed gun grip. "And that tosser Rayat."

"You know they've found some bezeri survivors, don't you?"

"Yeah. Not much comfort for them, I shouldn't think."

"I'd ask them what they wanted done with the bastards."

"What if they want all of *us* strung up?"

Ade hadn't thought of that. He'd started to accept Shan's view—and the prevailing wess'har opinion—that the marines weren't responsible for the destruction of Ouzhari.

But it didn't feel true.

"I could have told Lindsay Neville to fuck off," said Ade. "What's the worst she could have done? What's the worst Rayat could have done? Had us court-martialed."

"We could *all* have refused, Ade. You might be the sergeant, but we were all capable of saying no and we just obeyed orders."

"And we should have known better."

"You've seen more action than the rest of us. How many times have you thought, oh, sod this for a game of soldiers, I'm not doing that? We all think it and we don't act on it. That's why we're in uniform and civvies aren't, because if you argue the toss every time you can't fight."

"Yeah, and wess'har don't give a shit what your motives are, just what the end result is." He could see Barencoin making his way back down the Exchange, shuffling a pack of cards as he walked. He really didn't fancy a game now. He was troubled: he needed to talk to someone who'd done something unthinkable and had learned to live with it. "I've got to see Aras about something. I'll catch up with you later."

Barencoin slapped the cards against his palm to align the pack and held it out to Ade. "Gin rummy?"

"Nah, got things to do."

"Okay, I was well out of order there. Sorry. Now can we play?"

"I meant it. There's something I've got to sort out."

Barencoin didn't look as if he believed him. Ade didn't think Mart would spend a second worrying about what he'd done; or maybe he was like Shan, just good at looking as if he didn't. When he got back to the house—and he wondered why he thought of it as a house and not a cave—there was no sign of Shan. Aras was sitting on the terrace, Shan's swiss balanced on one thigh and Rayat's handheld on the other, the devices linked by a wire. A few shafts of pink late afternoon light pierced the cloud and gave one pearl face of the city a rosy luster.

"*Isan* has gone to see Nevyan," said Aras, not looking up. "I have been examining Rayat's handheld."

"Anything?"

"Nothing further. In the end, not having a named individual will not prevent Eqbas Vorhi intervening. It's simply a matter of detail."

"Can I talk to you?"

"If this is about Shan, we have discussed that enough."

"Actually, it's about Mjat."

Aras put the two devices down on the flagstones and beckoned Ade to him. "Are you having unpleasant flashbacks?"

"No. Well, yes, but it's not about that."

"What do you want to know, then?"

"How I came to roll over and just ship those bombs to Bezer'ej because I was ordered to. I never thought I was a bad bloke and now I just don't know any more."

"Have you followed orders before?"

"You know I have. I'm a marine."

"And how did you feel then?"

"I went where they sent me, and my targets were always ones who'd shoot me if I didn't shoot them." You had to be able to stop thinking about it after you'd fired. Most blokes couldn't in the end. Ade found women were much better at killing and moving on. "But *c'naatat* wasn't doing me any harm and neither were the bezeri."

"Humans follow orders, especially if conditioned to do so."

"I know. I *know* all that. But when you bombed Mjat, the isenj weren't a threat to you personally. So how do you handle it?"

For all Aras's human characteristics, he still had his unshakeable wess'har clarity when it came to cause and effect. "They were a threat to the bezeri. They wouldn't stop polluting the planet."

"But how do you feel about it *now*?"

"I regret that I had to do it and would do it again."

"So how should I feel about Ouzhari?"

"You know how you feel about it. You feel guilty. The question is whether you *are* guilty." Aras reached out and took hold of Ade's wrist, a loose grip, apparently unthinking. Ade braced his muscles involuntarily and had to remind himself that wess'har were touchers and huggers: there was nothing weird about it. But he still wasn't comfortable with another bloke touching his hand. "For wess'har to consider you guilty of causing bezeri deaths, you would have had to arm the devices. And you did not."

"I helped get the ordnance there. Lindsay Neville would never have managed it without us."

"And if you had a human lawyer, he would argue that you thought you were transporting neutron devices to an island without animal life, and that you had every expectation that the explosion would create minimal environmental effects beyond a few days."

"What's the word for that? Sophistry."

"And if you had known they were cobalt devices, and

Commander Neville had not set them to detonate, would you be guilty even though no deaths resulted?"

"Yeah. I would. It'd be like conspiracy to murder."

"Our two species have different views of reality."

It didn't help him at all. It muddied the waters. Perhaps that was an answer. Both sets of logic made sense in themselves but not side by side, and in the end it was the gut feeling that events produced that made guilt or innocence.

But Ade had a better idea of what he was feeling now. He was a kid at home again, not standing up to his violent father, not doing what he should have done. Aras let go of his wrist.

"You don't always follow orders," he said. "Shan said you held a gun on Commander Neville to stop her using the grenades."

"Yeah, and you know what happened next."

"Move on."

"I'm trying. It's funny how good and evil get harder to spot as you get older. I wish I had Shan's sense of black and white."

"It was part of her job to have one. And good and evil are concepts best left to the colonists. I prefer to think in terms of what I will personally tolerate and what I will not."

"How do you think the colonists fit that in with a god who's supposed to have a plan?"

"Does your god receive in packets?"

"Sorry?"

"Prayer. Perhaps God receives data in packets, like your communication systems once did. Or maybe prayers are heard only by the praying, which is perhaps more useful." Aras seemed distracted by the ideas. "If God is omniscient, why does he need prayer to make him aware of the things troubling people? And if he *is* aware, why are humans so presumptuous as to ask him to change events for them? Has he no firm plan for the universe? I asked Ben all these things, and Josh too, but they said I needed faith."

For a being with absolutely no concept of the divine, this was a twenty-four-carat piece of theology. Ade savored the moment of strangeness brought on by watching a pink pearl sunset with an alien brother in a caldera 150 trillion miles from home.

But there were no packets of prayers, and no god, and no-body was waiting for him at the Pearly Gates with a tally sheet of his sins. He wasn't going to die, and the only pearly gates were right here, and real.

Whatever peace he reached with himself would take some work.

"Fuck faith," said Ade. "It's as bad as following orders."

Boom.

The Eqbas vessel shivered slightly, causing several bridge crew to bob their heads. Ual found himself looking at an aerial view of Jejeno that spanned most of the bulkhead in front of him. A trail of vapor plumed up from the city and seemed to arc straight into his face, confirmation that some-thing had been fired at the warship.

Esganikan tilted her head side to side but she seemed per-fectly calm. Aitassi and Ralassi were not. They were seething, teeth bared, and Ralassi had taken over the com-munications position in front of the bulkhead. Ual found it hard to see how it was operated. There were no controls that he could identify, just an illuminated panel the size of a plate that moved when Ralassi did.

"You fired upon ussissi," he said. "This has never hap-pened before and it will not be tolerated. We will no longer fly your vessels. You will cease firing now."

There was absolute silence from the Jejeno ground sta-tion. Ralassi was right: nobody had ever fired on a vessel knowing ussissi were on board. The isenj were reliant on them as nonmilitary pilots and interpreters between isenj re-gions. But then no alien vessel had ever breached Umeh's airspace uninvited. The old protocols and assumptions had crumbled in a matter of minutes.

Jejeno looked as it always had. Its intricate towers and forests of bronze and brown buildings glittered in the afternoon light, and another vapor trail rose from the ground. This time there was no gentle shiver as the missile was deflected by the Eqbas vessel. It never reached them.

"God, it looks just like tracer fire," said Eddie, wandering up and down the bridge behind his bee cam. Ual watched and felt his courage begin to abandon him.

Then Eqbas Vorhi ran out of patience.

Bursts of yellow light stabbed a neat and precise path down to the vapor trail and the bulkhead dimmed the light from the explosion. Then a bright green beam picked out a target in the city below and a streak of reflected light flashed down it. Fire spread out from the point of impact and black smoke roiled up above the tops of the buildings.

Esganikan considered the image on the bulkhead. The view changed to a closer shot and Ual could see a crater fringed by twisted frames and shattered blocks of buildings.

"The point from which you launch your air defenses has been destroyed," she said calmly, as if she had done this many times before. "I see no point in causing more destruction than is necessary and we will not fire again unless there is another attack. Talk to your colleagues and explain that I would like to speak to the Northern Assembly *today*." She turned and took a few slow paces down the length of the bridge, her plume of red fur bobbing as she walked, and reached out to touch the bulkhead image of the only open space in Jejeno—its port landing fields. "I will wait. Now, helm, take us down."

"Shit," said Eddie.

Ual wondered if Esganikan had any comprehension of what followed when an explosion occurred in a densely populated city. If she did, then she showed no sign of anxiety about it. But he knew. He could imagine what was happening now and he was terrified.

Beneath them, water conduits would be flooding the streets. Homes, food production centers and offices ran right up to the walls of the defense station building, and they would have collapsed. Fires would be spreading. There would be no water to extinguish them because the pressure in the water supply would have plummeted. And there would be panic and crushing, fleeing crowds and many, many civilian deaths.

Eddie seemed to see his thoughts. "We'd call that *fish in a barrel*," he said. "Nowhere to run."

"That describes the situation for us all," said Ual.

They were attempting to bury Jonathan Burgh when Lindsay and Rayat arrived on Mar'an'cas.

Lindsay's trousers were soaked up to the knee. Barencoin and Becken had been in a hurry to deliver their prisoners to the colonists and she'd stepped from the boat into deeper water than she anticipated.

Rayat watched the burial party of colonists trying to dig in the thin soil. "No carrion-eating life on the island, I take it?"

Barencoin shrugged, chivvying him along like a sheepdog. "We're all carrion-eaters to the wess'har."

"Shall we give them a hand?" Lindsay asked. "I think they're going to have to pile rocks."

"You do what you like," said Barencoin. "We're persona non shit-pot with the colony."

He turned back down the path, Becken close behind him. James Garrod came down from the camp and grunted for Lindsay and Rayat to follow him.

"We haven't got much here," said James. Lindsay walked through the camp of oddly decorative tents, wary of a hostile response. People seemed subdued but purposeful. "And even if we're going home to Earth, we've still got a few years to wait out. So you pull your weight for the time you're here."

Rayat had somehow managed to grab a small bag of personal effects before he was dragged out of Umeh Station. He hitched it higher on his shoulder and Lindsay wondered if she could talk him into letting her borrow a fresh shirt. "No problem," he said to James. He seemed in his personable mode, probably grooming the colonists for some act of sympathy that would benefit him. "We'll do whatever you need."

James showed them to a tent. It seemed they'd have to share. Lindsay's distaste must have shown on her face.

"We don't do private suites," he said. "Will you be coming to services?"

It took her a few moments to work out that he meant *worship*. "I'm not sure I believe in God," she said. Rayat was carefully silent.

"Well, he's there, and you might as well start getting to know him before you go to him," said James. The kid said it with such casual certainty that her stomach tightened involuntarily. "You'll have a lot to talk to him about."

James walked away. Rayat tried the thin mattress on the floor and sat down cross-legged, hands folded in his lap. Lindsay wished for a change of clothing and an end to the new doubt that was starting to overtake her.

"Since I left Earth, I've taken more beatings than I did even in training," said Rayat. "My job's not usually this violent."

Is death really going to be the end of it? Am I ever going to have peaceful oblivion? "I noticed you don't fight back. Ever."

"No point fighting unless you're trying to escape or survive," he said. "Save it for when you really need it."

"And you don't really need it now?"

"I've never been this close to death before."

"Really?"

"Really."

She wasn't sure if she believed him. He appeared completely drained of motivation and color. So even a spook had his limits: it seemed that exhaustion and inevitability had finally ground him down as well.

"You're resigned to what's coming, then?"

Rayat made a distracted click with his teeth. "I know what you think of me, but I find it as hard as you do to come to terms with what we did."

"There's no *we* in this, you bastard. You loaded the cobalt primers in the ERDs, not me."

For once Rayat didn't argue. "I know."

"And all for nothing. Ade Bennett's infected and Shan's walking around large as life."

"Bennett?"

"I never told you in case you got stupid ideas again."

"*Bennett?*" The odd amalgam of revelation and dismay on his face was priceless. "Shit. *Shit.*"

"So we destroyed a sentient species for *nothing.*"

"You think I feel good about that?" She could have sworn he was genuinely anguished. "Okay, I've done things in my career that most people would find nauseating. But my priority is the welfare of *my country,* and I'm prepared to do whatever it takes to ensure that."

"Well, at least you admit it."

"Oh, I'll do more than *admit* it. I'd do it again."

"Why does that not surprise me?"

"Look, girlie, we don't live in a cost-free universe. We get our hands dirty just by living day to day." *Girlie.* That was Shan's dismissive term for her, too. Rayat had come as close to sincerity as Lindsay had ever seen, and it was disturbing: he was suddenly *angry.* "So, what if some states on Earth got hold of *c'naatat,* and we didn't? You think that's *not* worth paying a high price to avoid? If not for Europe, then for Earth? *You* must have thought it was, at least enough to use nukes."

"Some prices are just too high."

"And how many nice people get killed because they happen to be in the bad guy's army? There are *always* prices to pay and there's always an innocent bystander, but you can't let that stop you. You know something? I'd kill Frankland without a second thought, but at least she understands the stakes and she's got the balls to live with what she does. I'm not even sure we're after different things, either."

"For all her faults, she wouldn't have risked a species."

"Unless they're humans."

Lindsay hated him, and his logic, and his contempt, all of which reminded her more of Shan than she could tolerate.

Both had the same total, ruthless focus. They did dirty jobs: they risked their lives anonymously for their obsessive principles. And yet she couldn't see them as the same species as herself.

She shifted tack, worrying what her own motives truly were. "You going to go to have a talk with God, then? See what deal you can sort out with him?"

"I'm not a Christian."

"Neither am I. Well, not practicing."

"How do you cope?"

"I don't. I wish there was something I could do to make amends but it's a tall order, putting genocide right again."

Rayat tipped the contents of his bag out on the bed. His worldly goods consisted of two gray shirts, some unidentifiable balled-up fabric and a wallet. He sighed quietly. "What would we all give to turn back time, eh?"

"Pretty well everything," said Lindsay. *"Everything."*

19

Withdraw your vessel from our planet or face the consequences.

Priority message from Minister PAR NIR BEDOI
Northern Assembly, to Nevyan Tan Mestin

It was cold and the bezeri who nestled in the rocks off the coastline of St. Chad's island didn't know Aras at all.

They knew what he was, though.

He held the lamp and signaled to them, speaking wess'u for the lamp to shape into a language of color. *You asked for me.*

The rocks sparkled with concentric circles of pulsing yellow light that radiated from four or five central points. The bezeri slowly peeled away from the hiding place, hanging in the water a little way from him with their tentacles trailing in the current. Aras put his other hand out to steady himself.

One of them spoke. The lights on her mantle—the same lights that lived in Shan's hands—flared into complex patterns of red, green and blue that the lamp converted to sound.

So it's true. You are the creature that can live both here and in the Dry Above with equal ease, the one that never dies. One of those who saved us from the polluters.

I am, said Aras. *But I made mistakes and your people died. Who did this to us?*

He would tell them the exact truth. The generic *gethes* would mean nothing to them. Like wess'har, they were specific. *Humans who came here. We have already killed two as an act of balance.*

Are there others who are guilty?

Yes. What justice do you require for this?

We want them balanced too. And we will do this ourselves. We want all of those who brought this destruction upon us.

Bezeri didn't have that clear wess'har definition of responsibility any more than humans did. Aras knew they would include Qureshi and Barencoin and Chahal in that category—and Ade.

This was one occasion when the truth would serve no purpose. For the first time in his life, Aras lied like a *gethes*. He didn't lie by omission, as he had done with difficulty before. He *lied*, completely and totally.

There are only two of them. A female called Lindsay Neville and a male called Mohan Rayat.

Bring them to us.

I will.

There is one more thing. The bezeri took on her colors of quiet consideration, light blue rhythmic pulses. It was a while before she spoke. *There are too few of us. We need to rebuild, to recover what is left of our culture and our history. We said we did not want the help of aliens, but times are hard.*

Bezeri had a powerful sense of place. Being rooted in the coastal waters of these islands made them vulnerable, as did their fragile biochemistry. They cared about their clans and their territories and they kept detailed records. Faced with destruction, they needed to find comfort in their past exactly as humans did. It was ironic.

I will get you that help, said Aras, thinking of the Eqbas scientists.

We mean you. We want you to return to us. You can live among us.

Aras wondered if he had misunderstood. *Among you?*

The lights rippled, both fascinating and desperate. *You cannot drown. You can survive anywhere.*

Aras's wess'har candor almost betrayed him, but he bit back a refusal. His mind was filled with selfish preoccupations: he had an *isan* and a brother now. There was a time when he might have conquered his dislike of immersion and sought escape with the bezeri, but that time was long gone, and he was ashamed that his first instinct was to abandon them again.

That will be difficult, said Aras.

You said you would be there for us. You promised.

And so he had. *Give me time to think.*

A male bezeri at the back of the group came forward and reached into his mantle with one tentacle. He drew out a small flat oval and extended it towards Aras.

It was the ancient *azin* shell map that Aras had once owned. The shell was as transparent as glass and the bezeri had once made these beautiful complex maps by compressing colored patterns of sand between the layers of shell. Aras had given it to Shan, and she had returned it to the bezeri with one addition: a thin line of red sand, sprinkled carefully like a border, her way of telling them that she planned to protect them from outsiders. She called it her *exclusion zone.*

But it hadn't quite worked out. He took the map from the outstretched tentacle.

Why are you returning this? Aras asked.

Give it to the female who gave it back to us. Tell her that her red line did not hold.

But she tried very hard.

It was not enough.

Aras grasped the tether that reached down from the *niluy-ghur* and twisted it, the map tucked tightly to his chest. The line drew him slowly up through the water and he watched the lights dwindle beneath him. One of the Eqbas crew caught him by his tunic and hauled him inboard, watching fascinated as he coughed up the seawater from his lungs and shook himself dry.

He cradled the *azin* map in both hands all the way back to the ship, remembering all the times he had sat alone in his own vessel on Constantine and studied its contour lines.

Tell her that her red line did not hold.

Shan knew that already. And she hadn't failed them: *he* had, right from the time he had allowed the Constantine mission to survive.

Now the bezeri were asking for his help again. Aras thought of the concepts of *sin* and *forgiveness* and *mercy* that Ben Garrod had taught him about nearly two hundred years ago, and he remembered another one: *atonement*.

The Pajat coast, Wessej.

"I need some normal human DNA," said Shapakti.

"Don't look at me," said Shan. "Have you tried Eddie? Journalists share ninety-nine percent of DNA with humans."

"That is humor."

"You're catching on." The glass raft neared Mar'an'cas, skimming over a relatively calm sea. Clouds threatened to empty themselves any minute, and Shan wasn't sure if the raft was watertight from the top. Ade sat cross-legged aft of them, if the raft's layout could be described in nautical terms. "I expect you can get plenty from the colonists. You're almost in their good books for helping them fulfill their religious duty."

"Are they normal humans?"

"Apart from the fact they're as mad as a box of frogs," Ade muttered. "That's normal too."

Shan walked around the transparent deck, never having learned the sailor's discipline of not compromising the trim of the craft. Ade, frowning slightly, looked as if he disapproved.

"They're normal in the sense that most humans who could afford health care were genetically manipulated in some way, and that was the stock they came from," she said. "But I come from a Pagan family. They wouldn't have any truck with genetic interference, so my DNA was pretty well wild *Homo sapiens*."

"And this is what F'nar used to engineer the antihuman pathogen."

"Yes. They had a sample of my hair from the time before I caught *c'naatat*."

"As wide a range of specimens as possible would suit my purposes."

Shapakti had no hidden agendas; wess'har never did, as literal and unthinkingly frank as small children.

"And what *are* your purposes, then?"

"I would like to see if it is possible to stop humans becoming host to *c'naatat*."

That sounded sensible enough. But Shan's old ingrained misgivings about biological research began to nag at her. It was a little late for that, given that her DNA was currently doing a decent razor-wire job in quarantining Bezer'ej. It had certainly worked bloody well on the family in the church. She was aware of Ade staring at her.

"I don't like experiments," she said.

Shapakti appeared to understand her a lot better than she thought he did. "I only need to record a profile of cells. Then I can use models to explore the possibilities."

"And you developed that expertise on yourselves, eh?"

"Yes."

"Just checking."

"I can see why you doubt us. Life on your planet developed through competition. Ours developed largely through cooperation, symbiosis and sustainable equilibrium. Would you like to visit Eqbas Vorhi?"

She wondered what the payload from *Thetis* would have made of that. "Yes, I would. One day."

The raft beached and they stepped ashore. Ade kept glancing back at the vessel as if he didn't quite believe it. As they walked into Constantine camp with its bizarre jacquard tents and pervading smell of human waste, the marine slipped his rifle off its webbing and cradled it across his chest, looking worryingly prepared. Shan thought she'd be jumpy if she'd been stoned. She had faced a hail of missiles far too many times in her police career to take a restrained and sympathetic view of public disorder, and reached down her spine to the back of her belt to feel the comforting smooth grip of her 9mm. Shapakti stared.

"Yeah, you *bet* I'd use it," she said, anticipating his question and silencing it.

The colonists were about their business, mainly digging and shifting soil around in small barrows. They glanced up at Shan's party and then went back to their tasks. They were making deeper soil beds for crops, gathering up the thin top-soil of Mar'an'cas.

"It's a lot calmer," said Ade, but he still cradled his rifle and checked around him as he walked. "They can focus on going home now."

"Sooner the better," said Shan. "I'm going to find Rayat. Shapakti, you stick with me and we'll get you some samples."

"I'll stick around too," said Ade.

"Look, you know you wouldn't shoot an unarmed civilian." She couldn't be angry with him for being stiflingly protective. Nobody had ever given a shit about her safety before, not even when she was vulnerable to injury. It felt good. "But *I* can, believe me."

But Ade still trailed behind her, just the way she'd seen little wess'har boys trailing after an *isanket*, happy to submit to matriarchy.

Rayat was working when she found him. He'd never struck her as a man who liked getting his hands dirty, but then he'd never seemed to be a spy either; and she didn't usually get it that wrong. He was in one of the transparent composite crop tunnels, shoveling the contents of an old latrine over freshly dug soil. Ade stood at the entrance like a sentry and Shapakti followed her inside. The enclosed space concentrated the aroma wonderfully.

"You got five minutes?" said Shan.

Rayat looked up, still scattering the dark, crumbling mass. "I was expecting you to make some humorous comment about shit and my presence."

"I don't have a sense of humor. Fancy helping out a fellow scientist?"

"How?"

"Skin sample. Won't hurt a bit." She beckoned over her shoulder. "This is my chum Da Shapakti. Hold your arm out for him."

"What's in it for me?"

"Unbroken legs."

Shapakti put on his forensic glove and held up his forefinger like a proctologist; Rayat rolled back his sleeve. Maybe he didn't want to lose face in front of her.

"I'm glad your little EVA experience didn't affect your charm." Shapakti touched his arm and withdrew. Rayat looked slightly surprised. "Is that all you came for?"

"Here's your handheld."

"Found what you were looking for?"

"No." She was up against a pro in the interrogation game here. Rayat was even sharper than Eddie so she prepared a feint. "But in the absence of a named individual who gave you orders to cobalt Ouzhari, the Eqbas will probably fry the whole FEU when they get there."

It wasn't like that at all, but she lied anyway.

"I can see why you identify with them so strongly."

"Don't try playing the conscience card. It just pisses me off."

"And don't try to shock a name out of me. I don't much care what happens to politicians, especially ones who haven't even been elected yet."

Shan caught sight of her reflection on the taut-stretched surface of the composite, slightly distorted but all too detailed: not quite herself yet, too thin, too weak. She braced her shoulders. It was time to lob a pebble into the information pond, a trick she'd seen Eddie play too. She knew Perault. She could guess that if someone knew about *c'naatat* enough to brief Rayat, then Perault might know about it, and Perault's religious views would give her a very interesting take on microscopic eternal life. Shan had seen how the colonists behaved when confronted with it.

"I wondered if Perault thought *c'naatat* was her Christian afterlife." She gambled in her best throwaway tone, keeping her eyes fixed on Rayat's handheld. His scent said he was anxious. "Perhaps the idea of seeing God in a culture dish didn't quite do it for her, though."

She flickered her gaze as if she was trying *not* to look at the handheld. Rayat said nothing.

"Come on. Anyone you name is going to be long gone by the time the Eqbas get to Earth. Esganikan really wants to know."

I'm just thinking aloud.

"Nice try," said Rayat.

Ouch. "Can't blame a girl for trying."

"Like you said, it won't make any difference who authorized what." He smiled to himself, but it wasn't aimed at her. Either way, it was the sort of smile she liked to knock off people's faces the hard way. "You know Perault. She was obsessed with *c'naatat*. But she also understood that it was dangerous."

No, I had no idea she even knew it existed. She conned me. Fucking bitch. Shan felt abandoned, used, violated. "Did she really want it destroyed, though?" *Steady. Don't blow this. His scent's getting stronger.* "I reckon she lost her nerve."

"Yes, the gene bank ploy was clever, especially given the time she had to set it up. I really thought that was the genuine mission for a while and that *mine* was the bluff."

Your priority is Constantine and its planet, nothing else. Perault, pious and intense, gave her the briefing anew.

Doubt wasn't just nibbling away at Shan. It had started gulping down whole chunks. This was the point at which she threw in her real fears, suddenly grateful for her wess'har capacity to stand very still. "She knew I'd go for it. It was just a way of getting me here to make sure nothing happened to her Christian buddies. She didn't give a shit about Bezer'ej."

Rayat shrugged. "You've played this game before, just as I have. I wonder what elaborate cover briefing she'd have made up if the nearest foot soldier to hand hadn't been you?"

Shan found she could now control the involuntary dilation of her pupils. She concentrated on the sensation in her throat and jaw. She had to. Her stomach fell like a trapdoor opening on a scaffold.

"That's politicians for you," she said.

This was the onion-skinned conversation: Rayat knew she was interrogating him. Both were aware of the bluff and counterbluff but neither was sure where the layer of reality might be. It was distraction questioning, trying one topic to ease the suspect into answers before you switched to what you really wanted to know and they fell into the pit. He knew she did that. He probably thought he was smarter than her, though. He was probably enjoying telling her how Perault had set her up.

"Sure you don't want to name Cobalt Man?" said Shan, struggling with betrayal. "Last chance."

"Some things I take to my grave," he said. Spies had long been proven to be the most accomplished liars, able to control their reactions. But she was part wess'har, and she smelled the relief roll off him. He'd swallowed her line. "Talking of which, you're probably thinking up a suitable denouement for me."

"No, I'll leave that to Esganikan. Or the bezeri." She revealed it on a whim, but like all her gut reactions it had its roots in practiced strategy. "Yes, they found a few survivors."

Rayat's scent reaction was acid surprise. *Good.* Ade wandered up to her and stood in front of Shapakti, who looked welded to the spot.

"Want to go now, Boss? I can't stand the smell of shit any more."

"Wait outside, Ade." She'd found out what she needed to know. And she wanted to show Rayat that she could beat him at his own game. Childish: but she *was* a child again right then, hurt and lied to by the grown-ups. Perault had conned her, just as everyone said she had: but for entirely different reasons, for trivial, make-believe, *religious* reasons.

There was no government plan to break the agricorp cartel on patented food crops. She had been uprooted and sent 150 trillion miles from home because she was convenient and expendable.

It didn't even have anything to do with keeping Perault's terrorist sister, Helen Marchant, out of the frame.

But Shan still had the gene bank. And now she had powerful alien friends who could do something with it, so it was going back to Earth to bust the agricorps and their ilk. Her only regret now was that Perault was long dead and she'd never be able to see the shock on her face when she actually completed the mission. People who thought she was just another plod always got a nasty surprise.

And that included Rayat. *Now suck on this, you smug bastard.*

"I might as well tell you," she said. "*C'naatat* survived on Ouzhari too, and Ade's got a dose. I'm sorry your journey was wasted."

A scent-burst of anxiety. *Oh, this is good.* "I know about Ade."

"Okay, ask Shapakti about what he found on Ouzhari. Wess'har aren't very good liars."

Shapakti, ever literal, opened his mouth to speak but Rayat held up his hand to silence him. "Jesus, Frankland, I hope you've got a bloody good plan for keeping this thing out of human reach."

"I haven't, but Eqbas Vorhi has," she said. "And I'll go along with theirs."

She didn't stop to study Rayat's face. She walked out of the tunnel, reassured that she still had the edge and ashamed at giving in to professional vanity. Operation Green Rage was fresh in her mind again: she had kept her collusion with the eco-terrorists to herself, playing the incompetent right to the end, even when she was busted for letting them get away. She'd swallowed the humiliation. *You did it because it mattered, not so you could let everyone know how fucking noble you were.* She still felt cheated. *That* was what she didn't like. She realized that she didn't like being made to look a fool, and she wanted so much to be above those petty concerns.

Terrible events were sweeping whole worlds. Shan Frankland's personal anxieties meant nothing.

Ade caught her arm hard enough to jerk her back.
"Whoa, Boss. What's wrong?"

"Just doing a bit of growing up."

"Does it really matter why Perault sent you here? Isn't it
what happens that matters?"

"Very wess'har. That obvious, is it?"

"I know when you're upset."

"The bitch lost her nerve about the Suppressed Briefing
she'd given Rayat and she used me to salve her conscience
over the fucking colony, to make sure they weren't touched.
She manipulated my green sympathies to get me out here. I
fell for it."

"She SB'd you."

"A Suppressed Briefing isn't brainwashing, remember.
You can say no. She needed me to say yes because there was
nobody else she could send at the time, when she had to."

"So what's pissing you off? Just getting picked because
you were the nearest thing to hand, and not because you
were better than anyone else? Or being lied to by a politician? Happens to *us* all the time."

Ade was right on both counts. Soldiers lived with cynical
exploitation: and she'd automatically thought she'd been
chosen because she was so bloody perfect. *So this is your
come-uppance for conceit.*

She shrugged, humbled by his courage in telling her what
she really didn't want to hear. "You're right. It really doesn't
matter any more. Let's finish the job."

Shapakti tugged cautiously at her sleeve, clearly impatient with what he saw as a superfluous debate on motivation. "May we take more samples please?"

Shan nodded, and Ade steered Shapakti into the camp.
She went to sit on the beach and wait for them.

Bezer'ej was a huge crescent moon in the late afternoon
sky, as shockingly exotic as Wess'ej had been when Josh
Garrod had first pointed it out to her and told her that it was

inhabited. Ade and Shapakti returned about fifteen minutes later, talking quietly. Shan turned to smile at Ade, seeing him for a moment as the man she'd taken a fancy to rather than a test of her fidelity, but he looked shaken.

He was unusually quiet all the way back to the mainland. It was only when they had been picked up by the transport— more like a mattress on a hovercraft than a vehicle—that he spoke.

"If Shapakti can stop humans catching *c'naatat*," he said, "where does that leave us?"

Shapakti said nothing. Shan wondered what he had been discussing with Ade: but Ade was an open book. He never kept secrets, nor from her anyway.

"We'd be safer, Ade," she said. "A lot safer."

Things were not going as planned.

Eddie checked the fit of the ballistic vest. again. The Eqbas ship had landed but it hadn't yet lowered its ramp. He stared in carefully controlled horror at the bulkhead image as wave after wave of what he could only describe as gunfire hit the outer hull from the perimeter of the landing strip. He could understand how useful a see-through hull could be but that was scant comfort for his nerves.

It didn't seem to bother the Eqbas crew any more than it bothered the mindless bee cam. The camera wove slowly from angle to angle, taking its pick of the image: the Eqbas simply watched.

Ual was a Christmas tree of shivering ornaments, his quills almost at right angles to his bulky oval body.

"Please cease firing," said Esganikan. Ralassi repeated her request in isenj and Edie realized the message was being relayed outside the hull.

The barrage continued. Esganikan shifted on her seat and repeated the cease-fire request. Eddie had the feeling it was the Eqbas equivalent of a police officer's warning before firing; two of the bridge crew were taking great interest in a control panel.

"Very well," said Esganikan. "Cease firing immediately or we will respond. We wish only to meet your administration and to return Minister Ual."

There was a pause. Then the firing increased in intensity, peppering the illusion of a glass hull with thousands of exploding pinpoints of light.

"Suppress the fire," said Esganikan.

"Is that necessary?" said Ual.

Esganikan didn't even move her head. "We can sit here and wait for your people to run out of ammunition, or we can leave, or we can disembark and face the barrage."

"I would rather talk to them. Let me leave the ship."

"We are under fire."

"I'm an isenj minister of state. Whatever abuse my colleagues might heap upon me, it's simply words. I can walk out there and persuade them to hear you out."

"You're not our prisoner and you're free to leave, but I still think this is foolhardy."

Esganikan was a soldier. Eddie suspected she'd met quite a few welcoming committees like this one, because it didn't seem to bother her at all. "Why don't you let me talk to them? I'm human. I'm neutral."

"I'll do this," said Ual. "Tell them I'm coming out."

Esganikan's long hands were clasped in front of her chest and she was absolutely immobile. "Go, then. It will not alter what happens in the longer term."

Eddie got up and followed Ual to the hatch. "I'm still coming with you," he said, but he didn't know why. It was a reflex: something was happening and he had to rush to see it. He had a ballistic vest. There was no point scrawling MEDIA across the chest because the isenj behind the guns almost certainly didn't read English. If they did, he had no guarantee that his status would afford him any protection. It was like any foreign war.

"You have no protective headwear," said Ual.

The interior of the ship was as fluid and malleable as the external hull, an adaptable ship for a rigid people. They were now standing in a space that felt enclosed but there was only a thin transparent membrane around them, and Eddie's gaze was fixed on the exterior view that still filled the bulkhead.

It was like walking into a movie. "We can see them. Can they see us?"

"No," said Esganikan. "When you have composed yourself, we will create an opening."

"I will leave now and you will walk behind me," said Ual.

I should have asked Ade how to do this, thought Eddie. The bee cam was close to his head. *This is a beachhead landing. The front goes down and out you go. Oh God oh God oh God. Where's my breather mask?*

The bulkhead parted. It wasn't an image any longer. Eddie could smell burning and he inhaled dust. He was right behind Ual, close enough to notice his wet forest scent. The minister's beads were rattling as he made his inelegant way down the ramp that was forming in front of them.

There was absolute silence. The firing had stopped.

Ual let out a stream of high-pitched sounds. Was anyone close enough to hear him? Eddie didn't know what to look for at the perimeter fence and in the port buildings but he knew it was a battlefield and his instinct scanned for movement or any cue to duck or run.

Ual moved forward one slow pace at a time. Eddie followed. His feet were still on the ramp when Ual trod on the dusty landing field of Jejeno and a loud crack of expanding air and shrill noise deafened him.

Something straw-colored hit his vest. Something threw him flat on his back and the last thing he saw was the bee cam hovering above him. Something had gone badly wrong.

He had no idea that isenj blood looked like thin yellow plasma.

20

I now believe we can extract the c'naatat *organism from human tissue. This will reduce the risk of severe environmental consequences if more* gethes *were to become carriers of the symbiont. But we should still regard it as a life-form to be protected by quarantine.*

DA SHAPAKTI
biologist-physician, Wess'ej mission

Nevyan knew now that her *gut feel,* as Shan called it, had not been wrong.

And she had one question, a selfish one.

"Is Eddie hurt? What happened to him?"

Giyadas clung to her legs. Lisik and Livaor watched the communications link in silence. Cidemnet had gone to fetch their fourth house-brother Dijuas and the other children.

"He is alive," said Esganikan. The image showed calm routine behind her on the ship's bridge.

"Eddie, Eddie, Eddie," trilled Giyadas. "Bring him back. Bring him back. I will look after him."

Esganikan Gai had gone too far. The landing on Umeh had been opposed—and that was another *gethes* understatement Nevyan had learned, this time from Ade Bennett. *Opposed* was an odd way to describe a furious barrage of fire.

Esganikan didn't seem perturbed by it. "Minister Ual was shot. We neutralized the resistance at Jejeno airfield and we secured an entry point at Umeh Station. They have human physicians there."

"Ual is *dead*?"

"We believe so. They began firing when the hatch opened."

Isenj were fast-breeding polluters but they were also or-

derly, urban, and restrained with each other. Nevyan struggled to understand that they had opened fire on one of their
own. It was an indication of their fear, what Eddie called a
knee-jerk.

"What do you mean by securing an entry?"

"We created a corridor."

"I don't understand."

"My apologies, *Nevyan Chail*. I forget that you have obsolete technology. We have created an enclosed environment
to isolate Umeh Station, one hundred meters by their reckoning at ground level and a thousand meters into airspace.
That enables us to come and go without encountering isenj
for the time being."

Nevyan was beginning to understand just how much further the Eqbas had taken adaptive material technology. She
clutched the collar of her *dhren* to her throat, a nervous habit,
and the fabric reshaped itself. Like the tables that would
emerge from walls in the communal library, the technology
was the manipulation of molecular structure: but the Eqbas
could now use it to make fluid, ever-reshaping spacecraft and
sea-going vessels and impregnable corridors. Nevyan understood for a moment the disorientation of sudden inferiority
that the *gethes* had faced. Wess'ej had been the pinnacle of
technology in the Ceret system, and now it was not.

As long as the Eqbas were kin and allies, that was no threat.

"You shouldn't have interfered with the isenj on their
homeworld," said Nevyan. "There is no other species at risk
there. And, with the exception of Bezer'ej, they have never
attacked us."

"Ual asked us for assistance, and the isenj will not relin-
quish their claim on Bezer'ej. So we have choices—we
teach them to live within their own boundaries, or we confine them to their planet, or we destroy them."

"Targassat taught that the more choices you have, the
more restrained you must be in making them."

"Targassat did not accept the responsibility that comes
with power, which is why your ancestors fled here to avoid it.

Eqbas Vorhi accepts that if it *can* improve the equity and sta-bility of worlds, then it *must*. It is a matter of interpretation."

Nevyan felt she was losing the debate. Esganikan was comfortable in a warship millions of miles away, out of the influence of *jask*. Nevyan's defensive instinct welled up and the room fell into silence, even Giyadas seeming to freeze and hold her breath.

Nevyan pressed on. If Shan were here, she'd know what to do. "You don't have the military capability to take on Umeh with the forces here."

"Of course we have, and so do you."

"We have barely enough ships to sustain the defense of Bezer'ej."

"You have pathogens that can selectively target both *gethes* and isenj."

No. No, no, no. "Those are passive measures."

"We should discuss this later."

"Bring Eddie back here. We will care for him."

"As soon as he is ready to be moved, we'll return. We're assessing the *gethes* in Umeh Station at the moment." Esganikan's plumed mane tilted left and right. "They are *very* different to the colony on Mar'an'cas. How diverse human attitudes can be."

Nevyan could feel Giyadas's grip tightening on her leg. The child was scared. She was reacting to Nevyan's scent and she feared for Eddie. Eddie took foolish risks but he was, whether he acknowledged it or not, on *their side*. Nevyan had had to learn a whole new set of concepts to ac-company her knowledge of English, because wess'har had only one side to be *on*.

She switched off the screen and the living room wall re-turned to its normal state of gold stone facings.

"Lisik, is *Shan Chail* back from Mar'an'cas yet?"

"No, *isan*. Aras expects her soon."

"Has she activated her *virin*?"

Lisik checked his own device. "Yes. Shall I recall her?"

"No, I'll talk to her."

Giyadas suddenly let go and stood straight, pulling herself up to her full height and emitting a faint but definite scent of adult anger and *jask.* She was growing up fast.

"I know, *isanket,*" said Nevyan. "I fear for Eddie too. I fear for all of us."

But most of all Nevyan feared what she had unleashed. And she had to face it, and deal with it: she could never return to her past, her own world before.

Eddie knew he wasn't back in F'nar. The rest was guesswork.

At any given moment he was very clear what was happening to him, but when he tried to move from that single freeze-frame to a coherent sequence of events he wasn't sure what had happened at all.

He was in Umeh Station. He could just as easily have been back in his cabin in the *Thetis* camp on Bezer'ej if it had still existed. The walls had that same watery green light and the place smelled of cleaning fluid. The flashback impression was reinforced by voices he thought he recognized.

"He's not unconscious," said a male voice. "He didn't lose consciousness. The ussissi said so."

"Eddie? Eddie?" Someone had hold of his forearm. "It's Kris, Eddie. How are you feeling?"

"Where's Ual?"

"Come on, Eddie, talk to me. Can you see me?" She caught his jaw in her hand and turned his head to face her. It was Kristina Hugel, the medic from the *Thetis* payload, and she was running a handscanner over his head. He could hear it clicking, bouncing sound waves through his skull to detect fracture and hemorrhage. "Can you see me okay, Eddie?"

"Kris?"

"Good boy. You're okay. You were hit but you're okay. More blood than real damage. Any pain?"

His mouth was dry and he had a dull headache. "Hit where? Where's Ual?" He was aware his shirt was covered in blood, real red human blood, so it had to be his. "Who's got my camera?"

"It followed you in and we didn't know how to switch it off."

Eddie was damned if he was going to be kept flat on his back. He struggled to sit up. "Hit *where*?"

"You got hit in the head by something sharp. It's taken a slice out of your scalp but you'll be okay in a few days."

"You're not answering me. Where's Ual?"

"I don't know. The Eqbas brought you in and they're strutting round the place like storm troopers at the moment."

"Get Esganikan."

"Who's he?"

"She. The commander. The big female with the Mohican hairdo."

Kris smelled of old-fashioned antiseptic and stale coffee. She turned away to someone. "Vani, see if the ussissi can help, will you?" She caught Eddie by the shoulders just as he was about to put all his weight on his feet. "I wouldn't wander around if I were you. It's a bit chaotic here."

"Christ, that's par for the course. There's a war starting out there."

"Is it true they've recalled *Thetis* to ship us back?"

"God, I don't know. It'll take the best part of a year or more if they have, and it's going to be a hairy old year to wait out."

He listened. He couldn't hear firing. He wasn't sure if noise would travel through the sealed shell of the dome, but he thought he'd at least be able to feel the vibrations of explosions.

"Please, let me get up."

Kris Hugel offered him an arm to lean on. He caught a glimpse of himself in the mirror above the hand basin. He was in the infirmary. The gash in his scalp looked horrific, an angry stripe with the hair shaved away and the wound simply sealed with basic first-aid dermabond. He couldn't remember that happening at all.

"I'm a mess," he said. "How can I do a piece to camera

looking like this? I need to know what happened to Ual. I've got to find Esganikan."

"You're concussed, Eddie. Just take it easy."

No. It was his personal responsibility now. He had helped Ual arrange the snatch of Lindsay and Rayat. He was now so far across the neutral line that he knew he would never function as a journalist again, and he hadn't actually noticed the final point at which he had abandoned all the rules. It was incremental. The thin end of the wedge was very hard to spot when you were staring at it head on.

He tottered out of the three-room complex that made up the infirmary with Kris Hugel steering him by the elbow. The dome was surprisingly quiet, but packed with humans and more ussissi than he'd ever seen assembled in one place, even when they had last evacuated Jejeno when they thought Wess'ej would launch a retaliatory attack.

"That's not good," he said.

Ralassi sought him out. He was carrying a couple of bags that looked like rough-woven sacks. "Are you fit to travel?"

"Why? What?"

"No ussissi will serve the isenj now. That means no shuttles between Umeh and Tasir Var, or between continents. When we ask for our separateness to be respected, we mean it. Are you leaving with us?"

"What about us, then?" said Hugel. "What happens until *Thetis* arrives?"

"The same as would have happened otherwise," said Ralassi. "You survive. The Eqbas will protect the corridor until it's time for you to leave."

Eddie struggled for a grasp of reality. "What do you mean, *protect the corridor?*"

Ralassi pointed up into the canopy of the dome. The translucent filters and the tangle of vines obscured the view of the sky. "You can walk outside if you like. It's secure."

Adrenaline was a wonderful thing. Eddie shook off Hugel's arm and swayed his way to one of the exits. Normally he had to put on a breather mask to cope with the atmosphere outside, sulfur-tainted and low on oxygen even by the standards he'd acclimatized to on Bezer'ej: but the air outside felt . . . normal. As he looked out across the service road towards the building-upon-building city that crowded up to the perimeter, he couldn't work out what was different, and then he realized there were two notable things.

There were almost no isenj in the streets. Jejeno was usually heaving with bodies. And there was something familiar: the heat haze effect of an encircling barrier, like the one that surrounded Constantine, except he now knew this one would do more than simply filter out alien cells or trigger alarms. He followed the wall of haze above the level of the buildings, tilting his head back as far as the pain would allow, and saw the Eqbas ship holding steady in the sky right above Umeh Station.

It was how Eddie used to dispose of spiders. A glass upturned over the creature, a piece of stiff paper slipped underneath, and he could carry the spider to an open window and dump it outside. He never did believe in killing spiders. And now he was under the upturned glass, dependent on the kindness of big incomprehensible creatures who might allow him to scuttle away, or who might just as easily crush him.

Bronze droplets appeared to be falling from the ship. Three of them descended like elevators without cables. It was only when they were around 200 meters from the ground that it dawned on Eddie that they were more detached parts of the ship ferrying personnel to and from the dome.

"I hate this helpless feeling."

Kris Hugel stood beside him and looked up too. "I know I should marvel at all this but I just want to go home. I thought I was going back the first time and they thawed us out. But this time, I am absolutely *not* coming back."

Eddie's gratitude for medical assistance had evaporated. "If you'd kept your mouth shut about Frankland's parasite, none of this would have happened."

"Oh, and you weren't digging around and speculating about it. I hallucinated that, did I?"

"Okay, we all played our part in this fucking mess."

"Is it true?"

"What?"

"That she survived being spaced."

"Yeah. Right as rain."

"Jesus."

"Just walk away, Kris. Walk away, like she told you the first time."

Beyond the upturned glass of the Eqbas shield, isenj had started to venture out into the streets again. Eddie sat down on the curb that ran around the circumference of Umeh Station, feet in the gutter, and supported his head in shaking hands.

A shadow fell across him and it wasn't Ralassi's. He didn't need to look up.

"Just tell me what happened to Ual," he said.

Esganikan didn't sit down beside him. He expected her to, but then he realized why and reminded himself that for all her similarities with Shan, she was utterly alien and had none of Shan's capacity for psychological subtlety.

"He died," she said. "He was wrong. His countrymen *did* open fire, even if they did not intend him to die. The result is the same. And now the factions appear to be clashing—those who want to wage war on us and those who favor asking for our aid rather than the alternative."

"You sound like you've played this game before."

"We are seldom welcome. By definition, we arrive because matters have gone badly wrong."

"So what are you going to do now?"

"Wait and see what happens. There is no other species at risk here, and we can come and go as we please."

"You had a complement of two thousand crew, tops. This planet has a population of billions. Even you can't crack those odds."

"I had this very conversation with Nevyan Tan Mestin. If

we need a weapon, we already have one—the engineered pathogen deployed on Bezer'ei "

Eddie's scalp tightened and it wasn't because of the gash in it. *You promised. Shan, you promised they wouldn't.*

"No," he said. "No, you can't use bioweapons here, not that one—"

"I didn't say we would."

Esganikan wouldn't have been playing games like a human. She was simply answering his questions in a logical, literal order. *Shan, you said they'd never use it to attack Umeh.* That was why he agreed to get a sample of isenj DNA, to use his access to Ual. It was the ultimate betrayal. The guy was dead, and he had helped him reach that point, and now he was the procurer of weapons, every bit as bad as all the scientists he'd despised in history for creating bombs and diseases and other tricks for the use of politicians.

"Poor bastard," he said. He thought he meant Ual. "You poor bastard." And he sat crying quietly in the gutter of a besieged human enclave twenty-five light-years from home.

21

Superintendent Frankland,

I'm responding to your message, which was forwarded to me. I'm afraid Granddad passed away four months ago. He hadn't been well for some time. He used to talk about you all the time and I know it would have meant a lot to him to know you still thought about him.

Yours,

JAY McEVOY HARRIS,
granddaughter of Chief Constable Robert McEvoy

"He'll be okay, kid," said Shan.

Giyadas had a firm grip on Shan's leg and it was a measure of his *isan*'s discomfort that Aras couldn't smell her scent at all. She was suppressing it again. She didn't like being around children, not even little adults like Giyadas. Ade, taking excessive care over brewing the tea, caught his eye: they exchanged a glance, silently working out who was going to extract her from the grip.

"This was unexpected," said Nevyan.

"You bet."

"I am to blame for summoning them."

"No, they're to blame for going in mob-handed." Shan kept glancing down at Giyadas. It was clear that she didn't like being pinned to the spot but she seemed reluctant to push the child aside. "Maybe this is none of my business, but I'm bloody uncomfortable with the idea of Eqbas having the engineered pathogens. Isenj *or* human."

"Come with me. Dissuade Esganikan."

Shan's arms were folded tight across her chest. Aras could see the faint flicker of violet light leaking from her clenched fists, and he moved to steer Giyadas away by her shoulder. "I'll dissuade her, all right," said Shan. "They didn't need to go crashing in there. Do you think they can contain the isenj without needing to use bioweapons?"

"They say they can. But further support is years away."

"Y'know, I'm not someone who likes to talk their way out of trouble when there's a quicker way of doing the job, but I think talking is just what's needed now."

"I think you should stay out of it," said Ade.

"I'm not asking you," said Shan.

Aras intervened more from the disappointment of a broken promise than to back up his house-brother in waiting. "You promised you would leave Esganikan to pursue her own course unless she interfered with the gene bank."

"Let's get one thing straight," said Shan. "This is what I do. I sort things out. I can help Nevyan defuse this situation and I don't even need my gun to do it, so let me just do what I do best and then we can all get on with our lives. Right now, Attila the Parrot is considering wholesale slaughter and even I feel uneasy about that."

"Part of the ship will be back in an a few hours," said Nevyan. "The remainder is maintaining the corridor while more transports go to evacuate the ussissi. They're all leaving."

"Well, that'll give the isenj a few logistics problems to keep them busy." Shan seemed to soften towards Giyadas, or at least to feign concern very well. There was still no scent. She squatted down to look the *isanket* straight in the eye. "Sweetheart, Eddie's okay. He's probably very upset, though, but if he comes back angry it won't be with you."

"I know that," said Giyadas. "He'll be angry with *you.*"

Aras didn't think Shan cared what anyone thought of her, but he was wrong. The constricting blood vessels in her face gave her an instant pallor.

"Right again, kid."

She stood up and took the bowl of tea that Ade offered her. Aras thought he detected an attempt at placatory eye contact, but Ade was having none of it and wouldn't look at her. They all drank in silence.

There was a knock at the door. It inched open and Sha-pakti peered around it. "May I speak to *Shan Chail*?"

"She's a bit busy," said Ade.

"It really is very important."

"Not now, Shapakti," said Shan. "I've got something to sort out. I'll catch you later."

Shapakti hesitated for a few seconds then slid back across the threshold and closed the door. Shan drained her bowl and rinsed it under the spigot.

"Okay, Nev," she said. "Let's go. Mango time."

It was always a bad sign when Shan attempted humor. Aras and Ade were now alone with their doubts.

"She's put on a bit more meat in the last day or so," said Ade, transparently upset even though he tried to disguise the fact. "I reckon she's nearly back to normal."

"Don't be alarmed by her manner. She does care about us."

Us. Yes, it was a case of *us.* Once the current crisis had receded, things would settle down.

They had to.

There were an awful lot of ussissi.

They streamed down the ramp of the transport and moved across the plain in an unbroken column in the direction of the little Easter-egg domed village where Shan had nearly found out the hard way how they attacked. She watched them with Nevyan and Serrimissani.

"No customs control, then?"

"There are many more to come," said Serrimissani, ignoring her. She had collected a couple of sacks from one of the new arrivals, and Shan noted that without inquiring about the contents. Old habits died hard. "Some have joined the search for Vijissi's body. This is quite appalling. We have never been compromised like this before."

"Where's Esganikan?"

"I have no more idea than you."

"Have you got a problem with me or are you just always fucking rude?"

"My apologies." But she didn't sound as if she meant it.

Nevyan waited with her hands clutched at the collar of her *dhren,* her classic nervous gesture. *Come on, buck up,* Shan thought. But Nevyan was just a kid herself, thrust into adulthood a matter of months ago under trying circumstances. Shan wondered if she'd have been as capable of statesmanlike behavior at the equivalent age.

No, she didn't think she had. But she'd been well able to handle herself in a fight. And this wasn't even a fight: no blows needed trading and no guns needed to be drawn. All she had to do was want her own way, and mean it. The trick was not to become so aggressive that she overwhelmed Esganikan and found herself in command of an Eqbas army for the next five years.

What's going to happen when they reach Earth?

She put it to the back of her mind. Humans had asked for it. There was work to be done on Earth. Umeh was too far down the toilet.

They could wipe out humanity if they set their minds to it. Are you okay with that?

She found she couldn't get that worked up about it and waited in grim silence with Nevyan while the wind whipped up her trouser legs. She bent down and tucked them into her make-do wess'har boots. It was unusually cold weather for F'nar, they said. She found it pleasantly cool.

And it struck her that she was more worried about the isenj than her own kind.

Nevyan consulted her *virin.* "Esganikan travels on board the next vessel," she said.

"Okay, we don't let her disembark. We get her in her cabin. Enclosed space." Shan decided she could always hand control to Chayyas or Mestin if things went wrong. "Why does it work like that?"

"Work like what?"

"*Jask.* How come I face down Chayyas and she cedes her dominance, but we can take on Esganikan without her ceding to either of us?"

"Everyone's *jask* is unique. If matriarchs ceded to communal scents nobody would ever be able to take responsibility, which is how we're influenced by the common will. A fail-safe mechanism, I think you call it."

"I still prefer slugging it out, I think."

"Nobody is injured by *jask*."

"Okay, then let's make sure we don't go over the top with this."

"I can't take on her role. I know my limits."

"It won't come to that."

Shit, it might.

On the horizon, now deep turquoise with the failing light, three dark smooth shapes appeared and a characteristic boom shook the air. They slowed and hung almost motionless above a cluster of lava plugs. Then they came together and merged. And one ship landed.

"Jesus," said Shan. "How can any defense force deal with *that*? I mean, you think the enemy's sailing up the river in a bloody great destroyer and then you blink and they've got five frigates. Holy shit."

"As long as they are on *our side,* as you put it, this can only be good."

"And are they?"

Nevyan was a cloud of acid anxiety. "I believe they *are* fundamentally like us even if they're less restrained. They want to create a more permanent base here."

"Like the Temporary City?"

"Yes."

"And what have you said?"

"You can't ask for someone's aid and then deny them what they need to give it. And their way of life is too different for them to settle in the city for the next few years."

"It'll work out."

"I know I can rely on you."

It almost didn't make sense. But wess'har were full of non sequiturs.

The ship settled. Heat shimmered beneath the hull as the

craft lowered itself to the ground until it was as flat and solid as a building. Shan found herself standing at the hatch as soon as it formed in the bulkhead, even before the ramp extruded from it. The Eqbas who was on the other side of it didn't seem startled.

"Nevyan and I will be seeing Esganikan Gai in her cabin," said Shan. "Show me where it is."

The ship's interior still disoriented Shan because it was all shifting light and shadow, triggering her wess'har low-light vision but also leaving her with the unsettling feeling of being in a mirrored and deceptive shopping mall, a difficult place to pursue a suspect. A bulkhead melted and Esganikan appeared in front of her.

The matriarch focused on Shan with snapping four-lobed pupils, head tilting. *You really can't gauge me without the scent, can you?* Then she stared past her at Nevyan.

"You are anxious," said Esganikan. "Ual was most unfortunate but Eddie Michallat is recovering."

"Fine, but that's not what we wanted to talk to you about," said Shan.

The *Thetis* payload had been worried about Shan's lack of training in alien contact; they'd be shitting themselves now. Esganikan looked as if she was planning to walk past both of them but Shan stood her ground, feeling herself on the tightrope that separated authority from overkill. Keeping a rein on her scent was like trying to control a sneeze. She was aware of the physical sensations now: she concentrated on contracting muscles in her neck.

"Are the prospects for your own planet bothering you?"

"Depends what you mean by my planet," said Shan. "But right now we're not happy about the use of the isenj pathogen."

"I haven't used it."

"And we don't want you to," said Nevyan.

A few crew members wandering around the ship stopped to watch, and then stood very still in the wess'har alarm reflex.

"It might be necessary," said Esganikan.

Shan stepped a little closer, close enough to start a fight on Earth. "Let's get this clear. As long as they stay put on Umeh and don't bother us, or Bezer'ej, or any other planet, then you don't deploy bioweapons."

"That is the way it has been here for generations," said Nevyan. "Apart from Bezer'ej, they have never staged incursions."

"You fear for your fellow humans in Jejeno."

"I couldn't give a *shit* about Umeh Station," said Shan. "You understand that? I don't care. But the isenj will have to do something extreme to justify attacking them on their home ground. Mjat was their own fault. There's nothing left of Umeh to restore so I don't see what you stand to gain by wiping them out."

"I didn't plan to. But Ual consented to population control measures, ones we can take without culling."

Shan could taste the sweet fruit scent at the back of her palate.

Nevyan was standing very close to her. "We still want your assurance that you won't use the pathogen without our agreement."

Esganikan stood silent, gaze flickering between Shan and Nevyan. Shan could taste the pheromones getting stronger. Then the Eqbas simply cocked her head, forced to concede. "Yes," she said. "I agree. But we will still carry out the birth control measures."

Shan felt a bead of sweat trickle down her spine and she resisted the urge to scratch it. "Okay."

"Why have you stopped breathing?"

"It's just a habit."

"Do you wish to plead for your own planet now?"

"Where's this going?"

"We were told you were wess'har and that you lived in balance. Are you losing your resolve and reverting to type?"

"No. Believe me, just because the UN says that it's banned exploration it doesn't mean anyone will honor that."

"But even if Earth does curtail its expansion, we're still obliged to intervene. There are many other Earth species in need of assistance."

Yes, Esganikan was right, and it hurt: Shan *was* losing her nerve. But it wasn't because she thought they were wrong. It was because she was uneasy about the potential violence that would be on her conscience. And Esganikan wasn't taunting her: Shan had misunderstood the Eqbas's motive because she had slipped back into thinking like a *gethes*.

Esganikan was simply trying to explain the situation. Like all wess'har, she was seeking a binding consensus. "When you investigated crime, did you wait for the perpetrator to call you to ask you to aid their victim?"

And Shan *understood*. She understood not in the intellectual way of the legislator, or of the officer called to abide by laws of evidence, but at a gut level that said *coppers don't just stand by and let it happen. Fuck the rules.* She was picking up her baton again and sorting things out the old-fashioned way, because it was *right*.

She thought like an Eqbas and that made her uncomfortable.

But after a few seconds it didn't feel that uncomfortable at all. Humans would have to live with the consequences of exploitation. It was simple. It was what she had always believed deep down.

"You won't get any argument from me," said Shan.

Nevyan, steeped in the isolationist, mind-your-own business culture of Targassat, turned and walked away briskly. Esganikan took it as the end of the conversation and disappeared in the other direction. Shan was left standing alone for a few seconds, not quite understanding what had happened. The wess'har lack of valediction always wrongfooted her.

She caught up with Nevyan outside. The young matriarch exuded that vinegary scent that went with anger. Her pupils were dilated. She rounded on Shan.

"I find this very hard," she said. "Forgive me for my anger, but you encourage the Eqbas taste for interfering."

"Hey, it's my planet, and it's fucked. We *need* them. And the isenj could do with not knocking out so many kids."

"You haven't seen what the Eqbas can do."

"Oh, but I have. Eddie showed me the pictures of the worlds they've sorted out. Anyway, they're wess'har so whatever they do, they won't be screwing the underdog and exploiting those who can't help themselves, which is one hundred percent of the nonhuman life on Earth and a bloody big chunk of the human population, too."

"This intervention is why our two communities went our separate ways."

"I know all that. But your idyll is over, Nev. The galaxy changes. My filthy species is on the loose and it was only a matter of time before Eqbas noticed us. If they leave you alone, and they don't bother the isenj, will that make you happy? Because if you want them to be any different, then you're exactly the same as them—imposing your values on others."

Nevyan was walking fast towards the city, as fast as Shan could cover the ground: they were the same height, Nevyan short for a wess'har, Shan tall for a human female.

"I can't argue with your logic," she said. "But I feel afraid."

"You need to talk to someone who's faced real danger. Talk to Ade. Talk to Aras."

Nevyan stopped and swung round. Shan's instinct said *draw your weapon* and she knew it was stupid, but she felt it anyway and sidestepped instead. Nevyan didn't appear to guess what had flashed through her mind. She was fidgeting with her *dhren*.

"I know I'm afraid of change," said Nevyan. "For F'nar, I represent huge change, and to you I must seem like stagnation. But I can't help what I feel."

"It's okay." Shan wanted to comfort her. She was handling a situation that would have made seasoned politicians back home crap themselves, and the kid should have been proud of that. Instead she was scared, and Shan couldn't even bring herself to hug her. She gripped her upper arm instead. "It's okay. I understand. There are things that you take in your stride that scare me."

The still silence was awkward. "Shapakti is anxious to talk to you."

"I know. But I ought to apologize to Ade first. I was rude to him. He deserves respect."

"Yes, make things right with your *jurej've*. We'll talk in the morning."

Shan let Nevyan stride ahead while she ambled and finally fell behind. F'nar was speckled with pinpricks of light, utterly magical even in the dusk. She could be sure that dinner would be on the table when she got back, and an uninvited memory of her police colleagues at Western Division sprang into her mind. She was walking into the police sports and social club bar across the road from divisional headquarters, shift complete, pleased with herself, looking forward to a single beer, because she didn't like surrendering control to alcohol. *Did I have a busy day? Oh, I just averted interplanetary genocide, nothing serious. Who's buying me a pint?*

She missed them. She thought about them less and less these days, but it was still hard to accept they were probably all dead. Rob McEvoy was dead too. She didn't even know if she'd helped him step into the gap she'd left. She hoped so.

The world was still full of good people who deserved better. She was never sure if she was one of them.

Wess'har didn't have mirrors but Ade didn't need to shave now anyway. He could see very few changes that *c'naatat* had made to him, but he could tell that it didn't see the point of having body hair.

He'd get used to it. He propped the polished metal sheet against the wall and brushed his teeth, staring at a distorted reflection that looked near enough the same Ade Bennett he was used to seeing.

How much longer would the toothbrush last? He examined the bristles. If the wess'har could build self-repairing warships then a duplicate brush wouldn't be a problem. Salt and lavender oil made a good enough dentifrice, too; it was only for cosmetic purposes, because *c'naatat* would see off any tooth decay. He just wanted to be sure that he tasted okay if he ever got lucky with Shan.

He bent over the birdbath-shaped washbasin and rinsed, rubbing his tight-shut eyes, then stood up to bury his face in a *sek* towel. It smelled of cut grass.

"So *that*'s the tattoo that hurt," said Shan.

Ade clutched the towel to his groin, mortified. "I didn't hear you come in."

"My fault. I didn't knock." She seemed to be trying hard to look him in the eye and not succeeding. She made a visible effort to raise her eyes from his crotch. "I just wanted to apologize for telling you to mind your own business in front of everyone. Not nice. Sorry. I know you worry."

"It's okay."

"I don't think private apologies *are* okay, actually, so I'll repeat it when the others are around."

"Really, it doesn't matter." *Please, go away. Let me put my pants on.* "I've got something for you."

"You're not kidding."

"No, I *really* got something for you." He gestured towards the door with one hand, holding the towel in place with the other and knowing he looked about as stupid as he could get. "Go into the living room. Go on."

Shit, shit, shit. He could never do this right. He wrapped the towel around his waist and padded out after her. The sack was still on the flagstones by the door: knowing how much she was still the archetypal copper, he was surprised that she hadn't taken a look inside. If she had, she wasn't saying.

"This is for you," he said.

She held the sack slightly away from her body, two-handed, and opened it cautiously. "*Uhhh,*" she said. He'd never seen such a spontaneous expression of delight on her face before. It transformed her. She was illuminated. She reached in and lifted out the precious, hard-won pair of rigger's boots. "Aww, Ade, I thought you'd forgotten."

"I never forget that kind of thing."

"These are *great.* Just the job."

"Sorry about the color. I was working on getting them dyed black somehow."

"Brown's fine. Don't you worry about that." She seemed totally distracted by the boots and he wondered how much else he simply didn't know about her. She was a straightforward, practical woman, satisfied by sensible things, with no mystery or whim or mood to fathom out. "And I snarled at you. Sorry. Not sure how I can make up for that."

"I've thought of something."

"Saucy bugger."

"Okay, that was out of order."

"No, it's not out of order at all. I offered, remember?" She put the boots carefully by the door, side by side, still glowing with admiration as she gazed at them. Then Ade realized she was concentrating on them a little too hard. He wondered when she might say the word openly. "It's not you, Ade, it's me. I know it's what Aras wants and I want it to be that way too, but I just have to get my head straight before . . . you know."

Ade knew only too well. He was a complication. He was a dilemma in Shan's dead straight, old-fashioned right-and-wrong world; he knew without asking that she had never, ever cheated on a man. Her honest loyalty was both one of the qualities he loved and a barrier to getting what he wanted.

"I'm coming between you two," he said. He *knew* it. It broke his heart. He had her back, alive, the impossible fantasy of every bereaved person in history, and now he was about to make her deeply unhappy. He couldn't bear it. "I'm going to cause you both a lot of pain and I don't want that."

"Not at all. Not at all, sweetheart. It'll be fine."

Shan was the only person he knew who had to work out the moral argument before doing something. She never did what she wanted: she did what was *right*. It was one of those things that sounded clean and admirable until you were staring it in the face and it was about to say no to you.

And right then he found himself thinking not about being a moment away from having sex with a woman he worshiped, or complicating her loyalties, but about obeying Lindsay Neville's order to transport nuclear weapons to Bezer'ej.

"I'd better put some clothes on," he said. Guilt was a passion-killer all right. "I'm glad you like the boots."

Shan was staring at his shoulder now. "Did you know you've developed some bioluminescence?"

He twisted his neck to look at the top of his left arm. The tattoo he'd had done when he signed up as a marine—the Corps' globe and laurel, a defiant reminder that he was finally free of his dad's unpredictable drunken rages—looked backlit. Faint violet flickers escaped from under the dark pigment.

"Blimey," he said, desperate to lift the mood. "If it's in *all* my tattoos now, at least I'll be able to find it in the dark."

It was a legacy of the bezeri. And it wasn't funny at all. It just reminded him that he was a fighting man who hadn't fought when it most mattered: when he should have refused an unlawful, immoral order.

Yeah, guilt really turned you off.

Lindsay Neville stood on the Mar'an'cas shoreline and debated how far out she might have to wade before she couldn't change her mind and scramble back to shore.

There was nothing she could salvage in her life now. She had started to come to terms with David's death, and in time she might come to live with the knowledge that she had helped kill thousands of sentient beings. But it had all been for nothing.

The parasite had survived, and Shan had survived, and bezeri had survived. Now the remnant would remember what she had done, and hate her. That thought bothered her. It disturbed her that she found their survival another blow and not some measure of relief.

And Shan Frankland hadn't shot her when she was absolutely, utterly convinced that she would do it without a second thought. The bitch wouldn't put her out of her misery.

She'd do it herself, then. She cupped her hand and studied the bioscreen grown into her palm. The living screen was dead, just a patch of shivering green light, and there were no readouts from the marines. They were either out of range or they had deactivated their links, but either way it said the same thing: *you're on your own.*

She checked the cloud formation and the wind direction for a while, still a sailor, and decided now was as good a time as any.

Lindsay wasn't a strong swimmer. The cold made her catch her breath and she felt the current buffet her as she waded out into the shallows. *Why didn't you just jump? There's plenty of cliffs. Why pick this beach? Going to change your mind?* All she had to do was strike out and swim until she couldn't swim any longer. It wasn't going to hurt as much as living with what she'd become and it would be over, over, *over.* They said drowning didn't hurt at all.

The cold was starting to numb her. Two minutes, maybe five: that was all the time you had in cold water, or so they told you in survival training. She knew people survived a lot longer. It wasn't as grand a gesture as stepping out into space but it was the best she could do.

A wave hit her and she gulped in water, coughing and choking. The impulse to turn and head back to dry land was almost overwhelming. But she struck out further, surprised how much she rose and fell with the choppy waves. She was starting to slip from being in control of her environment to being overwhelmed by it, the point at which self-preserving panic would kick in.

No, she wasn't Shan Frankland, making a final gesture of sacrifice. She was ending it all, just running away. She could hear her own choking sobs. She didn't have a single noble thought in her head and she knew she had chickened out of dying the right way once before, but this time she was going to do it.

Every stroke she took brought her closer to a point where she couldn't get back. Funny: it seemed so much easier than pulling the pin on a grenade.

Seawater flooded her mouth again. For the first time she wondered what might swim in these seas. Maybe she wouldn't drown at all. Maybe she would fall into the transparent maw of a marine version of a *sheven* or an *alyat,* or worse.

She wasn't all that far out. It just felt like deep sea because the coastal shelf fell away sharply beneath her and the currents changed dramatically.

Then something grabbed her from behind. *Sheven. Don't be stupid:* shevens *live on Bezer'ej.* But a hand, a human hand with strong fingers, tipped her chin up and forced her onto her back. She lashed out. The hand became an arm round her neck and the next directionless kick she managed was greeted with a crack across the head.

"Relax or I bloody well *will* hold you under," said Rayat.

"Sod off—"

"Coward. Bloody little *coward.*"

"Let go."

"You're not getting out of this." He was pulling her backwards and she was running out of fight. "I can't stand a quitter."

"Fine time—"

"Shut up."

"—to play the hero."

"Shut up. You've got a job to do."

Lindsay kicked a few more times. This time he punched her hard, a fist right on the top of her head. She wasn't sure if she'd changed her mind or not. All she knew was that she didn't want to be where she was right then, with the things that wouldn't ever leave her mind.

Rayat hauled her back inshore, a textbook rescue.

"Bastard," she said, and coughed up water.

22

TO: the Representative from Eqbas Vorhi.
FROM: The Right Honorable James Matsoukis MAP, Pacific
Rim States Lead Delegate to the United Nations.

On behalf of our regional government, I invite your delegation
to land in our territory. This is a binding agreement on behalf
of the Australasian Republic and will be honored by all future
administrations. We share your concern for global ecology and
we will offer every cooperation. If there is any action we can
take now to prepare for your arrival, please inform this office.
*   We welcome to your assistance. It is a sad indictment of*
the ability of our nations to work in partnership when we
need to request the arbitration of an external government.

Rayat made Lindsay a hot mug of broth. She considered
checking it for poison because he wasn't a tea-and-sympathy
kind of man, not at all.

"Coward's way out," he said.

She sipped. "I bet you were great on the suicide helpline.
Don't you have a cyanide capsule you can take?"

They were huddled in the relative warmth of one of the
makeshift greenhouses on Mar'an'cas, but not so close as to
touch.

"Well, you either die well or live well, that's my motto.
Have you heard from Frankland?"

"What do you think? And how would she call me? She's
probably begging Esganikan to let her disembowel me."

"She could have killed you back in F'nar, but she didn't.
That tells me there's still room for maneuver."

Lindsay could see colonists going about their business,
blurred into an impressionist painting by the condensation
on the transparent sheeting. "I can't go on with this."

"So you're going to escape from the reality by topping yourself. Heroic."

"Well, seeing as I'm not good at rolling back the clock, yes."

"I hear the bezeri that survived are struggling. Ever thought of offering them a hand?"

"I don't think the Eqbas believe in community service orders," she said, and slurped the broth. It scalded her lip. "Or maybe I could go scrub Ouzhari clean."

"If you want atonement, maybe that's what you need." Rayat wiped his nose against the back of his hand. "But you'd need to have *c'naatat* to do that. It's a little hot."

"Look, I'm going to die," she said. "And you're going to die too. What are you playing at?"

Rayat had a habit of not blinking, just like Shan. Lindsay imagined that he was also as adept as Shan at getting people to do things they didn't want to do, and not by charm. Every conversation with him left her feeling as if he had done something terrible to her and then erased her memory of it, leaving only the impression that she'd been violated in some way. He was looking for an edge, even on the brink of death.

"I'm just not good at comforting people," he said, apparently contrite. "Sorry."

He stared into his mug for a moment, facial muscles slackening for a split second. For that instant she saw not a spook, but a man who did a dirty, necessary job that nobody else would do, and had no friends, no lovers, and nobody he could even trust to tell what kind of a day he had really had. Pity almost ambushed her. But she shook it off, knowing now what that feeling of violation was.

Wretched or not, Rayat was marvelously manipulative.

"You bastard," she said. She struggled to her feet and tipped the rest of the broth into the soil bed. "You think you're sliding out of this? No bloody way. You'll get whatever's coming to me too, don't you worry. I'll make sure of that."

Rayat stared up at her, still unblinking, and shrugged.

Lindsay stalked out and walked back up the path to the shore and settled down in the lee of some rocks.

Atonement.

The notion kept circling around her mind, looking for a chance to strike. You couldn't wipe the slate clean of tens, *hundreds* of thousands of deaths, not by doing a few good deeds. So did that mean she could just shrug and find release in permanent oblivion, and not even try?

She'd been around the colonists for too long. Perhaps she was worried subconsciously that there really was some higher authority she'd have to answer to. It seemed an imminent prospect. She'd seen crew in extreme danger switch from being openly atheist to begging some god or other to save them; death's threshold was the one point in your life when you found out whether you really believed or not.

What could I do, anyway?

She was a naval officer. Every scrap of training and every thread of her personality was bound up with responsibility and duty. She had to act.

But the Eqbas didn't need volunteers. And only Shan Frankland and her ilk could survive under water.

Lindsay paused.

It was an insane idea. She dismissed it, but it wouldn't leave. It came back and settled on her shoulder like a persistent pet bird.

Eddie didn't know if the Australasian offer was stupidity, arse-kissing surrender, a cynical PR stunt or enlightened thinking on an unprecedented scale. But he knew it was *trouble.*

Giyadas sat staring into his face while he watched the ITX feed, propped on a pile of blankets in Nevyan's warren of excavated rooms. He didn't find her gaze distracting now. He worked through the news channels and noted the sliding scale of fighting talk, from the slight regret of the Sinostates to the over-my-dead-body stance of the African Assembly.

"They're coming, whatever you say," he said to the screen.

Giyadas shifted position, but her gaze was fixed.

"I'm not going to drop dead," he said.

"I'm keeping an eye on you. That is the phrase, yes?"

"I'm fine. I've had worse head injuries falling over drunk."

"Yes, but you have emotional injuries too."

"Like I said, I've had worse."

"When will you visit Shan?"

Eddie wasn't sure why he blamed Shan and he didn't know quite what he blamed her for. Ual had gambled and lost. Shan had done what she thought was needed to secure Bezer'ej. It just didn't feel that way. "I'll leave it a few days."

"Esganikan has agreed not to use bioweapons on Umeh."

"Right."

"She *won't*. Nevyan and Shan made her concede."

"Bully for Shan, then." Eddie reached out and ruffled Giyadas's tufted mane. "I suppose I feel I let a friend down."

"Was Ual your friend?"

"Close enough to make me feel like a heap of shit for conning him over his DNA."

He didn't know if she understood that, but he imagined she'd be saying *shit* before too long. He took his rolled-up editing screen from his top pocket and flicked through the list of files waiting to be ITXed back to News Desk if only the UN portal would let him pass.

He hadn't looked at the bee cam's footage from the landing. To be more accurate, he hadn't looked at the footage from the point where the ramp went down. He was certain the bee cam had done what it was programmed to do and followed the action, which almost certainly meant graphic images of Ual being shot. Would he use it? The boundaries of what could be shown to audiences had been burst open centuries ago. A fat alien spider spraying body fluids wouldn't even raise an eyebrow.

But to use it, he had to edit it, and that meant looking at it. And that was what he couldn't do right then. He knew plenty of colleagues who had calmly cut sequences involving the graphic deaths of people they knew and even liked, and they considered it a duty and an act of respect, but Eddie found he was no longer one of them.

How many more reminders do you need?

"Eddie?"

So if you're not a journalist, what are you now?

"Eddie? Eddie, have you decided whether you'll return to Earth with the Eqbas?"

You know, it's not so bad to rethink who you are.

"I'm not sure, sweetheart. I'm not sure what I'm going to do at all."

He'd set Lindsay up to be captured and taken for execution, and not even spoken to her since. He'd pushed propaganda for one alien power and then helped a minister from another one defy his government. He'd helped the wess'har develop a bioweapon.

Eddie wondered what might be left of him when he put his camera down.

Shan didn't like herself much today. She had fewer days like these as the years wore on, but this morning she felt like a woman in the most negative sense she could imagine. She was messing men around. It was silly and girly and she should have known better.

She leaned against the wall of the washroom and let the single jet of cold water play on the top of her head by way of penance. It wasn't the physical stuff that bothered her as much as the voice deep in her brain that was still saying *slut, slut, slut.* She had never thought less of Nevyan for having four males, so why couldn't she extend that tolerance to herself?

Because you're still wired to believe that the best thing you can give a male is your exclusivity.

It wasn't. She could see that simply by looking at Aras and Ade eating breakfast, becoming increasingly . . . *synchronized.* The brother bond was as almost as important as the male-female relationship, and now she could see that more clearly than ever.

Watching Nevyan's household—quarrelsome, affectionate, apparently chaotic—was seeing aliens, interesting but separate creatures however much she admired and liked them. But this bonding was happening in front of her to people whose reactions and attitudes she knew intimately, and they were *changing*. Aras took some *gurut* from the range and Ade placed a tray under them as if by reflex. They were an instant team. They knew how to fit in with each other now.

And all she had to do was join that team, and everything would be fine. She didn't want to think the word *family*. It had no positive connotations for her.

"You approve of the boots, then," said Aras.

"Yes, just the job."

"Shapakti has called again."

Shan crunched on an overcooked piece of *gurut*. "Ade, you didn't bite his head off, did you?"

"Aras dealt with him."

"And I was most respectful."

"Okay," said Shan. "I'd better go and see what he wants. Are you sure there's nothing else you two want to discuss with me?"

Aras and Ade glanced at each other and shrugged, and Shan wondered if she was beginning to deal with a double act. They smelled a little agitated. Perhaps that was how wess'har males always behaved; she'd have to ask Nevyan for advice again, if she was in a better frame of mind today. Time was when she could do no wrong in Nevyan's eyes, or in Eddie's, come to that; and now she worried she could do nothing right.

But at least her *jurej've* thought she was okay. And that was what mattered. She gave Aras a playful swat that got no response and left to call on Da Shapakti.

It was a gray miserable day outside, the sort she actually liked. And it wasn't just raining. The drops pecked at her face, turning into sleet, a very rare thing indeed for F'nar. The pearl-shit icing on the elegant organic swirls and curves of the city looked like ice. It was the sort of day to come home to an indulgent tea by the fireside, and for a brief moment she actually missed home.

You must be joking. The apartment had five alarm systems and you only used one side of the bed. Don't kid yourself that you abandoned a haven.

Shapakti probably didn't run to toasted pikelets spread with lavender jelly. *Lavender.* Aras had planted lavender, and so all she needed was something sugary that would set into a gel. It was a noble project and one she intended to devote herself to when the current situation calmed down. She was still wondering whether *jay* fruit might be a suitable medium when she walked into the scattered camp of ship fragments in search of Shapakti.

He seemed surprised that she had bothered to come and see him.

"Do you have time now?" Shapakti always kept at a safe distance from her, a good clear meter. Now she had stepped down off the roller coaster of aggression, she realized what a stroppy bitch she must have seemed to him. Poor bugger: he was just doing his job, probably as dismayed as she had been at being diverted elsewhere, and missing his family. "It really is most important, and it is personal."

With or without the Eqbas, this was going to be her home for a very, very long time. She wondered why she had ever thought otherwise. And Ade had no more choice than she had, and neither did Aras, so all she had to do was shake off one more redundant attitude and get on with life.

"Certainly, son," she said. "Tell me all about it."

The request wasn't unreasonable, but it made Nevyan uneasy. She stood in the forest of lava plugs out on the F'nar plain and wondered how visible a small Eqbas settlement might be.

"It would look much like Surang," said Esganikan.

"No, it would be coated in *tem* deposits in a very short time."

"Very well, it would be covered in *pearl*. It would be disguised somewhat by the lava formations, and it would be *temporary.*"

Nevyan understood why the Eqbas wanted the comfort of a built settlement. Adaptable as their ships were, the environment was still limited. They longed for the surroundings of home. But it alarmed her because it brought them both a step closer together, and Targassat had been adamant that it was a life they should shun.

It had worked so well for so long.

"We won't intrude," said Esganikan. "We understand."

Nevyan imagined the billowing shapes robed in iridescence. But it would be demolished in time, and F'nar had built the Temporary City on Bezer'ej so she had no moral grounds for refusing this. "I asked for your military support. It's only reasonable that we should make your lives as easy as we can."

"So we'll begin," said Esganikan.

Nevyan thought of fetching Eddie to watch the beginnings of the settlement, to record the buildings constructing themselves out of the raw materials around them. Aras had said the original *gethes* city on Ouzhari—the one he had removed long before the colonists arrived—had been built in a similar way from the land itself, but with visible machines. Humans had their technical limitations. She called home and asked Giyadas to see if the journalist felt up to venturing out. Nevyan suspected it was his conscience that was still injured, because his head wound was healing quite well.

"We all miss home, and no doubt the *gethes* do too," said Esganikan. She scuffed her boot in the gold soil as if checking it for some quality or characteristic. "We brought back some Earth vegetation from Umeh Station for Shapakti's colleagues to examine. They want to create a small terrestrial environment to gain skills in restoring Earth."

"And where might they create this?"

"You have space in your hangars beneath F'nar."

"If you wish to use that . . ."

"Again, it would be temporary. When we depart for Earth, it can be dismantled."

Nevyan wondered if Shan and Ade might like the envi-

ronment to remain to ease a longing for home. Shan had
never shown signs of missing Earth, although she had made
much of being deprived of her favorite boots, but Ade Bennett seemed a more sentimental person. *Jurej've* deserved to
be kept happy.

"Proceed," said Nevyan.

She knew what it was like to miss home. She was beginning to feel on foreign territory already.

"Are you sure about this, Shapakti?" Shan found her arms had
crossed themselves tightly on her chest almost without her
noticing, just the way they did when an interrogation wasn't
yielding answers as fast as she wanted. "*Absolutely* sure?"

"It is *possible,*" said Shapakti. "I have only modeled the
procedure based on the specimen you provided. The bond
between the organism and proteins is tenacious, but it appears to be reversible. I believe we can remove *c'naatat*
without harming the organism." He looked at her as if she
had scolded him. "We would of course place the symbionts
back in the soil in Ouzhari."

He must have misinterpreted her dismay. She heard the
words *remove c'naatat* and her stomach flipped over. *No.*
No, it couldn't be this way, not now.

She thought of how she yelled and raged at Aras when
she realized he had infected her to save her life. If she'd been
offered the choice then, she would have grabbed it without a
second thought. She had her plans in those days. She'd
wanted to go home. She'd picked out a remote smallholding
on the border with the Cymru Republic, somewhere to grow
her illegal unpatented tomatoes, and she was getting out of
EnHaz because she had done a lifetime's duty and it was
time for *her.*

Then Eugenie Perault had intervened.

They were alone in the dark little bubble of ship that Shapakti had made his home. The bulkheads shimmered with
status reports and images; one picture, a live one as far as
Shan could tell, was of a billowing Eqbas building that

looked like a galleon on a stick. She suspected it might be Shapakti's hometown. He was like anyone in uniform, decorating his locker with comforting pictures of cherished people and places.

History. You can't change a thing now.

"What about the host?" Shan asked. "Selfish preoccupation, but I need to know."

"As far as I can tell without using live specimens, the hosts would revert to their original genome."

Now she didn't want the choice. *Is this me? Is this what I want? And why?* And then she didn't know if it was her opinion or if it was *c'naatat* urging her.

If it was influencing her, it was *sentient*.

The panic that threatened to make itself obvious to Shapakti felt as bad as stepping into space and feeling that total, searing cold that felt white-hot. What was inside her? And if it wasn't the parasite talking, what did she prize about being a host? She started to face the possibility that she wasn't simply being good old resilient Shan, always able to brace her shoulders and make the best of a bad job. She had to consider that she might enjoy being as close to a god as a pragmatic, disbelieving woman ever could.

She didn't have much time for gods. They were either absent or incompetent. She wasn't sure if it was a good idea to get too used to being one.

Then another sickening thought almost cut her legs from under her.

She hadn't even thought about Aras.

"What's wrong?" asked Shapakti.

"Have you worked out if you can remove *c'naatat* from a wess'har?"

"We don't yet know. It's possible."

"So . . . Aras could look forward to some sort of normal life, then." She swallowed hard. It took all her conscious will not to flood the room with the scent of her own anxiety. She lapsed into detached language. "He could be free to reproduce."

"If the organism can be separated from him, yes."

You're looking for an excuse.

It was almost a disembodied voice in her head. For the first time in her adult life, she didn't know exactly what she thought, what she believed, and what she wanted. There were no absolutes and no certainties.

Shapakti looked into her face, pupils snapping open and closed. Even if he couldn't smell her it was obvious that he knew the news had knocked her for six. "But you would like to go home, wouldn't you? I would. I have been away a long time. I want to see my *isan* and my house-brothers and our children again. I thought you would too."

Shan thought of Reading Metro and the admin workload and the gridlock riots and coming home to an empty apartment. Then she thought of the Wessex National Park and fried egg sandwiches and how large a plot of land her long-frozen pension would now buy.

"Who else knows about this?" she asked.

"My team, of course, and Esganikan—"

"Do me a favor. It's speculation as far as I'm concerned. You don't tell Ade or Aras. Not yet. That's my job. Understand?"

"Very well. But I thought this would please you."

She stood up and made for the hatch. "You've done a good job. But it's a choice I didn't think I'd ever be able to make."

"I am sorry for angering you. But they say you are a competent matriarch, able to make very hard decisions."

Shan stood on the threshold where coaming would have been on a normal ship, and felt the sleet against her face softening into snow.

"Well, they were wrong," she said.

23

I miss you. It's very wonderful here, very strange, and there are so many different types of people and plants that I sometimes forget myself and stop missing you all for a moment. But when I close my eyes to rest, there you are again. It's been too long. I will bring marvelous things back for you. I will let you know as soon as I have a departure date, so you can all plan a period in suspension. Thank you for waiting for me.

DA SHAPAKTI,
to his isan Jamurian Ve, his house-brothers, and the beloved
children of the clan

The snow was knee-deep. Wess'har didn't like the cold but a few brave souls had ventured out into the fields, swathed in layer upon layer of *sek*. Aras, who didn't suffer in cold weather and had been raised in Baral, took it in his stride. Shan could see him clearly through the scope of Ade's rifle.

"I hope he doesn't get the wrong idea," said Ade, taking the rifle back from her. "It isn't even loaded."

Shan sat on the top of the plateau next to her memorial, arms around her knees, and savored the exceptionally rare snowscape that ran across the ship camp of the Eqbas Vorhi mission to the city itself. A layer of snow on top of the pearl made F'nar look like a nostalgic window-dresser's rendering of a fairytale winter.

"What do you think of that, Ade?"

The growing Eqbas settlement, tucked discreetly into a stone forest of volcanic plugs, had begun to remind Shan of a wasps' nest. A slim base emerged from the ground and the structure was beginning to flare out from it, reaching into the air like an oyster mushroom just like the buildings of Surang. It was free of snow: they must have been using some sort of environmental barrier, and it was warm behind it, because *tem* flies had already begun polishing it with a pretty layer of iridescent shit. They swarmed to hot climates for the winter but some were still here and seemed to have been caught unawares by the weather like everyone else.

Ade puffed little clouds of condensed breath. Shan reminded herself to breathe again.

"Ade, have you thought about it?"

"I still think you should tell Aras right now."

"I asked if *you* had thought about it."

"Yeah, I have."

"You could be back to normal and going home. Wife, kids, the whole thing."

Ade had never been much good at hiding his feelings. Now he wore his expression of suppressed disgust, lips clamped tight and pupils wide. "How can you say that when you know what normal was for me?" His automatic camouflage jacket was now stark white with faint swirls of pale gray and blue, merging him with his background like an Arctic hare. He seemed perfectly adapted. *So this is what he really does. He's a mountain and arctic warfare expert.* "I didn't have a wife and kids and every woman I ever loved walked out on me. I'm coming up forty and I've been kicked out of the Corps. So everything I've got is here, even if they take every alien cell out of me."

"I was just asking. I didn't want you to feel that you didn't have a choice."

"You don't see yourself ever being my *isan,* do you?"

It was odd to hear him use the wess'har term. "Ade, I just thought it might all be a combination of a crush and loneliness on your part."

"Oh, and there was I thinking you didn't feel sorry for me."

"I thought you might see things differently if you could go home. You don't have to stay. Take *c'naatat* out and you could—"

"This *is* home."

"I'm sorry. I had to ask, just in case."

"Okay, do *you* want to have *c'naatat* taken out? Do you want to be regular Shan Frankland again?"

She'd asked herself that over and over again ever since Shapakti had told her it was possible. The answer had been immediate: *no*. It was a gut reaction. She still didn't know if it was the parasite colony talking, making a desperate bid to stay inside its host.

"No, I don't," she said. "And perhaps that's why I should go back to being a basic human. There's nothing worse than a bastard like me with a bit too much power. Maybe I need stopping right now."

Ade shut his eyes for a moment and she thought he was going to erupt. She knew he had been raised on violence and she knew it was within him; but she didn't want to see it emerge, not because of her and a few stupid comments.

But he simply opened his eyes again and gave her a smile that was utterly heartbreaking. "That's why I think the world of you. You're a fundamentally good person in a way almost nobody ever is. You think I can just pack my bag and leave, do you?"

"Stop it, for Chrissakes." She squirmed. "I know exactly what I am. Good doesn't come into it. You ought to bloody know, too. You've got enough of my memory now."

"Being good isn't always about being soft."

Stop it. "Come on, you miss Earth."

His lips compressed again. She wasn't getting anything out of him. "We've all got responsibilities here, but I'll go along with whatever decision you make. You're still the Boss."

"Great. Just *great*. That's a big fucking help."

"You still have to tell Aras. Where does that leave him?"

"Shapakti doesn't know if it'll work on wess'har. I don't want to get his hopes up."

"And if they can, you think he'll want to breed more than he wants you?"

"Possibly."

"You can't believe that. I've inherited some of his thoughts. So have you."

"So let's see what he thinks when he's got all the facts."

"He's going to go fucking ballistic when he finds out you kept this from him. If you don't tell him, he's going to pick it up from your memory sooner or later. I'd hate to find out that way. Tell him before he takes Rayat and Lindsay back to Bezer'ej."

They went back to staring at the snow. Genies didn't fit back into bottles easily. And she wasn't sure how she'd feel if Aras was given the same choice and then *took it*. She'd almost grown used to the status of an *isan:* she liked being adored, even if she knew that it was as much a biological mechanism as an emotional one.

C'naatat was showing her all the things she really didn't like about herself.

She got up and they walked back down the easy path from the plateau and down onto the plain again. Even 150 trillion miles from home, snow had lost none of its clean, quiet wonder.

"Want to build a snowman?" Ade asked.

She smiled. He was his old self again, trying to raise morale like a good sergeant should. "As long as we flatten it afterwards. Nothing intrudes on the landscape, remember."

And they built a snowman, laughing and pelting each other with hard-packed, vicious snowballs that almost burned when they caught bare skin. Shan stuck a stylus in the expressionless face to make a nose. There was never a carrot and a couple of pieces of coal around when you needed them.

"I've never seen you laugh like that," said Ade.

"I've never built a snowman."

"No?"

"I didn't really have a childhood."

"I can tell. Me neither."

"Oh." She glanced over his shoulder and he turned to see what she was looking at. "Shapakti."

The Eqbas scientist was walking unsteadily through the snow, the swathe of fabric across his face reminding her of the cowl of his biohaz suit. He made a few placatory bobs of his head and stopped to do a head-tilting stare at the snowman.

"Is this religious?" he said.

"No, and don't even mention it to the colonists if you meet them," Shan reached out and knocked the head off the figure, embarrassed. Ade retrieved the stylus. "You've got some news for me, haven't you?"

"I have something to show you—both of you. Somewhere much warmer."

"Sounds good to me," said Ade.

Shapakti turned and began walking back towards F'nar. Shan and Ade trampled the rest of the snowman back into featureless oblivion before catching him up.

"Why did you traipse all the way out here to find me?" she asked. "I've got a *virin*."

"You don't always answer," said Shapakti. "And I think you like plenty of warning of my interruptions."

It was Ade's first visit to the underground bunkers that housed F'nar's fighter craft and assorted weapons. He stopped to admire a vessel, but Shan took his arm and dragged him gently away. "You can play with that later." Shapakti led them through the maze of passages and they came to an opening that spilled bright light in exactly the same way that the subterranean colony of Constantine had when she had first ventured down into its heart.

"This was taken from Umeh Station," said Shapakti, and opened the hatch.

Hot moist air hit her face and she could taste greenness and life on the oxygen-rich air.

Home, her body said. *Home.*

Maybe it wasn't Reading Metro, but it was *Earth.* Rainforest vines and exotic greenery filled the chamber like some Victorian hothouse that had been shipped out to amuse an eccentric guest. Eddie was wandering about inside, stroking his fingers over the shiny emerald leaves.

"You okay?" said Shan.

"I'm fine," he said.

"I'm sorry about Ual. I never had chance to meet him, and I regret that."

"Yeah." He was subdued, not Normal Eddie at all. She didn't plan to divert any time to soothing him right then. She had enough on her plate as it was. "You can have your ballistic vest back now."

Shapakti beckoned them further inside and dug both hands into the ground, scooping up dark soil.

"This was the hardest part," he said. "We recreated terrestrial soil and some bacteria. It is far from ideal but the plants show every sign of surviving. They were grown in a fluid nutrient solution in Umeh Station."

"You're a clever boy, Shapakti." Shan took off her jacket. The air was tropically hot. "What now?"

"The gene bank," he said.

"What about it?"

"You said I might have access, with your supervision of course. I would like to see what we can achieve."

Shapakti was quite literally harmless. She knew he would do nothing to damage or exploit the contents of that precious store. He was even planning to put extracted *c'naatat* organisms back on Ouzhari; he was everything she could trust.

"Lovely," said Ade, closing his eyes and inhaling deeply. "Bit too quiet though. Jungle's all noise. I've done jungle."

"I shall find a single species to resurrect," said Shapakti. Shan thought it was a strange choice of words. "And its food sources."

"Better make it a herbivore or something, then." It was just a display of potted plants. It was quick familiarity when her guard was battered and falling, not a mystic sign she should go home again. "Want any help?"

"I would like access to databases on *jungle*."

"Umeh must have downloaded databanks, and if you ask the UN nicely they might put you in touch with biologists . . .

on Earth." Shit, she nearly said *back home.* It was getting too seductive. "Eddie's got a fair old library too, haven't you?"

"I have," said Eddie. "You're welcome to what I've got. And if you get through to the UN, they'll panic and wonder exactly where you're planning to invade if you ask too many questions about tropical environments. Try the Pacific Rim States. They think you're the cavalry."

"Maybe they are," said Shan.

"Saddle up, then," said Eddie, and walked out through the hatch.

Aras rested his head on his folded arms and stared along the faint grain of the table. He thought of the bezeri and wondered how much longer he could delay giving them his decision.

His duty was to go to them and help, but his wess'har instinct said his *isan* came first. What was it like to live under water, anyway? What could he give the bezeri, other than reassurance and an extra hand?

It was unthinkable to refuse them, and unthinkable to leave Shan even if Ade would be there to care for her.

I want my isan. *I want Shan. I waited so long for this.*

The door opened and he sat up sharply. Shan and Ade walked in, dripping slush from their boots and flushed from the walk in the cold air.

"Shapakti's built a rain forest," said Shan. "He's a clever little bugger." She paused. "What's wrong?"

"You startled me," said Aras. "I was thinking."

Ade went to boil water for tea. "Shan's got some news for you." He shot her a glance and she glared back at him. "Go on. Tell him."

She was suddenly angry: Aras could see that from her dilated pupils. She sighed air from her nose, irritated, and Ade suddenly smelled of anxiety. She wasn't happy about what he'd said.

"Okay, I'll apologize before I start," she said, and sat down at the table without removing her jacket. "Ade says I should have told you a few days ago. He's right. But I still don't have all the facts."

Aras waited.

"It's *c'naatat*," she said at last. "Shapakti thinks it can be removed from the host organism."

Aras stopped his thoughts racing ahead. He had heard this before, many years ago, when wess'har had found out what *c'naatat* was and that it did more than accelerate recovery. They thought they could stop it. And they had been wrong.

"Has he tested this theory?"

Shan scratched her forehead, looking down at the table's surface for a few moments. "He's separated it from a sample of my tissue."

"Ah."

"Go on. I know what you're going to ask."

"No need. I haven't given him a sample of *my* tissue. So he can't prove the same claim for the wess'har genome."

"I know. Are you going to give him a specimen?"

"Why should I?"

"It would solve the problem of accidental contamination if removal was possible."

"No," said Aras. "That's not what you mean at all. Don't lie to me. I told you once that you were a very poor liar, *isan,* and you have still learned nothing of the skill."

She sat looking at him and then got up and put her arms around him from behind. "It might be possible." She laid her cheek against his. He reached up and clasped her arms, thinking he might push her away rather than embrace her. "It's not definite, not by a long chalk. But I had to tell you."

"Why?"

She hesitated. He still couldn't smell any scent at all beyond her skin, sweet wood overlaid with female musk. "Because I want to know what you really want."

He could measure the time that he had wanted to be a normal wess'har again in *centuries.* The thought had obsessed him for years, so many years that it was impossible to explain to any other being—even Shan—just how overwhelming and intense and *sustained* that emotion was. He thought he wanted to be a father more than anything he could imagine.

And then he met Shan: and he made a rash, split-second choice to save her life and the agony of not fulfilling his instinctive biological purpose had eased so much that it was merely occasional pain, and one that he could brush aside by being with her.

Now he had a house-brother too, more or less. And they might learn to be content, and it didn't really matter that he had no children.

"Do you want to go home?" he asked. "Earth?"

Still no scent. She was sparing his feelings. "For the first time in my life, I have no idea what I think."

"You could go home. So could Ade."

"And you might have children. You can never have them with me, with or without *c'naatat*. That's one *never* we're certain about. If I stay a carrier, there can't be more of us. If I revert to normal, we can't reproduce anyway."

Aras knew exactly what he wanted. He didn't dare say so and influence her. He hadn't given her a choice about *c'naatat*, and she hadn't given Ade one either. They weren't bound by any obligation at all. But he had no right to think about his own happiness when the bezeri were still waiting for him to help them.

"I would very much want you to be happy," he said, and tried to keep his grip on her forearms neutral, neither letting go—a sure sign he was upset at the idea—or by gripping harder, and making it clear he didn't want her to leave.

"As long as I'm *c'naatat*, I'm staying here," she said. "I can never go home as long as I'm a biohazard, whatever countermeasures Shapakti thinks they can create."

She's going to leave me.

"You must make your own choice," said Aras. "It's too important for me to influence you and Ade either way."

She can go back to Earth as a normal woman and do what she planned to. She can have Ade and she can have her patch of land, and she can put the last few years behind her. I took that away from her once.

"You think about it," she said, and kissed the top of his head. "There's plenty of time."

No, for once she was wrong. Time had suddenly run out.

24

FROM: Esganikan Gai, Eqbas Vorhi fleet
TO: Marie-Claude Garces, Secretary General of the United
Nations

*We have been made aware that the order to use persistent
toxins on Bezer'ej was given by senior ministers and intelligence officers of the Federal European Union. Under your
own laws, these individuals are war criminals and so we
hold you to the obligation to arrest and punish them for their
acts of genocide and environmental destruction. Anyone
able to detain them must do so. If no action is taken, we will
find out who did not act, and when we reach Earth we will
hold all of them responsible for failing to take the appropriate measures of a civilized society.*

The atmosphere over lunch was tense. Shan had always
been one to speak her mind, but she wasn't forthright now. She
sat tapping her glass spoon against the bottom of the bowl.

Aras watched her discreetly from his peripheral vision.
Ade wouldn't meet her eyes either. Eventually she got up
and washed the bowl and spoon before pulling on her jacket.

"I'm going for a walk," she said, and didn't wait for a response.

The door closed. Ade counted visibly to ten, the time it
took for her to stride out of earshot. The crunch of her boots
faded.

"Aras, I swear to God, I'm not pressuring her."

Aras believed him. His face was pure distress. "You don't
believe in God."

"Look, I'll go. I can't do this."

"You will sit quietly and *listen to me*."

Ade's shoulders braced almost imperceptibly. He was

still instinctively ready to defend himself. "What do you want, Aras?"

"I want to see Shan content. She can't be content if she feels pulled by conflicting duties." He was clear now. It would be agony but it needed to be done, and the sooner the better. "I'll tell you something now that you must *not* tell her."

"Whoa, no—"

"She'll find out, but I want that to be after she can no longer act on the information."

"You can't lie to her."

"Oh, I've learned some useful human skills. I can lie by omission, and I can lie by false statements. I'm almost a competent human."

"I'm not promising *anything.*"

"I'll hunt you down if you distress her by revealing this."

"Mate, I've been threatened and beaten until I pissed my pants. You think you can do any better at scaring me than my dad did?"

"Listen."

Aras got up and walked round behind Ade, grabbing him by the shoulders. It was just to make him stay sitting, to make him listen; but Ade threw off the grip and wheeled round on Aras, sending the bench flying, and slammed him against the nearest wall. He was astonishingly strong for his height. Aras stared down at him, shocked by the instant white-faced anger he was looking at.

"Don't *ever* fucking touch me like that, okay? *Ever.*" Ade's face flushed. He let go of Aras's tunic and stepped back. "Just don't." His voice trailed off. He righted the bench again to sit and focus on his bowl of stew.

"I'm sorry," said Aras. There were things he didn't know about Ade at all and could only guess. He certainly knew about his violent father, and his shame for leaving his mother undefended as soon as he was old enough to join the marines. The old emotions seemed very near the surface. "I have to tell you this. The bezeri have asked me to live among them. I know Shan could go home as a normal human being and that you would look after her. If I choose to do what I ought for the bezeri, then she needn't feel she has to stay for my sake."

Ade looked up from the bowl and his mouth really was slightly open. Aras wondered why shock did that to humans. It was as if they were trying to taste the air because they didn't trust their hearing. "That would destroy her," Ade said quietly. "How can you even think of doing that? She loves you."

"And I love her, and that's the normal wess'har way, but Shapakti has changed that. I feared she would prefer you to me, as her own kind. Now I wish she would."

Ade lowered his head a little. His eyes were closed. "I'm the interloper. You can't do this because of me. And it's just a theory—"

"I've made up my mind."

"You're wrong. You're *so* wrong."

"I plan to take Rayat and Neville to the bezeri, as they asked, so that they can deal with them. And I'll stay. I want you to promise me that you'll explain to her why I did this and then take proper care of her while she adjusts."

"The fuck I will." Ade's voice sounded as if he had swallowed something uncomfortably hot. "*Adjust?* I know she doesn't look like the emotional type, but you'll hurt her. It'll rip the guts out of her."

"And maybe that's what it will take." Ade went to protest again, but Aras held up both hands. "You can't prevent this."

Ade didn't speak again. Aras began imagining how he might adjust to a life alone again, and in an environment more alien than he had ever known, but he knew he *could* adapt. He would cope.

The one thing he would never be able to cope with, though, was not being able to take his leave of Shan properly, and explain himself. He would walk out of her life with every indication that he would return again, and it would be the hardest thing he had ever done.

But he could lie now.

* * *

Mar'an'cas had taken on a distinctly purposeful air in the last week. Lindsay walked through the camp trying not to stare through open tent flaps, but she wanted to see what was happening.

Yes, the colonists knew they were going home. For all the privation and tragedy that they had been through in the past few months they seemed uplifted, and as much as the word nauseated her it was the only one that fitted their collective mood.

And it was nearly Christmas.

Christmas was one of those public holidays like Eid, Solstice, Hanukah and Diwali that had once interrupted her planning schedule because staff went on leave. That was all. Seeing it marked now by Christians who genuinely believed it was spiritually significant was both moving and frightening. And it still left her feeling like an alien.

Inside every tent was a light of some kind: a candle, a solar lamp, anything that created fire. In the charcoal gloom of an early northern winter, it looked reassuring and magical.

When she passed Deborah Garrod's tent she glanced away but the woman called to her.

"Lin," she called. "Lin, come in and have a drink. You must be frozen."

Deborah was simply a kind woman. She'd helped her through David's birth and she'd been there in the infirmary when he died. She knew what it was to lose someone she loved, too. Lindsay paused, then ducked into the tent.

"How have you been?" asked Deborah.

"I think you know."

Lindsay sipped the tea she offered. Its taste was irrelevant: it was hot, and that was wonderful. She felt like a fool because everyone knew she had tried to drown herself and that she had failed as surely as she had failed at everything else.

At least Deborah wouldn't ask her where she was planning to spend Christmas this year.

"You've had a terrible time, Lin."

"So have the bezeri."

"You didn't know."

"It was a bomb. I know what bombs do. The rest was detail."

"I understand a little of what you're going through. However awful it seems, there really is purpose, but you have to look at it from some distance to understand it."

"And God's the distance, right?"

"What do you think?"

"I think I've helped kill tens of thousands of sentient beings and focused the attention of an alien war fleet on Earth. If I've missed anything out, let me know."

"The bezeri have asked for you and Rayat to be handed over to them."

"I—I didn't know that. I thought they might as soon as I knew some had survived."

I'll drown anyway, then, or the pathogen will get me. Unless I ask the unaskable. What have I got to lose?

They went on drinking tea. Rachel, far more sober as a six-year-old than she had been at five, slipped into the tent with a battered handful of foliage.

"Decorations," she said quietly. She held them up on tiptoe, trying them against the ridge of the tent, and then dropped them in Deborah's lap. "We're going back to Earth, aren't we?"

"Yes, you are." Lindsay held out her arms to her and the child hesitated for a moment and looked to Deborah for approval before scrambling on to her lap. "You'll like it."

"You're not like Shan."

"Absolutely." As if she needed reminding. Shan never got in over her head or did anything without covering all the angles. Emotions never tore her apart. Lindsay struggled to put aside her fear and forced a smile. "What do you want for Christmas, then?"

"I want Daddy to come home," she said. "Or Aras."

Kids had a stunning sense of proportion. Deborah said

nothing. She fidgeted on Lindsay's lap and finally wriggled to the floor and skipped out again.

"That's what makes it hard," said Deborah.

Just being with Deborah was soothing in its way. Deborah didn't berate her or remind her of her failings. She just sat there and drank tea with her.

"What do *you* want?" she asked.

"To make things a little better. Perhaps I got my punishment before I committed my crime, by losing David, but it doesn't feel like that."

"If you won't ask God what's required of you, then you might ask the bezeri."

Lindsay gazed into the cup and realized she had been told something profound. Lancing this boil of misery would take more than just dying. She needed to hear what her victims thought of her. And maybe she could find a way to help the survivors.

Be certain you don't just want to stay alive at any cost.

Bezeri had faces. She knew that: they had eyes, like terrestrial cephalopods. All she had to do was to somehow look into them. But that meeting was a world away.

The wess'har would be coming for her. They would send Aras, as they always did, because the bezeri knew him and spoke to him. She would ask him, and hope that he understood that she wanted to share *c'naatat* not because she was afraid to die but because she was afraid for the first time that death would not be the end.

"I'd like to pray," said Lindsay, and could hardly believe her own words. And they were utterly sincere. "Please, Deborah, help me out here. It's hard for a mass murderer to know where to start."

The snow had stopped and the novelty had worn off even for the hardiest of F'nar's citizens. There was nobody out on the terraces tonight: lights shone from irregular, wound-like windows across the span of the caldera. It was really pretty. Ade liked it here.

He waited for a few moments before opening the door, listening carefully in case he interrupted a difficult moment. But Shan was sitting on that blue sofa that didn't fit in with any of the wess'har furniture, one leg tucked beneath her, head propped on her hand while she watched the shifting pattern of the screen on the wall.

"It's a brawl at the UN tonight," she said, not looking at him. "I'm waiting to see the African Assembly bloke slug the FEU delegate. He's close. I think he's got the form to take him. About five kilos, I'd say."

A humorous Shan was a nervous and unhappy Shan whistling in the dark. Ade slid off his jacket and fired up the range to reheat the stew. The white glass slab radiated heat immediately. "Where's Aras?"

"Talking to Shapakti before they deliver the prisoners to Bezer'ej."

"Did you have a fight?"

"No. He just seems very subdued." She switched off the screen. "I've tried convincing him none of this is going to change things. He'll come round."

Ade sat down next to her and offered his shoulder. She yielded slightly and settled into him almost as if they were already lovers rather than simply circling each other, nervous of the final step. There was nothing he could do. He wanted to blurt out everything, but she'd go storming after Aras and then there would be continual arguments. He didn't want that.

Besides, Ade had made up his own mind.

Earth didn't beckon him half as much as wanting to be with Shan and Aras. He felt a kinship now with the wess'har that was as strong as the sense of family in the Corps, and it wasn't just his burgeoning wess'har genes that were anchoring him. Aras was a soldier, an *abandoned* soldier, a man who knew what duty meant and what it was to be expendable.

And Ade knew he was in the way. And he didn't deserve any happiness, not after helping Lindsay destroy Ouzhari. It was time he paid for all the people he'd let down in his life—his mum, Dave Pharoah, and the bezeri.

"You really made this sofa?" he said, struggling to stay off the subject.

"Yeah." She looked into his face. "What color is it?"

"Blue," he said.

She managed a grin. "Wess'har vision."

"It's incongruous. But comfortable."

"Yeah, that's a good word. *Incongruous.*"

He checked himself. It wasn't a word he'd used before. He wasn't stupid, but he didn't use words for a living like Eddie did, and he wasn't as intelligent as Shan. He realized *c'naatat* was changing him in more subtle ways than he imagined.

"I'm going to go with Aras and hand over Lin and Rayat. I'm the one who took the bloody bombs there so—"

"I really don't need this now. Not again, Ade."

"I knew they stood a chance of getting used. So I'm guilty."

"Motive doesn't matter here. Just outcomes. How many times do we have to go over this?"

"So what about inept criminals?" he asked. "You try to be a murderer or a rapist or a thief or something, but you just can't manage the job. Does that make you innocent?"

Shan was silent. Then she made a slight *uff* noise that could have been a laugh or an expression of contempt.

"I'm buggered if I can answer that."

She fell silent again and he could see her jaw muscles working, her eyes slightly defocused. God, he'd stunned her with something *clever.* He reveled in the moment, not because he'd beaten her at something but because he had surfaced briefly in her intellectual league, and he wondered if she might love him for that. It was rare common ground, more heady than the one-of-the-lads feeling of both being in uniform. But now winning her affection didn't matter. He couldn't stay and prompt Aras into leaving. He needed to stop her feeling obligated to *him.*

She shook her head at last. "No, you've got me there. That's quite a question. Do you have an answer?"

"It still makes you guilty, because one day you might try it again and succeed. It's about . . . potential."

She turned her head slowly. "You do the simple soldier routine perfectly, but you're fucking smart, aren't you?"

"No. Not at all."

"Well, Hawking, wrap your IQ round this. What's the right thing I need to do for Aras? And you?"

"What about *you*?"

"I'll cope with whatever comes down the road. You know me."

Ade had managed brief excursions into Shan's mind since his infection and what he saw was the headlines, the big events that wouldn't leave her alone. But every day he saw new facets and they were much more emotional than people imagined.

He wondered when the memory of being spaced might surface in him. She'd bitten him and drawn blood: he expected it to well up any day now, and the prospect scared him.

He shared a plate of *netun* with her and respected the silence. With or without *c'naatat,* he loved her. Restored to normality, he wouldn't care about her any less than he had when he'd first seen her swing through that hatch, reassuring and in command, or when she'd treated him like a hero even though he crapped himself, or when she put his medals back in his pocket. He wondered what life might be like back on predictable Earth as a clever woman's bit of rough. It would be an Earth where they'd both be as alien as the Eqbas.

And he wondered what Aras might feel like as one of those weirdly likeable sea horses again, with none of the human genes that had made him what he was now. Maybe Aras wouldn't miss him and Shan at all: and maybe he would be devastated beyond Ade's capacity to imagine.

It was all a matter of what was right. Ade had a better idea of that now.

He'd spare her the explanation. He was never her real *jurej,* after all.

25

Let others praise ancient times; I am glad I was born in these.

OVID

"Oh," said Shan. "Oh-oh-oh-oh-*oh.*"

Two macaws fluttered among the vines, turquoise and saffron, looking like they weren't quite getting the hang of being macaws. Their colors were impossibly bright and she had only ever seen them on natural history programs, but they were as real as macaws could ever be.

"Now *that's* a miracle," she said.

"I knew they would delight you." Shapakti had the same air of embarrassed pride that Aras had displayed when he had first shown her F'nar. There was something fundamental in the wess'har male that needed to please a female. "They *are* perfectly beautiful beings, aren't they?"

Shan craned her neck. "It's one thing to recreate an arrangement of cells," she said. "But making it into a parrot that knows how to fly and be a parrot is something else entirely." One of the macaws made a crash landing on a branch and flapped, all screeching panic. "Well, more or less."

"We found a great deal of data on macaws. We recreated a virtual environment for them while we accelerated their growth."

"Instant parrot. I should hate this, but for some reason I can't."

"A word of caution, *chail.* Doing the same with each species in the gene bank will take a lifetime and more. This isn't Earth. There is no ecosystem for them to slot into and learn to be what they are."

"But the gene bank you take back to Earth will fit right in, won't it?" She wanted Ade and Aras to see this. They would love it. It was her first thought and then her second was that she still didn't know what was the right thing to do for Aras. It took the shine off a moment of pure wonder. "Even extinct species usually have a niche to fit into on Earth and close relatives that can socialize them."

"I believe you were right to insist on retaining a separate gene bank as—what is the word?"

"Insurance."

"Yes, *insurance.*" He clasped his long hands in front of him and wafted a scent of pure contentment. He was good at his job and he knew it. "And they speak."

"Parrots? Yes, they really can talk. Took us a while to realize that, and we didn't treat them any better for it, but yes, they can use language."

"An Earth without humans."

"What brought that on?"

"You said it a number of times, as did Aras."

"I just don't like people much."

"But we are having talks with people just like you, humans who are not *gethes.* Does that not give you satisfaction?"

So the Australasians had the sense to front up some vegan or environmentalist liaison. That was smart. "Only if I can shoot the rest."

"Human life is worth less to you than the lives of any other species."

"I'm a copper. You get that way after a few years."

"You have no more laws to enforce. How much longer will you insist on being a *copper*?"

"God, you do sound like Aras sometimes."

"Have you made your decision?"

The macaws shrieked and settled down to groom each other's plumage. It was hard to look at those exquisite birds and not believe there was something wonderful to look forward to, an extraordinary future for the planet she once saw as the entire universe.

Fast forward, she thought: *I'm back on Earth, all nice and cozy with Ade, and I'm part of the new world order, really putting into action all the things I truly believe in. It's everything I thought I wanted. And then one night and look up at the sky and I know Aras is out there, 150 trillion miles away. I know what he'll be thinking. I know how he feels. I know exactly what he's experienced, right up to the last time I slept with him.*

"How are you getting on with separating *c'naatat* from wess'har tissue?" asked Shan.

"I am beginning to think it is impossible," said Shapakti. "Each time I achieve separation, *c'naatat* survives but the host cells die. I will persist."

"Oh." *Will I remember him? If they take away* c'naatat, *will I really think about him the way I do now?* "Not looking good, is it?"

Shapakti held out his arms like a scarecrow and the macaws flew to him.

"They think you're their mum," said Shan. "You'll have a hard job returning them to the wild." *Just like me.*

"We will enable them to have a normal life somehow." Shapakti ran a cautious finger over one macaw's head. Both birds were jostling for position on his arm, feathers rustling. One caught his finger in its beak, more playful than aggressive, but Shan braced herself for a scream anyway.

"*Uk'alin'i che,*" said the macaw, very clearly, and they both took off for the vines again. *Feed me.* It was a regular Eqbas parrot, all right.

Shan sat cross-legged and watched the macaws until she smelled sandalwood overlaid with a little acid and Aras entered. He had something in his hands, wrapped in a piece of fabric.

"For me?" She attempted a reassuring smile.

He sat down beside her and placed the object in her hands. "The bezeri asked me to return this."

She could tell what it was even without unwrapping it. The weight and shape were familiar. When she peeled back the fabric the *azin* shell map was exactly as she remembered it, a beautiful piece of sand art. And she knew it wasn't a present.

She turned it over in her hands and remembered how strongly she'd felt she could honor her pledge to protect them.

"I can guess," she said, crushed, and wrapped it again.

Aras seemed to have developed Ade's habit of compressing his lips briefly before saying something difficult. "They said to tell you that your red line did not hold."

She'd promised them. She'd *failed*. "Is that what's been upsetting you? Why didn't you say?"

Shapakti busied himself talking to the macaws. Aras seemed distracted by them for a moment, his head tilted in curiosity. Then he turned his head very deliberately to her. "I thought it might upset you."

"I've got a thicker hide than Eddie, and that's saying something," she said, and grinned. Maybe he'd be happier now that she'd shown that she wasn't hurt by the bezeri's rebuke. By the time he found out it was a front, she would be comfortable with it.

He reached out and slid his hand into hers, almost edging his way as if she might round on him and hit him. She caught his hand tightly. Now was as bad a time as any to tell him.

"Shapakti says they still can't remove *c'naatat* from you."

He let out a breath, nothing more.

"It's okay, sweetheart," she said. "It doesn't change a thing."

Aras couldn't suppress his scent like she could. But smelling that acid-citrus fragrance didn't tell her why he was upset. It could have been that he really wanted to be normal again more than he wanted to be with her. If he did, she would have to accept that. They were both aliens: it was an unlikely relationship born of desperation. If it wasn't that, then she could only assume that he feared she would take her opportunity to reverse events and go home. She was, as she had been for days, torn between the life she had here and her duty to Earth. EnHaz, as brief a job as it had been, was where her soul lay if she had one at all.

She got to her feet and he scrambled upright beside her, but his eyes were on the macaws.

"This is the first time I feel that I've seen a real part of Earth," he said. "Not a farm, like Constantine, for the benefit of *gethes* alone. This is the Earth that is quite separate from humans, isn't it?"

"Yes," she said. "And there's so little of it left."

"You miss it."

"Good God, no. Reading Metro wasn't unspoiled rain forest. This is as new to me as it is to you."

"Eugenie Perault would be most surprised to see all this return to its rightful home," said Aras.

"Surprised?" said Shan. "I'll fucking bet."

She thought it would be good to visit Earth some time in the future, after the Eqbas had completed what they set out to do. By then, she might be able to return home safely.

No, it was *Earth* now. Just Earth.

Nevyan took Giyadas to see the growing Eqbas settlement. It was twice the height of an adult wess'har now, still looking ludicrously fragile but getting larger nevertheless. As Nevyan watched, she could see the gradual accumulation of particles building on the fresh edge of the construction as the nanites labored to their template, taking the soil from around them and converting it into a building. There was nobody around. The city worked alone.

"I don't like it," said Giyadas. "Does it have to be here?"

"I don't like it either. But if they are to help us, we must help them."

"We'll become like them."

"Not if we remain true to our principles." Nevyan had her own doubts. She wanted to withdraw permission. She felt she couldn't. "And they're not alien to us, not at heart."

"Are they building a city on Bezer'ej?"

It was a good question. The *isanket* had a sharp mind and was already confident and aggressive, an encouraging sign for her future. "If they build *there,* then they have no need to be *here.*"

It was an excellent idea. Nevyan turned and Giyadas followed her back to F'nar.

This was why her ancestors had parted company with Eqbas Vorhi. It was all too unnatural, too ambitious, too predicated upon continual expansion—and in that sense, it made them no better than the isenj or the *gethes*. The Eqbas managed environments without harm, but they were still spreading gradually throughout the galaxy, imposing their order—the correct order, but still imposed—on other worlds.

All I wanted was for the gethes *threat to be contained. And now we are the latest outpost of Eqbas Vorhi.*

She would suggest that they might be better occupied in building a temporary city on Bezer'ej, where the cleansing work still had to be done and the handful of bezeri survivors needed watching. If Shan joined her, the suggestion would become a demand that Esganikan couldn't ignore.

When Nevyan reached Shan's home, the woman was lying on her back on the terrace, hands clasped on her chest, with something over her face. It looked like a visor. Giyadas nudged her and she took it off.

"Sorry," said Shan. "Look what Shapakti's rigged up for me." She held the visor out to Giyadas and showed her how to place it over her eyes. "He's modeled what they might be able to do with the rain forests on Earth. He thinks they can be restored to at least their 2200 levels of coverage in five years. Isn't that amazing?"

Giyadas cocked her head back and forth rapidly, trilling with excitement. "It's green," she said. "So much green. And people!"

"Yeah, Shapakti likes his jungle," she said. "Gorillas. He knows that makes me feel odd."

"Why?" Nevyan had never thought of Shan as looking back. Now Earth had become something new and challenging for her. And if Shapakti was right, then she had the option of going home, and that was alarming.

"Long story. I saw a gorilla once and they'd taught it to use sign language. I didn't know what it was saying, but later on I found out, and it was asking me to help it get out of its cage." Shan raked her fingers through her hair: it hung down her back again, like a male's. Her *c'naatat* was reconstructing her as fast as Shapakti was fashioning new rain forests. "There's never a day goes by that I don't think about how it must have felt to see me walk away, so now I don't pass gorillas on the other side of the road, or bezeri, or cockroaches, or anything else that deserves the same respect as us."

Nevyan understood the sentiment if not the specifics. Shan was back in a world that had given her great torment and that she seemed to feel she could put right if she had the chance. The Eqbas had handed her a world of chances.

"You get on well with Shapakti."

"He's a decent bloke. We talk a lot about ecology, but that's all, okay? They're calling it the Earth Adjustment Mission. I love euphemism. I could watch it all day."

"That's still in the future. You know it will take their fleet five years to reach us."

Shan inhaled and her pupils widened into those black voids that showed stress in humans. "Hey, what is it?"

"You plan to leave," said Nevyan.

"No, I never said that at all."

"Eqbas has found ways and reasons for you to return to your home. And you will leave."

Shan looked towards the door leading back into the house as if she had heard something. She jerked her head back to look at Nevyan and she was visibly angry, wafting *jask,* but she lowered her voice. "I don't want to hear another word about it. I know Aras thinks I'm going to leave him as well and this sort of discussion doesn't help calm things down."

Nevyan knew she was outscented but that didn't stop her asking. "Do you *want* to return?"

"Don't ask me."

"Does Ade?"

"Ask *him*." Shan took the visor off Giyadas and the *isan-ket* made a disappointed *lrrrr*. "I'm not done here yet."

Nevyan's world was falling apart and she suspected that Aras's was collapsing in the same way. It was obvious: Shan wanted to go home. *If I were marooned on Earth, I would want to return to Wess'ej.* It was natural. But Shan was her friend, and she needed her counsel and her *jask,* and Eqbas was taking her away from Wess'ej as surely as it was changing the heart and soul of the planet. She couldn't help but resent it all.

"I won't discuss it, as you ask," said Nevyan. "But I need your help in more immediate matters. I want to ask Esganikan to move the settlement to Bezer'ej. I'm uncomfortable with their presence here. The whole city is. There's too much change, too fast."

Shan stood with fists on hips and nodded. "Okay. But we do this together, right? Because if I go down there and start a ruck with her then I'll end up driving the bus back to Earth, and that's one decision I don't want anyone making for me."

"Thank you."

"Where's Aras?"

"He's getting ready to take Lindsay and Rayat back to the bezeri. I'll be bloody glad when that's over."

Nevyan held her hand out to Giyadas to take her home. The *isanket* looked longingly at the visor.

"Can I see Earth?" she asked.

"One day, if you want to and Nevyan says you can," said Shan, instantly uncomfortable. Her eye movement gave her away. "It's a long time to be away from home, though."

"Do you like Ade more than Aras?"

"That's a very personal question."

"Ade's nice. Aras is nice."

"They're both nice."

"Aras can't go to Earth, can he?"

"True." Shan made a very definite move for the door. "Go and see Shapakti and he'll show you the macaws and get them to talk to you. They do talk, you know. Like we do."

Shan's finality always had the impact of a slap across the face. You didn't question it, not even if you were senior matriarch of F'nar.

"I'll meet you at the Eqbas camp after dinner," she said. "I need a bit of quality time with my *jurej've.*"

She was, at least, referring to them in the plural.

It wasn't Shan's problem any longer.

When everyone else was running away from a bad situation, she would be the one running towards it. It was what coppers did. That was what all professionals trained to deal with trouble did—police, firefighters, soldiers. She was never sure if she had learned to do it as a young probationer or if she had worked out from an early age that she was the little adult who had to make order out of the threatening chaos of her family. But whenever it began, her instinct was now to go and confront problems and sort them before they sorted her.

She lay on the bed, arms folded under her head, and waited for Aras and Ade to come back from the Exchange of Surplus Things. Ade was convinced he could make a barbecue. He was trying in his solid, dependable, reassuringly ordinary way to get life back to normal, to settle Aras down.

It's not even a decision. You don't run.

The isenj and the wess'har had been enemies for centuries, and the Eqbas had been imposing their sense of order on the galaxy for far longer. Humans had just stepped into the noisy bar and found the fight already in progress.

Walk around the block.

Her first sergeant, the only man who'd ever seen her really cry, said fights burned themselves out if you let them run on a little. If you piled in you could make them a lot worse. If you couldn't suppress the fight with numbers, then sometimes sending in a lone woman officer would do the trick and calm things down, because blokes still had that primeval reluctance to hit a woman.

Not all of them, though.

Walk around the block again. Let the fight sort itself out.

She heard the door open and sprang to her feet, not caring if she looked anxious or even smelled it when she came out of the bedroom. Aras had a bag of vegetables and Ade was carrying some metal grids and a strange assortment of cannibalized pipes.

"Okay, we're going to have a barbie on the terrace, complete with Eddie's shitty awful beer and a game or two of cards," said Ade. "Proper fun."

"I shall find this interesting," said Aras.

He wore a permanent scent of acid now. Shan made a point of wrapping her arms around his waist and resting her head on his chest. *You're still mine. Don't worry.* But it didn't prompt his usual *urrring* and his embrace was halfhearted.

There was the occasional metallic crash and swearing from the terrace as the barbecue resisted Ade's attempts to build it. Shan listened, expecting Aras to offer him a hand, but he ignored the noise and seemed simply to tolerate her touch.

"I could still go with you," she said.

"I think it's my proper role to deliver the prisoners."

"This is a bit more protracted." She slipped her hands inside his tunic and touched cool, suede-skinned muscle, hoping for some response. "Once this is over and done with, we'll concentrate on ourselves. You, me, Ade." The word *Ade* just slipped out. But it still didn't feel right, as much as she wanted it to. "I'm not on duty any more and neither are you after today. We don't run the universe. It's some other bastard's shift."

"One day you'll hate me for keeping you here."

"Don't be bloody daft."

"You will. Your loyalty is your greatest weakness."

"And there was I thinking it was my sloppy emotional personality."

"You think you're ruthless, but you care about some things very much."

"Whatever you say, sweetheart." *Don't do this. Don't.*

"Are you sure you don't want a hand with Lin? Rayat might cut up rough."

"I can manage. I have an Eqbas with me."

"Okay."

"I shall *get it over with,* as you say." He looked at her swiss on the table. "May I take that?"

"Of course." She'd made him take it when he parted from her on Bezer'ej, too. It was just a silly token. She wouldn't need it anyway. "It's only waterproof down to two hundred meters."

"I shall take care of it."

"Okay, Ade might even have finished the bloody barbecue by the time you get back." She hugged him. And now she would have to say what she had never been able to tell him. "I know I never say it, but you do know I love you, don't you?"

"Yes. I know. And I love you. And there is nothing either of us can do about that even if we wanted to."

It was an odd thing to say, but wess'har were full of strange comments and Aras had lost none of his wess'har idiosyncrasies. He was feeling insecure. She had to sit tight and let him calm down.

She went out to the terrace to offer Ade a hand with the barbecue, but he'd managed to get it standing on four legs.

"All we need now is fire," she said.

"I bet you say that to all the cavemen," said Ade, but there was something very like anguish in his eyes, and he smelled of acid. Aras's fears were clearly getting to him.

In its way the barbecue was a perfect image of their situation, a rickety approximation of Earth trying to re-create the familiar but failing. Ade succeeded in grilling *evem* and although the beer couldn't get them drunk it was an echo of what had been. But there was no raucous laughter or chatting, just Ade glancing occasionally at Aras and trying to crack a joke, and Aras not responding. Shan wondered if they ever argued in her absence.

She hadn't picked up anything from Aras's memories to

tell her if they had or not. She wondered what selection process *c'naatat* went through in deciding which recollections were sufficiently significant to bring to the front of the file. She suspected it was only the big stuff, the hard-in-the-face stuff, the images that plagued you like flash frames during the day and were the last thing you saw and tried not to see before you fell asleep at night.

But they'd work it out. Ade and Aras were both sensible, get-on-with-it sort of blokes. They were just like her.

She sat down on the wall and put on the visor that Shapakti had given her. She had seen enough of the city of pearl for the day. She wanted to rest her eyes on green forests, on Earth.

It was home. Whatever she did, it would never stop being home.

—————➤   ◄—————

26

TO: Esganikan Gai and Nevyan Tan Mestin
FROM: Minister Par Shomen Eit, Northern Assembly

The death of our respected colleague Par Paral Ual has been the cause of much strife and debate in Ebj and the rest of Umeh. We now recognize that we are in increasing need of outside assistance if we are to survive as a people in the long-term. If you now wish to begin talks with us about environmental recovery, we will guarantee your safety. If you can put aside your policy of occupation, then we can make efforts to change our cultural attitudes to population control. If we can achieve this, then Minister Ual's vision and sacrifice will be vindicated.

Shapakti wasn't happy about the change of plans, and it showed. Ade was new to this scent-signaling business, but it was now as loud and clear as a shout.

"I do *not* have orders to take you to Mar'an'cas," said Shapakti, standing at the main hatch of his vessel like a bouncer blocking a nightclub door. "Or Bezer'ej. Just Aras Sar Iussan and the prisoners."

"Think of me as the escort," said Ade.

"We are competent to do this alone."

"She was my commanding officer."

"That's irrelevant."

"Look, mate, I'm coming whether you like it or not." Ade wasn't sure if Shapakti was still afraid of him. He thought the rifle might have given him a clue. "I'm making sure Aras comes back okay."

"He can't be harmed."

"Neither can I. So humor me."

Shapakti made a little sideways jiggling movement of his

head. Shan said that wess'har did that when they were annoyed. "Very well. But you're lying."

I haven't exactly lied. It had taken Ade a while to understand that wess'har couldn't actually tell if humans were lying or not, only that they were upset or angry or afraid or any
one of a dozen states of mind that changed your body chem-
istry. They were like old-fashioned polygraphs. They told
each other exactly what they thought, but when it came to
humans they simply used their scent skills and other senses
to spot the emotion and then worked out the detail from context. They were getting very good at it, and he now had
enough wess'har in him for his scent signals to be an open
book to Shapakti.

"I have my concerns," said Ade. "I want to see Aras back
safely."

And that wasn't a lie, either. It had been almost impossible to walk away from Shan as if he was simply going for his
usual daily run, without a proper goodbye. Everything had
been left unsaid again: it was as if he had lost her a second
time, except that he knew she was safe and well. But he was
quite literally the spare prick at a wedding here. And he
owed the bezeri some substantial act by way of apology.

Shan would understand. She'd done exactly the same, although in a more spectacular way. The right thing was frequently the one that hurt most.

Aras arrived at Shapakti's ship and stared at Ade as if that
would be enough to send him packing. "Go home," he said,
and tapped the *tilgir* in his belt. "I need no assistance. I can
deal with this."

"I know," said Ade, thinking of the time they had hunted
down an isenj patrol on Bezer'ej. Wess'har had no Hague
Convention and they didn't take prisoners. "But I'm coming
anyway."

Aras paused for five long seconds. Maybe he resented being offered help; maybe he had plans for Lindsay or Rayat
that he thought Ade might resist. No, Ade was fine with
whatever he wanted to do. They'd asked for it.

And so had he.

"No interfering," said Aras. "And you'll return to Shan and do as I asked."

It was an awkward, silent flight to Pajat. It would be an even more challenging journey to Bezer'ej. Ade hoped Shan would understand one day.

Eddie packed his grip. Giyadas watched him for a while, subdued, playing with his editing screen and his handheld. He hoped she hadn't been annoying the UN staff on the ITX again. He couldn't imagine being annoyed if an alien called him for a chat; it would always be a wondrous thing for him as long as he lived. He had passed from amazement through familiarity and into a state of wonder again.

"You're going home," she said.

"No, I'm going to visit Jejeno with the Eqbas, if that's not an oxymoron." He'd explain that word to her later, if she needed it. She probably didn't. "I thought about it, and then I knew I had to stay here."

"You like us best."

"Yeah, I like you a lot. But that's not the whole reason. I've got to stop going home at the end of the day and pretending nothing is my fault."

"You confuse me."

Eddie closed the grip and tested it for weight. At least Umeh Station had real toilets with seats. He loved the wess'har but he hated their plumbing. "It's hard to explain, doll, but in my job you say things and write things that change what happens, but when those events turn nasty you never have to face the consequences. We go home, we go down the pub, we start a new story the next day, and the people we said those things about have to clear up the mess. So for once I'm making sure that I face the consequences by not going home. I've got as much to lose as you have now."

"And the Jejeno discussions will be a good story anyway."

"I know what you are. You're my bloody conscience."

"Will you teach me to do what you do?"

"What I do isn't worth doing."

"I *want* to do what you do."

"When I start doing it right, maybe."

Giyadas unfurled the editing screen. "Look what I did," she said.

Eddie smiled indulgently and held out his hand for the screen. She was a sweet, clever, funny little creature and he adored her. She had probably tried to edit some shots together, so he prepared himself to praise her lavishly for being a smart girl.

The smile evaporated on his face as he flattened the screen on his lap. He was looking at the locked-off camera shot of the BBChan foreign news desk, and it wasn't a freeze-frame. It was *live*.

"Giyadas, what have you done?" He turned over the screen: the handheld interface was active. When he flipped it back over, Mick was scrambling into his chair and looking pissed off.

"Eddie, for Chrissakes where have you *been*? Come on. Can't wait all day."

Giyadas preened. "I told the United Nations *gethes* that I was the next matriarch of F'nar and that I would tell Nevyan how helpful the UN had been if she would connect me to the BBChan."

"Eddie . . ." said Mick.

"Wait one."

"Please, teach me to do what you do," said Giyadas.

"Doll, you don't need to learn a thing." Tears pricked his eyes. "You're a natural."

"I like this reporting."

"So do I, doll," said Eddie, renewed. "So do I."

27

FROM: Esganikan Gai, Wess'ej Mission
TO: Curas Ti, Matriarch, Surang

At the request of Nevyan Tan Mestin and Shan Frankland, we are relocating our operations to Bezer'ej. Our presence is inconsistent with the life-style that Wess'ej has chosen. Out of respect for our kinship, and in the knowledge that they need no guidance in maintaining ecological balance, we have agreed to this request to withdraw. We will locate the new temporary settlement on the site of the previous wess'har base on Bezer'ej.

Lindsay Neville watched Aras walk down the path between the rows of tents. Shan wasn't with him, but Ade was.

Aras had that slightly swaying, almost feminine stride that she had noted in all the wess'har males she'd seen. Despite his height and solid build, there was nothing brutish about him and she felt no instinctive sense of panic, even though she knew that he was coming to take her to the bezeri for execution.

"I thought Shan might come," said Lindsay.

"This is my task," said Aras. "The bezeri are still my responsibility."

Ade stood beside him in silence, expression carefully neutral. A stranger would never have guessed that he had ever been under Lindsay's command. Aras had a pack over his shoulder and that big agricultural knife, the *tilgir,* in his belt.

"Where can I find Dr. Rayat? There's no point trying to evade the inevitable."

"He's working on the crops."

Aras cocked his head and walked on with Ade through

Mar'an'cas camp, Lindsay following them. He stopped and turned.

"You are quite extraordinarily compliant creatures sometimes," he said. "I genuinely thought I would have to subdue you."

"Like you said, there's nowhere to escape."

Aras said nothing and carried on through the camp until they came to the fields. Rayat was spreading human manure from the latrines. Lindsay was never sure if he took on the task to show how tough he could be, or if he was just doing a job that needed doing. She had never really reached the inner core of the man and she suspected she never would. Like Shan, he had a talent for making her feel inadequate.

He stopped and leaned on his shovel. "So this is it, eh?"

Aras beckoned. "Yes. Please don't try to bargain with me, because I am not open to negotiation."

Rayat glanced at Ade and his rifle, and then shrugged and drove his shovel into the soil. "Okay. No point putting on my Sunday best for this anyway."

The colonists didn't stop to see them go. They went about their business: they weren't the kind of people to turn into a mob watching the tumbrills passing. Lindsay caught the eye of someone she had known well, Sabine Mesevy, the botanist from *Thetis* who had joined the colony. And when she got to the shore, Deborah Garrod was waiting alone by the glass raft that had somehow attached itself to the pebbles like a perfect jetty reaching out into the shallows.

Eddie hadn't made contact since Umeh Station. Lindsay had been so sure that he would. She was hurt: she wanted a goodbye, even a forced one.

Deborah acknowledged Aras with a nod, then put her arms around Lindsay and hugged her.

"It'll be okay," she said. "It passes."

She didn't hug Rayat, but then that wasn't surprising.

Lindsay had never been so scared in her life: from her stomach to the core of her thigh muscles she felt cold and a sensation of pressure squeezed against the roof of her mouth. There was something in the brain that assessed threat far more accurately than the conscious mind, and this time her brain said *this is really it, sweetheart*. All the other times she had been scared for her life—and there had been a few of those—it hadn't felt like this, not at all. This was numbing, cold and completely disabling. But if Shan could go with dignity, and Rayat too, then so would she.

She needed to pick her moment to ask Aras for the favor that she suspected he would never grant.

She stepped onto the glass deck and wished she had been able to examine this engineering miracle when she didn't have dying to worry about.

The part-formed matrix of the Eqbas city stood frozen in time.

It was neither growing nor deconstructing itself. Nevyan walked ahead of Shan and Esganikan and stopped a few meters short of it. It still stood twice her height, a pearl-covered mass of swirls and billows that reminded her of the tree-sized fungi on Bezer'ej. The air around it was warm and pleasant: *tem* flies, caught out of season behind the biobarrier, went about their business of laying down more nacre on the smooth surfaces.

"I thought you were going to remove this," said Shan.

Esganikan tilted her head this way and that. "There is no core within this shell. Our materials have been deconstructed and returned to the soil. This is purely the *tem* deposits, and we will retrieve the remaining flies and release them further south where the climate suits them. And then we can remove the biobarrier."

Nevyan turned to watch Shan and the Eqbas commander, feeling excluded from the debate. She could always tell—as could any wess'har—when two matriarchs particularly liked each other, and for all the *jask* that had been emitted, Shan and Esganikan did appear to be becoming comfortable together. Nevyan imagined it was as much the shared experience of unnatural isolation as it was the kinship of dominance. A return to Earth with a powerful

new ally seemed a prospect guaranteed to test Shan's resolve to stay.

"Okay, let's get these little buggers packed," said Shan.

One of Shapakti's team placed a small square container
inside the biobarrier and within moments the *tem* flies began
struggling against an invisible force that was sucking them
into it. Then the biobarrier dissolved with a breath of warm
air that escaped into the winter chill of the plain, and only
the thin shell of pearl remained.

"Now, isn't that pretty?" Shan stepped forward and put
her hand out carefully, brushing her fingertips against the
rippled iridescence. Nevyan could see it was the lightest of
touches, but the shell cracked, and Shan stepped back with a
small sound of surprise and disappointment.

The pearl bubble began breaking up.

Shards shimmered to the ground from the uppermost level
and large cracks appeared at the bottom. The collapse picked
up pace and the three matriarchs stood back and watched as
the structure reduced itself to a heap of fragments.

Esganikan didn't react at all. Shan seemed upset.

"I hate physical metaphor," she said.

"It's just *tem* droppings," said Nevyan. "There is no such
thing as prophecy."

Esganikan left without a word. She and her people were
free to visit Wess'ej any time, but Nevyan had the impression that they would now keep *at arm's length,* to use Eddie's grossly inaccurate phrase. The Eqbas matriarch was
about twenty meters away when she paused and looked back
at them.

"*Shan Chail,* I have no doubt that we will talk again, next
time on Bezer'ej," she called.

"I'd like to do that," Shan called back, and Nevyan wasn't
sure if it was a statement of intent or a display of human
diplomacy.

Nevyan kept her thoughts about the nature of prophecy to
herself. It was a silly *gethes* thing, this superstition business.
The pearl shell had been an unstable structure made of *tem*

excrement, a thing doomed to temporary existence from the start.

No, she would not be swayed by it. She hoped Shan could ignore it too.

Aras had grown used to bezeri vessels over the centuries but he decided he preferred the *niluy-ghur.* However many times he submerged in the water-filled bezeri pod ships and felt the sea flood his mouth and lungs, he had never grown used to it.

It couldn't kill him. He had first found that he couldn't drown when he was a prisoner of the isenj.

"Do you know what they're going to do to us?" asked Rayat. He was sitting on the transparent deck, hands flat out behind him almost as if he was trying to look relaxed, but it wasn't working, not if you could smell a *gethes'* fear. Ade was kneeling down on one knee next to Rayat, rifle across one thigh, and Lindsay Neville stood with one hand on the column that housed the steering mechanisms. She, at least, was looking down into the water with some interest. She had been a naval officer. Perhaps she didn't fear the sea as much as a land-based civilian.

"What would you do to someone who had caused the death of most of your race?" asked Aras.

It wasn't a rhetorical question, although he knew how to frame those. He wanted to know. He had little time left to find out what humans might do in certain circumstances.

"There's only so much you can do to someone before they die," said Rayat, and sounded as if he knew that for all the worst possible reasons.

Aras sat on the edge of the deck and lowered the signal lamp over the sea to summon the bezeri. It was a dull day and he would be able to see their bioluminescence easily when they rose nearer to the surface.

If only he had been able to tell Shan what he intended to do; but he was adept at dishonesty now. She would have tried to stop him. She had been sent here on the basis of Perault's

lie to begin with, and then he had made her exile permanent
with another lie, by not telling her immediately what he had
done to save her life. When he looked back, it seemed he had
lied to her a great deal, just like everyone else had.

He distracted himself with Rayat's question. "It will be
relatively rapid. You'll drown before you suffer. Bezeri have
cutting mouth parts but they have no weapons, and they're
not as creatively cruel as your own kind." He paused. "You're
dead already, though. The human-specific pathogen entered
your lungs as soon as you landed."

"You could have left us on the shore, then," said Rayat.

"This will be much quicker. It's also what the bezeri
want."

"So who's going to help them now?" asked Lindsay.

"I am," said Aras.

"No, I mean who will be based here now that your people
have withdrawn."

"Me. I'm going below to help them begin the rebuilding.
I owe it to them."

Shan would be furious, devastated, but she would get
over it. Ade would help her.

"What about Shan? I thought—"

"You thought wrong."

Lindsay seemed shocked into silence. Even Rayat
smelled startled. Aras concentrated on not looking at Ade.

"What if I did it?" said Lindsay at last. "What if I went in
your place?"

Rayat and Ade both reacted at once. "The fuck you are,"
said Ade suddenly. "If anyone's going down there, it's me. Is
this some stunt to get the parasite? Did this bastard put you
up to it?" He shoved Rayat in the chest. "Did he?"

Rayat still appeared genuinely surprised. He certainly
smelled stressed, then scared. "I never—"

"I thought of it myself," said Lindsay. "I'll do it. If you
infect me, then I'll serve them—if they'll let me."

Ade stood up and took his rifle off his webbing. "Right.
So I just stroll away from all this? Not me, mate." His face

was suddenly pale and he smelled as alarmed as Rayat. "Shan said all she had to do was breathe in the water and stop panicking. I reckon I can manage that."

"You have no idea what you're taking on."

"I never do. But I do it, anyway. I front up and earn it. I don't know any other way."

Aras took it as an impulsive gesture by a fundamentally good man confronted with an unpleasant reality. But now he realized why Ade had insisted on coming. He had arrived at the same conclusion as Aras. He had looked at the messy, painful reality of guilt and the choices that were now open again and had made the same decision as he had.

Aras pushed him gently away. "I want you and Shan to regain the lives you had when you first landed on Bezer'ej."

"That's not going to happen." Ade stepped closer again, face-to-face with him now: the prisoners were forgotten for the moment. "You're not just staying here—you're planning to *live under water.* You thought about that, have you? So have I. It's going to be fucking awful and you haven't done a thing to deserve that. There's no way I'm leaving you down there, and there's no way you're abandoning Shan."

Ade started taking off his jacket, the one that changed color according to his environment. As it fell on the glass deck it made an attempt to become gray-blue and mimic the ocean beneath. Lindsay, a tired-looking remnant of a woman in a shabby naval uniform, grabbed his shirt-sleeve. "What the hell are you two thinking of?"

"They asked for *me,*" said Aras.

"Yeah, and they're going to get me instead," said Ade. "I'm a complication Shan doesn't need. And I want to look the bezeri in the eye and apologize."

Lindsay wouldn't let go of Ade's shirt. "No! Just *stop* this! You can't go down there. She'll come after you, you know that. Go home."

Lindsay let go of Ade and went over to Rayat, remarkably steady on her feet for a human walking on a glass floor.

"It's me and this bastard. My command, his idea. So we pay. Okay?"

Aras thought briefly of seizing both of them and taking them down into the water, leaving Ade behind: he was still bigger and faster than the marine, although he could put up a credible fight. But he knew Ade would pursue him. And one of them would still have to decide to return to Shan.

"I was just an accident," said Ade. "Let me put something right."

Aras found it was painfully tempting. Life would be impossibly hard without his *isan*. He had lost her once, twice, and now he was losing her for the third and final time. Human culture was replete with trinity. But if she had Ade Bennett, she would be cared for and respected, and—he hoped—she would find some peace with him.

Rayat was licking his lips nervously and blinking. "Lin, we're dead either way. You don't care what happens to Shan Frankland. You don't even like her."

"This isn't about her. It's about *me*." She put her hand out to Ade. Aras was getting agitated; if you took a terrible step, you needed to take it fast. Thinking was too painful. "Ask them, Aras. Ask them if they'll accept me."

"No, the bezeri need me. And Shan needs to have a decision taken for her."

"You selfish bastard," said Lindsay.

Aras couldn't see what was selfish about it. It was no more selfish than stepping out into space rather than hand over *c'naatat*. Lindsay spoke with the venom and pain of the human bereaved, who buried their anger at the dead for leaving them alone, and it always lurked hidden in their grief.

It seemed a desperate trick to avoid death. Aras stared at Lindsay, unable to equate this gesture with the woman who had brought bombs to Bezer'ej and thought it was reasonable. "You think being *c'naatat* is enjoyable? Desirable? Is this your bid to acquire it?"

"Nobody's ever coming for us. The Eqbas are going to see to that."

"You're not capable of this."

"Try me. Okay, the bezeri want justice. They can only kill me once. If I live down there, I can serve them, and whatever you think of me, I really, really need to be forgiven in some small part."

Lindsay grabbed Aras's wrist. No *gethes*—and no wess'har in recent memory—had touched his skin except Shan. He jerked back. "Go on, infect me," she said. "No tricks. Let me go down there and help them. Please, Aras. Then go back to Shan."

Rayat's scent was pure acid. Aras was about to seize both of them and plunge over the side of the raft, but something hit him hard in the head, once, twice, sending him to the deck and filling his vision with exploding light. He pushed himself up on one hand but the next agonizing blow was so hard he heard bone crack and saw a spray of his own blood spatter the deck in front of him.

A weight crashed onto his back, pinning him. His right arm was forced up his back. His shattered skull could recover in a matter of minutes, but he didn't have that time.

"Sorry, mate," said Ade, panting with effort. "Come on, you lazy bastards, give me a fucking hand. Rayat, get his legs."

Lindsay and Rayat were pinning him down now, sobbing with the effort. Ade forced his left arm higher, and as much as Aras struggled he couldn't get his strength back before Ade's plastic restraints—insubstantial, harmless-looking but horribly effective—cut deep into his wrists. He managed to kick out, but three bodies were more than he could cope with. The restraints snapped tight around his ankles.

Then the weight lifted off him. He was bound and helpless.

"You'll be okay soon," said Ade. He knelt panting, head tilted to look him in the eye as he lay on the deck. "But she'd kill me if I went back without you."

Aras knew that. He'd been working on forgetting it. "You can't do this."

"Watch me. Okay, let's have the signal lamp." Ade got to his feet and Aras expected Rayat to seize the opportunity to escape, even though the antihuman pathogen would kill him if the sea didn't claim him first. He picked up the device. "Does this thing interpret English?"

"It does," said Aras, recalling how Shan had used the lamp to apologize to the bezeri at least twice. It was getting to be a habit. "If the bezeri won't take her, then you must—"

"Here they come."

Aras looked down though the clear deck. There were lights, red and cyan and yellow, and they were rising nearer the surface. The last of the bezeri were coming. Ade knelt and projected the colored light through the transparent deck. Patterns flared into the water.

The human woman wants to help you rebuild.

The bezeri paused in their ascent. Their reply came in a curious flat approximation of human speech. *Is she the one responsible?*

Yes, and the man.

How will they serve us if we kill them? Or when they drown?

Ade paused. *We can make sure they don't drown. Like Aras. Like me.*

"Won't we contaminate them?" said Rayat.

Aras had moved among the bezeri for 500 years and none of them had acquired *c'naatat*. "Ade, I forbid you to go with them."

The marine looked at him and put a finger to his lips. He turned back to signaling. *Will you take them and me instead of Aras?*

Rayat reeked of acid. But he wasn't fighting. He wasn't trying to escape. Maybe *c'naatat* was better than death for him, because he had no chance now of ever leaving Bezer'ej.

How can we kill them if they displease us?

Ade shrugged, although the lamp couldn't interpret a motion. *Call Aras. He'll finish the job.*

"Ade, *stay*." Aras rolled a little so he could face him. *I know your past, Ade Bennett: I know your World Before, and I know what fears haunt you.* "Shan will never forgive either of us for this deceit. You abandoned your mother—and now you abandon Shan after putting her through hell. So much for your courage."

It was a cruel human ploy, a spiteful lie. Ade embraced danger every day to stop the voices, his own and his dead father's, that told him he was a coward. Adding Shan to those voices was almost too cruel. But Aras would have said anything then to stop Ade going into the water. He expected him to hurl back the same accusation—Aras was running, taking the coward's way out—but none came.

Ade's face fell for a telling moment.

"You *bastard*," he said. Aras could hear that faint note in his voice, the one that said he was struggling. "I'd never let that woman down again. *Never.*"

A vivid display of red and amber lights swirled beneath the raft, pulsing occasionally with green, getting brighter with each beat. The bezeri were shouting, *screaming.*

Give them to us. Give them to us.

Ade knelt back on his heels. *This will take a few minutes.* Then he laid the lamp aside and took out his fighting knife.

Lindsay shut her eyes and held out her arm to Ade. He sliced into her arm and then cut a flap from his own, exposing an area large enough to keep the blood flowing sufficiently to drip onto Lindsay's cut, just as Aras had done when he dripped his own blood into Shan's open head-wound. It wasn't easy: *c'naatat* stemmed blood flow fast.

"Hold your arm against mine, for goodness' sake," said Lindsay.

"No, I don't want your memories," said Ade. "But you're welcome to mine."

He sliced across his arm several times before he seemed satisfied that enough blood had flowed.

Mohan Rayat smelled panicky but no longer terrified. And his expression was relaxed, almost . . . content. Whatever Shan thought of him, she would have conceded that he was as capable as she was of facing the unthinkable with dignity.

Ade paused, staring into Lindsay's face for one minute, then two, then three. He grabbed her arm and examined it, frowning.

"Not a scratch," he said. His tone was flat and unemotional. He dunked his sleeve in the sea and wiped the blade clean on it, then turned to Rayat. "Now let's give you someone to keep you company on those dark nights, eh?"

"It's going to be one long night down there," said Rayat. "You lose the light at a thousand feet." He pushed up his sleeve to offer his arm. "Let's do it, then."

Aras could feel the warmth and slight itching as *c'naatat* reconstructed his skull and scalp. The pain was dimming. Ade busied himself cleaning Aras's blood from the butt of his rifle.

"Two more minutes, I reckon," he said.

Aras rolled a little further to watch Lindsay's grim, terrified face as she stared down into the water that was now filling with pulsing red, amber and gold lights. The raft was illuminated from beneath by angry bezeri, floating on liquid fire.

Rayat was gazing down through the deck into the glowing water as well. The scent of anxiety was overwhelming.

But Aras could have sworn he actually *smiled.*

28

Sometimes people need a few rehearsals to find out what they're really made of. Shan didn't, of course: right from the start, she took Horatius's view that there was no better way to die than facing fearful odds and holding that damn bridge. But I had Lindsay labeled as a regular human being, the sort who thinks the best way to die is in your sleep aged at least four score years and ten. And then she surprised us all. Who would have thought she'd choose an eternity under water to atone for the destruction of the bezeri? You never really know anyone at all. And I don't think Lindsay really knew what she would be capable of, either, not even then.

Was I ever tempted to try c'naatat?

You must be joking.

Eddie Michallat's Constantine Diaries

Ade watched the skyline for the approach of a small globule of bronze shiplet. Shapakti was late picking them up.

"You okay now?"

Aras was sitting on his heels, arms folded across his chest. Ade thought it looked weird, but wess'har found that as comfortable as sitting cross-legged.

"I'm no longer in pain," said Aras.

Ade knelt down beside him and braced himself to put both hands on Aras's head to examine it. Aras didn't flinch. Wess'har had few taboos about being touched. Ade parted the hair—barbed and vaned like strings of soft feather—and found nothing to indicate that he'd smashed the butt of his rifle hard enough into Aras's head to fracture his skull and rip it open.

"I'm sorry, mate," he said. "Only way I could bring you down for a while."

"I understand."

No, he didn't: Ade ached with misery. He had become his

father, resorting to violence in a moment. And, as Aras had pointed out, he'd run and left Shan to it, just like he had left his mother. He'd been so sure he was doing the decent thing. Now he saw what Aras had seen: another act of cowardice.

"*C'naatat* or not, that must have hurt."

"It did." Aras reached out and went to clasp Ade's arm, but he jerked it back. He was still edgy. "I regret what I said to you."

"Maybe it needed saying."

"I only said it to stop you. It's untrue."

It wasn't. Aras was becoming so human that he'd even learned diplomacy. But it was nice of him to try to lie out of kindness. Wess'har weren't good liars at all. *And neither am I.*

How could he ever sleep with Shan now? She'd pick up his memories. She'd experience those awful minutes. She'd *know.* It might not happen right away, but she'd find out before long. She'd realize that he handed over *c'naatat* to the two people she most despised, and that he and Aras almost competed to be the first to run out on her.

"What about you?"

Aras looked round. "What?"

"*Oursan.* You'll sleep with her and you'll transfer whatever it is that the cells transfer and she'll have your memories. She'll find out what went on."

Aras waited several seconds before replying, as if it had occurred to him for the first time too. But he must have thought it. "Perhaps not. Genetic memory isn't telepathy. And we will deal with that when it happens."

"Can you lie to her? *Would* you?"

Aras waited several seconds again. "I don't know."

Ade settled down again and waited, looking down through the *niluy-ghur*'s transparent deck at swaying weed in the shallows beneath. Shapakti's fragment of vessel could pick up the raft from the surface and set it down again without even getting the deck wet. The Eqbas would be one hell of an assault force. Ade appreciated that kind of detail.

He wondered what Lindsay and Rayat were doing right

then, and all he could imagine was that it was taking place somewhere cold, and dark, and terrifying, and *lonely*.

Dawn was coming to the roomful of jungle underneath the city of F'nar. Shan sat cross-legged on the floor and watched the artificial sunrise produced by the daylight cycle that Shapakti's team had created. The macaws stretched their wings one at a time, legs extended beneath them as elegantly as a dancer's, and fluffed their plumage.

C'naatat had many good points. The best she could think of right now was that it had erased all physical signs that she had spent an hour sobbing her heart out in the privacy of the jungle room.

"Do you want to go home that badly?" said Shapakti's voice. It made her jump. She hadn't smelled him coming.

"Forget it," she said.

"I understand. I long for home too."

She rubbed the back of her hand across her nose, still sniffing. "Not a word to Aras or Ade, okay?"

"Why?"

"I don't want them to know."

"The treatment will always be here for you."

"*If* it works. But not for Aras, though. And I won't abandon him, and I know Ade won't either."

"Then you have no reason to weep."

It didn't feel that way. But Shapakti was right. Shan patted his back, reassured for the time being by splendid wess'har pragmatism. The Earth she thought of as home didn't exist now: it probably never had, but it would exist one day and the Eqbas would see to that. She had almost completed the mission that Eugenie Perault had never intended her to fulfill. No, she had no reason to weep.

"Are those two buggers back?"

"Of course they are," said Shapakti. "They wouldn't let me accompany them on the *niluy-ghur,* but I brought them back as you ordered."

"Just checking," she said. *Ordered.* Yes, she *had* been insistent. "They can both be bloody daft sometimes."

"You have a good family. Cherish them."

Poor bloody Shapakti, years from home, and missing his brothers and his wife and their kids. Shan could offer him no comfort and fumbled in her pocket. She drew out the container that she had carried with her wherever she went, across years and star systems.

"I want to show you something," she said. She opened the cap and tipped the contents into her palm. Small, pale, round seeds—tomato seeds—settled on the background of bioluminescence that flickered within her skin. "Tomatoes. I always planned to grow them when I stopped being a copper. These are illegal, you know. Unregistered hybrids."

"Life-forms cannot be illegal."

"I like the way you people think. I really do."

She tipped the seeds back into the container and decided that she was going to spend today sowing tomatoes, just as she'd always planned. Shapakti beckoned her to the doorway, slipping behind her and herding her out into the passage. He had to start moving the habitat. Shan was glad it wouldn't remain here to remind her of Earth.

She walked out into the daylight, the real daylight of Ceret, the yellow sun they once called Cavanagh's Star before any human knew how many different names it really had. She wandered back up the pearl-encrusted terraces, rattling the seeds in the little box and greeting wess'har who she now knew as friends and neighbors. She paused at the top of the steps on the highest level of the terraces and turned to admire F'nar in the winter sun.

It was as every bit as beautiful as rain forest if you knew how to look.

Then she walked on, wondering about the feasibility of that lavender preserve. As she pushed against the door, the lights in her hands reflected in the pearl surface and she took a deep breath, determined not to look back at her own World Before. It was the first breath she had drawn in an hour.

"Hey, you two," she called. "I'm home."